secret 099 - goddess perfume

The Secret of Chocolate Series

maurllan

The Secret of Chocolate
Secret 099 - Goddess Perfume

MAURLLAN

ePub ISBN: 979-8-88619-004-5
A5 Print ISBN: 979-8-88619-005-2
LARGE Print ISBN: 979-8-88619-006-9
First publication date: 2022.05.24
Library of Congress Registered: 2022.05.25
Revision: 2023.10.25

STUNNED Publishing
Cover art, illustrations,
marketing content,
and storytelling are
Copyright ©2022 by Maurllan.

magnificent shadows
grabbing circling releasing
tangled in hurt and happiness

———

magnificent shadows

. . .

ONLY MAGNIFICENT LIGHTS cast magnificent shadows. Martee knew what strengths were in the shadows cast by her capacity to love.

Friday, late morning Sun rising high. She felt let down again by the most recent man, and continued to yearn for the Sky God's collection of subterranean treasures.

Martee's heart had reached a final place of resolve in her grieving. She needed to find a solution, even if it would break her heart to lose someone else close in making the change. Something just had to give.

She was holding her hands around a plate of hash browns and eggs after being stood up for an early morning ride. Unusually, the plate felt heavy, like her hands were full of rocks. She set the plate carefully on her breakfast nook table, the unusual feeling of heftiness growing in an otherwise sunny mid-morning day, slipped into the chair and crossed her legs at the ankles.

Martee rotated the plate thirteen degrees, murmured, "(I ever am / as I ever do.)" and gazed into the three easy-over free-range chicken eggs in hot grape seed oil covering pan-toasted black pepper hash browns, let her mind wander in the pattern, feeling for insights. The way the eggs had fallen from the grace of a sizzling skillet onto the plate and the way the criss-cross of pan-toasted potato slices had seared together showed the day was going to be amazing, unpredictable, potentially fun, and scary. It was rare to see an egg yolk break *after* arranging the plate, and the hash browns looked practically woven together except for a hairline tear along a ragged edge, which could be a weather front with sudden gusts of rain, or an earthquake along the boundary of someone's inner domain map. A lot was at stake, apparently, and not just for herself. She inhaled the luscious breakfast aroma through her nose, tongue-watering with anticipation of happily ever after changes, murmured, "(Let it be so.)"

The thought bubbled up with a slight passing frown, she would know the change was successful by the mousy whimpering in her own ears, and when had she ever done that?

grabbing circling releasing

. . .

BANELLE REGARDED him with her eyes upon him for a long time while her hands moved nearly automatically, grabbing, circling, releasing, plunging like a favorite sunny memory into the warm soapy water, grasping and lifting, working the cotton wash cloth in circles. Turn, massage again in circles, move the plate to the other sink bowl. The remembering was soothing, and the Sun outside combined with the tinted glass of her kitchen's window likely meant he could not see her.

He hadn't looked toward her house at all.

She felt curious why his bicycle with the red frame should have a flat tire there on the sidewalk in her suburban neighborhood, running through her mind the movie-like memories of her driving the black SUV out on errands and then back into the neighborhood.

There was only one practical way in and out of the community. She had kept her home here for three years so far without having seen in those memories his face, his way of moving, and she still felt like an outsider in the community herself.

He nodded while he worked, the rear wheel now removed from the bicycle, something in his hand while he held his hand against the rim and worked in semicircular yanks. He seemed very competent with his hands.

This morning had been different in other ways. Her two girls. She tensed her lips and looked into the sink, searching for any flatware which might be hiding. Her girls had been waving when they got into their daddy's dried rain, metallic sparkle dark blue car at the interstate restaurant where Banelle had agreed to meet him between cities, sound of trucks rushing harshly by. Her eyes felt wet. They were gone for the next six weeks, unless they just missed her terribly. That had happened before when blond-haired, green-eyed Jayenne was eight, impatiently growing up. But Jayenne is nine now and becoming independent. Then there was Boop, her little girl Bella. Brown hair and blue eyes in that nurturing face, courageous and competitive, Boop would be six next month.

Summer again. Banelle felt like sighing.

She glanced at progress outside. That man with spoked rim in his right hand was walking on her sidewalk towards her house. She felt a start of surprise, and alarm — felt excitement welling up also, watching him walk through the shade of the big oak, until he stepped off her sidewalk onto her yard. He had dark, close-cropped hair, walked with a sense of strength and purpose. As he neared the kitchen window, she could see he had gray eyes.

Then she felt the alarm return, bringing with it a feeling of embarrassment. She hadn't showered yet this morning, having felt instead like comforting herself with a pair of pink flannel loungers and a white poet's shirt, sleeves rolled up near the middle of her forearms.

She didn't feel comfortable at this moment. She felt dirty, like her bare feet had been walked around all evening and then slept them in her bed sheets, dirty. She felt her hair was oily and unbrushed, and part of her felt angry, because she also felt ashamed, a criticism from her youth. All the feelings roiled around inside her midsection, and she gripped the sink to steady herself.

She watched that man step between thickly budded rose bushes just on the left of her kitchen window and crouch down. *What the hell?* Unsure what to do in the crazy mix of feelings which had sprung forth in seconds and now swirled inside her with no particular focus, Banelle felt herself craning over the stainless steel sink — on bare tiptoes in her kitchen, the heels of her hands pressing at the sink, her pelvis resting along the cultured white marble counter edging, with the insides of her elbows toward the window — and she tried to see what that man was doing. She realized she was holding her breath.

The spell was broken an eye blink later when she heard inside the house the sound of water being turned on. "(Well, of all the cheek!)" she hissed in a whisper, rather than yell and risk his attention. The sound of water in pipes stopped, and she saw that man's back rise when he took a step away from her house and knelt on one knee in the grass facing her. She felt flustered, only a brick wall between her and a man kneeling before her.

She heard the clank of metal when he applied a tool against the rim of the spoked wheel, heard the squeaking of rubber and a deep snap sound, which was followed almost immediately by a, "Ha!" of triumph in a tenor register, then a deeper, prolonged baritone voice, "Ohhh, yeaahhhhh!"

The sound startled her with goosebumps, which only fired the anger she just realized she was feeling. Not only the affront against her sense of territory and feeling at odds about first impressions, she felt thwarted by her timing of the day and a brick wall: here he was, kneeling at her feet.

The familiarity he evidenced in the use of her home spoke to some deep part of her, a part which didn't like feeling vulnerable. Yet her anger lost the white-hot moral dignity, and she felt the tingling now relaxing. It amazed her how nice this prickle felt, sensed a subtle sadness from their departure.

The day being almost noon, she struggled with her desire for a shower and makeup to present her best self, and her more imminent urge to throw open the kitchen door and challenge that man just as she was. This was her house on her own merits and what else was at risk, her next marriage?

Another part of her shouted inside, *Don't get up yet! Yes! Of course I will!*

He was walking purposefully toward his bicycle, was it already too late?

———

Another feeling entered the lump, further muddling the inner conflict. "That," Banelle said, as she felt the sense of opportunity walking away. Now there was anger and self-reproach.

A moistness came in each eye. She balanced tears on the eyelashes, trying to feel where the hurt, frustration, or relief came from, felt the lump of a swallow in her throat. She wiped the back of her right wrist for one eye and the front of the wrist for the other, then remembered her poet's shirt, and put her face within the crook of her left elbow to damp her eyes drier and to feel the softness of the cotton for some comfort of her own.

When she pulled her arm down, she had the pleasure of watching that man's gorgeous ass as he bent away from her to reconnect the wheel into his bicycle. She noted the black knit of his riding shorts shaped snuggly around his hard-looking thighs and package bulging below, the hair on his legs, a refined blondish sort which glowed with a red hue where the sunlight caught in its strands. How would that feel on the fingertips?

She felt herself cross her arms. Her weight shifted with her left leg, and the inside of her right foot turned ninety degrees on the antiqued-white oak flooring. She rested her pelvis against the sink, bracing herself, left leg against the honey-pine cabinetry, the smell of stale soapy dish water wafting up.

His arms were moving vigorously, the elbows up and out. She could see the muscles in his shoulders and the taper of his back under the red mesh T-shirt. When the breeze caught the lower part of the mesh with his arms pumping, looking at him from behind she realized with a moistening feeling that man's waist was right-fingers tickling lean, a short reach to feeling everything from soft of the left wrist to hard tip of fingers.

"(Oh, Goddess.)" she heard herself say with the quiet voice. She blinked repeatedly to clear the visualization, flapped her left hand, sucked air into her lungs, huffed.

She felt the palm and fingers of her right hand slide through the unbrushed hair and stop at the nape with a clenching and re-clenching of a fistful of hair. Whispered, "(Now, this. This is about enough, you have tasks…)" She tried to remember what was important today, smelled again the dishwater, reached through the water into the sink with her left hand, pulled the plunger basket, then rinsed and dried her hands.

That man propped his bicycle leaning against the oak tree in her yard. He brushed the fronts of his thighs in two strokes, arched his back in a stretch, turned his head to look down the street right, then left. He relaxed. She could see him breathe in and out deeply in a deciding way.

He turned around and began walking toward her house, staying on the sidewalk to her front door.

She felt herself grab the edge of the sink as the roil of feelings came surging back with intensity: alarm, anger, excitement and that wet little flip in her abdomen which she wanted desperately to ignore, excitement at his being here in moments.

She looked around herself in the kitchen and remembered she had left a pair of leather sandals by the deep cherry round kitchen table. She saw hanging on one of the natural leather-covered cherry kitchen chairs the calves-length black wraparound skirt which had been draped there so long she had forgotten, probably earlier this spring when she came home from an office party.

She stripped the pink loungers off where she stood, feeling the cool air from her belly button downward, hustled to the table, started multitasking, scooching into left and right sandals while she threw the discarded loungers on an empty chair with her left hand, grabbed the black wraparound skirt with her right hand, and in a swirl tied the skirt closed with both hands. She sandaled her left foot, pulled her purse open with both hands, settled her right foot into its sandal; grabbed her brush out of her purse and gifted herself a few quick pulls through the hair, tilting her head for one side, then the other.

When she heard the doorbell ring, she tossed the brush onto her purse.

She felt the side of the mouth curl in a smiling, mysterious way. Here it was now.

Banelle made herself stop at the fridge and grab one of the two remaining apples in her left hand, took a bite as she pushed through the swinging kitchen door to her den, the aroma of freshness cheering her while stepping up into the foyer on her left.

She felt the day was different. Would she embrace a completely different understanding of herself over the long weekend? Would her girls even know who she was when they returned? Banelle imagined her two girls shouting in disagreement with each other about the way she had been and what Banelle was becoming, *I want* my *mommy! She is* our *mom!*

She grabbed the hard door knob with her right palm and fingers. And what was at risk? Just her relationship hopes and dreams since her doll-playing days?

tangled in hurt and happiness

. . .

DOLLAR WONDERED if the doorbell even worked. Should he knock?

He appreciated the solidly mortared pink-hued brick of the home, liked the color. The generous shady cedar canopy subtly teased the nose and likely explained why there was no glass weather door protecting the heavy, mellow-finished oak door, keeping Sun and rain away from the doorstep.

He did not like the cement he stood on though, the falsity of the material, he would have used stone for his dream home. He noted again the soon-blooming rose bushes along the walls of the front of the house needed trimming, fertilizing, a box of ladybugs added, and the lawn was improperly mowed, stressing the grass. He decided to knock loudly.

He heard a muted shriek, then heard the doorknob spin and rattle.

Dollar began to chuckle, felt the grin, felt the light of a smile around his eyes.

He heard a woman's coughing. There was the sound of the knob spinning in two directions accompanied by the soft metallic clicks of the internal works, then the door was pulled open.

The woman coughed once more, looking at him with a mist in her eyes, the back of her left hand against her mouth clutching an apple. He saw the natural nails, sandy, shoulder-length hair.

Dollar nodded. "You all right?"

She nodded repeatedly, her blue eyes clenched shut, swallowing. Her nostrils flexed, filling her lungs with air. She swallowed and opened her eyes, dropping her hand. "Yeh?" She swallowed once more.

"Did I startle you?"

She took a deep breath. "More than once."

He didn't know what he should say from here. He did not like feeling dumb, which happened every time he found himself face to face with a near Goddess.

His calm mental voice reminded him there were no actual Goddesses, and there were *rules* to dating, that a Goddess was some illusion of his own fickle imagination from another part of the mind. In real relationships, the man had to be loyal, honest, forthcoming, faithful, reliable, trustworthy, and ever present — those were the rules, and somehow the man was also supposed to be attractive, sexy, a great kisser, and know his way around a woman's erotic sensibilities, while keeping in mind her emotions were a huge part of her feeling attracted and allowing herself to be perceived as attractive. Apparently, the rules underpinned everything.

She was beautiful. His eyes scanned down her body, made quick turns around the curves, admiring. She wasn't perfect, just lovely, comely.

He still didn't know what to say.

She flashed a toothy smile. "We already have Girl Scout cookies."

"Hilarious." He felt the movement in his loins — hated feeling betrayed by his own body advertising where a woman could see. The physical movement reminded him thickly how much of the soft joy was missing in his daily rhythms. Three years of living *his* way on purpose, he wanted to rationalize their meeting was unimportant, and put the emotional fence back in place. The moment felt awkward, like now was the best time for leaving and dismissing the pretty opportunity he faced.

Except, her hot physical presence was nearly overwhelming, and he could feel the cooled air flowing out of her home passing his ankles. *She must smell good, or the Faie are at play.* Out loud, "I didn't mean to startle you. I was just curious."

Her head tilted left, the left wrist bent exposing the bitten apple, and he saw her blue eyes glance at his mouth, then scan each of his eyes.

He took a deep breath. "It's just that I have no idea where I am." There, a lie.

Her eyes got wide and her head dropped forward, sandy hair surrounding, looking at him incredulously. She didn't say anything.

"What?"

"You've got to be kidding."

He felt the warmth of embarrassment. He hated feeling stupid. "No worries. I'm supposed to be solving for World Peace somewhere else." He began to turn widdershins.

He felt that woman's right hand both firm and soft on his bare right biceps, smelled the scent of fresh dish soap. "Wait."

He paused, turned his head toward her.

"I just never heard a man ask for directions before." Shrugged her left shoulder.

He felt the awkwardness suddenly evaporate, felt himself held in a spell by the warmth of her hand, other parts of himself in complicit focus turned fully upon her.

Her hand dropped away. With the sound of her short inhale, the movement of her breasts within the white blouse caught his eyes, held them longingly.

He stopped his hand mid-air from retrieving her hand, the muscles all over his body tensing together, and dropped the hand to his side.

Her feminine form braced her right side against the door jamb.

He felt his desire and resentment bunching for an internal fight. He looked within her blue eyes, they came up. *Better salvage it*, he thought, knowing how the resentment got in his way. "I feel really stupid, is all."

———

The woman standing in the doorway wavered, smiled. "I've also never heard a man talk about how he is feeling."

Oh, Goddesses and their minor gods! Here we go... "Yes," Dollar said out loud. "Well, you'd better not listen or we'll start sharing how we feel back and forth and the next thing you know we'll be slipping into intimacy and then we'll be all tangled together whether good or bad, in hurt and happiness, fights and all, and suddenly the years will go by in a rush..."

Her head moved backward slowly while he talked, her eyes glancing upon each of his. Then dropping slightly, her eyes looking at the conversation of his mouth, then upward again within his eyes.

"...and who in their right mind believes in happily ever after? Because you can't *know* until the journey is over anyway, and then it's too late, it's over, all those years invested." He realized he was babbling, filled his lungs with air, pulled freshly in through his nostrils, and waited. *She is a Goddess, whether her own or the back of my head tricking my eyes, there's something of the Goddess going on here.*

His eyes were on her apple, bitten once, turned in her left hand with her wrist exposed toward him, her hand bouncing the apple up and down, weighing that choice.

She crossed her arms. The Goddess magick moved. He looked past the soft lilt of curves in the white shirt, past the bare of her throat and the upward curve below her mouth. He looked at her lips, where there was a bit of mystery to be known across a lifetime. He followed with his eyes the curve of her jawline, the lobe of her ear, and with the hairline, from there found her eyes.

Her eyes widened briefly. "Today is different, and so are you. If you meant even half of that, you'd better stop joking and elope with me before Monday." he thought he heard her say just now, the words seeping, filling his awareness — had her lips moved? Yes, yes, they had. Or they must have, because he remembered the enchanting bobbing of her jawline when his eyes swept along her hairline. Did she actually say, *Marry me?* He noticed she was smiling, white teeth.

He began to feel nervous and didn't know why, gazed within her eyes. Suddenly, like the sustained ring of an antique dinner bell which has been rung once by the encircling fingers of a graceful hand and then held expectantly in the air, he remembered he had only been curious why a woman in a white shirt would watch him through a window for twenty minutes while he changed a bicycle tire. It's not like she called the cops.

Wonder held his attention, hands clenching and unclenching hanging by his sides. He felt an exquisite tightness in his throat which seemed in the way of speaking further.

Bubbled up how it felt, believing someone was really interested in what he had been doing. He decided immediately upon remembering he was going to have the feeling again, if he could.

"Yes," he said, watching her blue eyes, her enchantingly enlarged irises' interest in him. He felt the intensity of his focus welling up inside him.

He noticed her right leg, the one most relaxed in the door-leaning position, how her knee began fanning back and forth under her black skirt. When his eyes looked again to see what her blue eyes were saying, he caught her for a moment gazing at his hardened loins, felt embarrassed by what was being said by a part of himself and felt turned on by the part of herself blooming subtly into his nose.

Then she was gazing at his lips momentarily, then at his eyes, this time not searching, just gazing. She leaned her head against the door frame, relaxed.

"Let's do lunch sometime," he suggested. Part of him fussed, *is that* it *for clever conversation?*

She nodded softly. Her right foot made a sweeping semicircle movement, her eyes looking at the cement landing. "Lunch sounds lovely." Her head leveled. Smiling, she pulled her right foot back and began bouncing it behind herself on the toe end of her sandal.

He held out his right hand. "My name is Aaron."

She took his hand. "I'm Bah-nel."

"Excuse me?" stopping at a single pump up and down with their hands together. The feeling of her hand in his was soft and delicious, and he continued holding her hand.

"Bah-nel." She started spelling that for him, "B-a-n-e-l-l-e."

"B-a-n-e-l…" he repeated, and stopped.

"…e-l-l-e. Banelle."

He pumped their hands once more. "Nice to meet you, Banelle." The feeling welled up, he was holding her hand a long time. He noticed what a comfortable feeling the connection with her was, and felt a subtle sadness about having to let her hand be free again.

"Aaron what?"

He released her hand slowly, fingertips dragging across her soft palm, smiling. "Aaron Horn."

She fought back a smile, fidgeting.

"Aaron Doucete Horn," he expanded, feeling an old indignation of being teased about his name, the feeling welling up again from a particular memory of his days as a boy in elementary school, being teased by two girls years older than himself while waiting for a school bus. He wondered how much older those girls were now and what had happened in their journeys while they aged ahead of him. Were they still pretty?

"Horn?" Her lips were restless.

He felt his lips firmly shut, a slight nodding at the school memory and the insight. "Nothing to do with Unicorns." The resentment was satisfied for now, dissipated. "Horn, four letters." He felt himself smile a bit, the best cuss words were four letters long.

She wriggled as she asked her next question. "Any nicknames?"

He felt himself smile more broadly and nod. "Not the one you're thinking of, I generally don't like that one."

"Oh?" Her eyebrows popped, her right hand covered her mouth, eyes merry.

"People's names should never end in the sometimes-a-vowel 'y'. Humorously, however, some of my friends back in college called me Der Füllhorn."

"Der Füllhorn?"

"Horn of Abundance."

"Ah," she nodded once, bright smile. "I see." Her lips covered her teeth smoothly, pressed together, her mouth opened. "What do your other friends call you?"

He felt a blush, bashful.

————

"Well?" Banelle's eyes look at his cheeks, then his lips, then his eyes.

He felt himself take the big breath. "I'm called Dollar."

"Dollar?"

"Long story, but it fits."

She tilted her head against the door frame once more. "Dollar." Her eyes glanced at his mouth, quick glance down lower, and then back within his eyes.

He remembered he had a pair of business cards along. He'd found it paid out handsomely to have cards with him at all times. Some people just went for the spontaneous. "I have a business card." He knelt, pulled the thin blue nylon sports wallet out of the velcro shoe pouch, his eyes noticing her bare left toes and ankle while his hands worked the velcro, so deliciously close he could feel the saliva on his tongue. The black skirt swayed over her foot, and he realized a little late he had unconsciously kneeled before her.

She didn't run or back away. Her toes flexed multiple times while he was watching. Was she trying to keep her balance?

He felt his lips part, and closed them purposefully. He pulled out a card and handed the card up to her, then put his miniature wallet away and retied the shoe.

He stood.

She held the apple with her left hand, index finger and thumb bracing left corners of the business card, the opposite edge pinched in thumb and index finger of her right hand. "Oh! Wait right here." She spun counter-clockwise away from the doorjamb and disappeared within her house.

The floor, he noticed, was a comforting water blue of large, rough finished glazed tiles. There were little girl shoes along the opposite wall of the foyer, clumsily cluttered. A small yellow rain jacket was crumpled against the wall. Shifting his stance right, he saw a stairway leading the eye up on the left, the steps covered in speckled gray Berber accented by a medium oak Mission hand railing.

She was gone for a short while. Then he heard the soft, rapid sound of her sandals clapping happily as she returned. She handed him a piece of white paper torn from some larger piece. She was smiling, her voice was firm. "You're supposed to call *me*."

Dollar felt himself chuckling and grinning, nodding. There was a myth men never call when they say they will. "Call." Frankly, he felt like running away. He also felt tingly and excited. "Later today, if that works for you also?"

"Great." Her eyes were checking his lips, then searched his eyes, the apple in her left hand low and tight at the end of her arm, almost hidden behind the skirt at her thigh. He looked within her eyes and noticed a slight shrug in her shoulders, the slight swaying of her whole body on the ankles.

There was an awkward feeling in the air, an unfocused expectancy railing against responsibility. He felt uncomfortable, restless. "Right. Well, I better get going." He turned and started walking, then smiled over his left shoulder.

She had been gazing at his ass, looked at his face, returned his smile. She leaned her right shoulder against the doorway, her head erect, smiling, then she crossed her arms.

He waved his right hand briefly.

She gave a little wave by freeing her right hand, then refolded her arms. Her right heel was bouncing, hinging at the toes.

He stopped by his bicycle, and wondered what to do with the piece of paper she'd given him. Facing away from her, he folded the paper once and stuffed her number down the inside of his black nylon riding shorts, within the shallow, tender spot where his right thigh met his torso, where he could feel the folded paper there and know the connection wasn't at risk of getting lost. He picked up his bicycle by the crossbar with his left hand, walked to the street, and mounted.

"Hey!" She was waving her left arm, apple clutched in the hand, index finger pointing in the direction opposite which he was facing, called, "The way out of here is down that way, two left turns and one right turn!"

He felt a brief surge of anger. He wasn't an idiot. Then he remembered the lie he'd told her about not knowing where he was. The anger relaxed and he smiled and waved once with the right hand. "Thanks!"

He resisted muttering to himself, grinned at the internal grumpiness of having to leave according to the rules. The right foot felt for the pedal. He smiled and nodded upward once and started out, taking care he turned around while she could see he was following her lead.

Would he have the courage later to follow up? Imagine explaining to others it was a flaccid tire which brought her into his life?! And there were *daughters!* He would be outnumbered! Was he insane?

~ goddess perfume ~

Secret 099

Historical Romance ~ circa 2003
The Midlands

———

Steam Rating: **Warm**
(moderately explicit)

whatever emotions were

. . .

BANELLE CLOSED the front door of her home, pushing the door with her hips and her back until the latch clicked, safely inside for whatever emotions were about to erupt after her shock wore off.

Her eyes transported her imagination through that man's business card, held with her right hand shaped like a half-rectangle around the end of the card, three fingers underneath to support the back of the card. Her left hand was down by her thigh, her fingers squeezing slow pulses against the hard shape of the apple, the taste of a recent bite on her tongue.

She felt like arching her back against the door, her hips swaying forward, to feel the private freedom of the skirt hanging away from her naked legs and secret self underneath.

Her eyes wandered toward the white ceiling while she rested her head on the door, searching the ceiling in a wandering way, after-glowing the connectedness she'd felt with the man just now. In her way, and using her own pace, Banelle imagined what this feeling would be like, to feel connected more often and longer with that man.

She got herself away from the door with a deep breath in-and-out and stepped down a step into the cozy feeling living room with the high sloping midnight-blue ceilings and quartz sand-colored Berber.

She slumped on the end of the overstuffed pine-green leather couch near the entry from the foyer, taking care not to bump her shins on the coffee table.

There was a difference in how she felt connected with him, different from the connections she felt with each of her girls. With the girls, the feeling was, well, higher in her chest almost in her throat. It was easy to speak of them often, and when she'd feel hurt by the older one, there'd be a clenching feeling in her throat along with the desire to call the younger one near for a hug. She also felt the connections with the girls in her hands, and the feeling brought her left hand up. "What am I doing with this apple?" She leaned forward, set the twice-bitten apple on the thick glass coffee table with black wrought iron. She leaned back, and slumped down on the couch into her interlace of feelings.

No, the recent feeling of being connected with that man was different from her chest and throat and hands. She felt her left hand, free of the apple, opening and closing slowly, the feelings of freedom and emptiness together. She opened her mouth slightly, ran her tongue along the bottom edge of her upper front teeth, and touched her upper lip with the tip of her tongue before closing her mouth. The texture of being connected with that man was eluding her, perhaps their brief time together just now couldn't have a lasting impression?

Something was peeking out. There it was, the sureness of the butterfly. She searched. There it was again – something revealed from the shadows, peeking out of the dark periphery of her inner vision of herself. "(What the hell is it?)" she whispered.

She did a quick breath in and out, sat up, and looked at the business card. 'I Own Your Lawn's Artistry,' bragged the motto. There was an impressionist landscape in various greens on the stone grey finger texture of the card stock. She spent a while tracing the patterns with her eyes, looking for hidden meanings, seemed everything was intentional about the design, more than just advertising. Eventually she sighed, murmured, "(Like hell he'll call.)"

She tossed the card spinning onto the coffee table, felt a short burst of adrenaline watching the card spin toward the far edge of the table, stopped with a long-edged corner hanging free of the tabletop. She stared at the card, her fingers fidgeting.

She felt the sense of loneliness come upon her, similar to the the feeling she'd had lying in bed earlier in the morning missing her kids. She felt she was missing something else, though she hadn't been able to think what was misplaced. She remembered how blue the morning had been, also how a sink full of dishes and sunny memories had begun dispelling recent sadness and loneliness. "Am I depressed?"

She felt a smile start, thinking how her Boop had said just yesterday, when they got inside the car to head for the interstate restaurant meeting place, "Momma, I think you'll do." Banelle had laughed when she heard her Boop say so. She had laughed and forgot about the sadness of her daughters leaving. Banelle had said, "Boop, I've known you'll do since you were in my arms the morning you were born."

"Exactly," her Boop had said, and reached over the car seat from behind and hugged her with the headrest in the way, and kissed Banelle wet on the right cheek. All Banelle could do in return from her awkward position in the driver's seat was pat her little girl on the arm and tell her she loved her.

Banelle had to ignore, for the moment, Jayenne's being jealous from the front passenger seat beside her. Because – and she always felt it wasn't fair and had tried never saying so – because she loved Boop much more than Jayenne, though she couldn't imagine how she could feel more love than she felt for both of them for exactly who they were, her daughters two.

"(God, what a feeling,)" Banelle whispered, and felt her eyes smiling while she stared at the carpeted floor, reliving the wet kiss on her cheek.

"(C'mon,)" she said, urging herself, pushing up from the slippery overstuffed couch. "Time for a shower and a day."

————

Banelle didn't go directly to the master bathroom, but instead paused upstairs on the color-speckled gray Berber carpet with eggshell-soft snow-white walls of the landing, looked into Jayenne's bedroom by leaning around the doorway, hanging on the hallway wall for self-preservation — and flipped the light switch on with her left hand. There were the familiar baby-breast pink walls, duck-foot cloud window curtains, Aztec-gold bedspread.

Jayenne's shoes were in an orderly line against the right wall by the six-panel white closet door. The pine writing desk sat under the window across from the doorway and left of the bed, pencils and pens neatly in the red wire cup on the desk, the back of the yellow-cushioned chair snug against the desk. Cleaner than Banelle's room, nothing out of order. The large photo book about whales sitting on the desk oddly angled was the only thing in disarray.

Banelle felt her nose squidge, turned the light off.

She did the same leaning-in at Boop's bedroom doorway, feeling through habitual guilt how she should treat each bedroom the same.

Banelle turned the light on, the cranberry-red lower walls came warmly alive, capped with birch chair railing, lace-white wallpaper reaching the ceiling, blue water-ripple curtains on the window, darker blue wedding rings-on-white quilt comforter on the bed. Then there was the clutter on the bed, clutter against the walls on the floor, and a disorganized collection of 1/64 scale cars around and on a plastic parking ramp, gifts from Boop's Grandfather. She sighed. The rooms *weren't* the same.

She felt it was important and comforting to walk inside Boop's bedroom, to stand in a clear spot in the middle of the floor. She marveled, Boop's room was much messier! Banelle turned slowly to take everything in with her eyes and with her sense of smell, feeling her deep breath, fought down the urge to pick things up, knowing deep in her heart how much her youngest daughter took comfort from having things stay exactly where her daughter put them, no matter how long they lay about.

Banelle had a rule about the rest of the house, though, how at bedtime Boop was to pick up whatever Boop had dropped and take things back into her bedroom. The self-care wasn't always consistent, yet here was a good rule which kept Banelle and Boop from fighting in more earnest ways.

Banelle scowled and wondered as she had many times while she looked around Boop's bedroom, was her youngest daughter like some side of herself?

Banelle had always felt, as she did now, her older daughter was most like herself, preferring things in order, making checklists and enjoying the pleasure of improving the lists with checkmarks, and for longer projects, the special joy of sticky stars at milestones. Banelle had also noticed in Jayenne there were hints of the little pleasures Banelle felt from following well-known, clear rules.

She felt herself gently sitting down on the corner of Boop's bed, being careful of not dislodging anything. Banelle felt her right leg crossing her left. It was after all a messy room, decided to cross her arms, leaned forward to rest her arms against her crossed knee. Her free right foot began bouncing up and down, swinging free of the black wraparound skirt.

Her eyes idly wandered around the things in the little bedroom. The half-dressed Barbies who couldn't stand by themselves, except for the one leaning against the pink accents doll house. The powder blue cradle with the brown curly-furred teddy bear. The beach ball slightly deflated and in primary colors, wildly out of color scheme with the rest of the room. The piles of clothes, one red blanket in a pile by itself with a rat-tailed light blue comb lying on it. The shoes scattered in a disorganized pile near the bed. "(Am I like how this room feels?)" her foot still bouncing.

She heard the phones. The one in the kitchen always started first with a sound of real bells, and about the time the kitchen phone was done with a ring, the phone on the upstairs landing would start with the more subdued artificial brrr-ing sound.

There was another phone in her bedroom which was also upstairs. She had turned the ringer for the bedroom phone off so long ago she couldn't remember which year she had done so, or if it was even the same house when she started the habit. This had just always been her way with bedrooms and phones.

The girls weren't allowed phones alone in their bedrooms yet.

Banelle eased off Boop's bed trying to not disturb anything, accidentally kicked one of Boop's shoes into a tumble and walked past the landing's phone on her way toward her blue-hued white bedroom, also with speckled gray carpet.

There was a dark cherry end table and headboard in sight in her bedroom, the quiet phone on top. The kitchen phone started the third ring even before the landing's phone had finished the second.

Banelle ran the last couple of steps toward the bed, covered with the old-world green comforter, four white lace European pillow throws hilling-up the head of the bed. She grabbed the white handset from the telephone base, landed on the bed in a half roll onto her back. "Hello?"

surging up was an unusual commitment

. . .

BANELLE HEARD her mother talking with someone else, so she repeated. "Hello? Mom?"

"Oh! There you are. I've been calling and calling."

"Mom, you have not."

"Oh, yes, I have, Nelli."

"Mom, you have not. I've been home all morning."

"I called you at work a hundred times today."

"Mom, it's a holiday. Friday is a banking holiday this week." Banelle pushed the sandals off her feet over the edge of the bed, each going bump.

"Ohhh! That's right. You aren't working today?"

"Mom."

"Oh, don't be so testy, dear."

Banelle felt herself roll her eyes. "Well, I'm sorry. What?"

"We're going to an art show and wondered if you would go along. I know how you get when no one's around."

Banelle didn't feel like responding. She felt compelled to speak and yet didn't, felt the strength of the standoff within herself.

"Are my granddaughters at Bill's?"

"Yes. Mom, I don't get 'that way' when no one's around."

She heard her mother sigh. "Nellie, don't try to fool the mother who loves you. What are you wearing? Your loungers, aren't you?"

Banelle didn't want to answer that. She raised her knees, crossed her right leg over her left shaking the mattress under her back and hips, felt the exposure of cool air around her legs when the skirt — still tied by the cinch at her waist — parted and crumpled in two piles around her ass. She felt the dawning exhilaration of being one step beyond her mother's attack. "Mom, I'm wearing a black ankle-length skirt and white blouse, and I'm looking pretty smashing," though as Banelle said this last thing she felt the words were partly a lie, wondered in the back of her mind where the confidence of feeling smashing came from?

Self-doubt, supported by contrary evidence already being submitted by her inner critical voice which didn't wait a heartbeat to remind her, there wasn't enough evidence to prove before a panel she was smashing.

"You're up and showered and well fed?"

"Yes." Banelle felt how big the lie was getting.

"And you're *alone* this morning?"

A fleeting feeling of being connected with that man with the bicycle welled up. She remembered how she hadn't felt alone when she had talked with him, Dollar.

The last thing she wanted on her first day off on a long weekend was to continue feeling exposed for external judgment under her mother's critical scrutiny. The thought of an afternoon taken out of her own element, and with her mother, brought out an old feeling of panic and, well, loathing, which made her feel guilty as well.

"No, mom." Immediately below the other feelings surging up was an unusual commitment from part of herself to explore throughout the long weekend how her life could be different going forward.

Banelle relaxed from the bigger lie into the smaller lie. "I haven't been alone. Everything's fine. I'm on a date today and need to get going." She felt her left hand clench around the handset, and her right foot start bouncing crossed calf-over-knee, felt how big a lie this last statement was. She wondered, would she regret having revealed this lie?

"Ohh! Well, who is he? What does he do?"

Banelle searched the ceiling above her, first left, then right, looking for a quick, convincing end to this conversation with her natural-born mother.

"His name is…" Banelle wondered which of the man's names to say, felt a leap inside her toward the one he had seemed most embarrassed by. "His friends call him Dollar."

"Dollar?!"

"He does landscaping for a living, and he's a real hunk…"

"He does seasonal labor?"

"…and I need to quit talking because I don't want him to hear." Banelle felt she had to swallow here and blink. "Mom, I've got to be somewhere at a certain time, so I can't talk now."

For a moment she could sense how her mom just knew there was a lie somewhere in Banelle's spurt of talking. The pause was palpable.

Then she heard her mother. "Well, have fun, dear. Give me a call this evening and let me know you are all right."

"I will. 'Love you."

"I love you, too, dear. I'll talk with you later, then."

"Bye, mom." Banelle felt for the phone base with her right hand, resisted looking, stared at the ceiling. With her little finger, she found the handset cradle for the phone, and with fumbling got the handset settled.

She uncrossed her right leg and flopped her arms and legs splaying outward on the bed, still staring at the ceiling. She wondered what she was going to do with the sudden lack of drive, felt so listless.

"(Youuuu,)" she hissed, narrowing her eyelids, feeling the glower and the firmness of her lips pressing together. She felt the comforter against her palms and crumpled handfuls of the bulky material in her fists. Whispered, "(This is a beautiful thing, lying to your own mother.)"

Banelle breathed in deeply and held her breath, then exhaled.

She felt she needed a short fantasy of what he would be like. She let go of the comforter and closed her eyes, rubbed her face with the palms and fingers of both her hands, took a short, deep, deciding breath, let the air out, and started unbuttoning her blouse.

The feeling on her breasts when the cotton fell away was a certain kind of freedom she'd almost forgotten about and didn't usually allow herself with her daughters home since she left the master bedroom door open most of the time, as it was now.

She pulled her blouse to the sides and ran her fingers lightly from her neck down across her chest and her midriff. With her eyes still closed, she unhitched the skirt and parted herself bare, arms still in the sleeves of the blouse.

She remembered she hadn't showered yet, felt grumpy. "(This would feel a hell of a lot better clean.)" Nevertheless, she smoothed her palms along the tops of her thighs, then lay still. Away in the distance, with her eyes closed and the cool air feathering her skin so softly, she heard a quiet hum. She realized the sound was the quiet rushing of the central air system. "(Wow,)" Banelle whispered, barely speaking the word, feeling her lips parted and the slight breath, awed by the unusual quiet of her home.

With her right fingers she made the softest slow circles dipping fingertips into her secret self, vision of the red mesh and his vigorous arms pumping, then her fingers were still.

The left fingers also found the curly hair, helped part lips, her scent blossoming on the nose. She became aware of the sound of her own breathing-in, breathing-out, felt how her nipples rose and firmed, her lungs expanding, visualized the sunlight through his shirt while he pumped with his arms, that tight ass bent before her hands, her stepping nearer and to feel under him where the heat hung soft and thick in her palm, hard and warm at fingertips.

In her mind he stood and turned himself before her in surprise, bulging hardness in his black stretch knit riding shorts.

He knelt at her feet, the skirt immediately coming off behind her. She imagined she turned to retrieve the skirt and felt his right hand press on the curve of her lower back, steadying her bent posture, then the kiss of his wet lips, then the wet of his tongue and brush of his left fingers.

When he rose and stood behind her, her right fingers guided his attentive interest smoothly into her, his thighs snuggled against her. Then she felt parted, messy on the left hand, guided intimacy in the right, felt his hands surrounding the curves of hips and she imagined his arms pumping repeatedly with the breeze catching his red mesh shirt tickling her curves. Her left fingertips chased the visualization deeper inside, she came in a tense rush and a gasp; it was like he was overhearing her heavy breathing, could smell the curl of her fingers by his intimate nose.

Whispered. "(Dollar?)"

only a different set of
shortcomings

. . .

DOLLAR OVERHEARING her was just her imagination. Had to be. People who had just met didn't have connections like that. The feeling had not departed. And why was his nickname Dollar?

There were only a few steps around the bed to enter the master bath on the left. Banelle paused just inside the doorway, flicked the overhead track lights on. She looked at her reflection in the full-length mirror on the left wall entering, first a sideways view past her left shoulder, then she turned toward the mirror, bent her right knee outward, and cocked her head to look at her secret self askance, before turning all the way around, putting her heels together, and with tensed leg muscles lifted to stand on her toes looked over her left shoulder at herself.

She turned, stepped across the gray slate flooring under the overhead skylight and braced her right hand against the wall, reached past the shower curtain with her left hand to grip the faucet, and paused, imagined having heard the kitchen phone. She listened. She heard the brrr-ing of the landing phone, then the bells of the kitchen phone.

"What?!" Banelle rolled her head back, mouth open, turned on her right heel, returned to the bedroom, around the bed, and picked up the handset in her right hand. "Hello?"

"Anna!" A woman's voice.

"Yes? Oh! Martee!" Banelle felt the little thrill, spun herself and sat on the bed.

"What are you doing?"

"Just slumming. The girls are at Bill's."

"For the summer?"

"Yes." Banelle felt her heart hanging on the word.

"I'm sorry."

"Thanks. You?"

"Stood up."

Banelle pressed her lips together to keep from laughing. "Really?! Who was it this time? I mean, who was it?"

"Same guy. You know, the one from the Help Desk. And what do you mean 'this time'?"

Banelle. "I thought that was off?"

"No. Well, it was. I called him last week and we did a dinner."

"You know you aren't supposed to call the guy, Martee."

"I know, I know. I just get so tired of starting new relationships."

Banelle didn't feel like responding, eyes misty. *At least* she *gets to start relationships.*

Martee's voice came nearer to the phone. "It's like the same thing over and over, and only a different set of shortcomings with each new man! For once I'd just like a step up in quality."

Banelle felt like she should say something. "There's no difference in any of them you've dated?"

"I don't know Anna. I'm frustrated. We were supposed to go biking today."

Banelle felt her eyes widen. "Biking or bicycling?"

"Bicycling."

"I didn't know you had one?"

"I don't. Benjamin does. He has two of his own and one from an ex-girlfriend."

"Oh?"

"Except he didn't call to confirm. When I called him he said he had a cold, but his voice sounded fine."

Banelle felt that was marvelous, Martee being stood up. "So, you're feeling frustrated?"

"Very much so! Anna, I know you never go out, but what do you say we go somewhere and do spontaneous flirting today? I'll treat. I made quota for the month moving new cars off the lot and I want to celebrate."

Banelle was surprised at the sudden restlessness which welled up hearing the question. "Oh, I don't know, Martee."

"Come on, Anna. Live a little! You never *do* anything! *Do* something for a change!"

Banelle felt surprised at the next feeling which welled up, a rise to engage a challenge, of wanting to *win*. "Martee, you'd wet your panties, if you wore any, if I told you how I was feeling right this moment."

"No way."

Banelle felt herself laugh. "Oh yes, way!"

"What time?"

First bubble. "Two o'clock."

"Stop my heart. Are you sure?"

"Martee, I have no idea whatsoever, and help me help you. Don't ask me again or I'll revert to being your poo-poo friend who never does anything exciting. It's easy to do."

There was a silence on the other end of the phone, and then she heard Martee say simply and quietly, "(Wow.)" There was another silence. "I want to meet this new woman! Two o'clock?"

Martee's comment made Banelle feel awkward. "Fine. I'll pick you up at two. What are you wearing?"

"Ummm… I guess I'll wear my red shorts, and white V-neck, and… black sandals?"

"Wonderful. What am I saying? I'll figure out what I'm wearing and see you at two."

"Good! Ohhh, I'm going to have a fun day after all! Bye!"

"Bye." Banelle hung up the handset, ran her left hand through her hair and flipped her hair backward with a twist-and-flip of head and hand, remembering at the flip her hair wasn't that long anymore.

She looked sideways at her right hand holding the handset on the telephone base and was quiet for a moment. Her eyes searched the finger marks in the dust on the cherry nightstand absently, then the edge of the Old World green bedspread, then the speckled gray carpet near the nightstand. Finally, she took a deep breath and got up.

On the way into the bathroom, Banelle leaned her head forward to see herself sideways when she came within view of the mirror again, turned right, stopped at the shower with her right hand on the wall, reached in and turned the shower on, then moved her left hand within the spray of the water to test the temperature, adjusted the knob almost immediately.

She shut the water off, thinking she had heard something. The sound of water dribbling and plopping from the shower head on the porcelain tub stopped, then she heard the doorbell. "(Damn.)" Banelle said under her breath, turned on her right heel, walked quickly back into the bedroom.

She grabbed her black skirt and tied the wrap, then grabbed her white shirt and whirled the shirt around, arms flowing into sleeves and onto her shoulders while she walked toward the hallway door. Not bothering with sandals, she began buttoning while she walked across the landing and started down the stairs. She stopped briefly on the stairs to continue buttoning her shirt, feeling the tingle of alarm. There was the sound of a key with a lock spinning and thunking.

The door opened a crack and she heard her father's voice calling, "B.B?"

"Yes, dad!" Banelle finished the last button.

———

Moving the door farther, her father saw Banelle was coming down the stairs, smiled his brown eyes. He stepped in, brown hair with a touch of gray by the ears, turned and closed the door, then spun the latch with a solid thunk. He turned toward her with open arms.

She felt this familiar compelling urge to enter his arms and be held by him. She did, and squeezed him around the waist with both her arms.

She felt him kiss her on the forehead. "How's my girl?"

"Oh, just as boring as I was yesterday evening when you stopped to check on me."

Banelle felt the resonance of his voice in her chest. "Boring, is it?"

"Yes." she squeezed him.

"I know I'm going to miss my granddaughters for a few weeks…"

She felt herself squeeze him again.

"…but you know, I'm glad to have my little girl to myself, again."

"Oh, daddy, you know how to compliment a woman!"

"Just my little girl, the rest are quite a puzzle."

Banelle leaned her head back and looked into his eyes, felt herself smiling, though inside she was feeling a sudden pang of being fundamentally unlovable. "Am I so different from other women?" Banelle felt the worry in her voice.

"Ohhh, don't be that way," her father said gruffly. "You know what I mean."

"No, really. Am I?"

He looked at her seriously, with concern and quiet thoughtfulness.

She felt guilty for asking, felt suddenly less pretty. Yet she felt his respect for her, felt overwhelmed by having the conflicting feelings inside herself together like this.

"Honey, I think it's that I enjoy being your father. Because I really, really like you and I'm almost always feeling damn proud of you."

"Almost always?"

"Yes, almost always."

Banelle swallowed, felt mistiness in her eyes. She felt like running away. "When are you not proud of me?"

"Times like this."

She felt the worry around her eyes, focused on the cut of his gray dress jacket and comfortably fitted blue shirt with simulated gray bark grain buttons. Was it her slumming he was talking about?

Such a warm greeting! Hugs and smiles and kisses! *What's wrong with me?* Banelle looked again into both his eyes, searching for that answer.

He breathed in deeply, huffed again, and nodded. "B.B, it's like watching someone feeling embarrassed. I almost always feel embarrassed for them."

Banelle felt caught out. "What do you mean?"

"When you aren't proud of yourself, like you are right now, how am I supposed to feel? Are *you* right, or am I?"

She ran the words around in her mind, touching them with these feelings. *Proud of yourself, like you are right now, am I right?* She felt her head tilt left thoughtfully while something began to clarify — an old belief unraveling, an old feeling unknotting, an undersized garment falling off. Banelle was not sure what to say next and wanted to say whatever this was with words so she could hear herself saying them, "You mean, when I feel proud, you feel proud?"

"Yes! Easily so."

"When I'm, what, less than proud?"

"Feeling low self-esteem."

"When I'm feeling low self-esteem, you feel this, also?"

"You've got it!" He pulled her against his chest with both arms and hugged on her strongly, felt his left hand rubbing her back, rocking the two of them back and forth.

She felt the warmth of his hug and burned the words into permanent remembrance, *When I am proud, my dad is proud.* Banelle saw it written in her mind with a magick finger on a blush scented wine glass, sound of glass squeaking and chiming, wavelets on the wine, said the words again and again with her inner voice while her dad's hug lasted, worried for a moment he wouldn't be there long enough on this visit to really let it sink in.

Banelle felt something sneaking out of the shadows of her mind, felt the sneaky part poking her deep in her belly with its finger, made her feel like smiling, the right side of her lips and face snuggled against his shirt.

"So, I don't smell coffee."

"You are correct." Banelle said, squeezing him with both arms. "I am proud to have just cleaned the kitchen. And I'm going to let you make the coffee again, because I haven't had a shower yet and that's what I'm going to do right now."

"Oh, so the old man's in the kitchen again?"

"Yes. Mind the door and the phone. I'll be back down in twenty minutes or so."

"Sooner is better." As she started bare feet on the carpeted stairs she felt her father's left hand pat her behind to send her on her way.

Banelle rolled her eyes, didn't let him see this openly. "(I'm thirty-two,)" Banelle hissed quietly. She wondered how young she was when he first patted her behind sending her on her way. Was it in the delivery room before her first bath?

Halfway up the stairs she glanced back and saw her dad pushing through the swinging kitchen door.

Banelle focused on making herself go upstairs faster. While she walked purposefully across the landing she began unbuttoning her shirt. She closed the bedroom door behind herself, dropped the shirt on the floor, continued walking as she unhooked the skirt and dropped it on the floor also, then walked into the master bath.

She gave herself a wink in the mirror when she passed by with the reflection smiling back at her, turned immediately, stopped at the shower with her right hand on the wall and grabbed the shower knob with her left hand, paused, and listened again.

Sound of a muted coffee grinder growling and whining. Then she heard the doorbell.

———

"Fuck!" Banelle said. She felt her right foot bouncing on the big toe behind her while she thought, chiding herself just to get her clothes back on and go see what the doorbell was about, then decided impulsively to let her dad deal with the front door like she had asked him to do.

She listened until the grinder stopped and the doorbell rang once more, then she turned the water on with her left hand and began adjusting the temperature. She stepped within the warm stream, pulled the curtain to catch the spray, closed her eyes and felt the satisfaction of reaching another milestone in her day.

The feeling of hot water pounding on her forehead and face was vital, and Banelle felt herself smile, felt the skin of her upper chest with her palms by crossing her arms at the wrists, and stood there, catching breaths of air by leaning forward slightly and then backing under the spray again. She wondered who had been ringing the doorbell, and felt a rush of curiosity.

The pleasure of the steaming shower engulfed her senses, moist air rich in her lungs, the feel of the slippery bar soap in her hands, slide of foaming soap on her skin.

The patter of water and familiar clean scents took her mind into a fantasy, what would it be like for Dollar to shower with her?

Minutes flew by. She shut the water off, listened.

Just the drip of water.

Banelle pulled a fresh towel off the rack, patted herself dry while thinking about what to wear. She felt this unusual sense of competition welling up further. "(How the hell to beat red shorts?)"

She hung up the towel, walked into the bedroom, slid the closet door wide. There were all the same things she always wore. Banelle felt annoyed. "(In here?)"

She paced slowly back and forth in front of the closet feeling scrutinized, criticized for having a small wardrobe, categorized herself as an inadequate dresser with dismal prospects, and she was beginning to feel hopeless. Something bright yellow on the left end of the closet caught her eye.

She moved clothes aside to get a better view and saw the sunshine yellow pleated miniskirt with matching panties and bikini. She paused and considered the conflicting feelings this outfit brought forth. When she sorted out feelings of disapproval from an opportunity for fun, she discovered this was just, how usual, a quaking fear of failing. A courageous part of her took over. "(Put it on, B.B.)"

She pulled the hanger with her left hand, pout on the lips. "(I'm not wearing just this bikini top.)" She cinched aside a few places along the rack, then paused at a dark suede vest with six silver buttons and a plunging neckline. "(I could wear silver accessories.)"

She pulled the vest hanger with her right hand, and tossed both hangers on the end of the bed on the way to the dresser.

She looked at the scattered collection of chains, rings, bracelets, and hair ties, then gingerly sorted through and found a silver ankle chain. She picked it up, thought about it for a moment, then knelt and hooked the tarnished glitter chain around her right ankle.

She stood and looked at the dresser again, spied a thick-banded silver bracelet and slipped it over her left wrist. Looking for something else, she opened a jewelry box. "(Aha!)"

Banelle pulled out a miniature glossy yellow and black bee with silver wings on a silver necklace, and hooked it around her neck while she walked slowly back toward the bed.

She removed the sunshine clothes from the hanger, pulled on the panties, surrounded herself with the pleated miniskirt, cinched and zipped, and while walking slowly in a circle to the bathroom mirror, slipped within and hooked the bikini top, arranging herself in the cups.

She pulled the suede vest off the hanger, and put it on, leaving the silver buttons open. At the closet, she crouched down and pulled a pair of dark brown leather sandals out, a leather ring on top of each sandal, six straps from the ring wrapping the top of each foot. She sat on the bed, buckled the straps on her ankles.

She stood, went into the bathroom while buttoning the vest. "(Not bad, not bad. I need a yellow tie for the hair.)"

She walked into the bedroom and opened the top drawer of the dresser, decided a bright yellow scarf rolled and tied would do.

She closed the small drawer and pulled open a bigger drawer farther down, looked at the collection of purses. She decided on a small black clutch and went to look in the mirror. "(More black.)"

She walked to the bathroom vanity, selected black eyeliner, and also touched up her eyebrows. Added mascara. She decided on clear gloss UV for her lips – and tossed the chap within her clutch.

Banelle walked back toward the bedroom, stopped at the dresser collection of jewelry. She searched the jewelry box until she found a pair of black chainmail earrings.

On a whim, she pulled open a drawer of belts and rummaged until she found a thin pliable black belt. Following her instincts, detached the sliding belt clip, then formed a loop with the leather straps hooked only on the right hip's belt loop, so the two ends dangled from beneath the right side of the vest down her bare right thigh, the soft leather brushing her skin lightly when she walked back to look in the bathroom mirror.

"(Wow.)" Banelle said simply, looking at every curve. She liked what she saw, felt out of sorts, like she shouldn't be looking so beautiful. *I wonder what dad will say?*

She continued to stare within the mirrored eyes, felt like reaching out and touching this reflection of the person in front of herself, yet by willpower kept her arms still. "(Do I know you?)"

Banelle noticed while she stared within these mirrored eyes how the lips and jawline had moved with the question, how the neck muscles moved, how the hair and earrings had a little bounce and jiggle about them, how the breasts rose and fell inside the suede vest while she breathed, the yellow accents of cleavage in soft black and brown deer hide.

Her left hand moved, she felt fingertips on the bare curves of her breasts, felt the hard bee pendant and chain between. She breathed deeply, smelling this pleasure in leather, staring within, seeing peripherally. "(Maybe I should know you,)" Banelle said, feeling this bounce of jiggling energy. "(Could anyone else come to know me?)"

she heard male laughter

. . .

BANELLE OPENED the bedroom door and walked across the landing, trying not to skip from her growing desire to show off to someone safe, her dad. She started down the steps, left hand sliding lightly on the rail and her feet pounding out a rhythm of feeling jubilant.

She heard male laughter from the closed swinging door to the kitchen, and realized with alarm that wasn't just her dad's voice she heard. She stopped on the stairs, felt anxiety, bent her head to tune in, stepping slowly down the stairwell. The laughter behind the closed kitchen door had died down. Instead, she was hearing her father's voice, resonant and muffled. She felt the curiosity pulling at her alarm and finished descending the stairs. Before she touched the kitchen door, she heard the phone in the kitchen begin the bell-characteristic ringing.

"B.B?!" she heard her father's voice call.

As the upstairs phone started the first brrr'ing, she put her left palm against the kitchen door and pushed. The sound of the kitchen phone's bells on the second ring grew much louder while the door swung left, wide open. She stopped there with the door firmly against the floor stop, staring across the kitchen at two men's backs crowded close around the stainless steel stove, blue and yellow natural gas flames heating pans. The men were chuckling.

Banelle's nose was assailed by the strong smells of chocolate and something other that she couldn't immediately identify. She heard the upstairs phone start a late second brrr'ing.

Her father's gray dress jacket was on one of the kitchen chair backs. His dress blue shirt sleeves were rolled up his forearms, black belt in tan slacks visible, the wallet outlined inside the left hip pocket, and black penny-loafer shoes.

The man on her father's right was wearing a green short sleeve twill shirt tucked into loose-fitting new-looking blue jeans, belted in dark brown and wearing matching rugged dark brown shoes with black nubbly soles. There was something familiar in the way the elbows moved.

"B.B!" her father yelled.

"Right here!"

"AH!" yelled the man on the right of her father.

"Shit!" her father said simultaneously.

Neither looked toward her.

The unexpected third person in her home had her feeling panicky, curious. Her eyes switched from the strange man's back to her father's back. Her mind raced to sort out her loyalty to her father from a feeling her territory had been violated when she had left him in charge of the doorbell.

The kitchen phone began the third ring, startling her.

"Are you going to get that?" her father said, his right ear canted toward Banelle while his eyes focused on the task on the stove.

"Yes." Banelle stepped left toward the wall phone, let the door close automatically. "What are you guys doing?"

"Making chocolate icing," said that man on the right of her father. Her father's left elbow and the right elbow of that other man were moving rhythmically to a sound of stirring pans.

Banelle lifted the handset off the wall mount with her left hand,

"Who is that other person?" Banelle pressed the handset against her ear. "Hello?"

"Hello," a woman's voice on the phone.

"Who is this?"

"It's me," said that man standing on the right of her father.

"It's your mother," said the woman's voice from the phone.

"No," Banelle said automatically, thinking that man shouldn't be answering.

"No, what?" her mother's voice.

"So, you two are going out today?" her father said, his head turning toward that man on the right.

"Correct." That man's voice was familiar.

"Nelli? Are you listening to me?" her mother said.

"Yes. Mom, wait." Banelle put the handset against her chest. "Dollar?"

"Honey, I'm home!"

She heard her father chuckling.

"Dollar, stop." Banelle frowned at his back.

"He can't stop," her father said. "His chocolate will burn, and I'll win."

"You aren't going to win. The new man must compete successfully with the daughter's father, consider it done."

"You think?" Her father glanced toward Dollar a moment, smiling toothily.

"I mean," Banelle said, closing her eyes and shaking her head to clear the amalgamation of excitement and annoyance. "Dollar, what are you doing here? Again?"

"I got your note sweaty. Since I didn't have anything more pressing than setting myself up for happily ever after, I wanted to stop back while the day is still fresh and see if you wanted to go for a coffee?" He bent his head, sniffed the pan. Dollar nudged her father's right arm, "Say, is that mine burning or yours."

Her father bent forward, sniffed.

Banelle blinked, eyes wide. "More pressing than what?"

"I think it's yours," her father said, stood erect, resumed stirring. "You are stirring backward."

Dollar's eyebrows arched. "What does that have to do with it?"

"Dollar!" Banelle said, stomping her right foot.

"What, honey?"

"Look at me!"

"Not right now, honey, and just remember I love you even when I'm working in the kitchen."

She huffed, put the handset to the left ear, heard her mom.

"Nelli?!"

Banelle felt more annoyed, mouthed, "(I'm not your honey,)" rocking her head side to side while the breath-silent words protested. She couldn't stop the smiling in the right corner though, the lips parting, a flip in her womanhood, *Remember I love you.* "Mom."

"Nelli, who's there with you? That man?"

———

"Yes," Banelle said, feeling annoyed with her mother also. Banelle felt her lips pressed together in critical watchfulness, standing with the feet together. "And dad."

"Your *father's* there?"

"I think it's your pan," Dollar said with a serious voice.

"You think?" Her father bent over and simultaneously raised his pan from the stove.

"Mom, it's really busy here right now." Banelle began to notice ingredients and formed a mental checklist. What had the two men been doing while she was upstairs?

Her mind was champion at the game of checkmarks and naturally believed itself supreme. She remembered the doorbell was first on the list when she finally entered the shower, mentally added a checkmark.

"I know, dear," her mother's voice.

On the counters near the men were a coffee cup on each side, two small knives, cracker crumbs and counted four, five, six crackers scattered, and a plate with only cheese crumbs left; a cream carton, a golden white ring of angel food cake on a plate, a bowl each with sliced strawberries in one and lumpy raspberries in the other; wrappers from baking chocolates; the bottle of Creme De Menthe, and… *My bottle of Grand Marnier!*

"Hey!" Banelle said.

"Ha!" her father said sniffing. "Mine is coming along expertly."

Dollar bent forward, raised his pan off the stove also.

"Ready?" her father said to Dollar.

Both men set their pans back on their burners, continued stirring.

"Hey, what?" her mother.

Banelle objected. "Mom. Dollar. Dad." her mind jumping like a leap frog: the raiding of her best liquors, her mom being snoopy, the tight buns in the new blue jeans, her dad cooking chocolate in *her* kitchen.

"Nelli." her mother's tone, which made her feel angry from memories of being scolded…

"Honey?" Dollar's voice, which caused the flip inside her midriff…

"B.B?" father's resonance, which caused her to look at her dad's tall back…

Everyone seemed to respond to her all in one choral chant, the feelings stumbling over each other trying to find their own place in the body through which to express every feeling simultaneously, her mouth caught open by the opinions of two minds, felt herself stomp her foot. "Everybody stop!"

"B.B." said her father.

"Critical moment with the chocolate," Dollar said.

"Nelli!" her mother shouted in the tinny sound of the handset, interrupted by a beep tone, like a piece of her mom was gone forever. Banelle lowered the handset, the ear freed from distraction. "Mom, I have another call coming in," Banelle said to the mic end of the handset.

"Nelli, I…" she heard her mother say, while Banelle's eyes rolled upward. She felt the lips pressed, her head shaking a tiny, *No,* of irritation. Her mind proudly reorganized the priorities, part of her feeling guilty. "Hold on."

Banelle used two right fingers, pressed simultaneously on the handset button until the mechanical click, released the button, switched hands, held the handset to her right ear. "Hello?"

"Hello?" Dollar echoed.

"Shut up," Banelle said, mentally noting that.

Her father laughed, leaning briefly back.

"What?!" from the phone, a familiar woman's lilt. Banelle gradually recognized Martee's voice.

"Martee, I didn't mean you. Things are crazy here."

"At *your* house?"

Banelle felt better connecting with Martee.

"Do you mind my trying yours?" Banelle's father said.

Banelle's mind flashed through checklists, comparing the homes, hypothesized her house was much better organized. Usually, there was a sense of doubt.

"Here, try now," Dollar said, and stopped stirring. He leaned aside while her father leaned toward the right and reached a ladle into Dollar's pan.

"Is it a party?" Martee's voice.

Banelle felt herself blink, eyes widening, felt pleasure waving a shadowy arm inside for minutes already. Her mind calculated the benefits of gaining attention from the men, smiled briefly, felt the touching sigh of chocolate melting into surrender. "Maybe it is." Banelle felt annoyed Martee had pointed out the party first. "Mom's on the other line."

"Oh, my word as a saint," her father said, "THAT is GOOD! Mmmm-yum-yumm!"

"Really?" Dollar said, bending toward the pan, sniffing.

Martee's tinny sounding sigh. "I wish I was there now. Do you mind if I just come over?"

Banelle's eyes narrowed. "I thought I was picking you up?"

"I don't remember that!" Dollar said.

Banelle clicked her tongue, irritated, squinted at the back of his head while scrunching her nose, realized she was smiling.

"I'm bored," Banelle heard Martee say.

Banelle felt exasperated, continuing to reorganize her day. "So, come now."

"Are you mad at me?"

Banelle sniffed, feeling of excitement under the right palm. "No, Martee, come on, it's just crazy right now."

"Very recently, yes." her father said.

Banelle felt her eyes round.

"Tell her, Hi," her father added.

"Dad says, Hi."

"Martee is a she?" Dollar's voice.

"Yes," her father said. "She does that 'e-e' thing with the name."

"'E-e', noted. Let me try yours."

Her dad leaned left, making room for Dollar's reaching to touch the stirrer into the steaming chocolate pan.

"You have the coolest dad," she heard Martee say, and the checklist improved.

Banelle felt herself shrugging slightly at this pleasure, feeling increasingly Martee should come over. "Now! Hurry up! You're missing out!"

"Five minutes! 'Bye!"

"Bye." Banelle felt for the button to change lines while privately watching the men's backs, released the button with a right thumb flick.

"Mmmm!" Dollar said. "Excellent!"

"Mom?"

"Thank-you-very-much," her father said with the rolling vowels Elvis voice.

Banelle felt herself smiling, lips parting slowly, privately shaking her head, the mind focused on her dad.

"Oh, Nelli, it's about time," her mother's relieved voice in the right ear.

Banelle's left hand slid to the pleats of her skirt, fingers pinching, swishing the skirt like a cape. "Is it done yet? Whatever you two are doing?"

"Yes!" the two men said simultaneously, startling her.

Caught out, the left fingers paused, tingled.

"You left me on hold for so long," her mother accused.

Banelle controlled her voice, part of keeping secrets. "Sorry, mom."

"I wanted to lie down. I was on the phone, and then the cat wanted me to let it out," Banelle heard her mother share.

"Ready?" her father said.

"So I had to open the door and let my sweet pussy outside where the other cats are, and it's spring, you *know* how cats are!"

"Mom, MOM…"

"Ready." Dollar said.

"What?!" she heard her mother say, Banelle jumped, narrowed the eyes.

———

Banelle's father put his right hand on the burner knob, steady eyes on Dollar. "Heat… *off!*" The two men each twisted a knob.

Both men moved left and began tipping the pans, pouring steaming chocolate over the angel food cake, clank of the pans bumped, twin drizzling streams of steaming chocolate smoothed onto the fjord-like round ring top of the cake, chocolate puddles forming around the base on the plate.

"Mom, I don't want to hear about that cat right now."

The men started scraping and banging the pans with the wooden spoons, the last of the chocolate goo dripping onto the cake.

I want to taste chocolate!

Her mother was saying something Banelle couldn't hear over the din. *Is this really important, mom?* Banelle thought, another part of her knowing *everything* is important, because if everything *wasn't* important then neither was she, or so that part of her believed.

"Voilà!" Dollar said, stepping back.

"Hound Dog!" her father said, stepping back also, arms

outstretched with a pan handle in his left hand and a drippy spoon extending from his right hand, chocolate drops falling from both onto the antique oak floor.

"Hey!" Banelle said.

Dollar put his pan on the right back burner, clattering the pan with the dropped wooden spoon. He scooped up the bowl of raspberries with his left hand and thumb, and in a graceful overturn at arm's length, dumped the berries over the cake, "Ohhhh, yeahhhhhhh!" in a booming baritone voice.

Banelle felt an instant frisson of goose flesh.

Her father slipped his right hand under the bowl of strawberry chunks, dumped the strawberries on the cake, echoing, "Ohhhh, Yeahhhhh!" her dad's voice in the bass range mimicking Dollar's, which put a tickle inside Banelle's butterfly zone, the tingling her skin raising the hair on her forearms. She shook back her hair, smiling freely, open, feeling the quake up into her shoulders.

Banelle heard a click from the handset. The right hand pulled the phone from her ear to a place against the right thigh, left palm on her pelvis, enjoying herself breathing and laughing. She inhaled deeply, closed her eyes, rested her back against the wall, sighed.

She switched hands, pressed the handset against her left ear, opened her eyes to look at her sandaled feet together, blinked twice, ignored the sounds on her right ear. "Mom?" Banelle took in another deep breath smiling, "Mom?" She half-turned left, hung up and held the handset against the wall mount base, the twenty foot coiled cord swinging at a doubled length, dragging part of its coiled loop on the kitchen floor. Banelle looked toward the men and realized with a start they were watching her.

"Say," Dollar said, staring at her breasts, his eyes flicking toward her legs, then her eyes.

She felt for the cool wall behind her with her right palm, turned her back against the wall to face the men more fully.

Dollar's face lit up. "You look stunning."

FINALLY! Banelle thought, looking at her feet and smiling at the natural shine finish on her toes.

"Yes to that!" she heard her father say. The vision of herself at the bathroom mirror earlier rushed to remind her how she didn't deserve looking this magnificent, looked up to see two smiles disagreeing, felt the shrug, smiled once for herself happily. Banelle felt herself wriggle, accepting this truth as found, the wonderful pleasure this is.

Her father looked at Dollar. "I was thinking of topping the cake with whipped cream. I've changed my mind."

Dollar watched her father. Her father's head jerked slightly in Banelle's direction, eyes gleeful, the wrinkles of being nearly two decades older than her gathering around his eyes.

Dollar grinned, nodded agreement.

The two men moved toward her, both grinning, arms down, palms out from their bodies, fingers extended.

She screamed, feeling alarmed and pleased together, started backing left along the kitchen wall past the recently hung up phone, and realized with another scream she was cornering herself. The men grabbed her wrists, each with one hand, Dollar pulling her right arm over his shoulder, and her father pulling her left arm over his own shoulder.

Banelle screamed again feeling Dollar's left hand sliding along the right calf between her legs, then strongly grabbing her right ankle, felt the thrilling of the leg being captured by Dollar. *Progress!*

"Ready?" her father said.

"Ready."

Banelle yelled, "Dad! Stop!" She felt her father's right hand cupping behind her left knee, and lifting her leg from the floor, while Dollar's hand lifted her right ankle, tucking her knee under his arm, the tingling of both legs shooting the surprise up her spine. "Stop! Put me down!"

…they carried her across the kitchen…

"No! Stop!"

"Spin her around." her father said.

The men turned her all the way around, backed her toward the kitchen counter…

She screamed, feeling helpless, falling as they sat her down abruptly with a hard bump, felt the chill of the white marble counter instead of hot cake, saw with a quick glance she was sitting safely away from the cake on her right, and felt herself laughing. She bent forward, chest near her legs, the bumble bee swinging below her chin.

Her father let go of her left leg and her arm. Dollar let go of her right ankle, left hand smoothing along the inside of her right calf, fingers brushing across the knee, and lifted away.

Banelle pulled her right arm away from Dollar, crossed her arms against her chest, heaving her lungs, breathing in and out. "Well!" felt her lungs fill deeply, eyes focused on her father.

"Are you all right?" Dollar said, catching at her eye with his gray eyes.

She ignored Dollar, continued smiling at her father. "So, you two seem to be getting on very well. In *my* kitchen, I might add."

"Yes." her father said, brown eyes wide, then relaxed them. He turned and sat in a chair on the near side of the round table, twisting in the seat toward them. He crossed his right calf horizontally over his left knee.

Dollar stepped past Banelle, interrupting her focus on her father, and leaned against the counter on her left, folding his arms facing her.

———

Banelle looked within Dollar's eyes and winked her left eye at him, immediately felt an internal criticism for encouraging him.

He smiled and winked back, his eyes with quick succession glanced at her breasts, thighs, feet, eyes. "You really look amazing."

Banelle took a deep breath and sat up. "Thanks." She crossed her right leg, right bare thigh where the eye-catching pleated skirt drew the attention. "So, tell me again how you come to be here?"

Dollar unfolded his left arm and waved dismissively, "I couldn't read the number you wrote because the ink ran, and I uncharacteristically really want to get to know you."

"How nice." Banelle's right foot began bouncing.

"Only, you weren't immediately available." Dollar re-crossed his arms, looked at her father. "So I've been getting to know Charlie."

Banelle looked at her dad.

Her dad shrugged, closed his brown eyes momentarily, then gazed at her. "I assumed you two had already dated. We just got to visiting, and I like him," eyes-closed nod. "Good choice this time," her father added, opened his eyes, looked at Dollar.

This time? Banelle thought. She glanced sideways at Dollar briefly, then looked at her father. "Dad, I haven't been dating."

"I know."

Dollar's eyebrows arced and his eyes rolled left, then right. He shuffled, unfolding his arms, braced his right hand against the counter, bent his right leg, resting the toe of his shoe across the far side of his left foot. He stared at her legs, then within her eyes, then at her lips, then within her eyes again.

She shrugged, shaking her head. "There's nothing wrong with me!" Banelle said hotly. "I've just been busy with my two girls. And with a full-time job, I might add," visions of Thursday's clock-watching from three in the afternoon until the end of the day to start a long weekend running through her head.

Dollar shook his head very slightly, closed his gray eyes and began opening them again while he spoke. "I didn't say anything."

"Oh, yes you did," Banelle snapped back, pointing the right index finger at him.

"Kids," her father said. "Wait until you are married."

The doorbell rang.

"Ah!" her father said, changing tack and putting his left hand up, closing his eyes. "I'll get it." Her father stood, quick eye glance toward Banelle, turned for the door, pushed the swinging door open, walked out of the kitchen letting the door swing shut.

Dollar stepped nearer, voice quiet. "(You really look stunning.)"

She liked him closer; she didn't like his being so close. She wanted to grab his shirt in her left fist and pull him toward her for a kiss and wrap her legs around him; she wanted to jump down and sit at the dark cherry table to gain some space from him. She wanted to stay on the kitchen counter, her head slightly higher than his head standing. She felt her crossed right leg start the bouncing. Banelle stayed where she was sitting, rooted with the conflicting inner feelings. Murmured, "(Thank you. Regarding my father, butt out. I did not invite you to meet him yet.)"

"(So?)"

She felt the fire roar alive. "(So?!)" Banelle mocked back at him.

He shrugged, put his left fist against his hip opposite the right hand bracing him against the kitchen counter. "(Deal with it, girl toy.)"

She blinked, the ire so instantly livid this surprised her, her whole body clenched, stilled for action. She felt her eyes narrow, looking at him, feeling fiercely disrespected. "(What?)" icy tongue stop.

Dollar smiled. "(Banelle, while what I am about to share is way early for any sane man to utter just after meeting a woman he might at worst case marry, whether you like anyone being sweet toward you or not, I really like you. I have absolutely no rationale to explain my just knowing what I know, and I'm determined to get to know you completely, if you'll let me. I would fondle your breasts any way you asked me to right here laying on the kitchen counter. You can imagine your clothes in a pile on the floor, along with the sandals from your gorgeous feet, or imagine laying before my clever tongue on the couch or any bed in the house. I haven't been in a relationship in three years, and it's spring, so consider this a heartfelt limited time offer.

He continued. "(Just imagine if Charlie wasn't here right now and the house was not filling up with everyone you know or ringing your phones. Just today imagine what we could learn about each other privately? If we make our way through the day together without having a melt-down, freakout fight and a short, scary, gut-wrenching breakup, I promise I will even strip naked and dance to your favorite grooves while you watch and play with yourself and you can toss small bills at me each time you orgasm. Furthermore, we wouldn't even have to consummate. I would insist on waiting until after our first date, which I am here in person to tell you can start any minute. Your call. I just want to learn what your cries of joys are, your moans, learn your smells, watch you find three moments of ecstasy back-to-back. You smell lovely, by the way, so natural, which for an outdoors guy like me is a total turn-on.

"(You could then tell me about the times you found yourself pregnant, terror and joy, share what it was like in the delivery room both times, those high stress moments had to be different. You can tell me about your experiences so far as a single mom for two girls you pushed into the world. Then about your career, what are your ambitions? What do you want to do with your home, next? That kind of thing. If you want my inputs, as a professional landscaper I already have ideas for your yard.

"(Then if you are still feeling amorous and want a go at me again, I promise there is a way I can make you melt into a chocolate-drooling puddle and have hardly touched you. I am an expert in the natural energies some other people use for Reiki, and believe me there is a turn-on from these magick hands. Just not now, we have company. Deal with it.)"

His face was serious when he finished speaking, the smile gone, moist lips slightly parted except for — Banelle's eyes widened realizing what he was doing — except for silently repeating her name, barely a puff of air on syllables, and then he would silently say her name again, his lips barely touching once, the tongue moving inside his mouth, opening again to suckle her name. "(Banelle,)" she could see him say, breathing her name in and out of his mouth staring deeply within her eyes.

She felt herself pulled within the black pupils before her, and the connection soul to soul sparked a tingling in her nipples, a moistness between her thighs.

———

Her dignity's far away voice reminded Banelle's romantic eyes he had just called her 'girl toy', so beside this wetness and tingling she also felt a deep resolve forming: he would never, ever, while ever he lives, within this lifespan dip his fingers into her treats or shake her tits his way.

She felt her leg begin bouncing with the increased inner conflict, and her hands moved forward and around her right knee, her fingers interlocking. "Oh, I'm dealing with it," Banelle said, feeling her whole body moving with agitation in the hopes of convincing herself.

He smiled and winked.

She felt the air rush in through her nose quite abruptly, responding to the spasm of instant readiness her core suddenly felt. Her fingers unlocked, and her hands moved from her knee to grip the edge of the counter on each side of her. She looked away from him at her naked knees and felt and saw the silver bracelet slide on her left wrist, and felt the silver chain around the right ankle, loose on the upswing and bouncing against her skin on the downswing. She could smell his arousal.

Banelle looked at his crotch without turning her head, saw that bulge in a long vertical hunk. Her eyes glanced at the closed kitchen door, then quickly looked at her knees. She imagined his hot breath was on her left ear, knew that he wasn't close enough to feel that breath no matter how close the bulging of his pants felt, and she gripped the counter harder, to will the fingers not to grab that belt and tempting bulge in his jeans. Then she realized she actually was feeling his breath in her ear, looked, and caught him with his lips shaped for blowing.

"(Stop it.)" Banelle looked at the floor quickly, the eyes without focus. *Stop it*, Banelle thought, *or I'll unzip your pants and grab you where you won't get away, then you'll be* my *handful!* Her eyes snuck a look at the jeans, then upward at his lips.

She wanted to feel her tongue part his lips; she wanted to push him away, both hands against his chest using all the strength in her calves, to feel the strength in her legs and pelvis and stomach when she pushed him away...

She imagined pushing him backward onto a bed where her hands could jerk the belt open, yank the brass fly down. She felt this powerfully. She wanted to wrestle his chin aside with her right hand, wrap her teeth around his left jugular and suck hard and mark him, pull with her left hand in jerks until he cried out for mercy, cried her name, *Banelle!* over and over. *Banelle! Please!* To just laugh in her throat with her mouth sucking his neck red for days after and jerking him with her hand…

"(Beg me.)" Banelle heard herself say. Her eyes went wide, felt the shock within herself realizing this decree had pushed over her tongue, just escaped her lips, out where he could hear.

She saw his head move back. His eyes looked at her lips, and he looked within her eyes.

Her mind raced, trying to remember what the actual conversation had been.

"(*Beg* to get to know you?)" Dollar.

She felt the rush of embarrassment on her neck and cheeks, her whole body stiffened still with alarm. Timorous, she felt afresh her sense of inferiority because a part of her knew she was unusual, not worth dating. Three years had proved this self-belief; a failed marriage proved this; an emotionally scarred daughter proved this.

She looked within the shiny black of his pupils, hoping to touch souls again, the sight of the shiny blackness reminding her of so much she felt deeply important, though her mind couldn't at the moment place what this missing ingredient was in any specific way. Yet the flickering, agitated white-hot flame within herself seemed to know *exactly* what the real issue was.

She felt this knowing expand inside and resonate throughout, flushing her skin again. She inhaled deeply through her nose, this inner debate clenching her jaw muscles, holding her teeth firmly together. Her eyes looked at his lips and then within the black pupils.

He moved even closer, his right thigh pressed against her knee and right calf where she felt the warmth of his hardness. Her forehead yearned for his lips, which spoke quietly, "(Banelle.)"

Her breathing stopped, their eyes together locked, spell-tied, heart to heart, felt her soul bared. Her eyes opened wider feeling the startlingly fresh raw winds of another person's soul momentarily wide open, a feeling of holding wide the kitchen door during an alarming spring rain driven by gusts of warm and chilly air alternating, buffeting her body, felt the urge to pull both of them into an embrace with her hands, feel his ass in her palms, to put her will behind her embrace and draw, feeling the rush of infinite power swirling within her, smell of his arousal swirling with the beauty all around her skin.

She told her hands instead to stay at task gripping the countertop, cowed from the feeling of infinite power but not believing she had the right. She wanted to shake her head, *NO*, but felt both sides of the equation: she hungered for that knowledge of fullness with him, his thigh pressed into hers, snuggled and familiar. Was it a mistake to receive contact from him?

She felt his left hand brush across her right kneecap, then clamp fully on her knee, gently, warmly wrapped around the bare skin, then a squeeze. She felt her sense of reason swamped, wanted to feel his hand part her thighs, her thoughts tied up in a visceral desire to lure his member into the wet part of her, to feel that naked hardness deep within her full power, the sanctity of her secret self wriggling around his arousal…

She sat still instead of lying along the counter and knocking the cake off into a chocolate mess on the floor, and realized within her body this white-hot mellowing fire was totally calming, totally ecstatic, and she began to feel poised. Was this a misty-eyed romance?

She had never felt this way prior to their shared moment, if it were even possible for the moment to remember anything which had ever come before.

Whatever had been her previous compromises in choices of men seemed to fade into gray distant regrets and disappear. She marveled at this new freshly bright sparkle feeling of mellow power clenched and growing within her left hand. Any further action suspended, hands clenching the counter, her breathing shallow here in this moment outside time, she looked at his lips, looked within his eyes.

"(Banelle.)" Dollar said quietly.

She felt the air rush through her nose filling the suddenly spasming lungs.

"(Please.)"

She wetly blinked.

"(Please let me get to know you. Please get to know me, Banelle.)"

Tears dripped on the cheek. She looked at his lips, felt her lips parted with his hand around her knee, felt herself smile, the lips opening more, felt the toe of her right sandal pry between his thighs and caress up and down once, then Banelle heard herself quietly shape the lips, "(I'm in.)"

It was so meek she just wanted to lie back and giggle. *All that fire and shit*, her inner voice said. *Would he fucking kiss me already?*

put her left hand on his biceps

. . .

ALL THAT FIRE *and crying about it!* Banelle put her chin on her chest, rolled her eyes privately for herself, brushed the tears from her cheek with her right fingers. Breathed in deeply, sighed, caressed her toes up and down between the thighs in his jeans. She felt herself smile with a hope Dollar wasn't seeing he'd won her happiness, carefully caught the smile between quiet lips of purpose.

Banelle raised her head, whispered. "(First, though, you need to get your hand off my knee and back up a respectable distance.)"

Dollar whispered also. "(Why?)"

"(Because my dad will foray in here any second and I'm in no mood to explain anything.)" Banelle felt the lie, felt the whisper was partly a lie, also, because she was barely riding control on her desires in this moment and would rather be screaming happily, mortally afraid of not being able to control her voice or herself with these wavering feelings. She also knew she had to stop whispering because Martee knows why she whispers, and that must have been Martee who'd arrived.

Banelle slipped her toes out from between his thighs, brush of denim on the top of the toes, slick feel of the naturally polished toenails.

Banelle tried for a normal voice. "How long has my dad been out of the room?"

Dollar smoothed his hand from her knee.

She felt an opportunity leaving, stopped herself reaching for his hand, regretfully watched him back a step away brushing the seat of his jeans against the counter, crossing his arms, turning his back against the counter. Dollar turned his head forward, watching the floor with wandering eyes. "Oh, three minutes or so."

Her eyes followed the dark hairline touching his ears, his relaxed strong neck, the breadth of his right shoulder and arm muscles, his lean abs which held her eyes.

Banelle felt curious to see if that arrival had been, in fact, Martee. "C'mon." She slipped off the counter, self-consciously straightened pleats around the curves of her ass, walked with concentrated balance toward the kitchen door, pushed the door open, stopped to look back, saw that Dollar hadn't followed her.

She took a step back into the kitchen.

He had put the tall plastic cover over the cake and was putting the plate into the fridge.

What? Banelle thought, feeling her eyes blink open wider, brief frown. *Is he so comfortable?* Her mouth was moist with the smell of cooked chocolate in the air.

She watched him back up. He crouched momentarily, leaning left and right, peering inside the stainless steel fridge.

She felt her eyes widen. What kind of mess was her fridge in? Her head tipped right, held this marriage of feelings fresh on her face when, in a moment, he closed the fridge door and turned and saw she was watching him. She silently communicated with a nod leftward and pressed lips into dimples.

He inhaled deeply, stepped in her direction, folded his arms, walked with intense downcast eyes.

She didn't feel particularly pursued. She wasn't having him hanging around in her kitchen with everyone else in the next room, either.

Banelle turned into the living room, discovered Banelle's father was sitting on the overstuffed pine-green loveseat.

Martee was sitting almost in his lap, shoulder-length dark hair draping with expensive styling toward Martee's shoulder blades, looked over her shoulder at Banelle. "Hey!" Brown doe-eyes alive with obvious curiosity, irises intensified by enlarged pupils. Martee was wearing the smoldering red shorts and white V-neck plunge blouse, and also a wide flat gold chain looping in a curve highlighting her throat, a thin gold bracelet on each wrist, a wide glossy black belt with the tip overlong, and sassy black sandals enhancing the wet-look red nails of the feet and matching fingernails.

Banelle smiled briefly. "Martee." Banelle realized she would have to introduce Dollar. She didn't want to. Martee looked exquisite, damn her.

Banelle's eyes glanced at the coffee table. Dollar's business card had been moved near the center. She looked at Martee, leaning into Banelle's father and Martee craning her head, expectantly watching the kitchen door.

Martee glanced at Banelle, waggled the eyebrows twice, then looked past her. That annoyed Banelle more than Martee's practically rolling into Banelle's father's lap.

Banelle turned on the spot with Dollar approaching, slid her right hand inside his left arm from beneath, molding her fingers around the beefy shape of his forearm. Banelle put her left hand on his biceps and pulled on him until he stood beside her. He uncrossed his arms, lowered them, slid his hands comfortably within his jeans pockets. He smiled, eyebrows raised, his gray eyes looking within Banelle's eyes, then at her lips. He bumped her hip subtly with his.

Banelle turned to Martee. "Martee, this is Dollar."

"Really? Well, hello, Dollar!" Martee spread her hands palms-up, arms wide and chest in motion like she would give him everything and take all of him for herself if he would only come closer.

Banelle felt his body move toward Martee involuntarily. Banelle clenched his arm, her feet stubbornly rooted, looked at him sharply.

"Hello." Dollar returned Martee's smile. "And you are?" He deferred to Banelle for the answer.

Banelle nodded toward Martee. "My best friend, Martee." Banelle looked at Dollar again, discovered he hadn't looked away from Banelle.

Dollar winked, smiled, then looked toward Martee. "Well, Martee, I don't know you yet but I can see already you are charming and beautiful."

"Oh!" Martee said, and giggled, leaning and wriggling and practically falling backward into Banelle's father's lap.

Banelle felt her eyes roll upward, inwardly seething at Dollar, feeling like his winking was supposed to disarm Banelle's feeling jealous so he could flirt. She was not accepting that. She sighed. *Practical matters first*, Banelle's inner voice said, the memory of chocolate smells from the kitchen. "I'm hungry."

Her father nodded. "Me, too," pushed himself off the loveseat around Martee's gyrations, and stood.

Banelle felt her hands let go of Dollar, watching Dollar's face. She was feeling a panicky need for space with her father now standing, worrying he would notice how close she felt to Dollar already, the hot scene in the kitchen cooking in chocolate bubbles just under Banelle's barely calm exterior, the feel of Dollar's jeans still on her right toes.

"I've been hungry for about half an hour," Dollar said, nodding while looking at Banelle's father and grinning.

Her father grinned.

Martee bounced from the loveseat, "Where are we going?" She wriggled coyly, and moved to stand near Dollar and Banelle.

"We?" Banelle said, and she looked first at her father, then quickly at Dollar, because she and Martee were going out, according to plans made earlier. Banelle realized there may not be a smooth way of disengaging from the men, and this wasn't her whole desire anyway. Besides, the other three would notice her being rude.

They were all looking at her. "I mean," Banelle said shrugging. "What does everybody like?" and by this she meant Dollar.

Here again this was already changing things, and the other three must be noticing. This was feeling discovered, even more thrilled. Banelle sighed, surrendering herself into further changing with the new events. This would have to follow along with the inputs of others, naturally. Banelle looked directly at Dollar. "What do *you* like?"

He smiled and winked. "(You,)" Dollar said quietly and leaned into Banelle, hands still in his pockets.

She looked briefly at her father then back at Dollar. "(Stop it,)" Banelle said quietly, and realized she had snuggled herself practically into Dollar's pocket. Banelle rebalanced herself, stepped apart from Dollar. "Mexican?" Italian?" She couldn't help feeling a wry smile. "Fast food burgers?"

Martee held her hand out to shake Dollar's hand, half-turning into the space Banelle had just made. Banelle could smell the perfume on Martee.

"Any independent restaurant," Dollar said, eyes on Banelle, watching past Martee, his right hand coming out of his pocket. When he took Martee's hand, Dollar began looking at Martee instead of Banelle.

Banelle felt annoyed. She didn't see what could be done about Martee having split the space between Banelle and Dollar, with hardly room to slide a hand between Martee and Dollar now. Banelle didn't see how she could regain being the closest with him without this turning into a cat fight right here on her own turf with her father watching. At the moment she wasn't sure she even wanted to be close to that man, and felt like running away.

She turned on her right heel and started toward the foyer, a step up. Banelle called over her right shoulder. "Well, come on." and turned to unlock the front door.

She felt a pat on her behind and rolled her eyes, not looking back. "(Why don't you drive?)" she heard her father say near her right ear.

"(Fine by me.)" Part of her was not fine, wondering who or what was driving together the foursome. Herself, she realized with a flush of feminine power leading them out of her home.

In a few moments they were all standing outside. Banelle had a brief glimpse of the odd collection of four cars in or near her driveway. Dollar stood near Banelle.

Her father was locking the house.

Martee sidled on Banelle's left, put her face close and said in a quiet voice. "(Where the hell did you get the hunk from?)"

Banelle felt like saying that was none of Martee's business. "(He just walked into my yard this morning.)"

"(Is that why you're all tens today?)"

"(What do you mean?)"

"(I haven't seen you looking so stunning since prom and that five thousand dollar dress, and don't remind me how long ago that was, either. I feel like scratching your eyes out.)"

Banelle felt thrilled, scrunched her nose at Martee, smiled and squinted, shaking her head.

Martee. "(No, really. You didn't tell me, 'Oh, Martee, for once I'll be dressed all tens!' You just asked me what I was wearing! I'm feeling angry with you.)"

"(I had no idea what I was going to wear,)" Banelle said defensively, quietly.

"(Right. You asked me what I was wearing. You never said…)"

"(Later.)" Banelle said quietly, turning further counter-clockwise, seeing her father had finished locking up, seeing over her left shoulder Dollar was watching Banelle and Martee.

Her father stopped with his hand still on the doorknob. He looked at Banelle. "The phone?"

Banelle felt her head roll back, her shoulders slump, knees bending slightly, heard her tongue click. Banelle waved her right palm. "Leave it."

She turned, completing her pirouette and looked again at the cars. Martee's new red Honda Prelude with a dealer's plate, Banelle's father's red Cadillac STS, and Banelle's glossy black Lincoln Navigator. "Looks like an expensive used car lot."

Banelle heard Dollar chuckle.

In her periphery Banelle noted Martee walking around to the other side of Dollar.

There was a lawn-green massive pickup with chrome wheels parked at the curb, partially blocking the view of the home across the street. "Yours?" Banelle said, looking at Dollar, inclining her head toward the largely stated pickup.

He smiled teeth bright with short enthusiastic nods, eyebrows up.

"No logo?"

"I took them off."

Banelle looked at the truck. "So what is it?"

"The work truck."

"Ohh, that'd be a Ford one ton." her father said, stepping between Banelle and Dollar and stopping so the four of them formed a line, Martee having sidled around the far side of Dollar — and who, Banelle noted, was standing so close with Dollar the breeze must needs go around.

Martee assessed the truck. "Power Stroke?"

Dollar nodded.

Martee grinned, nod. "Ford Power Stroke 7.3 liter four-by-four."

Banelle felt the name was innuendo, "Power Stroke?"

Martee caught Banelle's eye. "It's a diesel engine. The marketing is targeted at guys. Guys are more likely to stroke, so it is believed."

Banelle looked at Dollar. "So you bought it because it's called a Power Stroke?"

He grinned, shaking his head. "No. I like the rumble and clatter of the diesel. The name doesn't matter. I took the labels off, see?"

"It looks awesome," Martee said. "Well maintained and very masculine. It goes well with red."

Banelle felt her eyes roll, curled the side of her mouth in a smirk, bent forward and looked sideways at Martee.

Martee waggled the eyebrows. "Nice choice." using the eyes to indicate she meant Dollar.

Dollar was smiling, gazing at his truck. "It's a custom color."

"Even better." Martee quipped.

Banelle decided to change the topic. "Well, I'm still hungry."

Dollar turned his head toward Banelle. "I thought you were driving?"

Banelle felt defensive. "I was waiting on you guys."

"I was waiting on you to finish looking at vehicles."

Banelle glared at him, opened the clutch, started digging for her keys, felt nothing on the fingertips except soft corners, a lip balm, and identification inside the clutch, then remembered she had left the key ring in the foyer. She closed her clutch, took a deep breath, turned away from the other three.

———

"So." Banelle said, turned to face Dollar fully. "You're going to have to wait another minute."

Her father chuckled.

"Dad."

Her father shook his head, smiling. "Be right back," and he walked toward the house. He called over his shoulder, "Where are they?"

Martee broke out laughing, finally realizing what the segue was about. In Banelle's opinion, Martee made a little much of the wriggling, brunette hair bouncing, foot kicking and flying tits V-neck peeks.

"On the table in the foyer, daddy," Banelle called, feeling her head roll back, clenching the clutch with both hands.

Dollar was smiling, his arms crossed, looking everywhere except at Banelle.

A blue car cruised by, the horn beeped.

Martee looked at Banelle after that car had gone. "Was that for you or me?"

"What?"

Dollar's eyebrows arched. "You've been beeped at before, I'm sure? A hot number like you?"

"I think it was me," Martee said.

"I've never!" Banelle knew this was a lie. She tried to remember how long it had been since receiving an unsolicited honk. She looked down at herself briefly now trying not to be noticed doing so.

The horn on her black SUV beeped twice and flashed the lights, startling her. Martee did a short screech and physically shook like she'd been zapped, standing closer to Banelle's SUV than Dollar and Banelle.

"All aboard!" called Banelle's father. He walked up behind, handed the keys and remote around Banelle's waist into her left hand.

Banelle murmured, "(Thanks, dad.)

"(I think he likes you, B.B.)"

She felt the flush of a smile, turning to glance into her father's brown eyes. "(You really like him?")

Nod.

"All aboard!" Banelle echoed, turning toward the SUV and pushing with her left hand and keys against Dollar's shoulder.

She felt the same unusual sensation as the other times earlier when she had pulled or pushed on him, the tactile sense of thick muscles and inertia. She felt he would become aware she was pulling or pushing on him before changing his own direction; or like now, before going anywhere at all. She felt a strange thrill in feeling through the palm edge of her left hand how he had a sense of direction of his own, which she could influence. She felt the stimulation of his changing direction simply because she was touching him insistently.

She tried not to think on that overmuch or she knew she would falter, because who had the right? She heard herself click her tongue, knew immediately she had analyzed this overmuch already, and was feeling the rictus of dismay. She let her hand slip from his warm strength and fall near her side. She walked around the front of the SUV toward the driver's door.

Banelle felt the romantic fog roll back over her discovering Dollar had followed her around the SUV. He opened the driver's door with his left hand before she could connect with what was going on. He held the door for her, smiling and motioning with his right palm for her to enter the SUV.

She felt a rush of warmth, felt herself smiling and flustered sliding into the driver's seat, and nodded happily. When she was settled, he pulled the seatbelt out and held the belt for her. That surprised her even more. She felt her heart cede just looking at his hand holding the buckle. She looked within his eyes with wonder.

Dollar smiled, leaned toward her. His gray eyes looked from her left eye into her right eye, then toward what he was doing. She felt the pressure of the belt slide between her breasts and three-point belt across her pelvis. She watched his ear, smelled a blend cologne of roses and leather, heard the metallic click of the safety catch, felt the little fishtails swishing deep inside beneath where the safety belt crossed the hips. Would she ever want more than safety and security from a man?

His head turned toward her. Dollar looked within Banelle's eyes, backed away a step, closed the door and started walking around the front of the SUV.

Her father had gotten in the back seat on the right and Martee was directly behind Banelle, all the doors closed. "It's hot," her father said.

Banelle felt hot herself, though the heat of the Sun was running second place, and began fumbling with the keys. Her eyes were watching Dollar through the windshield as he walked around the front of the vehicle.

Martee's voice. "(He didn't open the door for me. And what was all that with the belt buckle? I've never had a man do that for me.)"

"(Oh, hush,)" Banelle said. "(I haven't had a man open a door for me since… I don't remember since when. Had to be before Bill. Maybe at the prom.)"

"(You think?)" her father whispered.

Banelle slipped the key into the ignition and started the SUV.

She felt the air blowing gradually cooler as the automatic air system kicked in.

"Dads don't count as men," her father grumped, looking at Martee.

"Oh yes you do," Martee said, and Banelle saw in the rear-view mirror Martee lean toward him, smiling, then sit erect again immediately, her dark hair flying.

Dollar opened the front passenger door and got in. "Done!" He pulled the door closed.

Banelle was watching him.

His eyes met hers. He smiled, buckled himself in, turning slightly to pull the belt around.

Banelle began backing the SUV out of the driveway, watching past Martee's hair in the rear view mirror, with glances out the left side mirror. "Martee, you know all the places. Where's the best independent lunchtime restaurant?"

"Kathy's?"

Banelle finished rolling the SUV backward, turned left, stopped on the street, put the SUV in drive, accelerated.

Dollar turned his head toward Martee. "What's Kathy's?"

"Sandwiches and soups. Or there's Rosebud's Delicious."

"That's a chick joint," Banelle's father said. "That's perfect."

"Dad." Banelle looked at him through the rear-view mirror.

He looked back at her through the mirror. "B.B, I've told you before, my eyesight is very good, and I'm going to continue making very good use of it."

Dollar chuckled.

Banelle rolled her eyes once, watched the road. "Dollar?"

"Oh, I'm going to bow to beauty and experience, Rosebud's sounds intriguing."

"Good!" Martee said, the sound of vain chuckling.

Banelle couldn't think up a response. She and Martee had eaten there before, and Banelle had her favorites. "Fine."

Everyone was quiet for a block.

———

"Dollar," Martee said, "what do you do for a living?"

He repositioned himself in the front passenger seat, turned himself enough for visiting. "I create landscape art."

Banelle looked at him, then back to where she was driving.

"Like statuary?" Martee said.

Banelle slowed the SUV and signaled for turning.

"Nope. It has to be living. Alive, like grass and trees and soil. Except for accents to accommodate humans, where I use stone and wood. Never cement."

"Why not?" Banelle's father said.

Dollar grinned. "Natural is powerful. No homogenizing of chemicals to create something which wouldn't occur naturally."

Banelle discovered a safe point in traffic, pressed the accelerator, turned left out of the subdivision. Banelle risked a glance at Dollar. "Really?"

"Really."

"And that landscaping," Banelle said, "would this beauty occur naturally if you didn't interfere?"

"Oh!" Martee said, "You're in *landscaping*."

Dollar spread his hands, faced Banelle while looking at his own palms, then emphasized with a shake, "I can't think of anything more natural than my hands teasing nature into full expression." His eyes refocused on Banelle's breasts, her thighs. He slowly closed his hands, forearms bunching muscles.

Banelle felt the naked exposure of his unwavering intensity building, tingling all over her skin. She had never felt anything like it. She glanced at him repeatedly, while also needing to watch the road to drive safely.

"That explains the muscles." Martee purred, sound of a cat stretching, ears and tail up.

Banelle would have laid her ears back if they were furry, feigned looking at the left side mirror. She felt something from Dollar more powerful than his words, and searched for her own words, having little experience with that.

"And the tan," Martee purred, vision of the cat's tail whipping.

Banelle felt the fur rise on her tail, it was *her* territory.

Dollar relaxed his hands, and the feeling of naked exposure and skin tingling faded for Banelle. She pressed her thighs together briefly and tried shifting her posture. Whatever he had done just now had her feeling horny.

"(Oh, Martee,)" Banelle said in quietly sighing words, peripherally glad Dollar's attention was distracted.

Banelle wondered why Martee acting like Martee bothered her more today. Banelle's mind analyzed this insight gladly. This was something her mind could understand in the moment, fretted at untangling that behavior out of her own hair.

"You know," Dollar said, talking toward Martee, "those are two of the things I really like about the work. Besides the artistic part." Dollar waved his right hand in a widdershins circle, palm down, set the hand flat on his left thigh. The movement was graceful. "And besides the people part." Dollar said smiling, with a nod of enthusiasm.

Banelle looked at him for a moment.

He winked his right eye.

She felt herself smile, breathed deeply, turned her attention fully back on the road.

"What two things?" Martee said.

"The muscles. The Sun on the skin, as you say. But I love the rain best."

"Oh?" Martee said.

Dollar opened his mouth to say something, hesitated, then closed his mouth. He turned in the seat facing forward.

"What?" Banelle said, bending her head forward, catching at his eye.

Dollar shook his head briefly, resisted her eyes, rested his hands palm-down cupping his knees. "Nothing." His fingers tapped against the jeans below his kneecaps.

Banelle signaled right, slowed down, turned the SUV into a crowded parking lot, slowed further.

"Take me with you sometime," Martee said.

Out of the corner of her eye, Banelle saw his head move back slightly. Dollar did not turn his head, or immediately reply. Banelle risked a glance from safely driving through the parking lot and saw his fingers had stopped tapping, and were instead gripping the kneecaps.

Banelle looked away immediately to pay attention in the crowded lot. There were people walking between cars.

She heard Dollar breathe in deeply. "Absolutely." followed by a sigh.

Banelle glanced at him, her eyes narrowing. She wasn't entirely sure he meant that.

"(Yesss!)" she heard Martee whisper.

Banelle saw a spot for parking and over-applied the brakes, all of them lurching forward in the seats.

"B.B!" her father said.

"Oops!" Banelle rolled her eyes, parked, taking longer than she usually did, being unsure of her foot in this uncertain bewitched landscape.

"There go three now," her father said, an animal growl in the voice.

"Three what?" Martee said.

Dollar chuckled. Banelle sighed, catching sight of the group of three women her father meant. The women were walking up the few steps there were on the sidewalk leading into Rosebud's. "Women, Martee." Banelle shut off the SUV.

"Good time of day to go." her father added.

The four of them got out of the SUV.

Banelle was standing already when she realized Dollar might have come around and opened the door if she had waited. *Ratz*, Banelle thought, glancing across the front seats and seeing him close the right front passenger door.

She heard Martee shut the passenger door behind her, and her father and Dollar shut theirs. Banelle closed the driver's door, mashed the remote. The SUV beeped once, flashed the lights, and she slipped the remote within her clutch.

Martee whispered into Banelle's left ear, leaning against her from behind. "(By the Goddess, he is handsome.)"

Banelle turned around counter-clockwise, staying close, and with a quick look into Martee's brown eyes, put her mouth near Martee's left ear. Banelle whispered. "(Yes, damn cute. And, girlfriend, my best friend for life, I saw him first. So keep your hands *and* your flirting to yourself.)" Banelle pulled back a bit and looked Martee in the brown eyes.

"(Awwe,)" Martee said quietly, shrugging the right shoulder, expensively cut hair flashing with reflected sunlight.

Banelle felt her eyes roll. "(You're hopeless.)" Banelle turned clockwise, putting her left arm within Martee's right arm to pull her along, and started them walking.

Banelle felt a frown, wondering why she was so aware of Martee's perfume today, a blend of hyacinth and nutmeg.

Dollar and Banelle's father followed.

"I take it you're not married?" she heard Dollar say behind her.

"No. B.B's mom and I divorced thirteen years ago."

Dollar chuckled. "Usually I say congratulations."

Martee turned her head, arm still linked with Banelle's. "You do?" Banelle felt the slight tug backward and pulled Martee along nevertheless.

"I rarely hear that," her father said, "and thank you. I think it's been the best decision all the way around. For everyone."

Banelle and Martee neared the three wood steps, painted adobe red, part of the flavor of Rosebud's, located thirty feet down the sidewalk from the main doors.

"(Not that it's been cheap,)" her father muttered, heard his sigh. "And yourself?"

"I've never been married, so I don't personally know the thrill of divorce, much less the chase."

"What chase?" Martee said, still watching the men behind.

Dollar barked a short laugh, "Out the door."

———

Banelle realized Martee was at risk of tripping on the steps, so she squeezed Martee's arm. "(Steps.)" Banelle said quietly.

"(What?)" Martee said, looking around. "(Oh. Thanks, Anna,)" and changed the timing of her step to match Banelle's. They climbed the three steps together without further calamity. The men pounded heavier on the steps behind them.

A skinny white young man was waiting at the doorway of Rosebud's doing greetings. He couldn't help his eyebrows popping when he turned from talking with someone further inside the green door and looked toward Banelle. He was trying unsuccessfully to be inconspicuous looking at her legs, and also made quick glances at Martee's legs, then looked down with restless green eyes, and shuffled his posture.

Banelle felt the corner of her mouth curl, a subdued smile. She looked down at herself for a quick peek. She felt this wasn't her right, to look more delicious than Martee did, the red shorts and black sandals walking beside her.

Banelle's right ankle bracelet and the pliable dangling thin black belt straps brushing her right thigh, the lively yellow miniskirt, these things made her feel she was definitely sporting the tens of life. She realized her little bee was swinging out in front of her cleavage, and she quickly straightened herself, feeling the bee bump against her skin.

"Good afternoon," said the young man. "Two today?" sound of hopefulness.

"Four," Banelle said.

Martee smiled toothily. "Nice tie."

Banelle closed her eyes and slowly shook her head. Black knit ties, tan shirts, and gray slacks were the uniform at Rosebud's.

"Thanks," he said, his left arm coming up, pointing at arm's length with a seating chart in hand which way they could go. "If you'll bear to the right as you go in, there are a few tables open on that side and someone will seat you."

"Won't you be escorting us?" Martee said.

He relaxed his arm. "I'd like that. I can't leave the door for a minute."

He looked past Martee and Banelle at the men, then looked at Banelle, then at Martee. "I'm off at four."

Banelle let go of Martee's arm and swiveled right to catch Dollar's eyes.

Dollar stepped forward and held out his left arm for her. Banelle slid her palm inside his arm, cupped her hand over the top of his forearm, the feel of his muscles under his skin at her fingertips. He led, snaked them through the remaining gap in the doors of Rosebud's, leaving Martee behind.

The foyer of Rosebud's was painted a farm chicken egg shell brown, with sweeping stucco walls, ferns hanging in wood-beamed skylights, with adobe-red tiles demarcated with black grout beneath the feet.

Banelle looked over her left shoulder, enjoying the smells of the restaurant and Dollar's closeness, and saw her father was walking briskly behind her. He smiled and gave her a pat on the behind as he walked around on her left, and joined them. They stopped when they entered the putting-green carpeted dining area.

"How old is Martee again?" her father said.

Banelle looked at Dollar, then turned her head left, looked at her father. "She's thirty-four."

"You think?" her father said. "When she turns forty, she'll probably wear *black* shorts and bright red sandals. And she may finally quit being shy."

Dollar chuckled.

"Dad."

He shrugged. "Just making the observations a man makes."

Dollar laughed briefly.

They were met by a teenage girl, Spanish almost-black eyes, Hawaiian black hair, trim energetic walk in the similarly styled uniform, and black athletic shoes which had seen plenty of use. "Three?"

Banelle felt briefly puzzled by how immaculate the styling of the girl's hair was, neatly rounded toward the neck, feathered from above like the wind. The girl was slightly taller than Banelle.

"Four," Banelle's father said. "Window, no smoking," he leaned forward, looking past Banelle toward Dollar "You don't smoke, right?"

"Tried it once when I was four," Dollar said, a decided nod.

"Non-smoking," Banelle's father said, looking at the teenage girl, straightening up.

Banelle tugged on Dollar's arm.

He looked into her eyes.

"(You tried smoking at four years old?)"

Dollar nodded enthusiastically, smiled. "(Thought I'd get it out of the way as soon as I could.)"

Then they were walking, following her father, a number of conversations going on all at once in the crowded restaurant, emotionally stirring exchanges of mostly female voices.

The tables were covered with thick white cotton tablecloths, different foods, some freshly being served. It was pink rose day, Banelle noted, seeing the pair of roses centering each table, lead crystal vases with water. The aroma of premium entrees was heavenly, the soft pink of the roses calming everything except her curiosity. Banelle pressed her cheek against Dollar's shoulder. "(Your parents supported that?)"

"(Supported it? I was a major pest when I had set my mind to something. I'm sure it wasn't a one-day topic.)"

"How about this table?" asked the teenage girl, stopping beside a four-chair round table in the back right corner where the large plate glass of the two walls met. The chairs were painted white with cream cushions.

"That's good," Banelle's father said, turning slowly, raising his eyebrows and scanning the room. He chose the chair in the corner with the view of the room and sat down.

Banelle decided to sit on her father's left, stepped past Dollar, stood by the chair, looked to her left at him.

Dollar stepped behind her and pulled the chair out. She sat as he pushed the chair in beneath her until she nodded.

Dollar chose the chair with his back to the room, opposite her father, pulled the chair closer to Banelle and sat down.

Banelle looked at the teenage girl. "When a woman in red shorts and a white blouse comes in, be sure to send her this way."

"Will do. What can I get you to drink?"

"Sweet tea."

"Water for me," Banelle's father said.

The girl smiled toothily at Dollar.

"I'll have orange juice."

"On the way! I'll be right back." The girl squinted her nose with a smile at Dollar when she turned, leaving.

Banelle felt her head fall forward, turned her head, catching Dollar's eye. "Are you a walking magnet or something?"

"Yeah?" her father said.

Dollar blushed. He shrugged briefly. "I have no idea. Sometimes." He leaned forearms on the table and turned toward Banelle. His eyes looked steadily into hers. "(Apologies. Keep in mind I'm here at all because of my *extreme* interest in *your* sexy aura.)"

She looked at her dad for a moment, who glanced within her eyes, and shrugged. She looked down at her hands, opened them to look at her palms, interlocked her fingers, closed her hands as a comfortably clenched ball.

———

"Ohhh," Banelle's father said. "Here comes Martee. Today in *red* shorts and black sandals."

Martee was smiling and walking energetically between tables, making her way toward them, the hair bouncing, navigating turns by swinging the red shorts higher than Banelle considered necessary.

Dollar was still looking at Banelle. When he had her attention his eyes pointedly stared at Banelle's breasts with eyebrows accenting his interest. Dollar was quiet and thoughtful, calmly returned her gaze, not smiling at all.

Martee joined them, sassing the shorts. She put her right fingers on Dollar's left shoulder, balanced on her left foot, right foot off the floor reaching for the empty chair with her left hand while smiling at Banelle.

Dollar turned away from Banelle, glanced at Martee's hand, then at Martee's face.

"Hello, everybody!" Martee said happily, sliding the chair nearer to Dollar. When she was settled, Martee took her right hand off Dollar's shoulder and clenched the hand in a little fist and propped the chin, elbow on the table, looking past Dollar toward Banelle.

Banelle felt they made a conspicuous cozy threesome, the chairs so close together, scowled briefly at Martee. Martee popped her eyebrows at Banelle.

Under the table — where Banelle with shock hoped nobody else could see Banelle's reactions — she felt Dollar's hand touch the top part of her left leg, forward near the knee. Trying not to show alarm and suppressing a knee-jerking response, she reached her left hand swiftly under the table and grabbed the top of his hand and simply held it firmly. She decided to not push that off, left bracelet cold on her skin because, she realized, that might be his way of connecting with her in private, where Martee couldn't see. Banelle liked this feeling. That hand on the knee gesture made her feel she was more important than Martee. She also didn't want him thinking it was time yet for exploring her body either, so she lightly and firmly held his hand where it was.

Banelle felt his reaction. He attempted to pull the hand away and her eyes widened slightly. She pretended to follow whatever Martee was babbling about, nodded while not hearing a word of it. Martee was waving the hands retelling the story of the door greeter, and Banelle knew in this instant she'd rather have Dollar's hand right where Banelle's knee was rather than off somewhere where Martee with her hands buzzing about could grab his hand up. Banelle clenched Dollar's hand more firmly and pressed down on the hand until he stopped his pulling away, felt his hand squeeze her leg reassuringly, then felt his hand relax beneath her palm and fingers.

"Amazing," Dollar said, interrupting Martee's retelling.

"Absolutely amazing!" agreed Martee, hair bouncing, body wriggling. "I'm *so* excited!"

"You think?" Banelle's father said in an uninterested, grumpy voice.

The teenage girl arrived with a tray of three drinks, surprised Martee by standing in the large gap of chairs between Martee's chair and Banelle's father.

"Oh!"

The girl gave Dollar his orange juice first, smiling sunnily at him. Then Banelle got her sweet tea in a huge sweating glass. Her father received a similarly large glass of water with ice nearly bottoming the glass.

The girl turned to Martee. "What can I get for you?"

"I'll have a light beer, in a bottle."

"Can do." The girl glanced at Banelle's father, quickly toward Banelle, then Dollar.

Dollar smiled sunshine warmth. "Can you bring us appetizers?"

"Sure." said the girl, responding happily, a lithe Hip Hop move in place watching him, palms crossed at the wrists near her thighs, footwork criss-cross, recomposed herself into the Waitress Attending lock move. "What would you like?"

Banelle felt her eyes widen.

"Lovely! What do you have?" Banelle's father said.

Dollar looked at him, then at Banelle, then back at the girl.

The girl shifted thoughtfully, putting all the weight on her left leg and tilting her head slightly. She began reciting, counting visibly by shaking her right hand, extending a finger for every item. "There are Spicy Thighs, Potato Skins, Spicy Cauliflower with cheese dip, Lemmings…"

"Lemmings?!" Dollar said.

"Yes," Martee said, touching his left arm momentarily with the fingers of her right hand. "Marshmallows lightly deep-fried in shredded coconut batter, sprinkled with powdered chocolate, drizzled with raspberry reduction."

"Lemmings."

"Yes!" bubbled Martee, bouncing, the hair jiggling.

Dollar looked at the girl.

The girl wrinkled her nose, smiling, squinted. "I like 'em."

"What else?" Banelle's father said.

The girl rolled the thumb out of her hand for all five fingers, palm shake toward Dollar, "And there's also Fish Bait."

"Fish Bait?!" Dollar.

Banelle squeezed Dollar's hand under the table and cleared her throat. "Gummy Bear worms and sashimi, with a small bowl of candied juice from cucumber, ginger, and mint leaves to go fishing in."

"Sashimi?" Dollar's brow furrowed as his eyes met Banelle's.

"Some people mistake sushi for being sashimi," her father said. "until they get the bill. With sashimi you know you're getting thinly sliced fish, whereas sushi is fermented rice with seafood and other ingredients."

Dollar stared at Banelle's father. "Not for me, thanks."

"How about the spicy thighs?" Banelle said, patting his hand three times beneath the table, squeezed his hand briefly, then rubbed her palm across the back of his hand twice.

Dollar chuckled. "Spicy thighs would definitely water the tongue." Below the table he lifted his fingers from her leg, palm against her bare skin, and intertwined his fingers with hers. "Probably I'll save the choice meat for the entree wrap, and munch the edges of a hot potato skin. If that works for everyone else?" Dollar added, looking at Martee, then at Banelle's father.

Banelle slipped her fingers fully between his.

"Ohh," her father said. "We could do that, and maybe have the spicy cauliflower, too." Her father patted his stomach. "A man with handsome abs treats them with dignity."

Martee giggled, covering her mouth and nodding at him.

"Skins and cauliflower," Dollar said, looking at the girl.

The girl smiled and nodded, turned to leave.

Banelle felt she could not resist having to say something which corrected the girl. "And bring me a smaller glass," Banelle said, a part of her wondering if this were important. *Everything is important,* another part of herself asserted.

The girl looked at Banelle, nodded smiling and looking bemused. The girl breezed away energetically.

The feel of Dollar's hand on Banelle's leg was the most natural feeling in her relationship history so far, she decided, after having gotten over the original surprise of it. She liked the feel of his hand on her skin, and decided to relax. She rubbed her left calf across his jeans until she found his foot, draped her ankle across the arch of his shoe snug against his shin, their hands together on her leg sliding higher along her thigh, hiking her skirt slightly. Her eyebrows raised momentarily, then smiled and looked at the thick white cloth, imagining what their hands and legs looked like under the tabletop.

That's as far as it goes! Banelle's inner resolute voice said, echoing in the canyons of her mind like a white-bearded prophecy predicting the next earthquake.

The miniskirt felt short, the heat of his hand on her skin like heavy desert sands forming a dune on the treasure map of her buried desires, the contrast of the cool air caressing the exposed skin on her thighs and calves and sandaled feet in the nighttime skies under the tablecloth. A brave feeling welled up, if he didn't expose her skin further himself, she would have to, and where would that get them?

the girl blushed and giggled

. . .

"WHAT SHALL WE TALK ABOUT NOW?" Martee opened her right fist and formed a curve of the palm with the cheek, propped her head and looked at Dollar, glancing at Banelle, and Banelle's father, then gazed at Dollar. Banelle could see from the way the upper body swayed rhythmically, Martee had crossed a leg and was bouncing the foot.

Dollar breathed in deeply and sighed, eyebrows up. "Let's play Revealing."

"What's that?" Martee.

He looked at Banelle, her father, then back at Martee. "It's about revealing ourselves. We each take a turn sharing something embarrassing."

Martee smiled toothily. "That might be fun! What do you think, Anna?"

Banelle felt herself shrug. "I don't know how dad feels," and looked at her father.

He was smiling, watching Martee with mischief in his eye. "I think that might be fun."

The teenage girl returned with Martee's bottle of beer and an empty glass.

"So who's first?" Banelle realized she shouldn't be asking, feeling awkwardly anxious about the game.

"We could start with the waitress," Dollar said, looking at the girl.

"What?" The girl set the beer and glass near Martee.

"We're playing a get-to-know-you game," Banelle's father said.

The girl smiled, hugged the round serving tray against her chest. "A game?"

"Yes," Martee said, leaning back in the chair, turning her body and including the girl with the group. Martee pushed the glass aside with her right hand, picked up the beer bottle and took a sip, set the beer down and held the bottle securely on the table. Her left hand came up, flipped the hair over her shoulder.

"So tell us something embarrassing that happened to you?" Banelle's father said.

"To me?" The girl bit her lower lip, looked briefly at Banelle, then at Dollar, where her eyes stayed. The girl blushed and giggled, released the lip and smiled, shrugged her right shoulder.

Dollar was smiling at the girl. "Yes? What's making you turn red like that?"

"What happened?" Banelle's father said.

The girl glanced at him, then looked at the pink roses, smiling. "This morning I was waiting on a customer who was being crabby at me, and I got flustered." She pulled the tray up, hiding her mouth, swiveled on her ankles.

"What happened?" Martee said, another sip of beer.

The girl looked at Dollar, pulled the tray down, shrugged. "I got nervous and spilled four drinks in his lap."

"Really?" Banelle's father said.

Martee laughed.

Dollar was grinning.

Banelle felt herself smiling, imagining what the man must have felt like, wet in the lap.

"They weren't even his drinks!"

"All at once? Or one drink at a time?" Dollar said.

"They were on a tray." The girl flipped the tray level, then backward toward herself, then gripped the top edge in both hands, renewed blushing.

"Wow." Dollar said.

"What did the man do?" Martee said.

"He jumped up and started swearing very loudly, and he wouldn't stop, so my manager had to ask him to leave." The girl giggled infectiously, wickedly, her black eyes darting around the group.

Banelle felt the right hand on her mouth, smiling privately.

"Exactly," Dollar said, raising his left hand off the table, his palm toward the girl. "Your first name?"

"Bernice." She shrugged, smiled at him, swiveled back and forth on her ankles.

"Dollar. Nice to meet you, Bernice."

She took his left hand with her left hand and they shook once.

Banelle's father reached with his right hand. The girl switched the tray, freeing her right hand, and shook his hand. "Charmed, name's Charlie." Banelle's father said.

"Thanks."

"Martee." shook the girl's hand and nodded, smiling.

Banelle felt compelled to shake the girl's hand also, though she was still annoyed how the girl kept looking at Dollar so much. "I'm Banelle. Pleased." Lied.

"I suppose you could stay while the rest of us take a turn?" Dollar said.

"Ahhh…" Bernice looked across the room, looked at Banelle, then at Dollar. "Maybe one."

Banelle felt like the girl meant she'd like hearing Dollar's story. Banelle felt like blurting out her own story so the girl wouldn't have a chance of hearing his; felt she shouldn't share anything at all — for him, or for anybody; felt like an outsider for wanting not to share of herself. "I'll go next." Banelle watched Dollar's eyes, felt her left hand grip his more tightly under the table.

His fingers responded, briefly squeezed.

"Wait." Banelle said, looked at her father for a moment, then at Dollar, at Martee, at the girl, then at the table. Banelle's mind seemed completely blank. She felt her mouth partly open, on the spot for saying something and nothing forthcoming.

"I can think of plenty of embarrassing things you've done, Anna," Martee said, taking another sip of beer.

Banelle looked at Martee. "You hush! I'll tell my own embarrassing story."

Martee chuckled wickedly, shook the hair back and smiled, watching Banelle.

"Martee." Banelle looked at the table.

———

Banelle got in touch with how this felt, feeling embarrassed. Images of high school. A bad date in her twenties. A day at work when she did something vengeful, blurring this now because she wanted not to dwell on that. None of the images felt right for sharing in this moment. She wondered again why she could smell Martee's perfume even from the other side of Dollar, idly thought how annoying Martee had been since joining them an hour ago. Banelle felt angry, felt jealous, felt embarrassed about Martee's flirting, and decided contact embarrassment wasn't appropriate for sharing either. The thing about the perfume had been nagging her, and suddenly an epiphany popped a butterfly wing in her mind why, and she felt herself turn crimson warm all over.

"What?" Dollar said, chuckled encouragingly, felt his fingers squeeze hers reassuringly.

She felt herself shrug. *Why not?* Her right hand covered her eyes. She pulled her hand down, breathing in deeply, felt her head fall backward and her shoulders slump, her eyes upon the black starry ceiling, strings of tiny white lights. "So," Banelle said, exhaling. She looked Martee steadily in the eyes, trusting the friend.

"Yes?" Martee sat alertly and leaned her elbows on the table, crossing her arms at the wrists with the bottle of beer sitting by itself to the side. Martee's left hand hung off the table, fingers restlessly near Dollar, a mischievous sparkle in her smiling eyes.

Banelle kept her eyes fixed on Martee's. "Martee joined us about an hour ago." Banelle nodded at Martee, "and ever since I've been thinking to myself, why is Martee's perfume so strong today?"

Martee's head moved back, a surprise in widening eyes, frowned prettily, blinking, frozen smile.

"Oh?" Banelle's father said. "I hadn't noticed."

Martee's eyes darted toward him and then back to watching Banelle, cocked her head right.

Banelle felt her lips tight, chin moving back and forth wrestling with having to expose herself. She inhaled, opened her mouth, "So…" Banelle looked at the table briefly and again at Martee. "I've been smelling Martee's perfume because I forgot…" Banelle rolled her eyes upward, looked at Dollar, felt his hand squeezing her leg briefly.

"Forgot what?" Martee said.

Banelle looked at Martee, felt her eyes widen with frankness, her lips firmly together. "I forgot to put on antiperspirant today!"

Bernice laughed.

Dollar was laughing.

She heard her father laughing.

Martee finally got it, and laughed, patted the table with the flat of her left palm three times. "Oh, Anna!"

Banelle felt herself laugh also, felt relieved somehow, felt accepted. She looked within Dollar's eyes.

He winked, his head bending briefly closer to hers.

She felt herself bonding with him. They both sat back in their chairs, hands together under the table.

Dollar looked at Bernice, his left palm up, "Bernice, this is my flame, Banelle." He turned his head, gray eyes looking within Banelle's eyes.

The words *My flame* lit in Banelle's mind, a giddy feeling swamped by shock.

Bernice extended her hand. Banelle reached her right hand out, grasped Bernice's hand and shook. Different than she expected, more like they could be sisters this time, an odd feeling. When she let go of Bernice's hand her inner resolute voice reminded her that was a teenage girl whom she hadn't been liking, and didn't know at all. The feelings disagreed: *Yes, we know her, and she knows us.*

Banelle felt the words *My flame* tickling warmly inside her belly.

Banelle looked at Dollar's ear, at his forehead, looked within his eyes whenever he turned, the gray eyes looking within hers. She could see he was having a good time. This felt sunny inside knowing she was helping him feel enjoyment even though her resolute voice was saying what a ridiculous idea this was, how could she possibly be the one enhancing his satisfaction?

A deeper, nurturing part of her which she'd forgotten was there resolved she was always going to facilitate this happiness for him, complement his delight in life. Her eyes widened and she felt herself lean back, savoring this feeling, trying to understand this better, negotiating such collaboration within herself. Where did this titillation come from? Why the rushing hot sense of nurturing?

This feeling seemed to come from her legs, not in the impassioned way, a feeling of firmly hugging her legs around his torso so her hands were free to fondle his face. Her eyes traced his hair, ear, neck, cheeks, nose, and chin with her thumb, holding this feeling of closeness inside herself, imagining her fingers fondling his handsome features.

Her resolutions melted into a warm chocolate puddle. There were no words with which to fight back against this nurturing resolve. She felt her right hand, which had been free and on the tabletop, now slipping backward off the table. With no one watching, the hand came softly to rest on his forearm, moved her palm slowly up and down the hair of his arm, squeezed. He looked within her eyes. She blinked, feeling misty wetness balancing behind eyelashes.

She felt him squeeze her leg. His eyes turned away, visiting, glancing with merriment at her father's voice. Then at Martee's happy laughter.

Home, Banelle felt. Completely loved, loving, the kissing breath on the tongue, lips parting. "(Aaron Doucete Horn,)" Banelle whispered, believing no one outside herself heard. Her resolute voice asked the unexpected, was she cast in a *faie glamour?*

leaned back nonchalantly like she

. . .

MARTEE WAS STARING INTENSELY. When Banelle noticed, Martee cupped her hands around her mouth so only Banelle should see, silently spoke words.

Banelle felt her lips part and move, imitating. She couldn't figure out what Martee was saying, and really, Dollar's words *My flame* were still reflecting brightly within Banelle's mind.

Martee nodded twice emphasizing the silent words, used the eyes indicating Dollar was connected with the topic.

"I've got another table," Banelle heard Bernice say.

Banelle felt her eyes go wide realizing Martee was also stuck on the same phrase, questioning, *My flame?*

Banelle pressed her lips tight, felt dimples, shrugged noncommittally watching Martee. Then Banelle grinned at Martee and bobbed her head up and down, feeling unusually catty.

"Table to wait!" she heard Dollar say.

"Lovely." Banelle heard her father say, and in the periphery of Banelle's vision, Bernice walked away energetically.

Martee signaled with the brown doe eyes and a short jerk of her head that she and Banelle should go somewhere and talk privately.

"Nice girl." Banelle heard her father say.

"Yes." Dollar.

Banelle shook her head ever so slightly and mouthed the word, "(Later.)"

Martee narrowed her eyes slightly and mouthed, "(OK.)"

Banelle was pleasantly comfortable, her fingers interlocked with Dollar's, their hands together on her bare thigh, her left ankle snuggled across his foot.

Actually, being honest with herself together in this moment, she wanted to sit on his lap surrounded by his arms, his flame held lovingly, leaning herself against his chest. *No way!* Banelle's resolute voice said within her mind. She breathed in deeply and exhaled, wishing just for once she could have an afternoon free of her own inner conflicts.

Martee leaned back nonchalantly, like she and Banelle hadn't been doing Secrets, beer in her left hand, took a sip, looking at Dollar while doing so, then at Banelle's father, pulled the bottle from her lips, swallowed, smiled toothily. "Who's next?"

"Ohh," Banelle's father said, "I suppose that would be me."

Dollar breathed in deeply, exhaled slowly.

Martee turned in the chair and struck a mirror pose of the one she had just been in, leaning back, welcoming toward Banelle's father. Martee glanced sideward at Banelle for a moment, returned her attention to Banelle's father. Martee's slight rhythmical swaying meant she had crossed her leg and was bouncing the foot.

Banelle felt like leaning her head on Dollar's shoulder, decided instead to simply turn and pay attention to her dad.

She was hyper aware of her fingers interlocking with Dollar's, her right hand glad of his forearm. Out of the corner of her eye, she saw him pick up the orange juice, and returned the glass partially empty. She felt thirsty and was enjoying where her hands were, chose against drinking sweet tea for the time being.

Her father looked at Banelle and smiled. "Once, back when I first started moving my advertising company from newspapers and magazines into a new business model which included TV commercials, there was the First Commercial." He looked at Dollar. "It's like doing your first full-page newspaper ad, only as I learned quickly, you don't have a natural frame to separate what you're saying from what the other advertisers are saying before and after you. Moving to film, that was a big step." He glanced at Martee, then Banelle.

"What a sight that first advert was." He looked at Dollar. "Thirty seconds of hell watching it on regional TV on its release." Her father looked at the table. "I remember it." he said, shaking his head thoughtfully, sighing.

He looked at Banelle, then toward Dollar. "A McDonald's 'vert played before ours. You know how they can be, smooth from the first second and filled with happiness and slow-motion, warm fuzzy feelings." He glanced at Martee. "And the one after ours just added to it: a Macy's classic with clear glass bulbs on a nine-foot pine tree, viewed through a soft lens looking in through a snowy Victorian window, an eight-year-old blue-eyed brunette with simple, well-combed hair, a tiara made of holiday-red berries crowning her head and some of the whitest teeth you've ever seen. 'Waiting for Grampa,' or something like that.

"Ours in between. Ha! I was embarrassed. What a spot for a debut!" He looked at Dollar and grinned. "We were selling toilet paper."

Banelle felt Dollar chuckle, heard Martee giggling.

Banelle's father gazed at Martee. "We were trying to help an in-state mill move its poplar tree surplus by appealing to state pride." He looked down. "We opened with an up-close on a stern-looking woman in her fifties, then panned out to include her tired-looking, equally-determined husband, and continued to pan out until you could see the husband held a three-tine pitchfork, and that they were in overalls with blue-and-red country plaid shirts. A barn in the background, a cow's behind sticking out of the darkened barn door."

Martee giggled, her dark hair bouncing and swaying, leaned briefly toward him.

"A live Guernsey milker." he said with a quick glance at Banelle. "Which as I remember took a lot of persuading to get her to stand still. Her udder was packed tight with unharvested milk. The tail, we never could stop the swish-and-flick, and there were bales of straw stacked around behind the couple forming a semicircle toward the barn door. 'Martha,' says the determined husband, never moving his eyes from the camera, 'I'm gettin' mighty tired of using straw.'

"'Henry,' she says, also not moving her eyes, 'It's all we've got and it's good enough for the cows. So put the bales away.'

"'So?' says the husband, 'I have a mind to do something with them trees over there,' tips the pitchfork a bit before returning it to vertical.

"Then we brought the product up from the bottom in a window by itself, sliding the farm couple's frame up and away: two rolls of toilet paper took their places, all lit up with soft gray-blue winter shadows and no farm yard in sight, just the softly white rolls of paper.

"Where the woman had stood, a tightly wrapped new roll in brand wrap, and where he had stood, an unwrapped roll partially unwound in a loose heap where the pitchfork had been, inviting the viewer to grab up a handful and use it. We did a voice-over at this point, using a confident male voice which said, 'We grow and roll our own.'"

Dollar broke out laughing, Banelle felt his hand shaking under hers and in her left ankle and leg all the way to her hips, his leg repeatedly bumping her softly.

Martee was another moment, then erupted with loud, carefree laughing.

Banelle was smiling, yet also feeling her father's embarrassment. She had seen that one in person while filming. An important event kicking off her father's business initiative.

He looked at Dollar, grinning. "After watching the 'vert before and the one after, I just put my face in my hands and pretended I wasn't beet red."

"That was yours!" Dollar said. "That was one of my favorites, and I'd forgotten all about it. I don't remember the commercials around it, though. That's just perfect."

"No? You may not have seen the first showing. I was on the phone as soon as I could get my composure. We did commercial schedule swapping, fast and furious. From that gaff I learned to always pay attention to which slot the 'vert is sandwiched into." Banelle's father breathed in deeply and sighed, his eyes on the table, lips in a wry smile. "Oh, what the hell." He sat up, grinned and winked at Banelle. "We did help sell a lot of toilet paper that year."

Banelle felt herself smiling. "Yes, *you* did."

"B.B." her father said, dropping his head lower and looking at her from under his eyebrows, "You contributed a lot to that. To many other efforts. That's part of why I enjoy my time with you, always coming up with ideas."

Banelle looked at his lips, at his unwavering watchfulness.

"You're in advertising, too?" she heard Dollar say.

————

Banelle turned, looked at Dollar briefly. "No." She felt her eyes dropping, looking at his arm.

"I've tried many times to get her there full time," she heard her father say.

Banelle looked within Dollar's eyes. "I don't see the room to be there," feeling more was being said than this quaint objection. "There are a lot of very talented people with years of experience working there already."

"No amount of experience covers for talent," she heard her father reply.

Banelle turned, looked at her father.

He was thoughtful, watching her. He looked toward Dollar, and the conversation paused. Banelle looked at the character in her father's face, not particularly in his eyes, though there was intelligence and attentiveness. Banelle noted the subtle expressiveness of the muscles in her father's face, and though he was nearly two decades older than she there was none of the wobbling laxity of undisciplined facial and neck muscles which she remembered from her mother's father.

Her father was in his prime – had been, and was still waxing with character every year. This she felt acutely, acknowledging the lies she had just told Dollar while her eyes continued a moment longer taking in again her father's strength, the real reason she couldn't work in her father's advertising agency. She felt herself waver, not believing she had comparable talents, feeling a certainty she wasn't measured in the same fathoms together with her father.

"What do you do?" Banelle heard Dollar say.

Her father's eyes looked at her. She realized Dollar meant the question for her. She turned and looked at Dollar, then at Martee, then at the table remembering how Friday had been at work. She sighed and looked at Dollar. "I'm a parts coordinator for an international logistics company." Banelle looked at how his lips parted, then within his eyes.

"So you're good with inventory?"

Banelle shook her head and smiled, her eyes captivated by his interest. "No. I'm good with patterns. Patterns in part numbers, bags, boxes, lots, canisters, shipping cars, warehouses, contracts, regional productivity, economic trends. There are patterns in all those concepts." She took her right hand off his arm and ran the fingers through her hair, flipping the hair over her right shoulder, reminding herself again her hair wasn't as long as it used to be. Banelle put her chin in her right palm and propped her elbow on the table.

She felt she had to move her left leg off his foot, because she was sitting up, slid her left foot around behind his heel instead, feeling the way with her foot, sliding her left shin against his calf from behind, then trapped his leg by also setting her right ankle across the front of his shin, snuggling tight, and shifted in her chair facing him more directly. The re-posturing also changed where his large hand spread. She felt his fingertips on her inner thigh, felt the intimacy increasing, tingly, wonderful. Her inner resolute voice searched for a way to object.

Martee smiled at Dollar. "Uh-oh."

Uh-oh, echoed Banelle's resolute voice.

Martee watched Dollar with smiling eyes. "It's down to you and me."

"I know it. Shall I go, or you?"

Banelle disengaged her fingers from Dollar's, pulled on his right thumb until he rolled his hand over under the table. She cupped her palm against his palm, intertwining the fingers comfortably. Now she could feel only the back of his wrist across her thigh, his touching inside the thigh a fond memory. *Much better*, Banelle's inner resolute voice judged.

She felt herself relaxing about contact with Dollar. The thigh, the tingling, his willingness to follow her wordless lead helped made relaxing easy.

Banelle saw Bernice walking toward them with the round tray balanced on the left hand.

Martee stared levelly at Dollar. "I think you should share yours."

Bernice arrived on Martee's left with the appetizers and smiled at Dollar. Bernice set two appetizer plates centered on the table, then four smaller empty plates in a stack.

Bernice had also brought Banelle a smaller empty glass, smiled with the eyebrows raised while placing the empty glass near Banelle's large glass of sweet tea.

"Thank you," Banelle said, appreciating the thoughtfulness, knowing deep inside she didn't really need another glass. Banelle had not touched her sweet tea yet, and regretted having asked.

"You're welcome. How's the game going?" Bernice glanced at Dollar, then at Banelle's father.

Martee nodded her head toward Banelle's father. "You missed a good one from Charlie."

"Darn." Bernice's eyes were smiling at him.

Banelle regretted Martee deciding Dollar should go next. Banelle kept quiet, though, wondering if Bernice would stay or hopefully leave right away.

Bernice looked across the room, then looked at Dollar, hugged the round tray against her chest. "Can I stay for the next one?"

"Of course!" Martee said.

"Just as soon as I think of one," Dollar said.

"Hurry up!" Bernice said, smiling brightly at him. "Just kidding."

Dollar smiled at Bernice, then looked at Martee. "My idea for the game, but it is devilishly hard to think of something when you're on the spot."

Martee reached out her right hand and rubbed his left forearm, then rested her hand on his wrist. "What's it gonna be?"

"Martee, I'm already major league distracted flirting with Banelle under the table, and your hand on my arm isn't going to clear it up any faster."

Banelle's eyes widened, feeling caught out, betrayed.

"How 'bout mine?" Bernice said walking around Martee, grabbed his left biceps. "Just kidding." Bernice giggled, pulled her hand away.

Dollar glanced at Bernice, and Martee. "If you girls don't stop, I won't be able to think clearly for a week."

Martee laughed wickedly and grabbed his arm with both hands. "Come on, Bernice!"

Bernice giggled, bent down, set the tray on the floor and stepped behind Dollar, hugged him from behind, her palms patting Dollar's chest.

"Ah!" Dollar said.

Martee laughed. "Wait for me!" Martee pulled Dollar's left arm away from the table and sat on his left leg, pulling his left arm around her waist, the cleft of her blouse under his chin.

"Nice!" Dollar said.

Martee put her right arm around both Bernice and Dollar. Martee looked at Banelle, smiling.

Banelle realized she had been holding her breath, inhaled sharply through her nose.

"Come on, Anna!" Martee's mouth open and happy. "Get your sunshine ass up here, too!"

Dollar was red, glanced at Banelle with bashful smiling. She felt his hand slip out of hers under the table, bringing alarms of change, and immediately felt his hand under her left thigh lifting her leg strongly.

Banelle screeched, feeling the electric charge run along the leg and into her spine, gasped and felt herself laugh. *Oh, what the hell!* Banelle thought. She braced her right foot, his hand pulling her left leg, trying to keep her balance. Her left hand found Bernice's shoulder, Banelle's right hand grasping for nothing in the air until she felt Martee's hand grab. Banelle sat on his right leg, bumping her left leg against Martee's right knee. Banelle wrapped her left arm securely around Bernice, her palm on Bernice's back, and felt Dollar's right arm slide around her waist. She felt happily uplifted, supported, affirmed.

Banelle heard her father chuckling.

———

"Now, how's a man supposed to think of anything?" Dollar complained, shaking his head and leaning back, rubbing the close-cropped black hair against Bernice's left ear, then the shorn stubble of his right cheek on Bernice's.

Bernice screeched.

Martee laughed. "Anna!" Martee jerked her head toward Dollar, then Martee kissed him on the left side of his forehead, holding the kiss. "Mmmmm!"

Bernice giggled, her right hand slapping his chest, swiveling at the wrist, then Bernice kissed him on the right side of his face. "Mmmmm!"

Oh what the fuck! Banelle thought, slipping her right hand around his neck, bending to kiss him on the lips. She chickened out, kissed him on the forehead instead, adding her voice with the other two voices. "Mmmmmmmm!"

The three girls laughed, and Banelle felt freely happy. Banelle playfully pushed on Martee's left shoulder. "You're crazy!"

Martee nodded enthusiastically, brown doe eyes, happy teeth.

"I think you all are crazy." Dollar said, "I'm in heaven, and I feel embarrassed."

"Anna." Martee said with a nod and mock sternness. "I think you missed a spot!"

Banelle felt her forehead furrow, tilted her head right looking at Martee, wondering what was meant.

Martee held her left index finger erect. "Here, I'll show you!"

Martee slipped her left arm across Banelle's left forearm, palm and fingers around the right side of Dollar's neck, leaned forward…

Dollar's eyes widened. "Now wait a min…"

…Martee kissed him on the lips and lingered, Martee's dark hair occluding Banelle's view…

"Martee!" Banelle gasped.

"Mmm!" Dollar said, eyes softening, "mmm," felt his fingers relax on Banelle's waist.

Banelle felt her eyes narrow, pulled her right arm from under Martee's soft breasts, tapped Martee between the shoulder blades. "Hey!"

…Martee continued kissing…

Banelle grabbed a handful of Martee's hair and pulled insistently backward.

…Martee came away from the kiss, laughing, looking merrily within Banelle's eyes. "See?!"

Banelle felt her eyes squint and gave a tug on Martee's hair before letting go.

"Aih!" Martee blinked, left hand clutching the head where Banelle had pulled. "What was that for?!"

Banelle put her right fist on the hip. "You know very well!"

Dollar was watching Martee's lips, then her hair, then her eyes.

Banelle looked at him, feeling of ire rising after that shock.

Bernice gave Dollar another peck on the cheek, pulled away from him.

Dollar winked at Banelle, felt his fingers dig into her right side, tickling.

"Hey!" Banelle blurted laughing, bumping her left breast against his chest. She decided to relax and enjoy that, leaned both breasts into him.

Banelle grabbed the leg above Martee's right knee and pinched the ticklish spot she knew Martee had.

Martee screeched and thrashed, jostling all three of them, nearly falling off. Martee's left hand quickly grabbed Banelle's right wrist and tried pulling Banelle's hand away.

Bernice crouched down and retrieved the tray.

"Anna! Stop!" Martee screeched.

Banelle let go of Martee's knee, wrapped her arms around Dollar, her head right of his, feeling a touch of vindication. Banelle winked at Bernice from beside Dollar's head.

Dollar murmured into Banelle's left ear. "(Lovely breasts! Can you stay all day?)"

Bernice looked over her shoulder, then back at Banelle, smiling, and jerked her head toward Dollar. She wagged her eyebrows at Banelle and held the right thumb up. "I better go check on my other table. You guys are so fun!" Bernice turned energetically, eyes briefly on Banelle's father, and walked away.

Martee wasn't leaving Dollar's left leg, so Banelle sat right where she was also. Banelle wished she had Martee's courage. She felt jealous enough to spit. This tongue of fire was mingled in with a feeling of enjoying herself.

"You girls ought to get down now," Banelle heard her father say. "Now. Before we get bounced out of here. And I'm not done looking at other women yet."

Banelle turned her head left and looked at her father over her shoulder. He winked and motioned with his left hand toward her chair.

"You, too," he said looking at Martee, pointing toward Martee's chair with the right finger. "Sit. Please." he added, turning his right palm upward, holding his arm toward Martee's chair.

"Ohhh," Martee said with a sound of regret and slipped out of Dollar's lap.

Banelle looked Dollar in the gray eyes. His lips puckered an air kiss.

She felt she'd like that, vision of their kissing. Felt like that'd be the day after hell is bankrupt and the gambling machines confiscated also, vision of Martee kissing him. Two conflicting visions. Which mirror to use?

Banelle looked at his lips, then his eyes. Under her thighs she felt his cyclist's leg. Inside her encircling arms she felt his strong shoulders and neck. With Martee away, Banelle felt his left hand warm on her right knee holding her legs near. She wondered, could she kiss him now? She knew her father was watching. She wanted that kiss. She looked at his lips, felt hers part ever so slightly.

She slid her right hand up to his neck, feeling the nape, her fingers slipping within the hair. She resisted grabbing his hair in her fist, resisted pulling his head back, resisted kissing him and parting his lips with her tongue, her lips meeting wetly around the tongue. She really, really wanted that. *Has it been so long?* Banelle's inner resolute voice said.

She looked within his gray eyes. How difficult to be so close, her eyes on his lips again. *Are you so damn horny?* Banelle's inner voice accused. She felt her right thumb caress the edge of his left ear, felt her left thumb caressing his back, the rough knit cotton shirt, felt her right foot hook around the back side of his left calf, turning herself closer to him, the left leg bumped high in his left thigh. *Holy shit!* Banelle thought, accidentally bumping the hardness between his legs, felt herself instantly unnerved, immediately felt her own arousal, fought with this sudden vivid yearning, panties in the way. *I am grown up,* Banelle's inner resolute voice said, her entire body tensing with the increased disagreement, the eyes unfocused, the thigh cautiously pressed again against his hardness, rubbing up and down once.

All his fingers reacted, the brief pull on her waist and legs.

Her smelling him, the mind swimming. *I am in control,* her inner voice said, the reprimand of that pride within the mind, *You don't even know the man!*

Yes, she does know, feels that man, smells that man. Sees that man close, touches.

I just met him! He just kissed Martee!

That is no longer. Here, this skin touches him now. To feel that hardness naked. To wet that kissing mouth.

Wait! Not here, I will be embarrassed.

———

Banelle felt the shuddering throughout her body, felt his palms react, grasping her more securely. Banelle, barely holding herself together, these breasts against that man's chest, the tingling nipples. She put her lips breath close near his right ear, shuddered, all of her agreeing. Banelle whispered wetly into that ear. "(Later, handsome. I promise.)"

Part of the mind wondered how the lips had gotten so wet wanting to taste him, felt the urge to swallow him, let the lips part with the tiniest wet opening sound in his ear, feeling how wet the tongue was, resisted sticking the tongue inside that man's ear, let the hot breath fill the space between mouth and ear.

She felt the reward of his body's response trembling at her mere breath and press of breasts, felt the certainty that hand on her knee and that hand on her waist both grabbed her more firmly, reaction of someone feeling their feet slipping, grabbing anything to steady vertigo. She rubbed her thigh up and down again, felt the hardness and his quiet moan in her ear. She smiled for herself where no one could see, feeling the victory over Martee, then she put the tip of her tongue between her front teeth, closed her lips to hide she'd been smiling, swallowed the juices in her mouth.

Banelle realized Martee and her father had been visiting. She inhaled deeply, pushed herself away from Dollar's chest, started untangling herself from his lap, felt his hands regretfully releasing her body, dragging her heightened senses through his fingers.

Banelle found her chair with the left hand, slipped off his knee, eyes focused on the hardness in his jeans.

When she looked up, Bernice was walking briskly toward their table. Bernice took one last step and made a little jump, landing with both feet together on Martee's left, holding the round serving tray by the edge, rocking forward and backward on the heels. "OK!" Bernice said, looking at Dollar, then Banelle, her father, then at Martee. "Have you decided what you're having?"

"Not at all!" Banelle's father said.

Dollar chuckled, eyes wide looking at the table edge, blinking. "I haven't even looked at a menu yet." Dollar reached for the stack with his right hand and passed menus around.

"Then I'll be right back." Bernice looked merrily at Banelle, walked away from them with a bounce in her step.

Banelle took the menu offered to her first, and her father got one, and Martee last. Banelle was looking at the menu. She felt her left hand touch his leg, smoothed her palm and fingertips along the length of his upper leg to near the knee, and back to the middle, feeling most comfortable resting her wrist across the top of his leg, her fingers lightly stroking the jeans of his inner thigh. She tried to focus her mind on the words the eyes had been scanning over and over.

"The salads are excellent," Martee said.

Banelle decided, to hell with the menu, tossed the menu aside, committed herself to order what she always did.

Dollar looked at Martee. "How about the steak Caesar?"

"I don't know about the steak. The chicken is heavenly, they put strawberries and kiwi, grapes and walnuts in with the grilled chicken and mixed greens, and their raspberry *vinaigrette* is house-made."

"I'm doing that." Banelle's father said

Out of the corner of her eye, Banelle saw Dollar nodding thoughtfully. He reached out with his left hand and retrieved a potato skin.

As did Martee.

"Ohh, wait," Banelle's father said. "Here's something even better." He threw the menu down.

Martee looked at Dollar. "So what's your embarrassing story?"

Banelle's father put some of the cauliflower on a small plate and drizzled the spicy dip on the side.

Dollar grinned. "Next time I play this game, I'll have The Story of Three Princesses to retell."

Martee laughed, rocking back in her chair, nodding three times.

Banelle smiled and looked Dollar in the eyes for the first time since slipping out of his lap. "No fair using that one now."

He winked at her.

"Ohh, here comes Bernice again," Banelle's father said. "Everyone ready?"

Dollar turned welcomingly for Bernice; Bernice smiled brightly at Dollar.

Banelle felt his right hand touch her leg, felt his hand softly relax on her inner thigh, tingles traveling up the skin of her midsection, nape, tickle onto her earlobes. She decided the anxiety was now open to letting his hand become that familiar with her body, despite what her resolute inner voice had been saying earlier about the inadvisability of this mutually teasing covert activity. There was a pattern to it and she was feeling increasingly drawn into the spell.

Bernice stopped by Dollar and Martee, looked at Dollar. "So, what have you decided?"

Dollar nodded at Martee. "Let the women order first."

Banelle spoke before Martee. "Bernice, I'll have the broiled shark and snow peas."

"Great!" Bernice pulled out an order pad and pen, gave the pen a flick and spin. "Baked potato with that or fries?"

"Actually, I always ask to have fresh baby carrots instead of potato."

"Got it." Bernice wrote on the pad.

"I'll have the chicken Caesar," Martee said.

"Great choice!" Bernice glanced at Martee briefly, and continued writing. Bernice looked at Dollar and smiled, eyebrows up.

"Does the steak Caesar come with the fruit and nuts I'm hearing come with the chicken Caesar?"

Martee sipped her beer.

Bernice paused writing. "No, but I'll get them to fix it that way if you like."

Dollar smiled, sat back. "Perfect!"

Banelle decided to have one of the flowerets her dad had ordered, reached her right hand.

Bernice looked at Banelle's father and smiled. "I already missed the best story. I don't want to miss the best order, too!"

He chuckled. "I'll tell you the story next time we are both here."

"Great!"

"I'll have the cottage cheese and dill chicken."

Banelle bit the cauliflower and spicy cheese, the taste buds admiring the sweetness and saltiness just before the head-clearing wasabi drifted into the sinuses. "Shit." Banelle blinked wide-eyed, looked at her dad.

Her father grinned. "Have another, B.B."

"What kind of potato?" Bernice said.

"Baked, please," he said, smiling.

"Can you bring me another beer, Bernice?" Martee held the bottle aloft, peering, gently swished the bottom in a circle.

"Can do. Is that it?" Bernice looked at each individually, smiling.

Everybody looking at each other.

Bernice turned with a bounce and walked energetically away. "Order up!"

Martee was watching Dollar. "Well?"

Dollar smiled. "Well?"

"Well?" Martee smiled brightly with the mischief.

———

"Well, well, well." Dollar smiled toothily, eyes on Martee, then he looked at the table.

Martee leaned forward, rested her arms on the table practically where Dollar was looking, still smiling. "Incredibly, thoroughly well." Looked at Banelle thoughtfully, then looked at Dollar.

Banelle glanced at Dollar's crotch, which seemed less aroused for the moment, and where her left hand draped on his leg. She felt certain by shifting her hand she could have the pleasure of his hardness again.

Dollar spoke, eyes unfocused. "My daughter's name is Katy."

Banelle felt the surprise of children. "You have a daughter?"

"Yes," Dollar said looking at her, glanced at Banelle's father, then at Martee. "Katy is twelve now."

"Has she started the 'I hate you's' yet?" Banelle heard her father say.

Banelle felt shocked, looked at her father. "Dad!"

He smiled with warm eyes. "Oh, don't act so innocent, B.B." He nodded at her. "You did that for a few years. Broke my heart the first time I heard it from you."

Banelle looked at Dollar, felt how wide her eyes were, couldn't help this feeling of exposure.

Dollar was grinning at her father, then Dollar looked at Banelle, still grinning. "No." Dollar shook his head. "Not yet, she hasn't." Dollar glanced at her father.

"I can remember your doing that, Anna," Martee said.

Banelle narrowed her eyes at Martee, scrunched her nose and shook her head.

Martee returned the face, imitating.

Banelle giggled. Martee chuckled.

Dollar was gazing at the table.

Banelle noticed Bernice approaching, a beer bottle on the serving tray.

"Katy was five once."

"Who's Katy?" Bernice said, stopping by Martee and Dollar.

Dollar looked at Bernice, smiled. "My daughter."

"Go onnnn!" Bernice said, handing the beer bottle to Martee.

"No, really. She's twelve now. She was five at the time."

"Time of what?" Bernice said.

"He's telling one," Martee said, took a sip from the new beer.

"Oh!" Bernice held the tray by the top edge in front of her, hanging down. She looked over her shoulder, turned back and looked at Dollar. "I'm staying for this one!"

Banelle felt her eyes closing for a moment and wanted to shake her head. Banelle opened her eyes and looked at Martee, who looked back at her. *Maybe it* is *time for a girl talk,* Banelle thought. Banelle looked at Dollar.

He was looking at Bernice.

"Katy was five." Dollar turned his attention back toward the table, eyes unfocusing, "And she and I and her mom…"

"You were married?" Banelle said.

"No." Dollar looked at Banelle. "We discussed it the year before Katy was born." He looked at the table, quiet. Banelle felt the fidgeting of his fingers on her thigh. "At the time of the story, we were a little family, albeit nontraditional, and we had gone to a theme park one Tuesday, thinking there wouldn't be anyone around. Angela," and here Dollar looked at Martee briefly, then at Banelle, "that was the former significant other."

Banelle wasn't sure at the moment why this novelty should be bothering her. "So even though you were never married, you have a daughter?"

"Correct."

"Any significant others since then?" Banelle heard herself blurt.

She heard Martee click her tongue. "Anna!"

He shook his head. "No. Not significant enough to have a daughter by."

"Oh." Suddenly Banelle felt inadequate, wondering if he expected to have another child someday, and she desperately wanted to ask. She was afraid of the answer, because she couldn't have any more, and this feeling inadequate made her angry. Her choosing to be selfish years ago might be an obstacle here.

Dollar chuckled, looked at her lips, then within her eyes.

"What?"

"Promise you won't say anything about what I am about to share when you meet them? Especially not to Katy?"

Banelle looked at his lips, his breathing comfortably, at his eyes. His asking this of her and not also of Martee implied a future together, and she felt excitement welling up. She also felt anxious about how horrible the secret might be, how of the other three at the table only she was going to be charged with keeping his forthcoming reveal, which bothered her, accepting responsibility for her father keeping the secret, for chatty Martee keeping the secret, and also for Bernice, whom she did not know much of. Yet the offer of trust was too much to resist. "Agreed."

"When I am by myself I've taken to calling her Angela 'From Hell' Marsh 'Now Dash' Davis."

Martee laughed.

Banelle heard her father chuckle.

Bernice giggled.

Banelle felt horrified. *What if he breaks up with me?* a part of Banelle worried. *You guys aren't even an item, are you?* said her resolute voice. Though another part of her knew for certain, yes, they are, and yet another part of her wondered if she couldn't have a child by him, what would prove she was more significant than his daughter's apparently awful mother had been?

The idea of his also privately calling Banelle names someday shocked her and pricked at an old feeling of anger over disrespect from men. Outwardly she smiled, pretending his share was funny, only she caught Martee looking at her, and Martee knew Banelle was just pretending. *Shit.* Banelle shrugged with the right shoulder noncommittally.

Martee echoed the shrug.

"So anyway," Dollar said, grinning, looking at Bernice, then Martee. "Angela wasn't working that summer, as usual, since she's a school teacher, and I didn't have anything going on that Tuesday, so I arm-swept my little girl and the three of us went to the theme park.

"Katy had never been, of course, so that was going to be her first time." Dollar scrunched his eyes closed and shook his head like he had just tasted something sour, then smiled with his lips. He breathed in deeply and sighed, eyes glancing at Banelle. "The park was absolutely full.

"It had taken us an hour to get there, so we weren't turning back. After fifteen minutes waiting at the gate we finally got inside and had wandered around about twenty minutes, taking in the sights, before we realized the whole park had been taken over for the day by a Baptist convention. Don't ask me which one, because I didn't know to ask at the time."

"My mom was Baptist," Bernice said.

Dollar looked at Bernice. "That's absolutely cool!" his left hand out and palm up. "This isn't a story about Baptists. I don't find them embarrassing at all."

Banelle heard her father bark a laugh, the ear hurting.

"Got it." Bernice fidgeted looking at Banelle's father, who was still laughing.

Martee leaned toward Bernice, fingers on Bernice's left arm. "Don't pay that old man any attention."

"He's agnostic," Banelle said to Bernice.

"Oh?" Bernice hid her mouth shyly behind the serving tray.

Banelle looked at her father briefly, looked down at the table. He had been watching her quietly.

Dollar waved his left hand dismissively. "This is not a story about Baptists."

"Tell me more," Bernice said, unsure, pulling the tray down, holding the tray by the rim.

———

"Trust me?" Dollar said, warm smile.

Bernice nodded once, then nodded a second time, smiling, demure.

"Excellent." Dollar breathed in deeply and exhaled with purpose. He looked at Martee. "Where was I?"

Martee grinned mischief. "The entertainment park had been taken over by Baptists, and the Governor activated the National Guard." Banelle could see Martee's head bouncing slightly, rhythm of the crossed foot.

"Oh, yeah-yeah-yeah." Dollar waved his left hand, palm down. "Priceless! Military intervention, hilarious. So there we were, an Episcopalian, a Lutheran, and an Undecided."

Banelle felt a pique of curiosity. "Who was Lutheran?"

Dollar looked at Banelle. "Angela."

"From Hell." Martee added.

He grinned, the eyes with glee glancing at Martee, at Bernice. "Exactly."

Banelle felt her eyes wide, feeling baffled by what should be done with this unholy revelation.

"So you were the Episcopalian?" her father said.

Banelle felt herself blink and looked at her dad, her head tilted.

"No. I was Undecided."

"About what?" Banelle heard Bernice say.

Banelle turned to look at Bernice, then at Dollar.

Dollar smiled at Bernice, his mouth open, teeth bright. "About becoming a Baptist, of course."

Martee laughed, leaned back in the chair. Took a sip of beer.

"Are you teasing me?" Bernice said.

Dollar touched his left hand to Bernice's right arm. "Yes." He nodded. "My apologies."

She tilted her head, looking at him, and her bottom lip puckered.

"No, really. My gaff." His hand squeezed Bernice's arm.

Banelle felt the ire.

"I was undecided about becoming any kind of Christian, and Angela and I had many arguments about the topic. Katy was Episcopalian by sacrament of baptism, it was just easier. The water wasn't very deep."

Bernice inhaled and sighed. "Go on. So what happened?"

Dollar pulled his left hand away from Bernice's arm and set the hand flatly on the table three times, "Funny you should ask."

Bernice cocked her head on one side and nodded, wryly looking out the window.

He looked down at the table, smiling. "So there we were, surrounded by our new friends from the Baptist Convention. And Angela…"

"From Hell." interjected Martee.

Dollar smiled openly, eyes fixed on the table. "…now Dash Davis, had already been after me about my language around Katy. I felt completely outnumbered at this point in the story and tried to keep my mouth shut." Dollar looked at Banelle's father. "Not only that, you knew who the preachers were."

"Why's that?" Banelle heard her father say.

"It was because one of their gimmicks that day was every preacher wore a button somewhere on his person which said, 'Ask me where I preach.' There were a lot of buttons! Seemed like every time I turned around, there was another person wearing one of those buttons.

"I was determined that Katy and I should have a great first visit to a theme park, so we three went looking for rides because that's what I was into and I hoped Katy would like rides as much as I do. There were long lines everywhere. We tried one, and after ten minutes standing and the line hardly moving, I told Angela and Katy we were going to try another one.

"We ended up in line for the water ride. It was one of the over-sized inner tube-shaped round boats with six seats facing inward that you had to buckle into. There wasn't as strict a height limit about that ride, and Katy was pretty tall for a five-year-old anyway. It was still early morning and cool, so not as many people were in line for getting wet.

"The three of us were strapped in, facing three other people, and wouldn't you know it, two were wearing buttons, and the one in the middle, across from Katy, turned out to be the wife of the button wearer on her left and the sister of the other one on her right.

"We had just got going, where the boat spun around twice and bumped us backward into the first obstacle, and that's when I learned Katy could do projectile vomiting."

Banelle felt her eyes wide, laughed, imagining the picture.

"Ewwe!" Bernice said, sound of experience.

Martee cackled a laugh, throwing the head back.

"The woman across from Katy got that morning's grapefruit juice, milk, breakfast cereal, and Oreo cookie."

"Ewwwwwe!" Bernice reiterated.

Martee slapped the table with the right hand and renewed laughter, eyes looking at Bernice, then Dollar.

He shook his head, turning red. He looked at Martee. "It was a ten-minute ride. It seemed like the Sun had climbed to high noon before we got off that first run. The woman was incredibly angry. Angela blamed it on me, which was her broken record playing. Katy was feeling a lot better, though, having gotten rid of what had ailed her. 'Daddy, can we go again?'"

"So what did you do?" Martee said.

He looked at Martee, shrugged both shoulders dramatically. "What could I do? I asked the man where he preached."

Banelle's father laughed.

Bernice laughed.

Banelle, the nervous laugh.

Martee had her head back, laughing, bouncing hair left, then right.

Banelle found herself wishing she had come up with a better story than forgetting antiperspirant.

Bernice's left hand happily mussed Dollar's hair. "I'll be back," walked energetically away, swinging the round tray from the right arm.

Banelle stared at Bernice's back.

Dollar patted his hair, looking at Martee. "So what about yours?" He grabbed another potato skin and looked again at Martee.

"Me?" Martee said, bouncing in the chair, fingers of the right hand on the bare V-neck of the white blouse.

had been struggling within herself

. . .

BANELLE FELT herself roll her eyes, tipped her head sideways, looked at Martee from the shadow of her eyebrows. "Yes, Martee, you!"

"Oh, Anna." Martee looked at Dollar with mischief, looked down, watched him levelly. "Tell you what. I'm going to take a quick girl break and freshen up." Martee looked at Banelle briefly with eyebrows up, then looked at Dollar, shrugging noncommittally with the right shoulder. "Then maybe I can think of *something* to share."

Banelle pulled her left hand from Dollar's leg. "I think I'll go, also." Banelle looked at him, then at Martee, turned her head and smiled at her father. His eyebrows went up, then relaxed, and he mirrored her smile.

"Perfect." Dollar.

Banelle followed Martee through the crowded tables toward the front of the restaurant where the bathrooms were located, one on each side of the foyer.

Martee looked over her right shoulder while they walked. "Someone sure has made herself comfortable with a man."

"Martee, watch where you're going." Banelle felt nettled. "Besides, I wasn't the one kissing someone else's boyfriend."

"Boyfriend?!" Martee scoffed over the shoulder, entering the restaurant's foyer.

"Yes." Banelle didn't feel sure she should be saying anything further about this.

Martee stopped and turned around.

Banelle stopped also.

Martee pointed with her entire right arm and finger. "How long have you known that man?"

Banelle's mind raced, conflicted, tried to think. Was the time ten o'clock in the morning when he was fixing the bicycle tire? She didn't need to say she was counting all the time she watched him outside her kitchen window. She wondered what the time was now, two, maybe? "Six hours." Banelle felt she was only partly lying, curiously felt like a lie in the other direction, her soul's knowing that man all her life so far.

"Really?" Martee turned on her heel toward the women's room. "Six hours!" Martee said over her shoulder.

"Yeah?" Banelle followed Martee into the bathroom. "Who is kissing a man within an hour of meeting him?"

"Anna," Martee said, shaking her head, pushing against the coral-pink bathroom door. "Kissing doesn't mean anything."

Doesn't mean anything? Certainly feels *like everything!* Banelle had been struggling within herself whether or not to kiss the lips of that man. She did not want him feeling in both his hands she was happy receiving his arousal until she knew how appreciative and consistently respectful he was.

The adobe-red floor tiles of the foyer gave way to a mosaic of seashell-colored miniature tiles inside the bathroom. Martee was holding the door for Banelle until Banelle pushed on the door also. Banelle let the door close behind her. There were beige stalls along the right wall, white sinks with the big mirror on the left. There didn't seem to be anyone else inside.

"Besides," Banelle said, hearing her own voice echoed by the hard sea foam-colored tile walls, "I can call him 'boyfriend' to my best friend who knows I *never* use that term."

Martee turned around, her mouth open…

"And, I can expect my best friend to be supportive, not thieving!"

"What?! I'm a thief now?"

"What the hell are you doing kissing that man?" Banelle said, left arm swinging toward the door, toward that man. "Dollar." Banelle added.

Martee spread her palms, shaking her hair. "Just having fun, Anna."

"Bullshit." Banelle felt this stubbornness, took a deep breath. "You've been all over him since you met him. This was supposed to be *our* day out, not yours and his."

"Oh? And who has her hands between his legs already?"

Banelle felt her eyes go wide.

"Don't pretend, Anna. That's as easy to see as rain falling on your big windshield. That man has been one-handed almost the entire time we have been at the table."

Banelle felt herself fold her arms and started tapping her left foot, then stopped and felt herself grin. "Yeah, so, I wish I wasn't sitting in a restaurant with him, I'd like to be holding more than his hand."

Martee grinned and put her fists on the hips. "Oh, Anna." Martee folded her arms like Banelle. "He is hot, isn't he?"

Banelle stepped nearer Martee, muted her voice. "(Are you trying to steal him?)"

Martee smiled and looked down, the lashes almost closed. She breathed in and sighed through her nose, then looked into Banelle's eyes. "The Portents this morning echoed my heart: I am completely fed up with losers, and from what I have seen so far Dollar is most *definitely* a successful human being. So, yeah, watch your step. He's mine if he will have me. And he's *smart*."

"What?" Banelle felt herself looking inwardly for answers, eyes down. There were some worries already. The twelve-year-old daughter. The former out-of-marriage significant other whom he still called by nickname. She wondered who else might be in his life or recently in his life?

Banelle pushed the imagining from her mind, not wanting to

dream about something which may not exist. *Give him the benefit of the doubt,* her resolute voice surprisingly said. She looked at Martee, shrugged. "I'm scared."

"Good for you! Fear helps keep the romantic fog away. Believe me about the dark things, I know."

"Yeah, you do. What else?" Banelle watched Martee's eyes for advice. "You're always dating."

"Yeah, yeah," Martee said, nodding, wobbling her head, hair alive. "I know, I know, always dating, and no Handfast."

Banelle looked from one of Martee's eyes to the other. Banelle felt it had to be said, "I hope to be married again some day."

———

Martee sighed. "What you do is date and really make sure before you go running off to a courthouse. It's that simple. Keep your eyes open, listen to the voices inside and they will keep you on track. As a reminder, this is your *first* date in five years, and by the Goddess of Self-Love, Anna, you're being chaperoned!"

Banelle heard herself chuckling, felt herself merry around the eyes. "Yeah, well, this is totally impromptu. You know how I feel about reckless spontaneity. If you weren't along I wouldn't be on a date today."

"Are you having fun?"

"Yes!" Banelle squealed.

"Yes!" Martee held Banelle's bouncing with her own style of flat-footed groundedness, fingers digging into Banelle's hips. "Just let's be sure you are going after what you really want, not following some rule book for princess fairy tales."

Banelle stopped bouncing, felt this catty wriggling persist. "How do we do that?"

Martee looked down, the eyelashes nearly closing. "You aren't going to like this."

"What?"

Martee looked at Banelle. "It will clarify in a very short time what your heart actually wants."

Banelle wondered where Martee was taking the conversation. "What will?"

"Clearly you need a fast, easy to understand answer."

"What?!"

Martee's unwavering doe eyes. "Shut up for a minute, and promise you'll think about this before answering."

Banelle took a quick breath with this impatience, feeling anxiety now. "I'm… whatever. I'm listening. And I'm thinking."

"Right. Here's what we'll do." Martee scrunched her nose briefly. "I'll continue flirting and kissing, because I'm having a great time, and your poo-pooing isn't going to ruin a fun day for me, nor run me off my future happily-ever-after highway Heroine's Journey with your reckless feelings all over the road."

Banelle felt her eyes widen and mouth open…

Martee held aloft her right index finger, shook her head. "And if Mister Handsome is Mister Right for Ms Anna's Heart, you'll know before the night is over, if you don't know it deep inside already, and then what's your worry, Gorgeous?" Martee curled the finger back within the hand and waited, looking from one of Banelle's eyes to the other. Martee's left hand still holding Banelle's waist.

Martee's idea aroused Banelle's jealousy. The idea also made her wonder why she couldn't be more like her friend and just relax and enjoy the flirting without glomming herself to him as soon as he knocked on her door and startled her hand on the knob. She wondered briefly if Martee was just maneuvering?

Deep in her heart Banelle knew their friendship's history and dismissed the idea. Banelle realized she was afraid he really wasn't sincere, and felt afraid of getting hurt. She remembered what he had said almost immediately, the words written brightly within her memory from their replaying in her mind over and over since she first heard them earlier in the day, when she had first wrestled with whether she would date him at all. *You better not listen or we'll start sharing how we feel back and forth and the next thing you know we'll be feeling like becoming intimate and then it'll all be tangled together, whether good or bad, hurt and happiness.*

Banelle wondered what would happen if he ever found out he'd been tested. She decided *caveat emptor* applied for any man who wanted *her*.

A part of her didn't feel so mercenary, though, just wanted to nurture and love him. She felt a moist moment, the instinctual part of her simply knowing who he was for *her*.

Another part of Banelle wondered how Banelle's and Martee's friendship would fare if Dollar went with Martee instead? The jealousy hadn't gone away, imagining Martee continuing to flirt with Dollar, visions of other kisses between them, this jealousy watching. Banelle looked from Martee's right eye to the left. Banelle shook her head slowly, marveling. Heard the tongue click within her mouth. "That's evil."

Martee nodded enthusiastically, smiling, smiles around the eyes with pinpoints of lights reflecting in the enlarged pupils, dark hair jiggling. "Keep in mind he may be *my* Mr Right. Well? What's it going to be?"

You will know. Banelle's resolute voice said. She took a deep breath and sighed, felt herself nod carefully once. "I can go along with that. But I'm probably going to be pissy with you, Martee. Just don't let our years together so far sour. You are my greatest love if that doesn't sound too weird."

"ANNA." Martee smiled toothily and thrust her face closer to Banelle, shook the hair. "It's not all about you!"

Banelle felt her eyes get wide, the impact of what Martee had just said trembling the footing of her entire self-image. "What?!"

Martee laughed wickedly, wriggling. "Anna, you are so *beautifully* vexing when you are innocent! But I need you to be as ravishing as you actually are, if you would just accept a wet handful of self-truths about your own Shadow. Suck it up! Sob wet snot if you have to! This isn't a game for two girls pulling the pants down on dolls: I know what *I* want, and so should *you*, if you'll let yourself. *Fuck* the rules! And stop trying to make up rules to apply to *me*."

There was the sudden loud echoing sound of a toilet flushing.

Martee's eyes got round. Banelle felt her own eyes go wide staring at each other.

Banelle, for one, felt particularly warm with rushing embarrassment.

Martee let Banelle go, stepped away from Banelle, braced her palms and thumbs on the hips, turned toward the sound. They watched the doors for the stalls.

An older woman backed out of the third of the four stalls, her face a toothless grin. "Song about a hedgehog?" The woman winked, shuffled toward the second of three sinks and looked at herself in the mirror, primped her hair, and shrugged. "Wish I had thought of that."

The woman looked at Banelle. "I might know a few tricks you don't know. You have to when you get past fifty and the entire skin of your body gets wet at the thought instead of just your loving grip, and it's no use blaming the man for a horse he never had. Invest the time to show him how to ride properly. I'm Luutsche. Are you open to introducing him to me?"

Martee bent forward in silent laughter, the right hand clasped against her mouth.

Luutsche turned her attention to the soap dispenser and faucet, the sound of wet. "I bet I could, too, while you two are still arguing about whose pussy is prettier. I'd let you visit, o'course."

Banelle felt herself smiling, wishing she could rewind ten minutes of conversation and play the tape somewhere else more private, with a pen and pad to write notes.

Martee twirled to Banelle, stepped near, whispered voice in Banelle's right ear. "(The boys are going to wonder what happened to us.)

Banelle whispered. "(I have to pee!)"

Martee grinned. Out loud, "Race!" dashed for the first stall.

Banelle felt her eyes roll and her head fall back. They hadn't played that game since childhood. She felt herself laugh, and felt the competitiveness rush back. "Race!" dashed for the next stall. "Martee, I hope yours is out of paper!" Could Banelle have her panties off first, captivating Dollar's nose, before Martee could grip his two fingers and thumb?

eyelashes almost closing, fingernails clicking

. . .

THE STEAM from grilled shark steak, seared pepper, and waft of lemon set with a ceramic clunk on the table went in Banelle's nose and turned into watering on the tongue.

"That's screaming hot," Bernice cautioned pulling the mitt away.

"*My* embarrassing story?" Martee looked down, her eyelashes almost closed.

Martee looked thoughtfully at Banelle, Martee's fork wavering back and forth, right forearm resting against the edge of the table. Martee put the fork down, shifted her weight, crossed the left leg over the right, and leaned attentively upright toward Dollar. She opened her mouth and paused, hair jiggling. "I love to be out.

"I go home sometimes, usually just to freshen up, like after work, or after something fun with fitness, the rowing team, or handball.

"There are people to meet and places to see, so I don't stay home much. I'm resilient in just about any situation and I like to laugh. I believe people want to have a good time, and if they aren't having fun either they don't know how, or they just haven't tried the right thing yet. Hell, I know people who haven't even given sex a good-time try."

Banelle felt Martee was doing more to introduce herself than just share an embarrassing story. The sound of Martee's warning played in

Banelle's mind. *Watch your step. He's mine if he will have me. And he's* smart.

Martee's eyes looked out the window on Banelle's right. Martee glanced briefly at Banelle, Banelle's father, then looked intently at Dollar. After a moment, the eyelashes almost closed, then looked at Banelle. "I've learned that if you can act like you're embarrassed once in a while, people warm up to you faster. You need an edge like that in sales."

Martee tapped the tabletop with the fingers, looking at Dollar, then at Banelle's father. Martee looked down at her fingernails and stopped. "Which brings me to probably the only thing I remember feeling embarrassed about."

Martee brushed away anything that might have been on the table where her fingers tapped.

"And I feel hugely cheated because I'm going to share that one thing. Where, I'm guessing, you have more than one thing." Martee shrugged, looked at Dollar. "So your sharing one thing isn't like you've shared everything which you are embarrassed about. Here goes anyway. Because," Martee said with a nod toward Banelle, "that's my best friend sitting next to you there, and she and I go all the way back to grade school."

"Toddlers." Banelle's father said.

Martee looked at Banelle's father, her eyelashes almost closing, fingernails clicking out a brief rhythm, then stopped.

Martee laid her palm softly on the table and looked at Dollar. "I want you to know something about me, Dollar, truthfully." Martee leaned back. "I never thought of it until today, when you and Anna's father told your stories, Bernice told hers, and Anna told her little story.

"I thought to myself, there's only one thing I can think of which I've ever been embarrassed about, so maybe that one thing deserves a lot more respect than I'd previously allowed."

Dollar raised his eyebrows, head back slightly. He frowned briefly, eyes down right.

"So anyway, one day I was selling this older couple on their next car. Usually that was so easy I wouldn't bother. It was my turn for the door that hour and we were short a few associates due to personal time and a firing, so I was working the old couple over by scaring them shitless with statistics about the make and model and year of the car they had arrived in.

It was in top shape, perfect maintenance record, of course. I made sure by having the service manager look into the car's history and then run it around the block. The statistics about their model and year was real." Dimples came and went on Martee's lips. "I imagine the husband was a meticulous provider, always a step ahead with preventative maintenance, even with his wife, she glowed." Martee sighed. "Where are the men like that now?" She tilted her head, eyes on Banelle, brief squint. Martee straightened her head and looked down. "Dammit all, anyway." Martee clenched the right fist, bumped still on the table.

Martee looked at Dollar. "I had that old couple sold on a similar, brand new vehicle, which had arrived in a shipment the day before. We had just pulled the car off the wash rack and the detailer was towel-drying the car when the couple arrived. It was a perfectly timed match: the couple would have more years of secure, reliable driving without feeling too shocked by change, they loved the colors outside and inside, and they were enchanted by me. They were another sale to help meet my quota for the day, and the couple and I were just visiting while the paperwork was being prepared." Martee turned only the eyes at Banelle. "Then Anna walks in. Of course I'm happy to see her almost any time, and I was happy about making another sale, even if it had been boring, so I put the two happy things together and introduced Anna to the couple." Martee turned the head fully toward Banelle. "What were their names again?"

"Bruce and Chelcia."

Martee nodded all the way back, and down almost touching her chin on her chest, shoulder-length hair flowing around, "That's right, how could I forget the names of *those* two customers?" Martee smiled cheerily, blinked her eyes, shook her hair back, waved the left hand dismissively.

...Banelle closed her mouth, seeing that an answer wasn't really wanted.

Martee looked at Dollar. "Anna had stars in her eyes about that Black Menace we drove over here in..."

Banelle felt herself smile.

"...and she had been saving her money like a good girl. I was going to give her the Best Friend for Life Deal, only I didn't know she was ready to buy that day, nor how excited Anna really was.

"She started telling the older couple about what she was buying, and why — I found that part out later after I had gone to check on the couple's paperwork. While away, Anna had convinced them the best sense of security is having the vehicle you really want because of what it does for your self-confidence, and as long as you were responsible and had saved your money, there was nothing more secure than having something in your life that you really wanted to be there.

"By the time I got back, Anna had up-sold the couple. They were stubbornly attached to a different vehicle they had been eyeing for months, had a chipper attitude, and a content bank account.

"The couple backpedaled out of the deal I had them in and bought the vehicle forty percent more expensive than the one I had been intent on selling them.

"Not only that. They took her to dinner!" Martee said, thumping the bottom of her fist on the table three times with the words, index finger out. "They all went in *their* two new vehicles, and I couldn't go because of the ratio of sales agents to customers that day.

"I was the punch line joke for the quarter and the intended recipient of much ribbing from my sales manager and the rest of the sales staff." Martee smiled briefly, turned a slight shade of red, pouted her lips, eyes downcast, a sigh.

She's so clever. Banelle felt puzzled, what was being done? She was not really able to put her finger on what that was.

———

Martee looked at Dollar, smiled toothily. "I learned something about the impact of values on sales that day. Since then I've outsold the rest of the staff every quarter, and damn near every day even when I'm goofing off." Martee put her left hand palm flat on the table. "Because *now* I make sure the older folks who stop in feel *real* security and *real* dignity, *before* they leave."

Martee nodded slowly once, her eyes intent on Dollar. She picked her hand off the table and waved palm-up in the air. "And nobody else has a clue! Serves them for the digs!" Martee smiled openly with white teeth and happiness, self-loving doe eyes.

"So now you know! I've only ever been embarrassed..." wavered the palm toward Banelle. "...by Anna!" Martee glared, tilted her head sideways, left forearm against the table edge, looked at Banelle, nodding with each word, "That. Must. Be. Significant."

Martee's eyes gazed at Dollar, her right hand disappeared below the table, looked like she was rubbing her hand on Dollar's knee. She paused, the forearm muscles clenched, relaxed.

Martee sat up, eyelashes nearly closed breathing deeply, the sigh of satisfaction, then a smile, propped her chin in her right palm, elbow on the table her gaze on Dollar, left fingers hanging off the edge of the table near him.

"So." Banelle's father said. "If someone can make you feel embarrassed when nobody else can, you should make sure they stay in your life?"

Dollar looked thoughtful, engaged, enthralled, eyes steadily on Martee. He rubbed his left palm on the back of Martee's left hand. "Thanks for sharing." Moved his hand a few inches from Martee's along the table edge.

Banelle felt lionized, felt alarmed by a depth Martee didn't usually share in socialized company, and worse, felt Dollar had disconnected.

Banelle's father looked at his watch. Announced, "It's three."

"Do you have to be anywhere, daddy?"

He shook his head, closing his eyes, then looked at Banelle. "I'm just done with this restaurant for now. The lunch crowd was prettier."

Banelle felt a sudden panic realizing she hadn't eaten any of her food. She sat up and grabbed the fork. "Can we hold on that for a few minutes?"

"Not a problem." his left hand spread in a relaxed wave.

Banelle held the forked chunk of shark steak near her mouth. She glanced at Dollar, then squinted at Martee, whose eyes moved from Dollar's and returned Banelle's gaze. Banelle smiled toothily despite a rise of anxiety, "I'm having fun! Let's think of something else to do next," pulled the piece of delicious meat off the fork between teeth, and even lukewarm, relaxed into this feeling of ecstasy.

Martee nodded happily, looked at Banelle's father, then Martee returned all her attention to Dollar, and shifted on her chair even further toward him, Martee's left fingers caressing his left pinky on the table. "What should we get into?"

Banelle, eyes widened, then noticed and watched Bernice walking energetically in their direction and realized Bernice wasn't wearing the hip apron with pens and pads.

Dollar smiled, glanced at Banelle, Banelle's father, eyes on Martee. "For sixty seconds let's take turns saying unique ideas, then we can go back and each pick our favorite thing from whatever comes up."

"You think?" Banelle's father said.

"Ohh, don't be such a grump." Martee.

While Banelle didn't really want herself on the spot to spout ideas, she felt something new deep inside herself which caused her to frown with curiosity. "Dad?" Banelle heard herself say, "you do something like this all the time with your creative teams, coming up with ideas?"

He nodded, the corners of his mouth dimpling while he looked at Banelle. He sighed. "You're right, B.B. I think I'm just overdone with this restaurant for today. It's got me feeling grumpy. I watched twenty girls leave and not one of them walked over to our corner and intro-duced herself to me."

Dollar chuckled. "There's plenty of cash, plenty of food. We can do this as easily outside, maybe easier."

"Oh, good!" Bernice said.

Dollar was startled. "Hello!"

"Why good?" Banelle said, still looking at Bernice.

Bernice looked at Banelle, head bouncing side to side, smiling. "I was just coming to tell my favorite table of people *ever* that I'm off the clock. I didn't want to leave and have you wondering when someone else came by to check on you."

"Off the clock?" Banelle's father said, looking at his watch. "You think?"

"Dad."

He breathed in and out of his nose a quick, impatient sigh.

"We need to tip you," Dollar said.

"And I suppose we should pay for our food, too," Banelle's father said. Banelle was watching her father when he looked at her, only the eyes turning. "My treat today."

"REALLY?" Martee, the eyes wide leaning away, left hand flat on her breastbone.

Oops! Banelle realized that indeed it was time to go, before Martee and her father turned their bickering buttons on. Banelle marveled, feeling her head shake. Sometimes her father and Martee acted as if they were married. *Speaking of marriage.*

Banelle leaned against Dollar's shoulder, whispered into his ear. "(Come on.)" She slipped her left hand under his arm and pulled upward. In a moment she felt him respond. He pushed his chair back and stood. She rose with him, blossoming togetherness. He stretched, leaning backward from vertical, bowing his body. Banelle's eyes widened seeing the lines of the muscles tense in his stretch, her right hand patted him on the abs twice.

"Ah!" Dollar laughed, stopped himself stretching.

Banelle's father was getting up, also.

Dollar pulled his wallet out.

Martee finally got the idea and started getting up.

"They have your ticket up front," Bernice said.

"We'll go up front." Dollar said. He pulled two twenty dollar bills out and handed them to Bernice. "I've never had better wait service."

Banelle felt her eyes wide, and watched the rippling emotions on Bernice's face accepting the pair of twenties. Banelle looked at Dollar's face. He seemed calm and at peace and purposeful.

"What's this?" she heard Bernice say.

"I think it's a tip," Banelle said, looking at Bernice.

Bernice's eyes became round with understanding. "Oh, this is too much!" Bernice pushed the money back toward Dollar.

"Here." Martee said, handing Bernice another pair of twenty-dollar bills.

"Uhhh..." Bernice looked back and forth at the two pairs of twenties.

In her periphery, Banelle saw her father's hand tossing another pair of twenties across the remainder of the table.

"What is this, you guys?!" Bernice said.

Banelle sighed, opened her clutch, remembered when she looked inside how she hadn't brought any money along, quietly closed the clutch, slid her left hand through Dollar's arm, snuggled herself nearer.

"Ohhh," Banelle's father said, "don't be a brat, Bernice."

Martee rolled her eyes and leaned her head at him with her lips disapproving, then pulled her head upright, looked at Banelle and leaned the head forward.

Banelle sighed, looked around Dollar toward Bernice. "Speaking for myself, Bernice, I have never before felt myself brought closer to so many people in such a short visit, including you. I'm guessing everyone had a great time here today and we are very grateful. " Banelle looked at Dollar, then at Martee, then at her father. "Is that right?"

floating on an anxiety of gradual emptiness

. . .

"ABSOLUTELY," grumped Banelle's father. "Now, let's say we all get outside. You too, Bernice." He smiled toothily.

"Door!" Dollar said, left arm and finger raised diagonally.

Banelle felt Dollar turning, let her hand slip free of his arm, followed him, eyes on the jeans covering his ass. With two steps Banelle was near Bernice, paused, looked into Bernice's eyes meaningfully, whispered, "(Come on.)" Bernice was looking at her, frozen.

Banelle jerked her head toward the front of the restaurant, imitating a sway dance move Banelle had seen Bernice do earlier.

Bernice's eyes got round. She picked up the third pair of twenties and folded the tips, stuffed them within her right pocket, then turned with Banelle and followed Banelle and Dollar toward the front. Banelle glanced back, saw Martee was following, stalked by her father.

The five of them wound their way through the restaurant, which, Banelle noticed while walking, wasn't half as busy. Floating on an anxiety of gradual emptiness deep down, Banelle was glad they were leaving for the day.

Banelle's father stopped by the register. Dollar pushed the front door open. Banelle and Bernice walked around Dollar outside, Martee immediately behind. He let the door close behind him and strolled with them in the mid-afternoon Sun, down the three wooden steps, then the four of them circled together on the parking lot, the sound of cars from the road nearby. There was a fragrance on the nose from lilac bushes.

Banelle noted Bernice seemed uncomfortable. "How old are you, Bernice?"

"Twenty-one now."

"Really?!" Banelle said, feeling a start of surprise and incredulity. "I had guessed you to be about sixteen."

"Thanks!"

Martee's eyes were on Bernice. "Got anything going on this afternoon?"

Bernice shook her head. "No. Not really."

"Seems a shame to have nothing to do," Dollar said, looking at Banelle.

Banelle smiled, felt mischief. "Yes."

Banelle felt compelled to turn away, the Sun over his shoulder. She looked at Bernice, blinking to clear the darkness which the sunshine had temporarily given Banelle's eyes, wondered if she should say more. Banelle wondered if the enjoyment she had been feeling might be, in part, from the jealously spiced laughter Bernice inspired. Where Banelle's jealously welled up from, she wasn't sure. *She's twenty-one...* began her resolute voice.

Banelle didn't let the thought finish, and shrugged slightly. Trust the instincts. "You need to come along with us, whatever we're doing."

"Yeah!" Martee said.

Bernice looked at Dollar. He nodded.

Banelle leaned her forehead against Dollar's right shoulder, slipped her left hand inside his arm and enjoyed feeling close, eyes down appreciating the cozy part of the parking lot circumscribed by their comfortable circling of feet. She heard footsteps coming down the short set of stairs, treasured the waning moment. A part of her wondered if they should find a pick-me-up somewhere. *Having fun can be tiring*, her resolute voice said. *You should be more conservative.* She felt her nose wrinkle briefly.

Banelle's father joined their circle of feet.

Banelle picked her head off Dollar's shoulder, let her hand drop, and stood apart.

"All right!" her father said. "Now that we're done with that, who's first with ideas?"

"We invited Bernice along," Martee said.

"Good!" Banelle's father said. "My thoughts, exactly."

Bernice giggled. Everyone looked at her. "I haven't accepted yet."

Martee looked at Bernice, narrowing the eyes, smiling. "Anna. You and I will hold her down and Dollar can tickle her until she agrees."

Bernice screeched, elbows tucked, fists under the chin, shaking her head, and grinning.

"You'd better say yes, quick," Banelle said.

Dollar took a step toward Bernice. Bernice jumped back, turning half away and laughed. "I accept!"

"Moving things along," Banelle's father said, looking at his watch. "Martee, why don't you lead us off? We'll go clockwise for sixty seconds taking turns with ideas. Ready?"

Martee flashed a smile. "Beer tour."

Banelle's father looked at her without raising his head, his left hand holding back the right sleeve, his right hand clenched and bent downward further exposing the watch face. "Canoeing." His eyes turned toward Banelle.

Banelle felt a rush of panic being put on the spot. "Coffee!" she blurted.

"Jogging," Dollar said, and everyone looked at Bernice.

"Movie." Bernice's lips squirming.

"Dancing," Martee said.

"Nine holes of golf." Banelle's father.

Banelle felt her eyes go wide, blurted, "Malling!".

"Rock skipping," Dollar said.

"Umm," Bernice said, "umm, I pass."

"Can't pass," Banelle's father said. "Anything."

"Sidewalk chalk!" Bernice, almost shouting, her hands shaking with the words.

"Caricature art," Martee said.

"Submarine tour," Banelle's father said.

Banelle felt caught out, realized she wasn't ready.

"Stumped or puzzled?" Dollar said.

Banelle looked at him. "Stumped. I mean puzzled."

"Can't be stumped or puzzled," her father said.

Banelle felt panic, anger from feeling pushed, looked at her father briefly, then down at her feet. She saw Dollar's rugged shoes standing to the left of her sandals with glossy nails, felt romance, envisioned flowers, shared bedroom smells, soft pillows bounced hard, flowers on the nightstand, his gray eyes staring down into hers, "Conservatory."

Bernice screeched and jumped up and down three times. "That was mine!"

"Shakespeare in the Park," Dollar said.

Banelle looked at him, wondering if that was a serious interest.

Bernice was bouncing the knees, feet planted, shaking her fists like a game show contestant. "Mini-golf!" Bernice blurted, grinned, stopped bouncing, smoothed the left hand palm down in a semicircle dance move, then leaned her head back, locked her move, eyes expectant on Martee.

Martee opened her eyes wide, looked left, right, left. She spread her hands suddenly, bending her knees. "Fish pond!" palms rising upward, fingers curling.

"Horse race," Banelle's father said.

"Casino." Banelle shrugged at an idea she wouldn't pursue on her own. *WE are not gambling!* her resolute voice intoned. She looked at Dollar.

"Skeet shoot," Dollar said, his head rocking side to side, a shrug.

"Live music!" Bernice smiled and bobbed her head up and down, feet in a one three dance step.

"..." Martee with the mouth open.

"Time!" Banelle's father said.

Martee closed her mouth, bounced once, the legs rocking forward-and-backward with pent-up energy.

Dollar pointed briefly at Martee. "I liked your idea for dancing."

Martee nodded, her legs changing rhythms, dancing a shuffle, twirled a circle.

"Is that your vote, then?" Banelle's father said, looking at Dollar.

Dollar nodded, smiling, eyes twinkling, a rhythm welling in the muscles, his head nodding smoothly with some private rhythm watching Martee.

"Bernice?" Banelle's father said.

"Dancing!" Bernice said, kicking her left foot, then shifting her weight back and forth rhythmically.

"I'm for Dollar's idea of rock skipping," Banelle's father said. He raised his eyebrows and looked at Banelle.

Banelle felt herself smile. "I'm voting for sidewalk chalk. I can't think when I did that last."

"Martee?" he said.

Martee's mouth opened and closed, then opened again and paused. "I like all those that were picked. And make it live music." Martee added between sways.

"As long as we get some coffee next," Banelle heard herself say.

"Any disagreements?" her father said.

———

Dollar's eyebrows elevated. "That'll make a long day."

"Are you griping, Tarzan?" Martee said, swaying side to side.

Dollar let out a single laugh of surprise, arched back and beat his chest, baritone voice. "NO! No elephants!"

Banelle felt her eyes go wide, the tingle of goosebumps startling skin.

Martee laughed, taking a step back from their circle, covered her mouth with the back of her right hand, nodded. She gave her hair a swirl and stood straight, stepping forward, rejoining the Council of the Circle of Feet.

Banelle heard her father chuckling, then looked at Dollar.

"Coffee first." Banelle heard Bernice say. "I would like to sit down. I've been on my feet all damn day."

The resolute voice reminded Banelle Bernice wasn't the younger girl she had taken her for. Bernice's opinions were more focused, like Bernice had been around much longer than she appeared physically.

"Or better yet," Bernice said, "there's a neat coffee parlor on the block where I live." Bernice sniffed the sleeve of her shirt. "I can duck into my apartment for a quick shower…"

"Agreed." Dollar said.

"…and get out of these skunky restaurant clothes."

"B.B?" her father said, "I believe you're the bus driver."

"Bus?!" Banelle said, feeling the ire.

She felt Dollar's right hand grip her left shoulder. "Bat Girl!" the baritone voice.

Banelle felt goose bumps tingling her skin, fire erupting where his thumb overlapped the suede vest and touched the bare skin of her breastbone. The fire ran instantly down her chest, her fingertips burning to touch his bare skin, yearning to feel his hands all over herself.

Dollar. "The Bat Phone is flashing red. Commissioner Gordon will be expecting us at the Undergrind Coffee Cave. Are you ready?" Banelle felt Dollar's hand and thumb slide away from her shoulder.

"Bat Girl?!" Banelle protested, feeling the game. She stood erect, putting her heels together and arched breasts, elbows slightly bent, fists at her hips. "Male-Crime Fighters!" Banelle looked levelly at Bernice, then Martee. Banelle pointed her left arm at the Navigator. "To the Bat Car!"

Martee shook her hair back, then rolled the head forward and looked directly at Banelle. "Have you lost your mind?" Martee was smiling happily.

Banelle felt happy, this moment now thick with *déjà vu*. She shook off the feeling, jerked her head shortly in the direction of the SUV. "Get going! Or I'll pull your mask off and everyone will know who you really are."

"Who is she?!" Bernice screeched, clutching the fists near the chin in mock terror.

Banelle felt her eyes narrow, staring at Martee. "She is the fabled Witch of Endor, she is just a bit ahead of her time."

Martee's eyes narrowed under the eyebrows, lips serious, glaring at Banelle. "*My* self-image is a full exploration of the magick of the cisgender pussy framework within contemporary romance locales. Remember, Anna, there is always one eclectic Wicca left to which boys must secretly ask their questions of masculine relevance."

Bernice lowered her arms looking seriously at Martee. "Do boys *ever* have relevance?"

They laughed.

Banelle turned toward the Navigator. "Come on, fellow *Relevants*!"

Dollar walked faster around and ahead of Banelle.

She pulled the keys out of the clutch, watching his legs and ass walking. "(Mmmm-hmm.)" Banelle hummed quietly, squeezed the clutch with a snap. She felt along the remote for the appropriate button, wished she had a remote for his zipper: down, up, down.

As Dollar approached the driver's side, the SUV beeped and flashed the lights twice.

"If you're opening doors!" Martee called from behind, "You've got to open them for all the girls!"

Dollar looked over his shoulder and grinned, flushing a shade of red. He turned his attention toward the driver's door, pulled the handle with the left hand and the passenger's door with the right, opening both. He dropped the right hand from the passenger door and backed up with a slight bow and palm inviting Banelle to get into the tan leather driver's seat.

She felt her head bow slightly, twice, watching his gray eyes while stepping past him, and climbed in. His left hand was halfway across her, dragging the belt across her thigh and breast before she had finished settling in.

Banelle heard Martee laugh, then Banelle heard a slap accompanied by Dollar's reacting startled, his hand jerked, Banelle feeling the brief increased pressure of the belt.

Banelle felt her eyes narrow, watching his arm, and imagined Martee's hand being so intimate with Dollar's ass, the visualization of Martee's hand lingering, groping, then gripping Dollar's ass. Banelle felt enraged.

He bent his head, caught Banelle's eyes, leaned nearer and kissed her briefly on the lips, finished buckling her in with the click of safety. His face was impassive, even with the shade of red coloring the cheeks and neck.

Banelle felt anxious not knowing what he was thinking, and also stunned. *He just kissed me!*

Dollar backed away and closed the driver's door.

She saw Martee through the rear-view mirror sliding onto the rear passenger seat, then slide again into the center, and saw her father getting in the right rear passenger seat, the sound of the door closing.

Dollar walked around the front of the SUV, his head bent watching where he was walking.

Banelle saw Bernice's shoulder move into the rear-view mirror, sitting directly behind the driver's seat, and the door closed.

The SUV was hot with summer sunshine. Banelle put the key in the ignition and started the Navigator, pressing her freshly kissed lips together, trying to remember the last time a man kissed these lips?

Dollar opened the front passenger door and climbed in, pulled the door closed, reached his left hand for the safety belt on his right.

Martee leaned forward and rubbed her left hand on his biceps, squeezed the arm, held her hand there. "You have a handsome ass. Are you offended?"

The automatic air smoothly began blowing cooler air.

Dollar turned his head and looked at Martee. From the way his eyes moved slightly back and forth, Banelle guessed he and Martee were searching each other's eyes. Dollar smiled, patted Martee's hand, squeezed, and held Martee's hand on his arm. Dollar glanced briefly at Banelle, then returned his eyes onto Martee.

Martee squeezed his arm one more time, then withdrew her hand slowly, and leaned back. Banelle watched Martee in the rear-view mirror. Martee saw Banelle watching and scrunched the nose, squinted the eyes, shook the head minutely.

Banelle mashed her rage against the foot brake, pulled the SUV lever into drive. She made a quick look around to ensure the way was clear of hazards. This extra care gave her time to fight down an urge to bark the tires, feeling the knotted tension in her right calf and in the muscle along the top of her leg. "Which way, Bernice?"

Banelle made the Navigator roll forward as normally as she could.

"Take a right at the street."

Banelle flipped the turn signal, acknowledging the dissatisfaction from the rest of herself, a part of Banelle again admiring Martee's skill. Banelle needed to focus on something charming rather than go far down that dark street. Yet who was bringing out the worst of whom?

eyes moved reluctantly from the jeans to look at his eyes

. . .

MARTEE WAS FEELING COY, and a little concerned, riding in the middle of the tan back seat, the smell of leather and tan colors all around the interior.

There was always a happy moment feeling with Anna's father's presence nearby. Martee turned her head right, feeling herself bounce in the pleasure of movement. She liked how her curves in motion caught others' eyes and had been intentional so long the movement of bounces had become unconscious competence. She looked at Anna's father who was watching out the passenger window. He unfailingly had an alluring smell about him. She was never quite sure if that was a masculine fragrance he wore or some quality of his virility.

Martee turned her head forward, looked at Banelle driving, and smiled feeling the little victory a few minutes back.

Martee tilted her head left, looked at the hunk of man in the front passenger seat who had, the way Anna told the story, just walked onto Anna's yard earlier in the day. Martee wondered who he was really, what his story was, how he got here today? She appreciated the contours of his face and neck, how his shoulders radiated strength. Martee leaned farther left to see better. She admired how strong his hands looked resting on the jeans, the muscular legs, watched the self-confidence quietly stated in the way he held his head. His every turn and movement seemed to be self-aware comfort, like a tiger at rest, calm, and confident of any future.

Martee grinned and spoke quietly to herself, "(Grrr!)" Leaning further, she felt her left shoulder bump Bernice. Banelle was weaving through traffic, moving the Black Menace generally faster than the traffic around them.

Martee didn't want to watch Banelle's driving today. There was an edge to it. Martee turned her head toward Bernice and immediately felt the shoulder bump again. Martee smiled at Bernice, whispered. "(Oops!)" Martee sat erect with a bounce.

Bernice shrugged, then looked from Martee toward Dollar. Bernice's eyes lingered on him for a moment until she wrestled the eyes away, leaned toward Martee, whispered. "(How do you know Aaron?)"

"(Aaron?!)"

"(Yes.)" Bernice's eyes darted toward Dollar and back to Martee.

Martee turned her head, saw Banelle's fuming eyes briefly in the rear-view mirror, and Martee watched Dollar. *Aaron, is it?* She glanced in the rear-view mirror and seeing Banelle watching, Martee scrunched her nose, squinted. *Too fun!* Martee tried to remember the last time she had Banelle so riled.

Martee turned to Bernice and leaned closer, whispered. "(How do *you* know Aaron?)"

Bernice didn't hesitate, leaning close, Martee watching the passing scenery through the left passenger window. "(Aaron works a bar called the Grape Hopper.)" Martee couldn't remember ever crashing a place named the Grape Hopper. She looked at Bernice's lips, then the eyes.

Martee leaned near Bernice's ear. "(Where's the Grape Hopper?)"

Bernice put her mouth near Martee's ear. "(Connected to the skyway of the city, about thirty minutes from here.)" Bernice leaned back.

Martee searched both of Bernice's eyes, leaned toward Bernice's ear. "(Did you date him?)"

Bernice shook her head vigorously eyes wide, then eyes on Dollar briefly, then on Banelle, and leaned near Martee's ear. "(I don't think I've ever seen him with anybody! Until today, not that I've been at the Grape Hopper recently.)"

My, my, MY, Martee thought, looking from Banelle toward Dollar. She was dying to ask Dollar about the Grape Hopper, loving the secret. He had *said* he was a landscaper. She felt the thrill of intrigue, feeling advantages. Martee patted Bernice appreciatively on the knee. "(Thanks.)"

…saw in passing Banelle was watching…

Martee whispered in Bernice's ear, "(I want to talk more with you in private.)" pulled away, looked in Bernice's eyes.

Bernice leaned toward Martee's ear. "(I need to change, want to tag along?")

Martee felt herself nod enthusiastically and bounced happily erect.

Bernice smiled, scrunched her nose, leaned briefly toward Martee. "(Jazzed!)"

Smiling openly, Martee turned her attention to the rear-view mirror, watching purposefully. She felt enlivened and energized with secrets! Concerns dropped away like scuffed old shoes. *Watch me! Watch me!* Martee thought, and began counting the times Banelle's eyes looked at Martee through the rear-view mirror. *One. Two. Wait – three – four…* Martee shook her hair back, *What a hoot! Anna is seriously unwrapped!*

Martee admired again Banelle's yellow scarf-tied hair, the dark suede vest. Martee leaned farther right, bumping her right shoulder against Anna's father. There was no sense of apologizing to him, felt so natural. Martee wrinkled her nose feeling jealous about Banelle's sexy legs, highlighted by the sassy-assed pleated sunshine miniskirt, and rediscovered the dangling black leather straps. *Nice touch*, Martee thought, remembering the gentle swish and slap of the leather straps when Banelle walked. Martee felt herself shake her head slowly. *I can't remember when Anna has looked as smashing as this.*

Bernice leaned forward, the left hand on the back of Banelle's seat. "Turn left at the next light."

Waiting at the light, Martee noticed Banelle gazing steadily into the rear-view mirror, and this time Martee smiled warmly for Banelle. They were friends after all.

Martee felt her right shoulder bump against Anna's father in Banelle's left turn after the light, accelerating between oncoming traffic, Martee unconsciously braced herself by placing her right palm and fingers on his left knee. After the corner was past, Martee unconsciously pulled her hand back.

"Park anywhere on the right side of this block," Bernice said.

Martee felt the Black Menace slow down, and watched Banelle pick a place and pull alongside the spot stopping near the car in front, the back end of that car almost at their rear window. Banelle put the transmission lever in reverse, and while turning half-around in her seat, looked at Dollar for a moment, then narrowed her eyes at Martee briefly.

Martee smiled warmly, shook her hair back.

Banelle watched past Martee, then past Anna's father, her left hand spinning the steering wheel right, then left, then right and left, then farther left for a few moments. Martee felt the Black Menace stop. Banelle turned forward, moved the transmission lever, turned the wheel right, pulled the Black Menace forward a few feet, and stopped.

Damn, Martee thought, with renewed respect for Banelle's driving skills, a big machine to hustle so succinctly into urban street parking with traffic whizzing by.

———

Anna's father opened the door and started getting out.

Martee pushed on his back playfully, heard and felt him chuckle.

When he was on his feet, he turned and offered Martee his left hand.

"Thank you kind sir," Martee quipped sweetly.

"The duty of a knight," he said, canting while saying so, the somber voice belied by his open smiling, his eyes watching her legs as Martee scooted out — landed with both feet near him feeling her breasts bump against his arm. She didn't pay the natural contact any conscious attention. She released his hand and stepped to the center of the sidewalk, turned and watched the others getting out.

Bernice scooted across the seat toward Anna's father. He held his hand for Bernice.

Bernice's face lighted up. "Thank you!" She used his hand to help pull herself the rest of the way out.

Martee heard a door whump shut and saw Dollar standing on the sidewalk. Dollar was watching Martee, his left hand falling from the front passenger door to the pocket of the new-looking blue jeans. Her eyes moved reluctantly from the jeans to look at his eyes which closed as he arched backward in a stretch, arms bending and muscles bulging.

Tigerrr!

Martee heard Banelle's door shut. She watched Banelle walk around the front of the Black Menace looking directly at Martee, stopped near Dollar and almost stepping on his foot.

He finished the stretch.

Banelle continued glaring at Martee, an angry jiggling in the hair.

Whew-eee, kitty! Martee thought, popped her eyebrows twice watching Banelle. Then Martee noted Dollar was looking at Banelle.

Banelle became aware of Dollar's gaze, turned her head toward him and smiled like the Moon rise chasing the afternoon Sun.

Oh, what a shit. Martee looked back and forth at the pair of them sideways while Dollar and Banelle gazed into each other's eyes. *Damn.* Martee thought. *It's like a wedding ceremony.* In Martee's periphery, Anna's father swung the rear passenger door shut, whump. Martee sniffed, straightened her head, looked at Bernice.

Bernice was watching Martee.

Martee shrugged, smiling.

Bernice's eyes darted along the street on Martee's right, then looked at Anna's father turning from the Black Menace. He stood near Bernice.

Banelle looked down, digging inside her clutch. The Black Menace beeped once, flash of lights.

Martee turned on her left heel facing toward the corner on what little of the sidewalk was left considering where they had parked. On the corner was a coffee shop with large plate glass windows. People inside were seated at small tables, paper cups in hands, yummy looking pastries on plates. *Sudden Brews* read the signage.

Martee looked at Bernice, bounced her head right. "This it?"

Bernice nodded happily. "I live around the corner." Bernice's head moved up and down twice, the short dance.

"ANNA," Martee said, seeing Banelle was enraptured again with Dollar.

Banelle blinked, turned her head toward Martee.

Uh-huh, Martee thought. *Jiggers, girlfriend.* Martee bounced her head left, watching Banelle's eyes. "I'm going with Bernice. We'll be back in a bit. Meet you in the coffee shop." and nodded toward the corner.

Banelle's lips were restless, the eyes wider. She inhaled. "How fortunate."

Martee rolled her eyes, shaking her head, looked at Bernice and shrugged.

Bernice touched her left fingertips to Anna's father's shoulder, "We'll be back in a bit!"

He lifted his right index finger, leaned past Bernice, looked down the sidewalk left, down the sidewalk right, then he straightened up. "How are the sidewalks around the corner?"

"What?" Bernice said, blinking twice. "Oh! Sidewalk art!"

He nodded approvingly, eyebrows up. "Exactly."

Bernice looked at Martee briefly, then back at him. "There's a huge courtyard. We can all spread out if we want."

He nodded. "How do we get there?"

Bernice took half a step forward, raised her right arm, fingers articulate toward the corner by *Sudden Brews*. "You go around the corner…"

"To the right." he said.

"…then halfway down the next block," waving her hand in that direction. "You'll see a sunny alley."

"Down an *alley*?" Martee said.

Bernice looked at Martee. "It's open to the sky, and wide. People go back there all the time to sit in the courtyard."

"Sounds lovely." Martee heard Dollar say. She looked at Dollar, noticed Banelle turn her gaze from Dollar.

"Turn right," Anna's father said, "half a block, turn down the walkplatz and into the courtyard. Got it. We can all meet there in thirty minutes. Work for everyone?" his eyes looking around their group.

Bernice's head bobbed up and down, a brief dance. "Jazzed!"

Martee felt a dimpling smile. "Ready?"

Bernice smiled toothily, tilt of the head and started walking.

Martee paced Bernice, smiling at Banelle as they walked past, Martee pointedly tipping her head and fluttering eyelashes.

Banelle scrunched the nose at Martee, then smiled with a nod.

"Bye!" Bernice said.

Martee glanced at Anna's father over her left shoulder. "See you guys in a bit."

He brought his left hand up, touched his forehead, lips, then stomach in a quick arching succession while bowing and smiling at Martee, stood erect.

Martee rolled her eyes skyward and shook her hair, feeling the smiling around the eyes, sassed her ass unconsciously, and turned her attention ahead.

They were at the corner already, turning right, coffee and chocolate aromas coming out of the door of *Sudden Brews*.

Martee turned her head right, cupped the left hand by her mouth, saw Anna's father's eyes were still on Martee — *Of course!* — and yelled, "Bring me a tall latte!"

His left thumb came up, nodded upward once.

Martee turned her attention toward the next sidewalk as they rounded the corner, saw more glass for *Sudden Brews*, people at tables inside, a glimpse of people standing around a counter in the back corner through the double doors.

Though Martee didn't notice this consciously she was, deep down inside, feeling warm toward the little things Anna's father always seemed happy to be doing for her. Breathed, "(He's such a wonderful man.)"

———

"Aaron?" Bernice said, turning her head.

Martee felt a passing frown. "Anna's father."

"Charlie?"

Martee looked at Bernice, felt herself blink. "Charlie!" Then pushed his name immediately out of her mind and returned to her habitual way of thinking about the man. "He's Anna's father," chanting the mantra.

Bernice was quiet for a moment. "What a cool man."

Martee looked at Bernice's lips, then at her eyes. Martee's head bounced, smiling openly feeling the happiness around her eyes. "Yes, he is."

The walkplatz wasn't accessible for cars. There were three waist-high foot round cement posts encased in pipe in a line between the two buildings. They turned down the sunny lane. Martee saw ahead a large open space with greenery, a fountain spraying water in the shape of an umbrella.

Martee couldn't get the picture out of her mind how Banelle kept looking at Dollar. "By the Goddess of Self-Love, has Anna got a case of wet panties about Dollar?!"

Bernice nodded, "Definitely!"

Martee looked at Bernice, not entirely sure Bernice was talking only about Banelle. "So, tell me about your apartment?"

"It's not mine. It's my roommate's."

"Boy? Girl?" Martee watching.

Bernice shrugged the right shoulder. "Girl."

They walked out on an expansive courtyard, the wide walkway leading toward a giant center circle of concrete slabs lain concentric, the center of the giant circle featuring the lively fountain, humid on the nose. Around the periphery were plants and flowering bushes, the mid-afternoon Sun shining from a mostly blue sky, scent on the nose from flowering wild garlic, indian paintbrush, and prairie milkweed with orange and black Monarchs floating between blooms.

"How lovely!" Martee said.

"Yes!" Bernice's head nodded, tilted her head left.

Martee walked with Bernice a short way clockwise around the periphery until they came to the next sidewalk left — leading diagonally to the nearest building, an intercross of pink brick and darker pink sandstone with bulging off-white wrought iron balconies going up. Martee counted, feeling her head nod, ...*four, five floors*, two balconies on each side of center. *Six floors*, Martee amended, noticing the ground floor hidden in the shadows didn't have balconies and was embraced directly by the gardens.

They arrived at the darkened glass doors at the center of the building. Bernice pulled a stiff card out of the back left pocket and slid the card through a card reader. When the light flashed green and beeped, Bernice pulled the door open and tilted her head to invite Martee inside.

There was a narrow, elongated lobby which connected the garden end of the building to the street side farther down the hall. Near the garden entrance, there was an elevator on each side. Bernice pushed a button, her head grooving ear to shoulder.

Martee turned around and looked out the darkened glass at the courtyard. She felt she might enjoy living here herself.

The elevator off her left shoulder rang. At the sound of doors sliding, Martee turned. Bernice did a spin on her left foot and energetically entered the elevator. Martee followed right behind.

Bernice pushed the top floor button.

"Martee?"

"Hmm?" Martee said, coming out of her musings on her sense of home.

"You never did say how long you've known Aaron."

Martee felt her forehead wrinkle. "About four hours?"

"Oh, go on!"

"No, really." Martee said, having a hard time believing how short the clock time had been. "We just all seem to click," thinking about Dollar.

The elevator stopped, the doors smoothed open. Bernice led them halfway down the building hallway, then left down another hallway which, Martee looking over her shoulder and then ahead of them, appeared to connect one side of the building to the other side. "So half of these apartments get to be on the courtyard?"

Bernice turned bodily while walking, looked back and smiled at Martee. "Yes! I was *so* excited to be accepted by this roommate of mine! After I saw her apartment, I was only too glad to agree to what she asked. Of course, I had to have one or two things *my* way." Bernice turned her attention forward while they walked. "I could never have afforded something like this myself, having it all built, the gardens shaped and planted, the ongoing grounds maintenance."

Bernice stopped at the second to the last door on the left, the last door being about four feet right, pulled the key card out and swiped the card reader on the wall beside the apartment's door. The door clicked. Bernice grabbed the handle and pushed the door all the way inward, stepped inside, and made room for Martee.

Martee moved past Bernice. Bernice turned and closed the door.

Martee found herself in an extended hallway of taupe carpet at the end of which she saw steeply angled sunlight and the glass of the courtyard wall of the apartment. On the left side of the hallway were four doorways, one of which was immediately by the entry door.

———

Bernice cozied against Martee, using the whole left arm with the fingers to point down the hall, quietly spoke. "(Martee, feel free to explore the living room,)" turning the palm upward, opening-and-closing the hand twice, then flipping the hand-palm downward, fingers curving left, "(The kitchen's the last door on the left, grab yourself something to drink if you like. If you need a bathroom use the next door here. My room is right here. I'll rinse off and be out in a few.)"

Martee felt her eyebrows up, nodded slowly, taking in the longest run of words she'd heard Bernice use, and looked back along Bernice's arm into her eyes.

Bernice searched Martee's eyes.

"(Thanks!)" Martee said with a bounce.

Bernice smiled and bobbed her head, the short dance.

Martee refocused her attention onto exploration, walking further along the hallway. She looked over her shoulder, saw Bernice's right leg disappearing into the first doorway.

Martee wriggled, stepping sensuously. The flat felt invigorating, delicious tingle on the skin. It was the feeling of going from black and white movies with distant screams of horror and blunt farmyard grunts into a Technicolor reality show of acapella musicians breathing binaural beatboxing at the back of the brain.

Martee paused at the second door on the left, a darkened guest bathroom, with a clean smell. She moved on, strolling along toward the next door, the sunshine getting brighter in the hallway with her progress.

The third doorway was another bedroom, a touch of cedar on the nose, dark, a large spaciousness on the ears, felt herself breathe in deeply and sigh at the call she felt for satisfying rest. Martee decided there was something subtly pleasant in the air of the apartment, couldn't place what the delicate energy was. Lovely, she just felt wonderful about herself.

The fourth door on the left was the kitchen. Martee stepped from the taupe hallway carpeting onto the pink-hued marble floor, the echo of sandals, oils and spices on the nose. She walked in a small circle widdershins taking in the wide dark wood counter opening to the spacious living room, copper fridge, stove, dishwasher, teak wood cabinetry, and culinary knives stuck magnetically to cherry wood slats. Martee felt she would love to cook here, not normally her thing, just here.

Martee stepped into the hallway, turned left and with two more paces entered the great room, felt stunned by the centerpiece room. She stopped, feet together. Whispered. "(Some roommate!)"

There was a spartan collection of dark wood furniture bound in black wrought iron. The floor was a lightly finished pink oak running from the right wall to the far left wall matched by honey pine boards running the length of the ceiling. The room put her in mind of an early-century sailing ship and she almost expected to see cannon guns.

Her eyes were drawn by the glittery chandelier over the central sitting area to her left, reminiscent of the fountain outside, hundreds of tiny lights in small crystal cubes. Under the chandelier was a twenty foot diameter sculptured deep pile circular black rug with a yellow Sun, white-blue stars, sweeps of red nebulae. On top, two loveseats, the far one in black leather and the nearer loveseat in white, adding a touch of leather to the corsage wafting under the nose. Martee wondered what kind of career funded such customization. Was the roommate an heiress of dynasty?

The glass view of the courtyard wall ran nearly the length of the room, two sets of sliding glass doors leading out onto the balcony. Martee walked to the nearest and peered at the courtyard below. The central timepiece over the fountain which caused the umbrella effect of jetting water was an oxidated brass sundial, top side sunny and dry, as if time were floating on the uprush of water. Martee wished she could float down and spin the dial's shadow with her middle finger, which meant the Earth would have to spin to keep up.

Martee turned her attention to the glass curios on the far end wall of the great room, reached the first curio, slowed. Old books in various languages, poignant figurines, rusty artifacts, embroideries.

Martee idly wondered if Banelle might indeed be legs in the air about Dollar, wondered with grinchy smiling what the rest of the man looked like underneath the ruggedness of the footwear, the intense blue of the jeans, and green of the knit shirt. Images of hard possibilities flashed through the mind bunched in sweaty joy, tangled sheets, her breasts body-pounded by his firm lifting muscles, soft bed beneath her ass.

Martee wondered, remembering back to earlier in the day, what the issue with rain had been? "(Well, we'll find out about that,)" in a whisper, and wondered why she was whispering.

She believed over the years she had not found anyone who satisfyingly filled her toes with lust, yet Dollar had her fancy more than once already today. She wondered why there was no man like that who simply walked barefooted onto her lawn, if she had a lawn, and he could mow hers every day, maybe twice.

Martee realized she wasn't just toying with the idea of actually stealing him for herself; a part of her had become *determined*.

At lunch, Dollar had pointedly asked Martee to share her story. His full attention had nailed her like a thunder crack starting a downpour, wet, a shudder and body-tensing feeling. Even now, she thrilled with the memory of his attentiveness! Felt the aftershock in her pussy.

Martee's eyes focused, a feeling a fresh shock running hands around her body, the sight of something extraordinarily familiar in the third curio, three glass shelves up from the bottom. Here was a lead crystal object, nubbly and dumpy in form, double-chambered by subtle demarcation, an unusual glass stopper which, instead of being on top, was tilted forward, curving toward her, shaped like a mushroom, playing with the back of her head and calling to her fingertips. Martee concentrated, feeling the gathering together of the eyebrows in coordinated observation, facial muscles pulling her lips into a curl on the right side of her face, whispered. "(It's a…)" Martee felt her eyes grow wide "(…scrotum!)"

Feeling fascinated, Martee crouched down at eye level. The liquid inside more than half filled the double cavity, merest tinge of a red hue, like a pale Zinfandel swirled with seven parts Sauvignon Blanc, and there was a great sense of antiquity. Or was that from the thickly ancient-looking leather pouch lying nearby on the glass shelf?

"Martee!" she heard Bernice call, what sounded like Bernice coming down the hallway.

Martee kept her gaze on the fascinating object inside the brightly lit curio, glimmers of glass, tasty-curious liquid, and turned her head left. "In here by the curios!"

"Jazzed!" she heard Bernice call from inside the great room.

"Do you know what this is?" Martee said, not turning. Martee tipped her head right, looked at the lead crystal scrotum from a new angle. It was so sexy, clearly crafted by masterly fingers.

Bernice arrived on Martee's left. "That's my roommate's." Gradually a feeling dawned on part of Martee's awareness there was something odd about Bernice's reflection in the curio glass. Martee turned her head toward Bernice, saw bare feet and knees, thighs, hands, arms, body. Martee felt her eyes go wide, and looked up further and saw all of Bernice naked, even the still-damp hair. "Bernice!"

Bernice jumped in place, body parts jiggling. "What?!"

"What the *hell* are you *doing*?"

———

Bernice turned toward Martee, hands cupped on hips — and in turning, Bernice presented *herself* at Martee's eye-level.

Martee fell on her ass, catching herself by propping the arms behind, palms on the hardwood floor, noticed the wood floor was warm. *"Why* are you *naked*?!"

Bernice erupted a laugh, backed away a step, hands clapped together, recovered a step nearer. "You noticed?!"

Martee looked at Bernice's lips, then Martee's eyes traveled down Bernice's curves to the immaculate toe nails, everything perfect as can be, alluring.

Bernice blushed.

Martee closed her eyes, shook her head vigorously, opened her eyes, looked again at Bernice's feet, then at Bernice in the eyes.

Bernice turned around, putting her hands on her face. She rolled her head back, relaxed her arms slack at her sides. "I guess I liked you so much…" Bernice turned around and looked at Martee. "Out of habit I am unconsciously as comfortable with you as I am with my roommate. My bad. And I'm *very bad* at times!" Toothy smile.

Martee's mind went through a series of thoughts in a flash, just as quickly dismissing all of them. *Keep an open mind a moment.* "Bernice, are you Wiccan?"

Bernice shrugged, gazed across the great room to Martee's left, lips calm together, inhaled. "It may sound strange." Bernice looked at Martee. "My roommate believes in nudity in the home. Emphatically."

"Really."

"Yes." Bernice looked across the room. She looked at Martee, shrugged the right shoulder. "I just got used to it. Now I like it."

Martee was quiet, looked at one of Bernice's eyes, then the other. "Nothing going on between you two?"

"What? Oh! No, no." Laughed. Bernice gave her meticulously styled hair a vigorous shake, did her dance move, then looked across the room, and smiled. She looked at Martee. "I'm told there is no greater pleasure than yourself."

"A towel at least for the loveseats, when reading Erotic Romance?" Another part of Martee decided it was just a thing, rolled to her right knee, got herself recomposed into a crouching position in front of the curio and gazed at the lead crystal scrotum, feeling a hunch. Martee pointed with the right index finger. "So tell me more about it," curled the finger into the palm. "And," Martee said, smiling, looking at Bernice. "Please excuse me if I don't undress like your roommate does."

Bernice waved her left palm, laughed. "I'm told there is no greater joy *on* the body than one's own choice of clothes."

Joy on the body, echoed Martee's thoughts, felt like there was more to know, and watched Bernice with unfocused eyes. "Bernice." Martee said, clearing her head, pointing with the right thumb. "*That* is what I'm interested in at the moment, not nudity and habiliments." Martee turned her head, and looked at the lead crystal scrotum. "Do you know anything about it? Has your roommate talked about its history?"

"I think it's ugly." Bernice crouched down bouncing her thighs near Martee, braced the fingers of the right hand on the wood floor briefly, then Bernice pulled the hand upward and rested her forearm on the right knee. "My roommate says it contains a love potion."

Yessss! Martee felt herself grinning, pressed the smile toward a restless sobriety. "Any idea which one?"

Bernice turned her head toward Martee. "There's more than one?"

"Oh, yes." Martee looked at Bernice. "Lots. Almost all dietary aphrodisiacs, or body secretions from animals. Chocolate, for sure, yet the strongest aphrodisiac is natural pheromone bloom." Martee turned her attention toward the curio.

"A real spell does more than enhance hormones, though, and shifts deeply held beliefs and self-defensive attitudes. That's when the pheromones *really* start getting up the nose. There's one spell I know of which actually does the magick unwaveringly, according to my research." Nod of the head. "My gut says *that* is it right there."

"That one?" Bernice said, left index finger pointing, eyes under the raised eyebrows.

"How did your roommate acquire the specimen?"

Bernice was quiet for a moment. She turned away. Then she turned back toward the cabinet. She pushed on the glass with the left hand to unlatch the glass door. The door opened swinging left. Bernice's left fingers pulled the door open the rest of the way.

Martee felt like babbling, because here it was, door of the cabinet opening. "Any idea where your roommate got it?"

There was a pause. "She says it was secretly featured at the Midlands Neopagan Fair eight years ago in an unmarked tent, and caused a number of life-changing events, so she had it removed from the grounds."

Martee felt disbelief. Those fairs were mostly trinkets and bawdy talent shows, including mock fights and beer.

Bernice turned away, then turned back toward the curio, pinched across the breadth of the lead crystal with right thumb, second finger, and forefinger, the sound of glass sliding on glass, and lifted the object slowly with a grimace of loathing.

Martee felt amused by Bernice's contempt.

Bernice presented the lead crystal scrotum to Martee's cupped hands. "Ewe." Bernice released the scrotum.

The weight of the object filled Martee's hands, surprising her with unexpected heaviness. She was glad of two hands. Martee brought the object nearer, not like she had never been close to the real thing before, and peered closer at the detailing. A man would have moaned by now.

Bernice shrugged in the periphery of Martee's vision, reached inside the curio and pulled out the ancient-looking leather pouch. "My roommate says it opens your eyes to love."

"I bet." Martee said, turning the object in front of her eyes. Whoever the craftswoman had been she was a master.

Bernice grimaced. "Feels weird, like natural rubber."

Martee cupped the lead crystal scrotum near her nose and sniffed lightly. A wafting sea spray of gut pounding ocean surf and subtle balsam entered her awareness immediately, the feeling her earlobes and forehead were suddenly damp with mist.

Martee felt her excitement growing, the lively salt and balsam scent jiggering her spine with dance, a moistness felt. Worse and worse, she felt what had previously mattered most to her was subtly shifting along a boundary where seduced sinuses touched the frontal lobe. "Bernice! This *is* the potion!"

Martee was shaking so much she had to stand. She walked around the black loveseat, and carefully set the lead crystal scrotum on the round glass coffee table, wiped her palms around the curves of her red shorts willing herself to not pick the potion up again just yet. She needed time to think, clear her sinuses of piracy, and assess the state of her mind. Was it still her own?

Martee turned and discovered Bernice was right beside her. Feeling affirming energy in the air, Martee grabbed Bernice's elbows. "Bernice!"

Bernice was impassive, and looked from one to the other of Martee's eyes. "If it's *the* potion, why a glass ball sack? Isn't that *sexist?*"

Martee took a quick deep breath, exhaled, turned bodily widder-shins where she stood for luck, and stared at the scrotum. "I've had the list of ingredients for a decade." Then turned her head and looked at Bernice. "I didn't have the quantities, or what the ceremony should be creating a batch, or even whether the list was complete. Rain water or sea water, for example?" Another thought bubbled up. "Sometimes symbolism is the *actual* catalyst for a spell. Would a crystal ball sack be the catalyst here?"

Bernice pulled an ancient papyrus document out of the leather pouch. "There's a leaflet here. It has the legend." Bernice looked at Martee. "Would you want to know the legend?"

Martee felt the shrug. "Of course!"

"Legend." Bernice said, and began the reading.

his touching her there barely-familiar

. . .

BANELLE STOOD near Dollar within the thickly sweet-toothed smells of Sudden Brews, waiting on her skinny mocha.

The walls were covered with wide stripes of chocolate and cream wallpaper with red-framed pictures of beans roasting and being harvested. Small round blue lacquered tables and medium-sized square red tables were addressed by green chairs. The walls facing the two streets of the intersection were mostly glass. High black warehouse beams overhead reverberated with a cacophony of barista screaming steam noises and conversation, and occasional laughs rising over the surf of energy. Outside, the bustle of vehicles waiting at lights or driving by added to the energy in the cafe.

Banelle felt a clash of socialized excitement and a longing for somewhere quieter with just her and Dollar. She was glad Martee was off with Bernice. Martee could be an ass sometimes. The respite gave Banelle a chance for cooling off. She knew some of the things Martee had been doing were just Martee pulling Banelle's chain. Banelle sniffed, the shared chain was attached to something inside both of them and this reality is why that mischief worked. She might love Martee, after all.

Banelle turned around and looked at the entryway, wondering where her father had gone. He had simply said he'd be back.

"Skinny mocha latte!" she heard one of the staff calling.

Banelle turned around and looked at Dollar.

Dollar had been watching her. "That yours?"

She felt herself nod, smiling.

He smiled, scooted sideways toward the coffee bar, then turned and stepped to the outbound beverage counter.

Banelle felt the smile around her eyes. *He's so damn nice.* Banelle felt her knees bending restlessly, tension in the calves, the clutch in front of her with both hands bouncing against her thighs.

She stopped a moment later when he turned in her direction, latte in his right hand, coffee in the left, and moved toward her with a nod upward, a glance of his eyes saying he wished them to be over by the window.

She turned, licked the tip of her tongue across her lips while she walked and scanned the cozy round tables by the window he had nodded at. She led through the mid-floor chairs toward one of the two currently empty tables against the window.

Leading with Dollar eclipsed behind her, Banelle felt a pang in her belly remembering the incident at lunch earlier when he had disconnected.

Banelle stopped by the empty table on the left, furthest from the door and saw he was following right behind her, which was comforting.

Dollar juxtaposed her latte and his coffee on the blue lacquer bistro table, stepped around behind her and pulled the green chair out with his left hand.

When she didn't move right away, Banelle felt his right hand on her right thigh pressing sideways gently. His touching her there barely-familiar evoked more strongly this desire to feel him fully against her, fogging her mind instantly. While intending to sit in the chair he offered, in the moment some part of her mimed along as his left hand pulled the chair backward beside her. She felt herself bump against him, she felt electrified and buzzing, and also embarrassment. She grabbed his wrist on her right thigh, and froze.

His hand responded, sliding around her thigh.

She felt her shoulders sag instantly, felt demur. She realized her hand encircling his wrist was being pulled around her own waist now, his arm crossing her under her right arm and sliding along the underside of her right breast, thumb brushing under her left breast. She felt instant comfort. His fingers wrapped around the left side of her rib cage, then Dollar pulled her firmly against himself, her eyes widening. Her head automatically snuggled against his neck, her racing mind in a spin with the physical surprise and swirling emotions of their moving so naturally into an embrace. She hugged his arm, squeezing that against herself.

Banelle thought to look around the room and saw the many people visiting over their coffees and lattes, a few of the women watching her and Dollar surreptitiously, peering over their paper cups and vented plastic lids. She felt conspicuous, and patted his arm. Banelle pressed her cheek against his, whispered, "(Everybody's watching.)"

She felt his cheek slide along hers. His lips kissed the left side of her temple and her heart melted into a chocolate puddle. As she felt him release her from their hug, she felt the inner conflicting arguments within herself fire up opening disputes about how appearances could be a good thing if she really wanted to feel proud of her being in a relationship with him.

She willed herself to sit down, scooting the chair with his assistance until she felt comfortably close with the table, looked toward him briefly, and smiled. She glanced at the snoopers who had been most obvious and the women looked away.

Dollar sat across from Banelle, scooted the chair twice, then turned in the chair sideways from Banelle to face the room. He crossed his left calf over the right knee and rested his back against the window, his right arm resting on the table near where her hands cozied the paper-cupped latte.

Banelle felt annoyed. "(I thought you wanted to sit by the window for the view?)"

He turned his head toward her, grinned, and spoke quietly. "(I love people-watching.)"

She glanced around and saw one of the snoopy women had been watching him. Seeing Banelle look at her, the woman turned away.

Banelle leaned toward Dollar. "(You're one hell of a magnet.)" She didn't like the jealous edge of her voice and felt she couldn't help herself. "(Could you just turn and visit with me, please?)"

He hadn't turned his head away from watching her. His eyes dropped down toward the table and the smile melted away. He looked at her. "You're a jealous woman."

She looked down. She realized she was fidgeting in the fingers, breathed in deeply and sighed, then looked at him. "(I hear that.)" Banelle shrugged her right shoulder. "(Maybe if Martee hadn't already fired me up today I wouldn't seem so bad to you.)"

Dollar looked away. Banelle watched his eyes moving, taking in the sights, seeing he wasn't fixated on any particular person. Her eyes traced the line of his neck, watched the muscles tense and relax, his head turning this way, then away. She heard him huff, saw his head nod once. "Yeah. Martee's one hell of a flirt." He looked at Banelle.

She wanted to ask him about that. The issue wasn't anywhere near her mouth at the moment, so she just smiled and looked down at her paper cup. She looked at his right arm resting on the table, feelings still humming from the surprise hug. She wished to feel that around her again. She removed her left hand from cupping the latte, touched the fingertips against his arm and smoothed the fingers back and forth along his hairy forearm. She smiled seeing the shiver run through his body and heard his sharp inhale.

He looked at her hands. She realized she had been softly stroking the hot paper cup with her right hand and stopped; smiling. She curled her left fingers against the palm and pinched her lips together restlessly. Did she really want to talk about this?

She lay the left palm flat against the table near her latte, and looked at him, inhaling.

He was quiet, his eyes looking within hers, unfocused. She felt he was looking through her with a deeper interest, black of the irises a nighttime glade.

She waited in the nocturnal vision, mist bubbles of winking green clouds around fireflies in a calm woods. A dark-sounding male chant and drumming called from a distant quarter. His eyes. She realized he had become focused. She inhaled sharply. She watched his eyes carefully, bringing the latte near her lips and sipping, hot on her tongue, looking from one of his eyes to the other. She set the cup on the table, swallowed, and looked down at the cup, then looked within his eyes.

He repositioned himself in the chair facing her, eyes right briefly. He looked at her, perplexed. "You have all these nicknames, what does 'B.B.' stand for?"

She felt herself grow warm, the breathing deepening. "I'd like to say it's an abbreviation for my first and middle names."

"What is your whole name, anyway? In this lifetime, so far?"

"Banelle Briena Lofine, B-r-i-e-n-a L-o-f-i-n-e."

"Banelle Briena… Lofine? From being married?"

"A last name I chose for myself while divorcing."

"Exquisite. 'Banelle Briena' isn't why your dad calls you B.B?"

She closed her eyes, feeling the warmth renew. She opened her eyes gazing on her hands around the cup, "No." Banelle looked at Dollar. "I'm quite embarrassed about this."

Dollar grinned. "I can see."

"My dad calls me B.B. He's the only one, besides myself, when I'm not thinking about it." Banelle shrugged, breathed in deeply. "It is short for 'Baby Belly.'" Her eyes flicked up to see his reaction.

He sat back erect and smiled, watching her. He leaned forward with the eyes aligned under the eyebrows, eyes in hers, and murmured, "(Beautiful.)" His eyelashes dipped lower, sharing only a slit of the eyes. She felt him rub his right fingers back and forth across the back of her left hand. "(B.B. Beautiful.)"

Banelle wiped her eyes with her right thumb behind closely held fingers, pretending to herself he would think she was covering her embarrassment. She worried again he might want children from his next relationship. She pulled her hand away, thumb chilly in the air and wet. She rolled her left palm under his fingers, laid her right wrist on top of her left, right fingertips on top of his and cozied his fingers between her hands.

He turned in his chair, fingers between hers, crossed his left ankle over the right knee, and leaned back against the window.

She sighed, feeling the warm pleasure of their being together.

Then she was suddenly afraid he would unplug from their very new and quite precious, for her, core relationship. She realized with a widening of her eyes, more precious for having come together on such delicious, stimulating timing. A total windfall, the girls away for the upcoming weeks. More sumptuous than she'd imagined. More reward than she'd expected for herself, more than she'd hoped for even when she was feeling upbeat: a gift from the Universe. And what does a girl do with a wrapped gift?

she was indeed on the right track

. . .

MARTEE PROCESSED what she was hearing as Bernice read the ancient papyrus, a pleasant voice in Martee's ear. Bernice seemed to be familiar with the story, her eyes glancing at Martee frequently.

In the days before Kokopelli, *there was the first god, who was the god of the sky and all future things, and his name was Ouranus.*

Ouranus imagined a blue-eyed lass, and Gaeia the Goddess of Fairness was born, watery and green. When the age for it came, Ouranus and Gaeia joined.

The younger gods began to be born.

One of these younger gods was the Goddess of Ambition, and there came a day when the Goddess of Ambition, on some wrath of vengeance, swung with a scythe meant for the fields of Gaeia's grains, and the testicles of the sky god were cut off. They fell a great distance and landed in one of Gaeia's vast oceans.

The frothing of change from the vital part of the sky god's creativity landing in the sea was terrible to behold. The churn involved both deep sea and lofty winds, and there were storms which were started at the twist of water and sky which still wander the earth today, immortal, filled with lightning. They only pause to breathe, then spin large as hurricanes again.

From the roiling waters, according to the appropriate time, rose the Goddess of Self-Love.

From that day forward, the mortals were no longer content with the handful of Gaeia's grain which fed them fairly every day, and the mortals became aware of appearances. Each sought to make changes in the manner of anything's visage, any odorant, any textures, each according to their own Individuating whim, and from that day forward the mortals were compelled by a desire for beautiful change.

The potion of the Goddess of Self-Love acts to sharpen the distinction between pultrichude and repulsiveness and thereby make choosing more certain.

The effects last until the willfulness of Sol returns. Those who inhale from the potion will see any love which has been hidden, and if a love is discovered unrequited, the power of desire is redoubled and redoubled again until requited.

Martee crouched in front of the lead crystal scrotum, her fingers crowded on the edge of the glass table, balancing her body, and murmured, "(Well, no worries there.)"

"…and it says…" Martee heard Bernice giggle.

Martee looked at Bernice. "What?"

"'May stain the soul beautifully. Test in an inconspicuous place.'"

Martee laughed. "When love comes to mow my lawn, Bernice, do you think I'm going to worry about a grass stain?"

Bernice chuckled, turned the leaflet, her brow furrowed. "There are instructions on how to use it." Bernice looked at Martee briefly, crouching down. "One. Open the bottle. Say, 'Welcome Goddess.'"

Martee felt comforted, she was indeed on the right track, the words began according to the ancient ways.

"Two. Place one drop on the forehead. Say, 'Love and scorn garments, attire my naked soul.'"

Martee glanced at the parchment. "That's new."

Bernice looked at Martee, then scanned the leaflet. "Three. Place one drop on the concave of the breast. Say, 'Love and scorn garments, attire my naked soul.'

"Four. Place one drop on or in the belly button. Say, 'Love and scorn garments, attire my naked soul.'

"Five. Seal the bottle. Say, 'I am the pearl.'"

Martee felt her eyebrows pop up.

Bernice watched Martee for a moment, then looked at the papyrus. "It says you must be naked during the ceremony."

"Really." Martee thought about the chants which the leaflet required. The pattern of threes of real magick was involved, and there were balances of oppositions. The part of Martee which *knew* the potion was legitimate felt more heard.

Despite what Martee had told Bernice earlier, Martee now felt a satisfying and compelling requirement for nudity. "Well, Bernice." Martee tilted her head left, and pressed her lips together looking at the scrotum.

"What?"

"When in Acropolis."

"You're going to try it?"

Martee turned toward Bernice. "Of course! Unless you feel your roommate will object?" Martee watched Bernice carefully.

Bernice stretched herself upward slightly and closed her mouth, looked toward the hallway entry, then bounced down, and looked at Martee. "No objection." Bernice's eyes glanced toward the doorway briefly. "This time." Bernice added, looking at Martee.

Martee stretched upward and looked over the white loveseat to scan the opposite end of the great room. She couldn't see what Bernice had looked at, bounced back down into a full crouch, searching Bernice's eyes.

Martee mused with the most expressionless face she could placidly muster, wondered at the puzzle which paraded itself in the moment. Here was Bernice who was comfortably practical with nudist house convention. The evident wealth and history around the apartment seemed at odds with Bernice being just a roommate and only making waitress wages. And the phrase about, '*This time.' What the hell was that?*

Martee looked from one to the other of naked Bernice's eyes, smiled, put her head on her right fist, propping her elbow on her right knee. "Bernice, are you going to try it?"

pecked an air kiss

. . .

"PERFECT," Charlie said, clapping his hands and rubbing them together. "Everybody is invited to pick a section of sidewalk anywhere around here…" Dollar watched Charlie turn around half-way, his head and eyes exploring what 'around here' meant. Charlie looked at Dollar, Banelle, Bernice, and Martee in quick succession, "… and pretend we got rich recently from contributions while we drew chalky pictures.

"Today is no different than any other day in the entrepreneurial career which found us. We are just doing another gig in another city with fresh chalk in our hands. Any questions?"

Dollar felt himself chuckle, appreciating the scrape of wealth and chalk.

Banelle was laughing, song in Dollar's ears.

Martee was watching Charlie. "None here!"

Dollar noted, turning around, Bernice was chuckling quietly, a latte in her left hand, her eyes watching Charlie, eyes darting around the group of them, then back on Charlie. Bernice looked briefly at Dollar, and her eyes fell. She swiveled on her ankles holding a classy green paper bag hanging straight down at the end of her right arm, the bag bumping against her calves while swiveling.

Dollar admired Bernice's change of clothes. His eyes followed her ankles from where they emerged from brown leather moccasins, how nicely the lines of her legs flowed toward her knees, thighs disappearing under a brown leather skirt which started inches above her knees, flopping sexily, then turning hip-shaping at her waist where an intense blue silk shirt bloomed from her narrowly taut waist upward, flowing in billows around breasts and arms, and ending with a conventional set of white buttons up the front of an open-button classic collar, matched with button-down wrist cuffs which echoed the tautness of her waist. There was something of a Cinderella transformation, and he idly wondered who the Fairy Godmother was.

Dollar's eyes budged to Martee, her lips pressed together with the corners of her mouth dimpling thickly, her eyes an uneven perplexed look, holding a paper cup in her right hand almost at chin level. Martee was watching Dollar, the gorgeous doe eyes, scutter of eyelashes glancing down and up Dollar's body.

"B.B," Charlie said, turning toward Banelle, "please hand out the chalks."

Banelle pulled the glossy white plastic bag to waist level, peered inside, and reached in with her right hand. Her eyes met Dollar's. She smiled.

He felt himself smile. On impulse he decided to blow her a quick kiss with his lips, choosing to leave his hands in his back pockets.

Banelle smiled more warmly.

"Bernice..." he heard Charlie say.

Banelle pecked an air kiss back at Dollar, pulled the first box of chalks out of the plastic bag.

Dollar looked at Charlie, then turned his head toward Bernice, following Charlie's gaze.

"...make sure everyone gets one of those hats."

Bernice looked into the green bag. "Is that what these are? Hats?"

"Here," Charlie said, reaching his right hand, stepping toward Bernice.

Bernice smiled with her lips pressed together, crouched, set her latte on the cement by her feet, fished with her left arm inside the rustling paper bag, ignoring the hat on top, pulled the next hat out, and handed the hat toward Charlie.

Charlie stopped at arm's length from her, took the hat and put the hat on his head, slightly crooked — an artist's hat, squat and rounded, black felt with a red tag sticking out of the top center where the triangles of the material came together, a short rim by the frumpy forward edge. Charlie looked at Martee and waggled his eyebrows.

Martee laughed, leaned back and kicked her right foot out. When she put her foot back down, Martee swirled her hair around, stood erect.

Dollar marveled again at the connection between Martee and Charlie. *Like two souls out of the same hornet's nest.*

"Here," Dollar heard Banelle say almost in Dollar's back pocket. Her voice was so close and warm, sent a shiver down his back along with a spasm of pleasure, a ripple through the muscles of his body tensing his legs and arms in rapid quivering movements. He suddenly felt clumsy, breathed in, let the wave of joy dissipate, and turned with some normalcy widdershins halfway toward her, being mindful of including the rest of the group.

Banelle handed him a box of fat chalks which he received with his right hand. He held the box at waist level and looked at her with his head turned toward her. He looked at her lips, at the breasts mooning from beneath the sexy dark suede top, noted the fragrance of suede and natural skin on the nose, saw the bare curves of her breasts teasing his eyes to plunge lower and rising for his attention, a swooning allure breathing the soft joy, tasty tangy yellow bikini. Banelle squeezed his left biceps briefly with her right hand, then slipped her hand back within the glossy white plastic bag, and started walking toward Martee.

Dollar shifted the box of fat chalks into his left hand, looked around himself to assess the cement he was standing on, and briefly looked toward the sound of the handsome fountain splashing soothingly thirty feet away.

He glanced back at the way they had come in, turned himself all the way around with the long shadow of the late afternoon Sun stretching away from where he stood. He trusted his instincts, walked along his shadow away from the group thirteen paces, stopped, then turned toward the fountain. He looked over his right shoulder to assess again how far he was from the giant circle's periphery, looked briefly at the sky overhead, then took two strides toward the fountain, feeling the spot beneath his feet was exactly in the sweet pocket of overlapping energies from trees and bushes, glad the spot wasn't in the fountain splash itself.

Dollar realized he had forgotten to get a hat, looked left toward the rest of the group. He saw Bernice handing a hat toward Martee. Banelle, like Charlie, was already wearing one canted to her left eyebrow. When Bernice looked around, Dollar raised his left hand, holding the box of chalks aloft to catch her eye. "Help!" Dollar felt himself grin, lowering his arm.

———

Bernice smiled toothily, still crouched down, reached deeply within the rustling bag, pulled a hat out, leaned in his direction and launched toward Dollar at a run… when she came near, her feet pattered out a faster rhythm, slowing herself, and she stopped so close beside Dollar he felt her breath on his left arm. "Here." Bernice pushed the hat against his shoulder and smiled openly.

Dollar grabbed the hat automatically, yet he did not take the hat from her. He felt himself shrug, speaking like his nose was inside diving goggles, "I don'd know how to wear an ardisd's cap."

Bernice laughed, leaned backward, dipped her body left and right in a dance move, dropped the bag and used both hands for cramming the hat on his head, chuckling wickedly.

Dollar laughed from his gut, delighted hearing her merriment and feeling her energy, her fingers in his hair again.

Bernice gave the hat a slap with her right hand, making the hat perfectly squashed and secure.

Dollar felt flattered. "Thanks a lot."

"You are welcome a lot!" Bernice nodded in a bobbing dance,

smiled openly, bent her knees together and picked up the green paper bag, pulling the last hat out of the bag.

Dollar nodded toward the hat she held. "You want help with that?"

Bernice looked at her hand puzzled, then at him and her face lit up. "No!" She turned toward the others and walked away, swaying her ass, the leather skirt alive which tickled him. He felt himself smiling.

Dollar saw Banelle was watching, then saw Martee intently walking toward him. He waited.

Martee came near, smiling.

He canted his head left and looked sideways at her eyes, then her hat, at the way her hair bounced wavy, and looked within Martee's eyes. "That looks smashing."

"Thanks!" Martee stopped where Bernice had stood so close to him, turned on the spot facing the same way he was facing, looked down at her feet, close together, holding the latte paper cup in the air in her right hand, bending her upper body pointedly, white blouse exposing more of the curves of her breasts, and aligned her toes with an imaginary line from Dollar's toes.

Dollar bent his head near her shoulder to see what she was looking at, noticed a subtle wild pine smell, part of his mind automatically inventorying by name all the trees and shrubs he'd seen so far in the expansive square surrounding the giant cement circle and couldn't think where he'd seen any coniferous species. He hadn't actually walked around the grounds yet, though.

Martee stood erect, swiveling her body slightly toward him without moving her feet. "So, what are we doing here?"

Dollar looked at her openly smiling lips, then within her languid brown eyes so sweet. He looked over his left shoulder. "What we are doing..."

Martee turned her torso right more, her head turning.

"...is finding..." Dollar nodded at the periphery of the circle, "... the sweet center of the energy flow, which happily is not in the water display." He turned forward and nodded at the splashing fountain.

"Really." Martee made a point of swiveling toward her left, then toward her right, leaning to look past him, the white-bloused décolletage catching his eyes and nodded. "What about that way?" Martee stood erect, eyes on his.

Looking steadily at her eyes, Dollar tipped his head toward the left, then right, "Direction is academic, since our place on the circle is relative to time, time being something I can't control in this situation." Dollar looked at her lips, closed, still smiling. "I just felt it important to be out of line with the entry path to preserve the balance of my own chi, so here we are."

Martee nodded approval. "Perfectly reasonable."

Dollar looked down at his feet, finding a feature he could keep his eyes on, a dark flat rock embedded in the surface of the concrete. He took one step backward, put his right foot across his left foot and sat down vertically, folding his legs in a smooth motion.

Martee mirrored the procedure, ended by sitting near him, her right knee touching his left thigh which spread an unexpected warmth throughout his leg, adding to the pleasant warmth of the late afternoon Sun and warmth of the sunshine stored in the cement beneath them.

The tribal hat of the newly formed sidewalk artists' clan felt tight on his head. Dollar leaned his head toward her. "Could you do something with this hat?"

Martee laughed, reaching for the hat with her left hand, the dip of her blouse baring breast curves under his nose. She set her latte on the concrete behind them. "I was going to ask you about that."

Dollar smiled, inhaled Martee's lovely pheromones through his nose and watched the energy in the breasts as she made adjustments to his hat. Clearly Martee was aroused. He wondered again where the pine tree was hidden.

Dollar felt a need to chatter. "You just can't get good help these days."

He felt her lift the hat with her left hand, felt her right fingers smooth his hair, then she disheveled his hair with her right hand, smiling. He felt her set the hat carefully on his head, patting the hat gently with both hands, smiling openly. Her smiling eyes met his inches away, then looked at his hat again. She administered a soft two-handed pat. "There." Martee pulled her hands down. Eventually she pulled her eyes down also.

Dollar opened his eyes wider in mock panic. "Is that actually an improvement?"

"Of course!" Martee laughed, leaning leftward.

He shrugged.

She swirled her hair, sat erect, swiveled right, breasts under the taught blouse, retrieved her latte, turned forward.

Dollar looked at the cement in front of himself. *What the hell to draw?* He heard footsteps and looked up. He saw Charlie, followed by Banelle, who was watching Martee with angry eyes, and then Bernice walking energetically to catch up. He watched all three select places not far from himself and Martee.

Charlie picked a spot between Martee and the fountain, fifteen feet away.

Banelle looked around and picked a spot closer and more toward the right of where Dollar was sitting than Charlie had picked, a dozen feet away.

Bernice slowed and assessed where everyone was. She sat even nearer to Martee, off to the left, ten feet away.

Dollar looked at Banelle and smiled. When she noticed his watching her, she didn't immediately smile, then smiled briefly in passing, and looked down quickly.

He shrugged his shoulders. *Woman, if it bothers you so much, do something. Don't just fucking fume.*

Dollar's eyes wandered around the tiny stones embedded in the cement immediately in front of him. He really wasn't into cement. He patted the slab with his right hand, the sound of skin on roughly felt concrete.

He felt Martee looking at him. He turned his head and saw her perplexed expression, her eyes alternating between looking at his hand flat on the cement then his eyes, back and forth.

Dollar made an effort at a serious artist's face. "Always check to ensure the canvas is stretched properly."

Martee laughed, slapped the cement in front of her with her left palm twice. "Damn right!" She made a little fist with her hand and smote the slab once, also. "There!"

Dollar chuckled. "Right!" Nodded largely once, watched her eyes. "Any idea what you're drawing?"

Her eyebrows went up, shaking her head gently back and forth, the hair waving and full of life. She sipped from the latte in her right hand.

He looked at the cement, and shrugged, decided to be whimsical. He set the box of chalks down near his right thigh, opened the lid, and shook out the chalks clinking, fat cylinders tumbling loosely rolling about. He picked the yellow with the left hand.

Dollar leaned over his chosen flat of cement, eyeing the black stone marker he'd picked for centering. He drew a large yellow Sun, then twelve equidistant detached line rays. He drew the eyes and flatly expressive mouth of a smiley face in a tiny spot at the center of the Sun's large circle, the embedded black stone as nose. This looked like something he would have drawn at age three, except for the cynicism of the flattened smile. He felt himself smile flatly, crosschecking his work. Now, though, he added the patience he didn't have as a child, and began meticulously adding hundreds of detached rays, with careful scratching sweeps radiating outward from the solar flare perimeter of the Sun.

Martee watched his drawing until it was clear he was deeply involved in the redundant part of the self-challenge, until, apparently, she had finished her latte. He heard the click of her empty paper cup somewhere off beyond his left, not bothering to look. He heard her opening her box of chalks, thinner ones, by the sound. More colors also, he saw with a glance. Martee picked up the black chalk.

He returned his attention to flaring the Sun. He heard her begin drawing, the thin-sounding scraping of the chalk while she worked, pleasured in the thicker click and scrape sound of the chalks he had for drawing, smelled the intermixed odors of the chalks in the air.

He smelled again the subtle waft of wild pine, the continued feeling of her knee shifting, pressed against his thigh as she and he worked together, the comforting warm feeling of creative togetherness.

Dollar's mind and muscles plunged fully within the art he was rendering.

Time passed.

Finally he had all the Sun rays drawn which his heart wished to see and which his patience would allow for. He set the yellow chalk down, felt inside himself for the next color, picked up the fat sky-blue chalk.

On the inside rim of the Sun, a quarter of the way around the left curve he drew a tiny stick figure posed in alarm at having been discovered! He added what he hoped looked like a flute in the figure's left hand. He fiddled with the flute's image until he saw there was no improving the flute further from that far away, from where he was. The flute looked like a short stick so far, and needed to communicate recently discovered music. He drew an eighth note floating away from the figure.

He selected the fat black chalk. Among the Sun rays on the bottom left of his art, he drew two seafaring seagulls flying together in the sky — Jonathan and what's her name, Pansy for now — highlighting their wings with the sky-blue.

He put the chalks down and afterglowed, contemplating his art, thinking about the symbols, tracing what he had rendered against the vision which had been evoked at the beginning of the current effort when he had felt whimsical, and before the necessary diligence of practical art, feeling now the whimsy as a distant memory, felt ache of muscles from diligently plowing through the activity of engaged self-expression.

He could look at the Sun and the alarmed stick figure, touch the memory of how he'd felt when he'd started drawing, compared the results on the cement with the memory of the feeling, shrugged accepting the art work mostly was faithful to the original vision.

The memory had a life of its own, though, meaningfully enlarged by the perspective of the actual chalk rendered, deepening internally. The drawing wasn't perfect like the vision had felt. And who knows, maybe his *memory* of the vision had been redrawn during the work?

Dollar became conscious again of the feel of Martee's knee against his thigh, his eyes wandering across his artwork, and thought again how settling it felt having her contact. He realized also he had felt her drawing and energy throughout the session. While he gazed at his art, he felt his left hand slide across the inside of her bare right knee.

––––––

Dollar heard and felt Martee stop drawing for a moment. He felt the brush of the back of her right hand across the back of his left hand, a loving touch in the periphery of his awareness, felt his fingers wrap around the front of her shin near the knee, then stopped himself, and felt his eyes go wide. Yet deep inside he knew what felt right, and relaxed. Presently he heard and felt Martee resume drawing. Could he imagine a creative future with her?

He looked at what Martee had been drawing. His eyes pulled away from his art by the dark intensity developing on the cement to his left in front of her. Dollar was struck by two things immediately. One, how her drawing skill was crude, and two, how her art had an intense sense of action which spoke through the crude panel of chalk. So real, at any moment with a snap of the fingers the drawing could become a living scene. He saw in her picture three dark wolves running toward him, intense greenery with moonlight-green high-lights beneath their running feet.

A third thing struck him about her drawing. He felt his eyes blink, considering the implications, looking from her work toward his own and back several times. Checking the flow of the lines, he saw quite plainly how in her drawing all the shadows drew their lines and perspectives from the bright sunshine of the drawing *he* had made.

He turned his head and looked at Martee's face. Her hair was moving with her drawing, a wavy life of its own a moment or two behind her active expression. When she would pause for a moment, it was like her hair could finally catch up, and that dark hair would be still for a moment, playing with a light breeze. Then she'd begin moving, that wavy hair following along half a moment's breath behind her own movements.

Martee looked at him briefly, resumed filling in details in the picture she was working on.

He felt himself pull his hand off her knee, felt his left hand slide along the small of her back until he found the curve of her left hip, and rested the curve of his hand there, energy soaking through the palm, enjoying how her body moved. She leaned forward, sideways, the other way, back nearly erect. She would glance at him briefly, swirl her hair around felt as a surge in his left palm. Then she would lean forward again and draw. He watched her hands move, enjoyed the feeling of Martee connected with him.

After a while, she leaned forward less often. Finally, he heard her put down the last chalk with a clink, felt her warm right hand slide gently onto the inside of his left thigh.

He watched her features and how she was entranced by her chalk.

"(That looks magickal.)" Dollar said quietly, continuing to watch her face.

"(Thanks.)" Her voice had a distance of preoccupation.

He looked at her hair at rest, the cute nose of her face, the sweep of her cheeks, the rounding of her chin. Finally, she turned toward him, looked within his eyes, at his lips, leaned toward him. He felt her kiss on his left cheek, wet. Her breath withdrew, she sat erect. "(You're sweet.)"

Dollar smoothed the palm of his left hand all along her back, ending with a final quick back and forth rub. Then he realized he and Martee had gotten chalk colors on each other and pulled his arm away. She had not complained.

He leaned forward, rested his chin on the right hand clasped over the left fist, propped his two elbows against the insides of his knees and stared at Martee's art.

He felt her hand move from his thigh and rub the underside of his arm slowly while he gazed at her picture. "So," Dollar said. "I see magick here."

"Yesss!" Martee said. She cupped her right hand around his biceps, and relaxed, holding on.

"What's the symbolism of the wolves?"

She turned her head and looked at him. "Do you have an hour? Or a week, even?"

He chuckled.

"(A lifetime?)" Martee added, much quieter, privately leaning into him.

Dollar felt himself inhale sharply. He looked at the other three artists – Bernice, Charlie, Banelle, all drawing in rough sounds of dragging chalk sticks. He glanced at the fountain, looked back at the other three, at the cast of their shadows lengthening across the cement plaza toward his right.

He gauged the brightness on their left, saw how the Sun had descended importunely toward the clear skies beyond the reach of the building on the west side of the expansive courtyard. There was a waft of wild pine, the feeling of the possibility of love revealing a future together.

Dollar turned his head, pivoting the underside of his chin on the bunching of his hands, his eyes looking within Martee's eyes. "(Maybe.)" He turned his attention back upon the drawing she had rendered. "(Give it a go and we'll see how far we get.)"

Martee tugged on his arm. "(All the way!)" He felt Martee squeeze his biceps once. She stretched, her left arm out, her left hand a little fist reaching toward the late afternoon Sun. He felt her pulling against his biceps while stretching, felt the tensing of her body through her knee against his thigh. She relaxed from that stretch.

Martee put her left hand on the ground and scooched herself closer two bounces, pulling on his arm, until her leg was pressed all along the side of his leg. He felt her shoulder brushing his shoulder, her right hand relaxed cupping inside his elbow, felt her head snuggle his shoulder, her hair tickle his arm, soft, then she sat erect.

Martee began bouncing against him regularly while she explained. "There are three callings in Wicca, as I see it. Not that I'm mainstream, I have a busy mind." She put her left thumb out, then the index, the second finger, "Rituals, symbols, and earth naturals — anything genuinely of Nature."

———

Dollar looked at the right wolf which seemed the closest to jumping out of the picture. "Tell me about earth naturals?"

He felt Martee's knee nudge his as she spoke. "You may know some of them already, certain herbs."

Dollar saw Charlie looking at them. Charlie noticed Dollar's looking at him. Their eyes met briefly, then Charlie turned his eyes upon Martee.

"Homeopathy?" Dollar said, continuing to watch Charlie.

"You're thinking rosemary, St. Johns, or something everybody talks about."

Dollar nodded several times, rocking his head on his bunched hands. "Naturally."

Charlie returned his attention upon chalk drawing.

"Yesss!" Martee said, bouncing enthusiastically. "That all changes with awareness, with the intricacies of time."

Dollar rested his right cheek on his bunched hands, looked at Martee's restless lips and impassioned eyes. "For example?"

"Pick a spice."

"Cinnamon."

"Excellent! Seems innocuous, right?" Martee bounced. "Well, suppose you cook with it. You have, haven't you?" Martee bounced, leaning forward a bit and catching at his eyes.

Dollar nodded. When she wasn't looking, he felt himself roll his eyes. *SO elementary!* he thought. He breathed deep and set himself to pretending interest. Boundaries were being crossed, and he wasn't about to share, pulling out the evil instead.

"With cinnamon, you can't be obvious." Martee added emphasis with her left hand jerking to a stop, fingers splayed, palm up. "The amounts matter as well as timing, because awareness matters. So you cook with cinnamon very subtly, on days when you have to, say, enforce discipline in some employees." She made a little fist with her left hand, extending her index finger downward.

Dollar felt himself becoming interested, mind on employees. "Oh?"

"So you cook with it before you go to work…" Martee looped her left hand and stopped with her hand cupped, palm upward. "…then you lay down the law." Martee turned her left hand over and slapped her left calf.

"Cinnamon helps me instill discipline?" Dollar felt his words thick, resting his chin on his bunched hands, his mouth not as free to move. He felt content being thoughtfully at rest.

"Not at first. Never, if you also joke around and act nice that day."

"Or take a shower first, I'm guessing?"

"Exactly." Martee bunched her left fist and pointed the index finger toward his idea. "Change the awareness."

Dollar reseated his right cheek against his bunched hands where he could comfortably watch her. "And I'm guessing eventually I won't have to say a word. Just cook cinnamon rice, with raisins, sugar, and milk."

"Ahh!" Martee said, raising her finger vertically and holding her mouth in a wide, open smile, canting her head left, happiness around her eyes watching his lips and his eyes. "Now you've changed the spell! Are you sure you know what will happen?" Martee rolled her left hand around in a little circle, stopping with the palm upward inviting his input.

Dollar felt himself staring, his eyes tracing the lines of her red shorts and crossed legs. He looked at her eyes, wondering if it was safe to tease, shook his head propped on his bunched hands. "Well, no, I shouldn't think I'd know, not being Wiccan." Dollar fought the curving of the smile, press of lips.

"Right!" Martee bounced, clapping her left hand onto his left biceps. "My point is that to have effective discipline, the discipline results from spells you have built upon acting responsibly, which means consistently." Martee canted her head with a bouncing stop on the right. "Authority and responsibility are the yin-yang of an Independent Wicca." Martee canted her head left, then right once more. She straightened her head and smiled, breathed a sigh in and out, looked down, the eyelashes almost closing, then she looked at him, sitting still. "I can do magick because I'm an authority on it. I engage with authority using magick because I'm self-responsibly consistent."

He felt himself shake his head back and forth, closing his eyes. He opened his eyes, looked at hers, took a deeper breath and sighed out through his nose. "Dice that differently for me?"

She looked at his lips. "You only truly learn when you accept total responsibility for yourself, of course." Martee looked within his eyes, leaning her head closer, canting her head left, her eyes glancing at his lips from under the shadows of her eyebrows, her mouth slightly parted, waiting, alternately checking his lips, his eyes.

I wonder if that's the keynote? Dollar thought, taking a keener interest in what she had been sharing. *An engaging authority and treasured consistency offered to* me? *Does she mean that?* "(You know, Martee.)"

Martee matched his quietness. "(What?)"

"(All this sharing…)" Dollar leaned his lips near her left ear. "(We better watch out with that, or next thing you know we'll be feeling like getting intimate.)" He pulled away a few inches, watched her lips, relaxed back into the self-composed centeredness he was feeling, the side of his face on his bunched hands, the elbows of his arms comfortably braced on the insides of his knees, his legs folded and grounded.

He had shared a line the two of them should not cross, yet he could see while watching her Martee wasn't accepting his comment as he intended.

Her eyelashes were almost closed, lowered right. He felt her left hand squeeze his biceps once. She looked briefly at his crotch and smiled, then set about organizing the chalks with her left hand.

He felt himself breathe in deeply, and sigh. "All right," Dollar said with his normal voice. "How about the other boring sounding…"

"Boring!" Martee's eyes flashed, body straightening upright with a bounce.

"…rituals?" Dollar felt himself grin. "Apologies. 'Boring' just seemed… earth natural."

He watched her press her lips together and squint her eyes at him, then she scrunched her nose briefly and returned his smile. "Rituals *can* be boring, actually. They can also make you feel really silly for trying them…"

"For example?"

"…yet they can be powerful. Oh!" Martee bounced. "Well, there's 'I Love You.'"

———

Dollar felt his eyelids close slightly and wondered if Martee was using magick on him. He opened his eyes more normally, looked at her lips, then at her eyes.

"You misunderstand." Martee bounced. "The ritual 'I Love You' is one of the Mirror Chants."

"Mirror?"

"Correct. Whenever you see yourself in the mirror, you say, 'I Love You…'"

He looked at her lips.

"…and it can make you feel damn silly for a long time at first while getting comfortable with the ritual."

He looked within her eyes. "What does that do?"

"Here…"

He didn't understand what 'here' meant, because she hadn't gestured, hadn't chanted, hadn't sprinkled him with cinnamon, and she hadn't changed the way her eyes were upon him. Presently, he saw come over Martee the most joy he could remember ever experiencing from any woman anywhere in his life, and that pulled at him. He felt he wanted to wrap his arms around her just to capture, for a moment, that kind of joy for himself.

He also discovered — with a widening of his eyes in alarm — whatever she was doing without anything overt, like loosening a blouse button or flashing a breast, was moving him thickly to a full sense of desire. He felt himself swallow, lips parting like a parched man after patiently walking miles, days, months, years without the wet joy, wanted to kiss her *now* because he was sure a summer rainstorm smile like that could make him forget he had ever been thirsty on any day of any previous Moon.

Martee watched his eyes, his lips. Her eyes lingered on his crotch, which had become aroused, then looked into his eyes. Martee's pupils were dilated. "There. What did you feel?"

Growl of the Animal in the night woods, he closed his mouth, feeling and hearing himself clear his throat, opened his mouth… There was nothing to say verbally. He closed his mouth. She did, indeed, know magick. "Martee." Then more quietly, "(Dammit, Martee, you know… physically.)"

Martee brought her face close to his, then her breast pressed against his arm, lips near his left ear. "(Feel *amazing*, handsome? Like to feel that every day?)" felt her moist breath, the warmth of her cheek near his, heard the lips part near the left ear, felt her wet lips suckle his earlobe, shivers down his spine. She pulled her lips off his earlobe and sat back.

He looked from her eyes toward her lips. His eyes descended lower, savoring for the moment how the cut of the white blouse opened the plunge of her breasts as she breathed, felt within himself a new level of appreciation for the warmth of having her right hand cupped around his forearm, her thigh and shoulder pressed against his.

He looked within her eyes. He looked down at the red shorts. How easily would they part into his hands, her thighs exposed to their merging, her pheromones on his nose? He looked within her eyes, one, then the other, felt he'd like to always see those sweet brown eyes upon his. Dollar fought down the desire for now, leaned toward Martee's right ear. "(I'm in. There's something to this.)"

"(Something to this!)" Martee said with a bounce, felt the tug of her hand on his forearm, saw her hair alive and full of happiness.

He felt himself exhale through his nose, grinned, and accepted the win. "There is. So, someone who wants to learn that one, they have to feel silly for a long time?"

"Wellll," Martee said slowly and carefully. "If someone wanted to learn that one..." He felt her left hand softly rest on his biceps. "... from someone else..." He felt her left hand pivot at the wrist, the heel of the left hand never leaving his arm while patting three times, "... who, say, knew all the convolutions of how and why it works..."

Felt himself smile, murmured. "(Like she knows kissed raisins and sugar gravy.)"

...Martee stopped, closed her mouth. She withdrew her right hand from his elbow and stuck that out for him to shake.

He took her hand.

Martee immediately gave his hand a shake, up and down hard once. "Done!"

"Martee!" he heard Banelle say. "Why don't you tell him about one of your spells which didn't work out?"

"Oh, the Goddess!" Martee looked toward Banelle with wide eyes, the back of Martee's left hand against her mouth. Martee leaned backward, then pulled her hand down and swirled her hair, tugged her right hand in the crook of Dollar's elbow, sat erect, cupping her left hand over the top of his biceps, her eyes gleaming. She looked at his eyes, then at his lips, and within his eyes, breathed in deeply and sighed.

Dollar inhaled sharply, taking the cue. Actually, he was working hard to feel uninterested in order to settle the arousal, and Martee seemed to be having such a good time, which tugged deftly at his continued interest, and he liked Martee. One of the facets about Banelle, which he was coming to appreciate, was how Banelle attracted wonderful people.

Even Bernice, he saw now, was a wonderful, fun person. Dollar remembered Bernice's face from the Grape Hopper, had never been acquainted with her personally, figuring her for just another kid with no clarity of values or life experiences. His previous presumption was erroneous.

He was hoping Banelle considered him, also, among those worthy of attracting, because within the short time since their morning when he'd first met Banelle, and here he felt his eyebrows pop with the realization…

Martee, watching him, reacting like he'd just popped his eyebrows on account of something Martee had been saying.

…he realized how since the morning cycling and bicycle tire repair, since chumming in the kitchen with Charlie, since lunch out as a foursome, since the adventuring had continued as a fivesome, how since all these things had begun transpiring, his life, he realized, had in mere hours been tremendously enriched. He liked feeling wealthier emotionally. An epiphany welling up: he wanted more networked wealth in his life.

He realized he hadn't been paying attention. "What? Wait, say that part again?" Dollar focused on Martee, shaking his head, and closing his eyes momentarily.

"I put in the red alabaster…" Martee stopped, mouth open.

Dollar shook his head to clear the wandering mind, and leaned right, watching her. "I'm not tracking yet. Could you start that one over?"

She tilted her head left and squinted at him. "Are you paying attention?"

———

What to do, what to do? Dollar shrugged, centered himself. "I was entranced by the way your hair bounces, and got lost in an afternoon fantasy."

"Really?!" Martee bounced once, vanity perking.

He heard Banelle cough wheezingly twice.

He decided it would be best to resist turning to look at Banelle for the next few moments.

"I think," he heard Charlie say, "he got lost in the complexities of time and awareness."

Dollar felt himself laugh, turned only his eyes toward Charlie.

Charlie winked.

Shit, Dollar thought. The joke Charlie made was prime. Dollar looked at Martee.

She was leaning away from him, hair draped beyond her left shoulder, a skeptical look while watching him.

He smiled at her and shrugged. "I apologize. Actually, I was totally zoned. I want to get deeper into the sharing. Apologies." Dollar clamped his right palm on Martee's fingers in the crook of his elbow, Martee on the way toward a pout. "Wait! I really am interested." He realized in his sharing, he was, although his interest wasn't only because of the storytelling. He watched how quickly Martee dispensed with the pout, lighting up almost instantly.

Dollar glanced at Banelle briefly. She was intent on her chalk work again, bent almost double down upon the concrete canvas.

He turned his attention back upon Martee's enchanting him, Martee flattering him... *Uh, oh!* He sat up, folding his arms loosely.

She removed her right hand from his forearm, started patting the inside of his left thigh with her hand, adding emphasis to the things she was sharing to him.

He hoped his loosely crossing his arms made it look like he had an itch on the underside of his left forearm. Underneath on the soft skin where nobody could see, he grabbed some of the skin between right forefinger and thumb, pinching hard, painful enough for the eyes to water.

The pinch grounded him immediately, pushing away enough of the romantic fog which had wafted seemingly from nowhere. *No brain? Use pain!* And here he was not paying attention again, knew there would be a cold walk in the rain before he admitted inattention a second time on the same story, from the same woman.

Dollar noticed now the smell had been here all along, bobbing for awareness every so often, the subtle scent of unspeakably wild pine in the air, breathed in deeply through his nose, to be sure of the pine, curious. He wondered again where in the expansive courtyard the pine was growing, and what species, because — inhale without being conspicuous to Martee's storytelling — he couldn't place his ever having smelled that particular pine fragrance before, as if the source pine was from a different millennia.

He noticed while he was musing how some part of Martee's body was always beautifully in motion. He wondered if she would be in motion even if it was the middle of the dark morning long before dawn and they were actually trying to get some rest. He could awaken himself and watch her sleeping, would she still be in motion?

He looked at how her breasts rose and fell, how they shook and kept moving whenever she turned her torso quickly, and she did that a lot he had noticed. He imagined for a moment reaching his fingers into her curves as she slept beside him, looked at the way her shoulders sloped toward her arms, how feminine they looked. He noticed again how trim her waist was, how well the white plunging blouse met the red shorts slipping inside them, looked at her legs emerging below, how the muscles flowed and were noticeable without looking fierce. He liked especially, the size of her feet and hands, felt like kissing all four repeatedly, suckling the fingers.

A realization struck him now, looking at Martee as a total person, how there was one and only one category he could put her in. "(Gorgeous.)" he said out loud, surprising both of them.

Martee smiled toothily, squinted her eyes in happy lines, opened the eyes and continued sharing her story.

Martee's wasn't the same beauty which Banelle had. He turned his eyes for a quick refresher. Banelle's form, movements, gestures, and symmetry were all burned richly within the mind's eye, along with her smells and the feel of her against him, the feel of her hands on his body anytime Banelle touched him. All these impressions of Banelle were soaking richly within him and permanent.

He turned to watch Martee, thinking himself polite. His mind was still fiery with the glow of Banelle's features and femininity. He felt strongly there was only one category to put Banelle in: *Gorgeous.*

Dollar glanced at Bernice briefly. Despite his enjoying her around and all the fun they were having as a group, he felt unusually compelled toward listing Bernice in the only other category which seemed to be available at the moment: *Repulsive.* He felt guilty as hell, convicted three centuries back because he really, really liked Bernice and enjoyed her company thoroughly — one-on-one, and the five of them as a group. He had admired her attire, the cut of her hair and other details all day so far. The realization of feeling repulsed made him feel evil, which was not how he normally thought of himself. The feeling of repulsion was, at the moment, irreconcilable with how he had felt about Bernice on their ride over here, and irreconcilable with the rest of himself any day or night.

He shuddered and turned his attention back upon fucking gorgeous Martee, idly wondering what the barely discernible wafts of enchanting pine were from, somewhere upwind in the city, if not from this courtyard, his current guess.

———

In turning back toward Martee, Dollar saw she had finished the story and was looking at him for a response of some kind. *Oh, fuck.* He wasn't quite sure what should be done. He looked at her lips, which at the moment were parted expectantly.

He looked back within her eyes, and in this moment he felt himself drawn powerfully within her awareness, the hands of alarm spreading fingers wide, paralyzed, reaching to brace a feeling of falling...

...Felt their souls blown open like doors kicked in by the crash of a thunderstorm. In the instant after the thunderclap he knew she knew. He knew also what she knew, though there were a million things. Much more than words could be found for in the poignant, timeless span the doors were open. Here were two budding relationship loves previously partially hidden in flirtation, fully revealed with chest-slapping skin into each other, hers and his.

…There was a great sucking of the winds, doors slamming shut with echoes of their closings reverberating within the mind, a few leaves whirling around in circles inside the doorway on the floors of the vision. He blinked his eyes and refocused on Martee.

She looked crestfallen, shoulders slumped down, gorgeous eyelashes almost closed.

Goddesses! Dollar thought, feeling a powerful compassion welling inside his heart. He had not seen Marty so quiet since meeting each other. He had a few too many years' of failed relationship experiences himself to let the moment become a permanent part of their emotional baggage. No matter how briefly he had known her so far, his instincts told him there would be many, many years ahead, it was worth investing further in what they now had together. Dollar felt instant resolve.

He drew from the reservoir of the unexpected within himself something surprising to tell her with energy instead of words how enduringly he felt connected with her. He put the bottom lip out, let his head hang down, and watched her with the sad eyes.

Eventually she looked up. When she saw what he was doing Martee said, "Stop it, you." She tried squinting her eyes and started laughing instead. Martee climbed to her feet on the concrete and pounced on him, digging her fingers into his ribs, and she had guessed right — or did she now *know* he was ticklish? He was instantly laughing and on his back, head bump on concrete, hat lost, yelling, "Martee, Stop!"

He laughed more.

She finally relented when his chest was emptied completely of air from laughing so hard. Her face was over his, kissing close. He watched her eyes while he began to get his wind back. She looked at his lips with her mouth parted, the tip of her tongue touching her teeth. Her eyes looked within his and he felt her shift her weight, her breasts so soft, that joy pinning him to the ground.

Her left hand came near his forehead, felt her fingers brush his hair toward the side, the feeling of her gentle fingers sending ripples through his core, a part of himself melting inside. He felt Martee's left fingers pinch his nose. "(Beep.)"

He laughed, rolled her off himself away from their chalk art. He rolled himself to a sitting position and looked at Martee. Her right hand landed on his knee, smiling up at him, laying on her back.

He turned his torso and saw Banelle was livid.

Dollar looked at Charlie, who had been gazing at him. Charlie raised his eyebrows and turned back to what he was drawing, the sound of chalk.

Dollar saw Bernice was watching, smiling brightly. He felt a brief wave of loathing and a frown, feeling he should not even have the emotional vocabulary for loathing. He had never felt loathing at any of the times he'd seen Bernice at the Grape Hopper. He remembered she always looked attractive to him, just not now. What the hell?

Dollar returned his attention to Martee. He breathed in deeply and sighed. "(Thanks.)" Quietly, not sure why he said so. The gratefulness felt correct for both of them. He rubbed his left hand along Martee's forearm, shrugged. "(There is a lot to process. I do want to hear your stories from your *lips* sometime.)" What was there he didn't know about Martee now?

He stood, reached his left hand down for Martee. She took his hand in both of hers, rolled onto her feet, light and bouncy. She landed close, her breasts pressing against his abs. She smiled, pulled his left hand to her lips, and kissed the tips of his fingers, then her eyelashes almost closed. She looked within his eyes, then pulled away, turning her body, then her head. She bent over with him behind her and started gathering the disorganized chalks.

Dollar stood there for a moment, aching with the unspoken invitation. *Shit.* He forced himself to turn and face the others, partially folded his arms and gave himself another sharp, squeezing pinch of tender skin under the right forearm, decided with the boost in clarity it was time to reconnect with Banelle.

He picked up his artist's hat with his left hand, walked over and stood close behind Banelle's left shoulder.

She was just putting her chalks within the box. She looked up so he could see she was crying.

He held out his right hand.

She took the hand finally. He pulled her onto her feet, the feeling of grace and naturalness, like they had rehearsed a ballroom dance opener countless times. On impulse he pulled her against himself…

"Wha…?"

…and wrapped his arms largely around her, kissed her forehead. Then he just held her close, felt the thickness in the jeans pressed up against her. At first the feeling was of a rag doll. Soon, though, he felt her arms slide around his waist, the left arm around the small of his back, her right arm across his back diagonally, felt her hand between his shoulder blades, felt her body melt against his. The feeling of her being close just about bringing tears to his eyes now, another delicious feeling in a deepening connection with her.

———

Banelle released the hug, though Dollar did not, his hands at her waist. She put her palms against his chest, arching at the waist enough for searching his eyes. She looked at his lips, then her eyes dropped toward where her hands were flat on his chest, fingers splayed. She brushed with the palm of her right hand smoothing his shirt. She found something which shouldn't be there, apparently, though he couldn't see what that was because he was watching her face. He felt her fingers pick something off his shirt and rub the fingers toward the cement below, then Banelle smoothed his shirt some more. She looked within his eyes, searching back and forth. "(Are you sure I'm enough for you?)"

He looked at her lips. He smiled into the feeling of pressed lips with dimples. "(I have never felt so turned around, with you in my arms, your arms around me just now. We are just starting to know each other. Am I going to be enough for *you*?)" His eyes searched hers. He felt her sigh in the press of her lower torso against his loins, looking at his lips, then the pat of her hand on his chest three times.

He felt himself shrug, took a step back, turned left to look at the running art Banelle had drawn in chalk on solid concrete: a horse galloping toward the right in a style touching on cave art. There was something particularly well done about the ochre coloring of the horse, about the horse's lines, about the black night which the horse ran in with one lone star shining ahead. The rendering was vital. Dollar felt deep admiration. "(Wow.)" He looked at her, feeling his eyebrows arch in surprise. "(Are you an artist?)"

Banelle's head moved back slightly, "(No.)"

He looked at the horse. He felt his head shake slowly feeling the intensity of the imagery, tracing the lines of the horse's movements with his eyes, looking to discover what piece of the picture moved him so. "(Do you ride horses?)"

She smiled brightly, leaned into him momentarily, shook her head, stood erect and poised. "(No. I never have. Someday.)"

Dollar saw Bernice had gotten up. He turned and watched Bernice walk to Charlie. Bernice approached close behind Charlie, crouched down and gave him a long hug from behind.

Dollar looked around, waving his right hand behind himself feeling for Banelle's hand. He caught her eye over his shoulder, then felt Banelle's hand slip within his. He pulled her along to look at Bernice's art.

Bernice had drawn two large distant hills, and from between them a river flowed wanderingly toward the viewer becoming wide and filled with whitewater. On the left side of the brimming river there were hundreds of wildflowers, birds flying about, and even one bee with a curly flight line. On the right side of the chalky river, pine forests crowded the bank, dark shadows inside darker shadows, some of them coloring the water reflectively.

After a few moments, he felt Banelle pulling on his hand, and when he consciously noticed Banelle required something of him he turned his attention away from Bernice's art and allowed Banelle's leading them to go look at the art Dollar had drawn, and the art Martee had drawn. Martee's art was powerful and moving, and so obviously shadowed by his gigantic Sun he felt embarrassed.

Banelle spent a long while looking back and forth at the two pictures. He felt her drop her hand from his. He panicked inside, though he would never show the panic for anyone else to see. He was profoundly relieved a moment later when he felt Banelle push his left arm back, slipping both of her arms around his waist, and squeeze. "(Just remember you are mine.)" felt her squeeze herself against him.

Dollar wrapped his left arm around Banelle's shoulders, turning her toward him, placed his right hand on the small of her back, and squeezed her to him. Banelle looked up at him. He pulled his eyes from the two artworks side-by-side and looked within her eyes, moist and searching his eyes. He heard and felt her sniff. Then she turned her head left, laying the right side of her face against his chest. He felt her squeeze him.

He watched the other three while they walked around looking at the various art works. He continued holding Banelle. Finally, she pulled her left arm away from him and patted his stomach. "(C'-mon.)" Banelle led him by the hand toward Charlie's art.

Charlie had drawn a giant tree on a tall sturdy trunk with expressive wrinkles in the bark growing hundreds of feet above small figures of cows and sheep and people below, the canopy of the tree spreading widely, a single fruit falling.

Dollar looked at that for a long time.

Martee swung in close orbit around Banelle and Dollar, stopping on the right side of him from where Banelle was. Martee did not touch Dollar while quietly studying Charlie's art.

Banelle continued holding Dollar's hand. Dollar saw Banelle ease forward, gazing quietly past him at Martee.

When Martee noticed Banelle's watching, Martee did so with only a glance, her arms folding, then Martee was looking at Charlie's art again. "Anna, you have such a wonderful father."

Banelle sidled closer to Dollar's left side and slipped her hands around his left arm. He felt her forehead rest against his shoulder.

Dollar smelled faintly the wild pine, wondered how long the pine had floated so subtly before he had noticed the aroma again.

Charlie walked near from the direction of where Martee's and

Dollar's art was. Charlie looked at his watch. "My turn. Everyone having a good time?"

Dollar knew he was, felt himself nodding. He looked at Bernice who was nodding vigorously beyond Banelle. Dollar turned his head right, looked at Martee who swirled her hair and smiled, then turned his head left and looked at Banelle, her nose against his shoulder waiting for his eyes. Banelle was looking at him with smiles around her eyes, pupils enlarged, wagged her eyebrows once, spoke quietly, the warmth of her words muffled in his shirt. "(Dollar, you'll do. You *are* enough for me.)"

Dollar cleared his throat hoping no one else had heard that, looked at Charlie. "What's left on our finalized pick list?" Then Dollar kissed Banelle's forehead.

Charlie arched back, his eyes toward the sky, leveled his head and looked at Bernice, flexed his knees and stood. "There's dancing." Charlie turned only his eyes to look at Martee. "Live music." Eyes on Dollar. "There's also rock skipping. Which is my favorite, by the way."

Dollar was processing, where to find live music and a dance floor tonight?

Charlie continued looking at Dollar, somewhat piercingly Dollar felt. "It was your idea," prompted Charlie.

Dollar felt his eyes go wide, stopped his mind's wandering from imagining having left the dance with Banelle under his arm to naked in a tent with the rain all around them, smell of horses, his fingers feathering her hair — from there to splashing rocks in a pool of water. "Goddess, yes! My idea, wasn't it?"

Dollar heard Martee laughing, her sandaled left foot momentarily off the ground in his periphery, felt Martee's right hand rub his right upper arm, touch of feminine attention on both shoulders.

Dollar tried to remember, where the hell had he seen lots of skipping rocks near a body of water?

whipped her arm, twisting her body

. . .

BANELLE PRESSED HEAVILY on the brake, bringing the SUV sliding to a halt on the downward slope facing the inside of a river bend, rocks in the dirt spitting out from the wheels. The windows down, she could smell the dirt in the air while the SUV made the last couple bounces.

"Damn, Anna!" Martee yelled from the back seat.

Banelle looked in the rearview mirror and saw Martee had her hand braced against the roof, smiling happily. Banelle chuckled. She had never driven the SUV off paved roads before.

She slid the transmission to park.

Banelle looked at Dollar riding in the front passenger seat, his eyes wide with mock alarm, right hand clinging tightly to the overhead handgrip. "Ohh, stop!"

He laughed, opened the right door and climbed out.

Banelle shut the SUV off and dropped the keys on the floor mat. She heard the right rear door open, then the left rear, and felt the vehicle jostle as the others stepped out, heard the whumps of three doors.

She looked at the mowed park slopes along the wide river wandering lazily in the bend, at the woods around the clearing. She could see rocks all along the shoreline, running uphill four full-car lengths in some places, depending on how steep the banks were. None of the banks seemed particularly dangerous.

Bernice appeared by the driver's window, looked in at Banelle, put her right arm on the frame of the window. "Jazzed!" Bernice did the bobbing nod. "Can I drive on the way back?"

Banelle felt her head jerk back. "Hell no!"

Banelle regrouped. "I mean, no. Because, Bernice, I like you a lot." Banelle put her right hand softly on Bernice's arm. "You are twenty-one? My insurance doesn't cover anyone under twenty-five." Banelle felt the lie, even though the facts were absolutely correct. *No, this is about vanity, baby.* It was *her* ride to drive.

Bernice looked at Banelle's lips.

Banelle wondered if she hadn't said, "baby," out loud.

Bernice looked into Banelle's eyes.

Banelle wondered again where she had been smelling something subtly pine-like. *Where the hell is Dollar?* Banelle wondered. "C'mon." Banelle pulled on the door handle, Bernice jumped back, and Banelle swung the door open.

She saw her father was the first down to the waterline, Dollar nearing the water also and busily picking up rocks. Martee already had a rock and was giving the rock a body-shaking overarm throw. The rock flew in a high arc and dropped with a splunk in the center of the riverbanks.

Banelle slid off the seat and dropped to the ground, turned around and slammed the door shut. On intuition, having given the challenge of Martee's bouncing hair a lot of thought during the afternoon, Banelle reached behind her head and tried untying the scarf, but found a knot.

Bernice's voice. "Let me get that for you."

Presently Banelle felt Bernice tugging at the knot. "Ow!" Banelle felt the dimples of her smile…

"Oops!"

…because nothing had hurt her. Banelle scrunched her face to keep from laughing. Some lies were fun. She heard other rocks plunking the river, and for some reason this longing to laugh more pulled at her. "C'mon, c'mon, c'mon."

"Wait…"

Banelle felt more tugs, then felt her hair come loose. She shook her hair and turned toward Bernice.

…Who handed her the scarf. "Thanks!" Banelle tossed the scarf through the driver's window, turned, and ran down the slope. She felt herself start to laugh.

"Clear!" her father said, leaned back sideways, then he powered a rock at a low trajectory…

Martee pulled back similarly…

…his rock caught the water with a zipp'pock sound, then the rock skipped another three times in smaller splashes.

…Martee's rock was right behind, skipped five times and passed over where his rock sank out of sight.

Banelle crouched, grabbed a handful of rocks with the left hand, stood, and walked near the river's edge joining the line of her father on the far right, Martee, and Dollar, making herself the leftmost.

Banelle hauled back with her right hand and threw a rock toward the river — the rock went splunk without a bounce.

She heard Martee laugh and clap. "Good one, Anna!"

Besides feeling nettled, Banelle noticed there was an echo of Martee's voice on the large lazy curve of the river. Downstream to the right, rock bluffs rose on the near and far banks. Ahead of them across the river the bank was open and flat for nearly a hundred yards, until the far wood line caught the view, burying the line of sight within thick foliage.

Bernice stepped near on Banelle's left, hauled back, threw a rock…

On Banelle's right a rock Martee had just thrown was skipping lightly across the river.

…Bernice's rock skipped once and plunged under on the second contact.

Banelle picked another rock out of the left hand and, watching how Dollar and her father were leaning sideways and throwing, tried to emulate the motion. She whipped her arm, twisting her body, immediately feeling a conflation of emotions from the instant pleasure of her pelvis muscles tensing quickly and pulling hard, which was contrasted soon after by the dissatisfaction of the rock doing only a single skip followed by a splunk. *Progress!* Trying for a self-boost.

Dollar's last rock was still moving, and after six skips the rock started a waddling curve of splaying water. Then the rock's energy was completely spent and sank.

Bernice threw another rock…

Banelle caught Dollar's eye. "How come yours skips?"

…Bernice's rock went thunk and disappeared. "Yeah?"

Dollar shrugged, palms up. "What rocks?" Dollar turned toward her father. "Did you see any rocks?"

Her father looked at Dollar with a deadpan countenance. "Oh, hell no!"

Banelle heard Martee laughing. Banelle picked another rock out of her left hand, hauled back with the right hand, gave the rock an angry whip. The rock skipped twice, and sank.

"ANNA." Martee's voice.

Banelle looked. Martee was leaning forward and squinting at the place her rock had hit the water.

"What?!"

Martee turned her head, looked at Banelle. "Are you using flat rocks?"

————

Banelle looked in her open left hand at the two oval rocks remaining. "No." She heard her father laugh.

Dollar stepped nearer to Banelle. "(Here.)" He handed her a flatly smooth ovoid rock about the size of her palm.

She looked at him, squinting her eyes. "I thought you said you didn't have any rocks?"

"WHAT rocks?" Dollar shrugged, arms at waist level, palms up. "Bernice." Dollar leaned to look past Banelle.

"Yes!"

"I ask you, do you see any rocks around here?"

"Hell no!"

Banelle turned to look at Bernice, who was shaking her head slowly, eyes wide.

Banelle heard Martee laugh, turned to see a rock Martee had just let sail skip three times, then sink. "Martee." Banelle felt her lips pressed together and looked at Dollar. She looked at the river and hauled back to throw…

"WAIT wait wait wait WAIT!" Dollar grabbed her arm. "If you're not going to throw any of the stones we don't have, you've got to not throw them like we actually have some to throw away."

Banelle stopped herself and stood erect. "What the hell are you talking about?"

Dollar shook his head, eyes wide. "Not rocks!"

She felt like dropping the rock on his foot and punching his arm. Then she felt his right hand around her right forearm. Another part of her had something else in mind which she'd like to do with him in the river, just his naked body and this naked body, wet and tingly. She felt his left hand pull her right hand up, then both his hands fiddled with the way she was holding what was obviously *not* a rock. She felt herself grin.

"Don't expect to find any flat rocks held in your hands like this around here." Dollar shaped her hand so the index finger and thumb were wrapped around the edge of the flat rock in opposing directions, the other three fingers curled supportively underneath.

Bernice had stepped closer, watching with interest what wasn't going on with the rock that wasn't in Banelle's hand. Banelle laughed, a joyful feeling having her hand and mind played with.

"NOW." Dollar looked her keenly in the eye, his face leaning toward her, and kissed her on the forehead. "Don't imagine for a minute that even if there were rocks around here, they had any chance of floating at all, especially if one happened to fly from your hand spinning flat like the river." Banelle felt his hands drop away.

She saw Martee hauling back sideways, looked at how low by the ground Martee was when she threw the rock in hand, how her face became intensely focused throwing, then Martee's eyes followed with alacrity what she had just let loose across the river.

Banelle blinked Martee out of the mind, put herself in these shoes instead, touched on what kind of pleasure this must be next, threw with all her strength the rock she did not have, feeling this unfamiliar spasm of muscles in her calves, thighs, midriff, forearm. The rock whizzed, spinning flatly away from her... Caught the first pock water spraying... Struck again... again — felt her head nod, watching intently the rock catching the river — again... then the rock sprayed water in an arc, spinning against the river's current and sloshed under. She let out a scream, dropped the rocks from her left hand clattering on the shoreline and jumped at Dollar, grabbing him with both arms.

She heard Martee clapping. "Hooray, Anna!" Heard the echoes of Martee's voice.

"Excellent!" yelled Banelle's father, and there was the echo also of her father's voice.

Banelle grabbed Dollar's head with her left arm and right hand, then she kissed him full on the lips. *Oh, what the hell,* pushed her tongue in through his lips and tasted his tongue, enjoyed his start of surprise. She pushed away, palms against his chest with a bounce on the flats of her feet, smiling and looking within his eyes. He reached for her, his eyes on her breasts. Banelle turned abruptly and started looking for flat rocks. She needed time to process her own shock.

Bernice had found one, hauled back and threw. Banelle heard the first pock, saw Bernice's rock flying through the air from one circular ripple toward a next... the rock struck three more times.

Banelle jumped up clapping and yelled, "Hooray, Bernice!"

"Yes! Bernice!" Martee yelled.

Bernice jumped, clapping for herself.

Dollar had his thumb up. "Oh, yeahhhh!" the baritone voice.

Banelle felt the ripples on her skin, still busy looking for and picking up flat rocks, with several in her left hand, searching strides away from the waterline in a century of glacier travel.

Bernice jogged to be near Banelle and stopped, rocks crunching under Bernice's feet. "Find any here?"

Banelle laughed, and stood. "HELL NO, Bernice! There are no rocks around here!"

Bernice laughed.

Banelle felt herself laughing.

Her father clapped his hands once. "Hoy! Everyone grab a rock that's not there, then let's try not throwing a rock together!"

Banelle crouched, harvested one more flat rock she had just seen, stood, then jogged back the few yards toward the waterline, gaining a century of youth at an age of wisdom. She heard Bernice following immediately behind and to the left. Banelle prepared a fresh ancient rock, encircling with her thumb and forefinger and bracing with the other three fingers in a curl beneath, then turned her body sideways to the river.

Banelle saw her father watching down the line at Banelle. Banelle nodded, smiling. She saw Martee was waiting at the ready, the red shorts taught around spread thighs in the rocky setting.

Banelle's father looked past her toward Bernice.

"Ready!" she heard Bernice call.

Dollar had been watching her and Bernice. With a quick look at how Banelle wasn't holding the rock she didn't have, he turned and didn't ready the one he didn't have, then gave a single nod upward toward Banelle's father.

Her father returned the single nod, body turning away. "On three! Not one! Not two! Don't… throwwwww!"

———

Banelle turned her attention toward the river, threw with all her strength what she didn't have in her right hand.

Five rocks flew away from the shoreline, roughly synchronized… They all hit with sp-sp-splocking sounds… hit again with less synchronicity… after the third hit, Bernice's fell out… Dollar's chunked under next, three more rocks flying… Banelle's went under on the next hit, the rocks from her father and Martee continuing in converging lines... the two rocks skipped, danced in passing... Banelle's father's rock went under on the next skip... Martee's made one more skip before whirring in a small sliding clockwise arc, and dropped out of sight.

"Yesssss!" Martee yelled, jumping repeatedly, the crunch of rocks underfoot.

On the lazily moving river, concentric circles rippled outward, the expanding rings of water floating slowly downstream and crossing through each other.

Banelle turned, smiling and breathing deeply, saw Martee leap at her father and hug him. Martee kissed him on the left cheek and jumped back, then ran up the bank.

Banelle picked another rock out of her left hand, readied this resolve, hauled back and threw again...

"Who doesn't have two rocks?" Banelle heard her father yell.

"I don't!" Banelle said, feeling two pair in her left hand. Her recently thrown rock skipped high and, on the third skip against a water ripple, leaped head-high in the air and went plunk-under.

Bernice called, "I don't!"

Dollar raised his left arm, his hand full of rocks and turned toward Banelle's father. "I know I don't!"

"That makes four of us!" called her father, turning. "ARE you READY?"

"Wait!" Martee called.

"Too late! Not one! Not two!...

"Wait!"

"...Don't throwwwwww!"

Banelle threw with a whipping strength, then she had to listen for the rock while juggling quickly to get the next rock ready. She had the grip correct and hauled back and threw this rock also, an exquisite feel... saw the first rock was on the second skip already, how Dollar had actually lagged behind her getting his second out, a feeling of victory.

Her second rock skipped, the first rock skipping again...

Bernice sent her second rock flying...

Rocks were smattering all across their area of the moving river, pucking and splashing.

Banelle felt herself jumping, the sound and feel of crunching rocks beneath her sandals, a faint smell of pine in the air.

There was the sound of Martee's feet running down the slope of rocks.

Banelle looked at her own hands, readied a third rock, hauled back and threw. Banelle felt elated, seeing she had beat Martee's first throw, "Yes!"

Martee was quick, though, and threw two more stones as follow-ons, each time shaking herself head-body-feet, the violence of throwing.

Goddess, what passion.

Dollar threw his last rock. Then he turned around and went looking for more rocks which weren't there.

Banelle assessed the last rock in her left hand. She tossed the rock upward... caught in the right hand, felt the shaping of her fingers the way she had learned the new grip. She backed away from the shore a few steps, ran toward the river and threw the rock like she lived in the wild. The rock skipped... skipped... Banelle counting, "...five, six, Sevennnnnnnnnn!" Banelle threw her head back and whirled, shaking her hair back and forth. "Yesss!"

She turned around, saw Dollar coming back with flat rocks the size of both her hands spread. "What?!"

He laughed. "We don't have even bigger rocks! Here!" Dollar stepped near, set the stack on the ground, an offering of worship. "I'll prove it to you." Dollar handed her one of the overlarge flat stones.

She took the stone by the edge, almost dropped the stone before getting an adequate grip. Banelle laughed. "What?!"

Martee had stepped back from the river with her feet apart. She saw what Dollar had brought back and laughed, bending backward, her left foot off the rocks temporarily.

Banelle's father looked to see what the joke was and grinned. "Hell no! I don't see bigger rocks here!"

Martee turned toward Banelle's father. "Race ya!"

He laughed, palmed Martee on the ass as she passed, and jogged after her.

Dollar hauled back with one of the big rocks. Banelle saw how he had wrapped his entire right hand against the edge of the large rock, how his left thumb and finger pinched the rock, how he threw two-handed. There was a huge splash and the rock skipped... splashed again... on the third hit the slab of stone went SP-lun-K loudly and gurgled under, swirling water.

"(Holy shit.)" Banelle whispered. She heard Bernice laughing and clapping. Banelle looked at the monster in her two hands and tried wrapping her right hand against the edge the way he had. Her hands were smaller, so she found she had to pinch her left thumb and forefinger and also cup her right hand around the edge a few inches behind from the left thumb, bracing the rock's edge with her right wrist. She hauled back, doing her best with short running steps toward the river's edge and threw the rock... wobbling, spinning lazily, a heavy splash, she jumped back with a screech feeling water spattering her shins and toes in the sandals, the sound of the rock going under while watching her wet skin with shock. She laughed crossing the arms over her breasts, backed up, and turned around.

Dollar was grinning at her. "Ain't that sweet?"

———

Banelle felt herself nodding happily.

Martee was jogging back in short steps with two large flat rocks in her hands, hair jiggling, happy passion in her eyes. Banelle felt herself leaning backward, laughing at the sight of Martee's breasts bouncing carrying the rocks.

Martee stopped near the river and let one big flat rock slip to the ground with a clinking thunk. She withdrew a few paces, arranged the other rock in her hands, then stepped aggressively toward the river, spinning bodily twice, threw the rock wobbling through the air, and stepped backward to catch her balance. The rock splashed and skipped… splashed, and sloshed out of sight. Martee bent her knees, feet wide, bending her arms at the elbows, fingers spread and tensed upward, leaning back. "I! Love! This!"

Banelle felt her eyes go wide, felt her lips pressed, dimpling. There seemed no limit to Martee's passion for rocks.

Martee bent over and picked up the second big flat rock…

Banelle turned around, saw her father walking back, smiling, carrying a stack of seven similarly large, flat rocks. Banelle turned further right and looked at Bernice.

Bernice shrugged.

"Had your fill?"

Bernice nodded, smiling.

"Me, too." Banelle stepped nearer to Bernice, slipped her right arm within Bernice's left arm. The two of them walked up the slope toward the SUV. Banelle heard a big splash behind her, then heard Martee scream and clap, heard Dollar laugh, heard her father chuckling.

Banelle walked around the Black Menace, opened the back of the SUV, hatch rising above them, feeling she'd like to sit down and also feeling she'd like a break from the others. She sat on the left side of the carpeted truck bed, making room for Bernice.

Bernice leaned against the tailgate beside Banelle, hips braced by legs.

Banelle noticed with a fleeting scrunch of her eyebrows and nose there was a subtly pine-like aroma in the air. Her eyes scanned the tree line, wondering what the source was. She breathed in deeply and held her breath, looking along the dirt-packed slope of the trail she had followed driving them here, at the trees which crowded along the top of the hill where the woods ended and how they obscured the curve of the trail.

She sighed, then resumed breathing regularly, feeling the coolness of the light breeze, felt the tickling evaporation of water on her toes and feet in these sandals, and on her shins. She looked down at herself, extending her feet out in front, pointing her toes. *Nice.* She let her legs relax. Her calves felt the SUV's back bumper. She began swinging her feet lazily.

Banelle noticed Bernice's fingers fiddling with a small flat rock, Bernice's eyes down and the focus faraway, braced against the tailgate with her feet on the ground, legs straight and close together.

"That a leftover?" Banelle looked at Bernice's face, at the side of her mouth, then at the corner of the left eye. A feeling surged, struck Banelle how if she was forced only to use two categories of beauty, she would have to call Bernice beautiful.

"I thought I'd keep it." Bernice folded her right hand around the rock in a fist, cozied her left hand across her right hand, the hands together resting on Bernice's leather skirt. Bernice looked toward the woods, her eyes randomly scanning the tree line.

Banelle heard a series of loud splashes from the river, Martee's characteristic short scream, and felt herself smile.

Banelle looked at the wood line also, at various individual trees, how dark the woods behind the trees in front were, how the foremost trees were catching the late afternoon Sun setting from beyond the curve of the river behind her, and admired the increasingly red-hued barks of the frontmost trees. She was quiet a few moments, then remembered what she was going to ask Bernice. "Are you in college?" Pulling her eyes away from the wood line, she looked at Bernice.

Bernice looked at Banelle unexpectedly quick, then looked down. Bernice raised her eyes to the tree line again. Bernice glanced at Banelle briefly. "No." Bernice looked down, feet shuffling, jumped onto the tailgate beside Banelle, started swinging her feet also. She looked at Banelle. "I want to go again, though."

Banelle glanced at Bernice's lips, then at her eyes. "Pursuing what?"

"Astrophysics." Bernice leaned toward Banelle, smiling, touched Banelle's right arm with the fingers of the left hand. "Just kidding." Bernice sat erect. "Mathematics, probably."

"What's holding you back?"

Bernice looked at Banelle.

"Ohhh, yeaahhh!" Dollar yelled from the river, Banelle felt the goose bumps, alarms of the lover touching, voice freshly wet from the river. Banelle sniffed, watching Bernice, felt herself smiling and shook her head back and forth slowly. She heard Martee's full-hearted laughter and clapping.

Bernice rolled her eyes and looked away, shook her head back and forth, canted her head, looked at Banelle, then looked down and patted the back of her right fist.

Banelle's smile relaxed. "So what's holding you back?"

Bernice shrugged, looked at the tree line. "Emotional support." Bernice looked at Banelle briefly.

Banelle wondered what that meant, then thought of her mom, how sometimes there didn't seem to be an end of the stream of criticisms. "Is it your mom?"

Bernice looked down at the ground, feet hanging still. "No. She's dead."

Banelle stopped swinging her feet, became quiet, fighting with the fear of losing her own mother. Banelle kissed the fear inside and spoke. "I'm sorry."

Banelle looked away, let her eyes wander across the red-hued tree line, shadows growing. Banelle looked at Bernice. "What about your father?"

Bernice shrugged, studying her own hands closed on her lap. She opened them, quiet, watching the rock lying there on the right palm. "My father went fundamentalist, about a year and a half after my mom died." Bernice wrapped her right hand around the rock, turning the clenched fist downward, and rested it on the right leg. "It's just so damn extreme, choosing ignorance."

———

Banelle felt herself shake her head, the feeling of knotted empathy.

"Yesss!" she heard Martee screech, and smiled.

Banelle looked at Bernice's eyes, staring away at the trail. "What does that have to do with emotional support for your going to college?"

Bernice slapped her left leg three times with the flat of her left hand, "I DON'T KNOW." bumped the right leg with the clenched fist of her right hand. Bernice looked sideways at Banelle, with eyes of pain.

Banelle and Bernice searched each other's eyes.

Bernice's eyes became moist. "I just wish he'd hug me once in a while. You know?" Bernice's chin sagged to the chest, the shoulders jerked, then jerked again.

Banelle felt herself sniff wetly, looked at the clenched fist, thought about how their day had been so far. She remembered seeing Bernice hug her father from behind while he was still sitting on the cement plaza putting the finishing touches on his art work, remembered her father wasn't even aware Bernice was near him when Bernice spontaneously hugged him.

Banelle remembered earlier in the day when they were first getting to know Bernice waitressing for them, remembering all the times Bernice had demurred regarding Dollar — how Bernice smiled for Dollar first, looked at him first, brought his things first. Banelle felt the jealousies revived, remembering those moments, then looked at the occasionally shaking shoulders and at what she could see of Bernice's face which wasn't covered by the short black hair falling forward. Banelle felt the revived jealousies twist with the new insights, then they transformed, becoming something which felt equally powerful.

Now these feelings reached out to hold Bernice protectively, instinctively riled because some unknown face who was supposed to be a father – she felt her eyes narrow – supposed to be a father for a young *woman*, who, despite her natural and striking beauty also looked so young Banelle had mistaken Bernice for a teenager. Banelle slid the palm of her right hand across Bernice's back, cupped her right hand around Bernice's far shoulder, pulled Bernice within this loving hug, cupped her left hand around Bernice's neck, accepted Bernice's head against her shoulder, felt Bernice surge from the crying, knot up, and surge again, felt Bernice's left hand cup around Banelle's left arm. Banelle caught the faint odor of pine, instinctively turned her eyes toward the tree line.

While holding Bernice, Banelle found her mind wandering. She watched the red hue on the trees, and found herself imagining Jayenne being hugged at that crying couch years ago. She felt compassion welling up, felt a grudging forgiveness for the father who should be hugging. It was complicated. *Maybe he thrashes himself with that memory like I have.* Banelle found herself hoping someday that father would have a chance again, whoever he was.

Banelle smiled, enjoying a moment of warmth reliving the day the five of them had been enjoying together. She thought about the two times she had tongue kissed Dollar so far, and pressed her knees together.

Banelle thought about the chalks, how Martee had been bare-assed close against Dollar the whole time. Banelle remembered him pulling Banelle upward from the concrete plaza – his eyes gazing powerfully within hers – pulling her erect to stand with him, then pulled her close, remembered herself feeling water in the eyelashes, how he had pulled her against himself in his refreshingly warm, loving hug. The kind of hug only her dad had previously been able to give her. *Like this hug.*

She looked at the reddening trees, feeling in this moment the happy smile around the eyes. Banelle wondered what the time was, realized with a start this day of uniqueness was a long way from over. They'd be dancing next, and the thought tripped her anxieties into a free fall, imagining she'd have to sit on a stool and watch Martee having all the fun with Banelle's father and Dollar. Bernice apparently enjoyed dancing also.

Banelle felt angst about looking foolish, in her mind wobbling like a clumsy office girl trying to dance in front of a crowd of judges, more afraid of foolishness than she was of seeming like a dead weight for her dad, imagined herself looking pointlessly foolish in those supportive eyes of his instead of relaxing into spontaneity.

Banelle looked at the coarse black hair of Bernice's head, feeling Bernice calm in her arms. "Bernice."

"Hmm?"

"Can you teach me to dance?"

"Oh!" Bernice freed herself from Banelle's hug, sat up and wiped her eyes. "Like, here?" Bernice spread the palm of her left hand.

Banelle felt herself nodding, smiled, lifting her eyebrows up and down. "I'm a chicken about flying, scared to death of dying, and horrified of making a fool of myself this evening." Banelle raised her eyebrows. "Know what I mean?"

Bernice scrunched her nose, smiling, shook her head back, then tilted her head forward, eyes shadowed with eyebrows. "Not a bit. Be glad to." Eyes closing, she began bobbing her head.

Banelle felt herself roll the eyes, nodded slightly several times, and watched Bernice. "You open all the doors. I'll get the CD pouch."

"Jazzed!" Bernice jumped off the tailgate, turned left around the back of the vehicle toward the passenger's side doors.

Banelle hopped off the tailgate, walked around to the driver's door, opened the door, reached across the seat of the SUV and retrieved the stiff black nylon pouch from the floorboard console. She pulled the pouch near, unzipped the pouch and started looking through the collection. *What to dance to?*

———

Banelle heard Bernice open the two passenger side doors while Banelle searched through CDs. Out of the corner of her eye, she saw Bernice walking around the front of the SUV while Bernice watched the other three down at the river splunking and skipping rocks. There was the sound of visiting between throws.

Bernice turned her attention toward Banelle and walked around the open driver's door and pushed in beside Banelle on the right. "Barry Manilow?" Bernice looked from the CD pouch toward Banelle, then at her lips. "Is he even alive?"

Banelle felt herself get warm. "My mother…" Banelle stopped herself telling a lie, how her mother gave the CD as a gift, which was true, but this wasn't about her mother. Banelle looked at Bernice's lips, looked within Bernice's eyes. "*He* is for me." Banelle felt this knowing shrug. "I hear the songs in my head." Banelle smiled, felt a sway of music. "I wish *I* wrote the songs." Banelle marveled how true this felt, and shrugged both shoulders again.

Bernice shook her head with wide eyes. "WELL," leaning nearer, "that's not dance music." Bernice looked at the case, her eyes scanning, her fingers helping flip pages. "What *are* these?" Bernice's eyes kept scanning CDs.

Banelle started to feel defensive. "What?"

"There's your dance problem. Look at all these! Here." Bernice pulled out a CD, and spun the jewel. "Yeah, play the Call Me song." Bernice handed the Tracy Chapman *Give Me One Reason* CD to Banelle. Bernice continued looking at Banelle, "It isn't dance music, per se. It has a fun groove for learning some shakin' on the river bottom, though."

Banelle felt herself laugh. "Ass shaking?"

"Yeah!" Bernice raised her hands, snapping fingers. Banelle felt Bernice's hip bump against Banelle's, felt her head fall back, her mouth smiling openly. Banelle pulled her head forward, still smiling, and bumped her hip against Bernice. "Call Me!"

Banelle slid the CD into the player, picked the keys off the floor, found the ignition key, pushed the key in and aligned the ignition with Accessory, mashed the CD play, then pressed the repeat song button, grabbed the volume and waited. The guitar bum-bum-bum-bum-PAH riff started, then Banelle cranked the volume until the music hurt her ears and she backed out of the SUV.

Bernice pulled the left-side passenger door open.

Banelle skipped around Bernice and went to stand higher on the slope behind the Black Menace, stood on the hard-packed dirt path in the shadow being cast by the setting red-ball Sun shimmering on ripples from the curve of the river.

Bernice danced near.

Banelle shrugged, tried swaying, feeling bashful about dancing with a younger dancer. There was so much that she didn't know about Bernice. Would Bernice think her silly?

"SHAKE." Bernice said, talking over the music. "MOVE." Then Bernice grabbed Banelle by both upper arms. Banelle laughed, feeling the push and pull of Bernice's full-hearted on-the-beat energy.

Banelle relaxed, began moving with the music. "I HAVEN'T DONE THIS IN YEARS."

"YOU SHOULD PRACTICE AT HOME, BUM-BUM-BY YOUR-SELF, GOT-CHA GOT-CHA GOT-CHA..."

Banelle remembered Jayenne's criticizing scowl when Banelle tried dancing at home with her daughters. She *knew* Boop would dance with her. *Maybe Boop and I will have a girl's dance night at home, without Jayenne around.* Banelle felt herself relax further.

"HEY." Bernice said.

"WHAT?"

"I'VE HEARD YOU CALLED B.B. AND ANNA..." Bernice changed up her dance moves, dipping and rolling her torso in a circle, bouncing the beat. "I DON'T KNOW WHAT TO CALL YOU."

Banelle thought about that, watching Bernice and trying to emulate the swaying and bouncing. She felt she was doing pretty well. "CALL ME ANNA."

"IS THAT YOUR NAME?"

Banelle shook her head, felt this nostalgic smile of old memories. "NO. PART I PLAYED. COLLEGE PLAY."

"Jazzed! SO, ANNA, PICK YOUR KNEES UP. UP! YES! NOW SHAKE YOUR ASS WITH YOUR FOOT UP." Bernice flipped the feathered hair, smiling openly, widely swinging the hips, Bernice's eyes on Banelle's body. "YEAH. YESSS. SUPERB!" Bernice waved her hands from breasts toward thighs, fingers fanning. "DESCRIBE YOUR CURVES."

Banelle copied, feeling bashful.

"YES. NOW. SCRUNCH YOUR FACE UP ON THIS CHORUS..."

Banelle felt the surprise of hands squeezing her hips, this screeammm! She turned around and found Dollar was right here. She felt the thrill of tingling, he was dancing with Banelle, his focus on Banelle's lower body, eyes narrow and intense, a shadowed smiling dancing man...

Banelle laughed, leaning back, right hand on cleavage, and kicked her right foot off the ground. Grounded again, she shook her ass feeling amorously wet, felt a beating pulse.

She stepped in close with him, danced at him, and bumped his body, wriggling her whole body. She scrunched her face at him when the favorite line came around, wriggled her breasts with the beat, leaned toward him pleasing herself, felt breasts brush back and forth against his chest, felt his hard jeans bump her pelvis three times with the beat. She reached around with her right hand and grabbed his ass.

selfishly dancing against his body

. . .

MARTEE WAS chair dancing to the beat. She took another sip of beer, enjoying the slow-swaying deep rumble music, felt the fizz on the tongue, the beat buzzing in her clit from a decent band on the far wall stage. The bar area was off to the right from the dance floor, exits through the crowd of tables on the left, and she was in no hurry to leave.

The dance bar was smoke-filled from a fog machine, people-filled, featured dark wood floors, a black loft ceiling and air ducts, and three glittery spinning lights showering the dancers with colored sparkles.

Martee was seated next to Dollar on tall chairs on one side of two square high tables end to end.

Banelle sat on Martee's right at the end of the two tables, facing down the length watching the dance floor. Martee noted Banelle was blissfully watching Banelle's father and Bernice dance slow, hugging each other. It annoyed Martee how Banelle seemed completely open with that.

Martee had gotten dances on the hardwood floor of the club, both with Dollar and with Anna's father, then the three women together while the guys chatted, and then danced by herself once because she was the only one of the group who liked a particular song and very few other people in the club were out dancing that time either.

Then the five of them had sat out a bunch of songs and talked about whatever came up, none of it memorable to quote except the five of them sharing time, which was very memorable.

Goddess, what a night! Martee watched Bernice with Anna's father. Bernice had gladly said, "Yes!" when he had asked her. Something about that was making Martee scowl, although she couldn't put her finger on the source of the disquiet at the moment.

Martee took another sip, beer bottle in right hand, while cupping her left hand on Dollar's leg. Her doing so wasn't the first time during the evening. After she had startled him with her touch a first time, he seemed welcoming. She liked the feeling of his closeness. Her hand had been on his leg quite often the last couple hours.

Banelle generally seemed content and pleased and happy. Martee wondered about that again. It wasn't like Martee had stopped flirting. Martee felt her own smile, afterglowing from having gotten Dollar out on the floor for more than one slow dance, rubbing herself all over him, feeling how hard Martee made him, selfishly dancing against his body. She felt her hand slide up his inner thigh to feel again the closeness of his heat on the back of her hand. "(Grrr.)" Martee murmured, aware of the growing sense of closeness with him.

Martee looked again at Anna's father and Bernice. There must be thirty years' difference, give or take a few, not that he looked particularly old, just her knowing how experienced he was. And of course everyone in their group knew Bernice was twenty-one.

Or so Bernice had said.

Martee looked at her collection of six empty beer bottles. *Glad I'm not driving!* She rubbed her hand forward-and-back on the inside of Dollar's thigh.

He looked at her.

Martee set her beer on the table freeing her right hand, leaned her left cheek against his right shoulder and blew him an air kiss.

He puckered an air kiss back at her, then he looked at Banelle briefly, and turned his attention toward the dance floor. Martee felt his right hand settle on her left wrist on the inside of his thigh, felt his fingertips lightly brush the length of the back of her longer fingers.

Martee touched her right palm and fingers on the bare part of her inner right thigh, the smell and feel of Dollar's shoulder on her cheek. She tunneled her thumb inside the right leg of her shorts and brushed her secret self in time with Dollar's fingertips stroking her left hand, glowing wet, wishing in the moment his pants were off so she could just feel the hairy naked skin of his thigh instead of jeans, and smell him more directly. In the fantasy she imagined his hands removing her sporty red shorts in his jerking impatience.

The music climaxed, resolved. She felt herself shudder. There was light clapping.

Martee moved her right hand to her right knee and sat erect. She watched Anna's father leading Bernice's very happy smiling face back toward their group's two tables. Martee was fleetingly aware of a subtle aroma reminiscent of dark cool pine forests, then the notion floated away while she focused her eyes intently on Bernice being led by Anna's father arriving at their tables.

Martee grabbed the nearly empty seventh bottle of beer with her right hand and drained the mouthful left, felt the frizzy lukewarm liquid on her tongue, slightly sweet with a hoppy after-bite. She set the bottle down, swallowed, breathed in deeply and squeezed Dollar's thigh twice with her left hand. She sighed and squeezed again. Martee bunched her right hand and propped her chin on her fist, resting her right elbow on the tabletop.

Anna's father helped Bernice into Bernice's chair opposite Martee, his left hand cupped under her right hand balancing her as she got situated. Not that Bernice needed any help. Bernice was smiling widely and openly.

There was a twinge inside Martee. She felt her eyes get round. *Am I… JEALOUS?* Such an intense feeling! The shock, Martee was *never* jealous of anything!

Anna's father sat down across from Dollar, looked at Martee, winked the right eye, and smiled.

"Hey!" Martee heard on her left, not recognizing the voice. "OLD MAN."

———

Martee turned her head left and leaned forward to see where the voice came from.

There was a younger man six feet from their tables, unkempt clothing, looking with an angry glare at Anna's father.

Martee glanced at Anna's father, saw a hardness in his eyes and countenance which she almost never saw. He hadn't turned his eyes from Martee.

She looked again at the intruder, to see why she felt the young man was badly dressed. He had an overly worn shiny black leather jacket, unzipped, with one side nearer the floor than the other, because it may have been torn. Underneath the jacket he wore a tattered white T-shirt on with a faded local band name, then blue jeans with large oil-stained dark areas and abrasions, scuffed work boots, and a belt which hung sloppily long, drooping away and downward from the buckle.

Martee looked at Anna's father. He wasn't looking at Martee anymore, his focus was on the intruder.

"You, THINK?" he said.

Martee felt the strength suddenly alive in Dollar's leg and there was a suddenness of movement from his leg. "I'm not an old man," Dollar said, in what she had come to think of as Dollar's Tarzan voice, the sound of his words reverberating off the low dark wood ceilings in the local part of the bar.

Martee noticed there was another young man, similarly dressed, standing behind the first.

"I'm not talkin' to you," said the first young man, looking at Dollar.

"YOU ARE." boomed Dollar. Other eyes at other tables turned to the scene.

Anna's father and Dollar exchanged a glance. Anna's father looked at the intruder.

After a moment watching Anna's father, Dollar returned his attention on the intruder.

"What are you fired up about?" Anna's father said.

"You," said the young man.

Anna's father's countenance was harsh and composed. "There's a lot about me which you don't see," an edge on his voice which she had never heard before.

Martee felt her eyes widen.

"So?" the young man said.

"So?" Banelle's father said, uncannily imitating the sarcasm of the young man, and then his voice was completely his own. "What is it that you *do* see that bothers you?"

The young man was quiet for a moment, his eyes steady, glaring. "I'm sick of seeing old men dating younger chicks."

There was a pause.

Martee looked at Anna's father, then took a quick glance at Banelle on her right. Banelle was angry. Martee glanced at Bernice across from her, saw how Bernice — beautiful Bernice! — was leaning back and staying out of view, watching the back of Anna's father's head. Martee looked at his ear, at his face, at how erect he sat and immovable-looking. He stepped off the tall chair.

Martee pulled her hand off Dollar's leg with a sharp inhale, felt the palm of her left hand nervously rubbing the bare skin of her left thigh.

Dollar hadn't moved, except to swivel his barstool to put his full attention on the intruder, and she had a sense of instant potency held in check by the merest of whiskers, like a rat trap's quirky unbendable copper trigger.

Anna's father stepped close to the young man, and stopped. "NOT that this can ever be your business…"

"You're in my space, old man," warned the intruder.

"…One of these three beautiful women…" and here he canted his head and pointedly looked at the young man's clothes with disdain while he spoke, then looked in the young man's eyes "...is my daughter."

The young man opened his mouth...

Anna's father continued immediately. "The second is a friend of my family whose nose I used to wipe and who hasn't found a man who's WORTH A SHIT." Martee jumped, seeing his body bounce with unexpected energy with the last three words.

...The intruder closed his mouth and glared at him.

"The THIRD is MY WIFE."

"WHICH one?" said the young man.

"THAT," Anna's father said, "is definitely NOT your FUCKING BUSINESS."

The two men stared at each other, Anna's father and the young man.

"Hey." said the second young man, slapping his buddy's arm, sound of leather. "Told you it was a bad idea."

Martee felt herself jump with the slight sound, and clutched the edge of the table tensely with her right hand.

"What?" said the first, not relenting in his glaring.

"Let it go, man," said the second, who was turning his head, watching the other people in the immediate area who were now watching the scene.

"NO." Anna's father said.

There was a look of self-doubt about the intruder's eyebrows. The second young man snapped his head from looking around, brought his attention back on Anna's father. The second young man looked even more unsettled than the first, who was still for the most part glaring in the countenance, although he apparently had now been taken past his own script.

"What I meant..." began the second.

"Where do you work?" Anna's father said, continuing to stare at the first young man.

She saw the young man waver, and how he immediately regrouped, yet something in the air had changed even though the hostilities remained.

"Like you said," he spouted, "none of your business."

"You're not working."

The young man shifted his weight, then he centered himself again. The young man looked like he wanted to say something, but didn't have anything prepared or rehearsed in front of mirrors which could be said, so he was simply glaring.

"Any of you ladies feel like dating this unemployed young man?" Anna's father said, keeping his attention on the intruder.

———

Martee felt her head shake emphatically, watching the events unfold.

The young man glanced at her briefly, noticing. Then he looked at Anna's father, and narrowed his eyes briefly, then looked presumably at Bernice, whom Martee saw out of the corner of her eye was shaking her head sadly, eyebrows up. Martee glanced at the young man. All this was happening very quickly.

Almost as quickly, Martee heard Banelle's voice on her right, loud and clear. "Oh, Goddess, no!" the divine bell of doom.

Martee felt herself cringe.

There was an end of all conversation in this side of the club, dying a gasping death immediately. Martee's searching eyes took in shocked and cringing faces. Martee turned her head and looked at Banelle.

Banelle was glaring at the intruder, her eyes lidded, her neck vital and elongated, her head tilted back slightly. The look of scorn which she focused on the young man agreed completely in volume to her voice and in the untouchable, unreachable beauty in the clarity of her icy words just decreed for all attending the scene.

Many new heads in the crowd turned on hearing the decree to see who spoke and saw that beautiful woman regarding the unpleasant reality of some unlucky man. The eyes of those new heads turned again, following the line of Banelle's discriminating gaze, and fastened themselves in blinking stares upon the intruder.

Martee felt the shiver, turned her attention on the young man. His eyes had changed from hard and glaring to merely angry and brimming with a slight hue of facial features.

Holy shit, Martee thought.

The intruder was fidgeting, his eyes seeing in glances the rejection of all three women.

"Let's go," said the buddy, slapping the young man's arm and looking around at the growing interest.

"NO." Anna's father said, continued staring at the young man. "How much money were you pulling down at your last job?"

"None of your…" began the young man.

Anna's father nodded impatiently. "HOW MUCH?"

The young man fidgeted. His eyes searched Anna's father's face.

"Twelve an hour," said the young man, spitting out the words.

Anna's father's head nodded slightly several times, his eyes on the intruder. "Education?"

The young man shifted his weight slightly, then re-centered himself. "Two years of college."

"Plans to finish? Would you resume if your employer paid for some of your classes?"

The young man fidgeted more, and glanced at Martee. His eyes started glancing at Banelle, then quickly averted them. He narrowed his eyelids briefly, then openly stared at Anna's father. He cast his eyes down slightly and immediately glared at Anna's father again, steadily. "Never had an offer like that." He looked off toward his left, and looked back at Anna's father. "Why're you asking?" fidgeting.

Anna's father didn't answer for a moment. He took a deep, deciding breath. "Because I'm a profitable judge of character. Don't tell yourself you are anything like I was at two years of college, because you wouldn't believe yourself." He pulled his wallet out of his pocket, pulled a business card out of his wallet, looked at the card momentarily, then handed the card toward the young man.

The young man didn't move.

The buddy slapped his arm, sound of leather. "Take the card."

The young man took the card. "What's this?"

"Call my human resources lead," Anna's father said. "They'll check you out. If you're worth a shit like my gut tells me you will be after you get some hands on experience, then my H.R. Director will decide where she wants to put you, and for how much. Bring your friend there. Maybe he can keep your hindquarters out of other trouble. Questions?"

Martee realized she'd heard that manner of talk from a high school principal she'd known in younger days.

The young man was reading the card. "Who am I saying sent me?"

Anna's father didn't answer, simply loomed with the same mountain-hard air which he'd had from the young man's first words. He looked at the second young man and pursed his lips in disapproval.

"Hey," said the buddy, "maybe they're special cards."

"What a clue." quipped Anna's father.

Martee wondered why he wasn't already coaching football.

The young man looked at him. The anger the young man had been exuding was still there, though conflicted, his feet rooted on the spot.

"Let's go," said the buddy, and this time the buddy had a fistful of leather collar and was pulling persistently. "Don't fuck up another opportunity for us." The buddy's eyes glanced at Anna's father, gave a nod, then focused on the young man, pulling harder.

The young man, angry and glaring, watched Anna's father until his turning body couldn't allow his head's turning so far. Then he turned around completely and followed his buddy through the parting crowd.

Anna's father watched them go, not moving, stillness exuding from the mountains, mist from the dance floor swirling at their feet.

The crowd folded together behind where the pair had walked away, eyes watching the retreat, the voices of the crowd renewed.

Finally, Anna's father turned clockwise and stepped back toward the table, his eyes unfocused in thought, the countenance hard. He climbed onto his chair. When he was situated, his eyes cleared. He interlaced his fingers, smiled, returned his attention with present-moment alacrity to the five-some. He looked Dollar in the eyes.

Dollar was watching him intently. He swiveled his chair square with the tables again. "If they don't fit the business plan at your place, have their applications sent over my way."

Martee was suddenly aware of an aroma, eyebrows tensed momentarily, in her inner ears the sound of wolves converging, yips, brushing feel of dark forested pine trees welling up within her inner landscape, strong in the nose.

Anna's father nodded firmly once.

"They need some of those rough edges ground off." Dollar added.

Martee watched Dollar. She realized with a ringing snap of clarity in the left ear he was one of the very few truly handsome men in the world, marveled how she hadn't noticed that before. She pulled her eyes from looking at him and scanned the faces of men in the crowd, none of whom seemed to notice her looking at them. She felt herself reacting internally at the sight of each of them, something bordering on nausea, which, she realized was not the way she normally looked at men. There were usually so many opportunities.

———

Martee felt more like retching as she glanced around.

In her mind she saw again the faces of the two intruders, felt in her gut now the same powerful revulsion she had heard Banelle enunciate crisply and loudly minutes before.

"Correct." Martee heard Anna's father say, sighing. "We need a national military draft, to refine the blunt edges of the knives coming out of high school."

Martee's attention was attracted back upon Anna's father by the rich winter-fires chocolate-feel of his voice. She looked at him, though she didn't consciously notice, except in a fleeting joyous girls-playing laughter inside her mind, how glad she felt to be instantly free of the revulsion she had been feeling a moment before when scanning the faces of the other men in the crowd near their table.

Anna's father's countenance relaxed. He looked at the table, then he looked at Martee. She felt from his gaze a strange connection with him, a secure feeling carrying many complex threads, like a sturdy blanket inherited from a great-grandfather passed down through the generations. He then turned and looked steadily at Banelle.

Martee continued looking at him and marveled how he represented so much warmth to her. Such a contrast, she felt, from the dauntless weathered giant he was a few moments ago. She could still see that there, also. She had felt the same inspirational awe while visiting the Rockies years ago. Her eyes looked at his shoulders, traveled across the breadth of his chest, came back toward his neck, and followed his jawline. Martee saw the peaceful centeredness reflected in the calm of his cheeks and eyes, and thought how much she would have enjoyed having a father like Banelle has.

Martee's eyes became a startled-bird flurry of eyelashes, her eyes fixed on his eyes which were currently gazing at Banelle, then Martee felt her eyes become round like Moon rise, feeling a quake in her stomach, the spasm of her legs… "(Charlie.)" Martee whispered, before she realized consciously her lips were even parted. She put her right palm over her mouth quickly and her eyes darted to see if Dollar had noticed her whispering — Dollar was watching Charlie at the moment.

Charlie turned his head farther left, to look steadily at Bernice.

Bernice smiled briefly, and her lips became impassive just that quickly.

Martee turned her head right and looked at Banelle, discovering Banelle was already quietly watching Martee.

Before Martee could think, she said, "Oh!" loudly within her hand over her mouth and it sounded like a small animal had gotten thumped by a brick. Banelle had been channeling the Scorn of the Goddess just minutes ago.

"Sorry you girls had to watch that kind of bloodshed," Martee heard Charlie say, the words resonant, his tones calling her tingly spine with chocolate promises of deep pleasure, dripping caramel in her secret self, Moon tides pulling at Martee's breasts to feel his experienced hands, blouse buttons popping free, gumdrops tingling for his chocolate flavored tongue.

Bernice exhaled sharply through the nose.

Martee could only peripherally see Bernice because Banelle had Martee's entire focus at the moment. Banelle really was the beautiful queen, Martee realized. Not what Martee always wished to believe Banelle was, the dumpy turtle safe in its shell in a world filled with the elephant's thickly raised trunk.

Banelle was simply and quietly watching Martee, Banelle's recent icy regality currently gone and a certain soft mistiness was in Banelle's face while she held Martee's eyes.

"Jazzed!" Martee heard Bernice say, and there was a soft slapping sound which followed a blur in the periphery of Martee's eyes as Bernice's hand playfully slapped Charlie's shoulder. Everyone at the table laughed except Martee, who watched Banelle loosen into laughing, eyes closing, the queenly mouth opening prettily in a happy release.

Martee heard Dollar's laughter, a sound like rich, strong leather furniture. Martee was feeling shock, too alarmed by the revelation of Charlie to enjoy the joke Bernice and…

"(Charlie.)" Martee's lips whispered.

…had made, and with Banelle's laughing, her eyes completely shut, Martee was able to pull her own eyes away. Martee looked immediately at that man across the table from her.

Charlie was watching Martee. He smiled warmly for her when Martee turned her eyes back to his. His eyes were merry and thoughtful, the face she had habitually and previously overlooked — so handsome. Martee felt powerfully compelled to put her palms around his head, to touch his ears softly with her thumbs, to pull his lips closer for kissing his…

Martee blocked the imagery with panic, clenching her legs beneath the table with both hands, covering and pressing her knees together. She felt a shock which rode over all these observations, felt her head shake slightly, and here was an epiphany: however long the letters of his name had been kept secreted, she had to push the name out of her mind again. "(Anna's father.)" Martee whispered.

He continued to gaze at Martee. She couldn't meet his gaze any longer, lowered her eyes to his hands on the table.

"So, where are you two love birds going on your honeymoon?" she heard Dollar say.

Martee felt her eyes grow round.

"Oh!" she heard Bernice say. "We'll go to Bermuda…"

"(ANNA's father.)" Martee reminded herself.

She heard him chuckling, her eyes on his chin, the happy toothy smile.

"…and then up to Tripoli."

"Tripoleeeee?" Martee heard Banelle say, then heard Banelle's happy, beautiful laughter.

Martee felt Dollar's hand touch Martee's left hand on her knee. She felt startled.

"Oh, yes!" Martee heard Bernice say, laughing. She saw movement at the periphery of her vision where Bernice was swaying aboard an imaginary ship.

Martee grabbed Dollar's forearm and clutched his arm against her body with a spasm, his hand accidentally pulled between her thighs. Martee didn't care. She just needed to feel his arm clutched against her body. She felt his hand between her legs and that helped her look down, steadily fighting her eyes downward from the strong desire to reengage with Charlie's eyes, forcing herself to look down, insistently: *Look down!* Willfully. Look. Down. Martee finally was able to pull her eyes completely from…

———

"(ANNA's FATHER'S eyes.)" Martee whispered as she looked at Dollar's arm, clutching that, squeezing his hand between her thighs, saving herself from a vertigo she couldn't remember ever feeling before. Her breaths came in short shallow intense runs, her hands squeezing his forearm with pulsing. Martee felt Dollar's leather-smelling handsomeness there, treasured his arm and hand strongly as she could, willing the spin to stop, barely an antidote for the powerful desire she felt to fuck that other man…

"(*ANNA's* father.)" Martee reminded herself in a whisper.

Martee willed herself to stare at the handsomeness of Dollar's strongly muscled arm, kept her eyes fixed on the ripple of his sinews as he turned his palm and fingers to cup the inside of her left thigh, squeezed her thighs around his hand…

Presently the room stopped spinning. She realized consciously how strongly she had been squeezing Dollar's forearm. Martee's eyes made short side trips up his arm, feeling her head turn slightly, then feeling her eyes casting downward along his arm where her eyes were safer from seeing…

"(*Anna's* father.)"

Martee allowed herself a few cursory trips visually farther up Dollar's arm, practicing her focus before she could glance at Dollar's gray eyes, and then only for a moment. Her eyes raced back down his arm, bending her head downward…

Try.

She looked more fully at Dollar's eyes.

"(Are you all right?)" Dollar said quietly, his head leaning closer to her face.

She nodded slightly in rapid succession, smiled briefly and blinked her moist eyes, feeling heard.

Martee relaxed her right hand and slid her palm along his forearm to clutch the crook of his elbow. She snuggled his arm against herself, then she realized what she was doing she had seen some mothers do snuggling their newborns. The realization didn't change how she snuggled his arm. She just appreciated the secure feeling he brought her at the moment was profoundly what she needed. She didn't release her left hand clenching his wrist, either. She kept his hand snug against her pelvis securely between her thighs, the strength of his hand snugly against the desire, here.

However beautiful, however handsome, however outstanding that knight commissioned as her escort, however overwhelming Dollar's incredible handsomeness was at the moment, the desire in the pelvis was for…

Martee stopped the name from emerging in her thoughts, the

chocolate winter fires image of kissing and intimacy, then the blink of nothing.

Martee smiled for Dollar, holding the smile meekly. She blinked her upturned moist eyes for him, hopefully showing him she couldn't explain she was deeply and profoundly glad he could be here for her. While at the moment she couldn't say the obvious concerning his extremely handsome features, his leonine heart, his protective spirit, she wanted him to know she had given her love over to him. She hoped he could see from her wobbly smile that what she held with Dollar was a new love she wanted to deepen. Martee felt herself press her lips together, felt the happiness around her moist eyes. She was just a bit busy at the moment facing down an old love.

Finally, she felt Dollar's hand squeeze her inner thigh reassuringly and felt sparkles of starlight. He returned his attention away, visiting with the others.

Martee continued to watch Dollar's face, or she watched his arm, or she watched her own arm snuggled around his. Or again, she watched his neck, his ear, the way he tipped his head back for a laugh, felt the way he bounced when he chuckled like an equestrian when the horse is set for a chortling trot. Then she would watch the edge of the table and try to tune in, trying to understand the others' visiting, yet her mind retreated every time her emotions came close to identifying who the others were by names, except that one man.

Dollar, Martee would whisper in her mind every time to keep her focus, and then she would snuggle his arm tight as before, clutch his wrist against her pelvis with her left hand, squeeze her thighs feeling breezes before the rain.

Martee did not visit with the rest of the group for the rest of the evening, because, for the meanwhile, for the moment-by-moment, she could only know Dollar's arm in her awareness or lose herself again to the vertigo; to focus with all her will on the sense of Dollar's being here, for her.

magick of a very real love potion

. . .

DEEP DOWN IN Martee's sense of herself, in the moment she remembered with a rush of years Charlie was not just Anna's wonderful father, Martee felt the vertigo of free fall and the descent through the nighttime of her inner vision, landed with bare feet on the cool dew-covered grassy shadows of a glade in a redolent pine forest, recognized the smell of musty pine thick within the nostrils, thicker than she had ever smelled her own pines before, knew the exaggerated fragrance for what that was: the magick of a very real love potion.

Echo in the mind. *The effects last until the willfulness of Sol returns. Those who inhale from the potion will see any love which has been hidden, and if a love is discovered unrequited, the power of desire is redoubled and redoubled again until requited.*

Martee had felt during the fall how the orange-hued horizon toward the west had within the glowing a threat of an imminent rise in Moon energy, and the Portent carried powerful erotic childbearing yearnings.

There was an icy-blue, intensely bright star in that part of the sky. Martee knew that star was the real source of the threat she felt, the source of the potion itself. She knew the impending shift in Moon energy was the threat's consummation. She knew with all her soul she must flee immediately, while also feeling no strength in her limbs at all.

Her lands were not the star's lands, mind you. She recognized them as her own from her own frequent, happy travels and adventures here, smelled their familiarity, heard her own familiar lands' night sounds.

She knew she had friends here.

She gathered the strength, and yelled, *NIGHT WOOOOOLVES!* and Martee's inner voice lingered loudly.

She was answered almost immediately by two howls, one toward her left and south, the other north on the right, and the animals were very close.

The howl from the west ahead of her added to the chord of the other two before her own call was finished, from deep within the woods dark below the star.

Two dark forms came running on their wolves' legs upon the clearing on either side of her. When they got near, they turned as she was and stood guard on either side. They growled, each of them in their turns, voicing their feelings, sensing the threat posed for their mistress.

There was the yip-and-bark in the wood line a hundred yards in front of her. Finally, the dark form of the third wolf came bounding out under the starlight. Upon seeing her, he redoubled the run and flew, tail shifting from small circles one way then the other, keeping the balance accelerating across the glade, then tail horizontal behind.

When the third wolf arrived, Martee held out her right palm. The third wolf stuck the cold nose within her hand happily. Sensing her apprehension, the third wolf turned to face the west with the others, the three of them together with her, and she felt a thick furry tail slap her bare shins twice.

She looked down, saw how she was fully naked, felt the completeness of her vulnerability. Having her night wolves near helped considerably, and she drew some courage against the long task ahead.

Outrun the Moon.

Martee drew in a deep breath and yelled, "SOUL LOVERRRrrr!" and she waited, knowing how even the fastest of manly legs weren't as fast as the wolves had been. After a time, she heard the pound-pound of running feet drawing near behind her and stop. Heard the heavy, manly breathing in her ears, felt his heavy exhale on her neck.

Quickly! Martee said, *I cannot move! Carry me to our ship! We must outrun this change of Moon!*

The Soul Lover moved around in front of her, ducked, a strong shoulder against her torso, and arms around her thighs scooped her aloft. She watched the western skyline, how that seemed to throb with the orange glow. She felt vertigo, felt dizziness, felt buffeted in the running.

The wolves turned and ran guard in weaving lines behind her. They ran together swiftly off the glen through the nose-filling pine woods for a long while, then across a beach, sloshing within gradually deepening waters swirling below, wetness splashing the souls of her feet and toes, knees, and fingertips. Then, with feet pounding on a wood gangway and wolves' paws clattering and scrabbling, she was carried higher and onto a dark wooden deck, the smells of the sea about.

Martee found herself set on her feet near the main mast. She grabbed the mast with both arms and pulled herself around the mast, feeling it between her thighs.

She was distracted by the sudden warmth, movement, and strength of the mast, and broke her gaze from the horizon. She looked up the grainy wood of the main mast, in gradually farther views, and finally when her eyes had traveled toward the very top, she saw Dollar's face like a vision, strong, in a hazy hole in the black night sky.

He smiled, and she heard him call to her, was she doing all right?

She wanted to answer, knew he couldn't hear her from her universe, so she smiled, hoping he would see the gratitude and felt the moisture in her eyes. She drew courage from his being there, and set her heart to endure the task ahead.

Now. *Sail!* Martee commanded. *I will fight the Goddess magick with my own, but I am not strong enough to fight so close to the western sky where the star rules on this night. Sail!*

She clutched the warm mast with her arms, sliding her right arm higher than her left, pulled her left hand down low for leverage to keep the pelvis firmly safe against the powerful call, the thighs firmly snuggled around that safety.

She knew the danger posed by the desire was most insistent here, and she instinctively felt the mast was her only chance while she fought against the unexpected turn of the Goddess' magick.

The ship turned away from the west, slowly at first. Then Martee commanded the winds. Soon, there were foam caps on the freshened waves. She changed its coming from the west so the wind blew from the southwest, strong and soulful warm, angling the wind to move her sailing ship faster.

The strong winds grabbed the sails heavily, listing the ship. She felt the wind's surges and choppy vibration in the mast. The crew of forty-two men which manned the Night Ship cheered with hearty masculine voices when the wind fully caught the sails and the lurching ship found her new bearing.

Martee knew the Soul Lover was at the wheel, steering their true course. The wolves on her right and left lay down on the deck, ears alert. The third wolf sat in front of her, eyes watching the western horizon.

Clinging to the mast, the mist from the freshened waves softly falling occasionally on Martee's naked body. She felt the slow rhythmic list, a sigh of the big ship in the quickening waves, and she took time to regroup.

———

Martee remembered now the mutual realization with…

Anna's father.

…fourteen years ago, simply a truth which they both had come to recognize and not the resurging, long-buried, magick-evoked desire which now was upon her with all the vengeance of the long-frustrated years of denial.

Martee also remembered Banelle hadn't been emotionally ready to accept the reality about the best friend and the father. And still wasn't, Martee knew.

The situation was worsened a year later when Banelle's mother and father executed their divorce, and Banelle had required more emotionally from her father than before.

The divorce had shocked Martee, also, because by then Martee had pushed the truth out of her awareness. He had not been available legally, and Martee liked Banelle's mother and father, both of them. Nothing had happened between herself and…

Anna's father.

…as Martee persisted in calling him, willfully.

She had seen right away fourteen years ago how nothing practical could conceivably happen, and shortly after the simple truth of the soul love had surfaced Martee had found the inspiration for, created, and soon used consistently the Forget-the-Man chant, well-embedded in her emotional life months before Anna's father had begun dissolution proceedings.

Over the years, she had even forgotten why she had created the chant, and so the chant fell into disuse.

Martee wondered if the spell would work again now, yet in renewing her clutch on the wind-driven mast in both arms and legs, anchoring herself from the nearly overwhelming waves of desire and gusts of soulful connectedness, Martee knew there was no way in hell the presently flaccid chant would gather the chant's full strength. For Martee, chants drew strength from consistently repetitive use across many Moon cycles, and then they became incredibly powerful in her hands and on her tongue.

She felt a brief smile recalling how the early chant was a fond chant of hers: the First Chant, she remembered now. Martee had begun in earnest her journey as an Independent Wiccan. She doubted the chant's current power because the chant had dropped from renewal long ago.

There just wasn't time for everything, and her excitement and quickly deepening journey within the Independent Wiccan experience had enthralled her and kept her increasingly busy with new insights.

Martee wondered how thoroughly the desire for…

Anna's father.

…had been hidden by her own magick compared to the surging power of the Goddess' spell. Martee held a deep fondness for the first spell, the principal spell, the spell of her initiate self-training. Might there also be a hidden reservoir from fourteen years ago of the spell's potency within herself?

Martee determined to try the chant, speak the words inside the vision. As she began to recite, the vengefully-awakened desire spiked her chanting words with oddly timed surges while she uttered the syllables now under the dark starry skies of the mind:

Forget the Man.
   Old WHAT's-his-name
   What's that NAME?!
   Was that a man, or a woman?
   With THIS breath THAT forgets,
   something known is gone,
   hundreds of susurrations
   in whispered meetings fading.
   Who sees WHAT gorgeously naked?
   What IS she chanting?
   Such words brought together NOW!
   A Mirror of Freedom!
   KISS depression,
   this new feeling accepting.

Martee felt the renewed chant had worked enough to get the man's name off her tongue; to keep, for the moment, her speaking that name accidentally, to keep such a name, whatever it had been, from inflaming the resurgent waves of desire for...

Martee smiled, accepting herself.

She wondered what else she could do. She hugged harder, pressing her pelvis against the warm mast, felt the chill damp from the foaming waves, felt the soft falling baby mist on her naked body, soft as feathers stroking her skin, felt the tug of the Soul Wind against the mast's sails, felt the wind's gusts pull at her hair, saw the wind in the tufts on the furs of her wolves.

The wolf on her left was watching her, concern within the amber eyes.

Martee looked at the icy blue-white star above the horizon, gradually sinking. She knew the star Goddess by name.

Venus.

Martee felt her eyes narrow in focused admiration, feeling a stubborn willfulness she was born with. *Not THIS night, Venus!* Martee wondered how Venus could be so close to the horizon with such a rising of Moon energy?

Venus never wandered far from Sol. With Venus bright in the west and Sol already darkening below the horizon, orange colors fading fast, then where was the Moon?

Martee could feel powerfully how the Goddess of Consummation was on the rise, yet where was the reflected sunshine?

Then Martee remembered: it was a New Moon weekend, when for three nights and three days the Moon was Dark, racing to her lover Sol. She knew now the Moon was someplace below Venus' clearly laughing voice, sea waves heavy with adoration, scorn slapping the sides of the ship.

Unless... Martee felt her eyes get wide, felt her hopes weighed down heavily. *The Dark of the Moon!* Martee remembered the Spring Eclipse was upon them, when the Goddess of Consummation seduces in totality the entirety of Sol's will and self-expression

Shit, Martee whispered, and renewed her grasping the mast. They were in a solar eclipse event: the course of lives were changing, pregnant with opportunities, the seeds of wills were being captured, inevitably gestating toward fruition.

The Black Moon.

The urge to fuck was overwhelming.

The wolf on her right began growling long and low.

Martee knew consciously now the Will of Sol, which could neutralize the love potion, was passionately absorbed in the Moon's titillating embrace, unavailable to cancel the Goddess' spell.

Martee became aware of the smell of the three wolves, how the normally woodsy, lusty musk of running through grasses and leaves was pungent with an acrid odor of seawater in their fur, how blending with the musk there was also a tang of pine in the wafting odors of her gorgeous wild wolves, the bell chime laughter of the Goddess Venus in Martee's mind.

A lot was at stake, and not just for herself. Martee filled her lungs deeply with the pungent, pine-hued tangy vitality of the wolves' immediacy and closeness.

One happily-ever-after was already fourteen years past due, the amount of time necessary for the Goddess of Fashion to change her mood. That now out-of-fashion happily-ever-after would not be aligned again for another one hundred sixty-eight years, and even then other cycles were at play, a window missed. Martee felt some hope rise in her heart. She just needed to ride out the weekend without fucking a love no longer in fashion. The window would finally be closed.

Only magnificent lights cast magnificent shadows. Martee knew what strengths were in the shadows cast by her capacity to love. She needed paranormal help to resolve the Goddess spell. To whom could she turn?

A name came to mind.

Let it be so.

she slipped from the chair
at his pull

. . .

BANELLE LOOKED at the seven empty bottles in front of Martee. Martee hadn't let the waitress take any away.

Banelle noticed in the periphery the watching stares of various men in the surging, laughing crowd of the noisy dance bar. The flashing eyes came from the undesirably gray, packed crowd of men and women in the bar. The band was on break.

Banelle watched Martee. Something was wrong. *Seven drinks in three hours*, Banelle's resolute voice intoned. She sensed something *that* wrong wasn't the alcohol, though. Banelle could remember a number of occasions over the many years of their friendship where more than a few drinks had been consumed and Martee had never clutched at any man's arm like she was doing with Dollar's arm now.

Banelle looked at him. Was he doing anything to encourage Martee with his arm, his hand? Banelle leaned left discretely, pretending she was simply getting more comfortable, and took a quick look around the left edge of the table.

Martee's thighs were wrapped tightly around Dollar's hand and Martee was clinging onto his arm, but it didn't look like Dollar was doing anything actively.

Banelle sat erect and looked down at the table. Her fingers

fidgeted, she felt her eyes narrow, and glanced sideways at Martee. Then Banelle looked steadily at Dollar. If he was doing anything, by the sureness of hell it didn't show in his face. He was pleasantly visiting with her father, with Bernice, and with herself.

Banelle looked steadily at Martee's face, feeling more than a little annoyed with not being able to catch Martee's eye for the recent twenty minutes.

There were no moments of pleasure crossing Martee's strained features. A feat, Banelle felt, which couldn't be accomplished after seven beers. *In only three hours!* added Banelle's resolute voice. Was Martee enjoying herself?

Banelle gazed levelly at her father until he looked at her, chuckling from something just said in conversation. "Dad, maybe we should go."

Her father nodded, still grinning, and he glanced briefly at Martee, then at Dollar, then at Bernice, then looked back at Banelle. "Duly noted." He looked at Dollar again. "Everybody ready?"

"Yes." Banelle heard Bernice say.

Dollar nodded, then Dollar looked with concerned eyes at Martee.

Martee simply clutched Dollar's arm.

Banelle slipped left off the tall chair and stood with a clear, uninterrupted view of Martee clinging to Dollar's arm.

She watched him lean his head near Martee with concern on his face. He stepped part way off the tall chair, and pulled his arm, like pulling slowly on a wooden spoon stuck inside bread dough, with Martee physically sliding on the barstool.

He finished stepping off the tall chair. Martee clung tightly onto his arm without looking at him, relinquishing only the grip her legs had on his hand as she slipped from the chair at his pull, then stood unsteadily, as near to Dollar as Martee could get, bumping against him with eyes down.

Dollar glanced at Banelle, then turned his attention back upon Martee, flexing his hand in the air below Martee's arms. Dollar leaned his head nearer to Martee. "Are you all right? Martee?"

Martee looked shyly at him, the unsteady smile and grateful eyes, then Martee returned her unfocused gaze toward the floor.

Banelle walked around Martee and Dollar while he was backing away from the tables a step, clearing himself and Martee of the chairs, and Banelle cozied near on the other side of Dollar. She wrapped her hands around his left arm above the elbow and pulled on his arm until he bent toward her. She put her lips near his ear. "(What the hell's wrong with Martee?)"

He straightened up enough to look into each of Banelle's eyes. "(I don't know. Has she ever acted this way before?)"

Banelle wanted to say, *Hell yes!* Instead, Banelle felt herself shake her head vigorously. "(No.)"

He looked at Banelle's lips, then within Banelle's eyes. "(Any ideas?)"

Jealous and frustrated with Martee, Banelle couldn't think of anything she could contribute which would improve the situation, felt this shrug of anger. "(No. Let's just get out of here.)"

Dollar nodded past Banelle toward the exit. Banelle felt his left hand slide down her back, felt his hand push the small of her back toward the exit. "(You lead.)"

Banelle turned and began walking, winding a path through the crowded tables, continuing to feel his fingers familiar and safely at her back. She took a moment while walking to turn and look backward past him.

She saw Martee was shuffling along, clinging tightly to his right arm, with Bernice right behind Martee, and her father behind Bernice.

Her father's eyes caught hers.

Banelle had to return her attention leading them through the crowded floor.

She led the five of them outside, under the glaring parking lot lights into the dark night.

Banelle stepped left and waited for Dollar's arm to wrap more fully around her waist, then stepped smoothly into sync with him, a natural ballroom dance move. She looked at his eyes, and felt the odd tugs through his arm at her back from Martee's scooting along beside him on the other side, clinging bumpily. Banelle leaned into his embrace. "(Were you doing anything to her in there? That energy thing you do with your hands?)" Banelle said quietly, feeling the edge in her voice.

His eyes looked at hers quickly, shook his head fractionally, looked at Banelle's lips, then within her eyes. "(This is weird.)" Dollar said quietly. He turned his head and looked at Martee.

Banelle leaned forward while they walked and looked past Dollar.

Martee's eyes were downcast.

"Martee," Banelle said, low, intensely. "MARTEE." Banelle straightened up, looked at Dollar.

———

Banelle saw they were nearing where the Black Menace was parked. She opened her clutch and felt for the remote with her left hand, and mashed the proper button. The SUV beeped twice, flashing the lights, then she withdrew her fingers, and clicked her clutch closed. She stepped ahead, walking around to the driver's side, and felt his hand slip around to the small of her back, following her. Banelle stopped at the driver's side passenger door and opened the door.

Dollar pulled Martee along the last step, Martee stopped against him, clinging on his arm.

Dollar looked at Banelle briefly, then focused his attention upon Martee. He crouched down, slipped his left arm under Martee's knees, stood, and slid Martee onto the passenger's seat. He tried extracting his right arm.

"MM-MMM." Martee said, shaking her head vigorously, her arms renewing their grasp.

Dollar looked at Banelle, his eyebrows up. "(This is your friend,)" he said quietly, annoyed, jerking his head toward Martee.

Banelle narrowed her eyes at him. She stepped nearer Martee, put her hands under Martee's face, lifted upward gently and looked intently at Martee's eyes.

Martee's attention swam toward Banelle briefly. Almost as quickly,

Martee's eyes became round and unfocused. She shook her head back and forth, pulled away, and buried her face on Dollar's arm.

Martee's simple, emphatic reaction retreating from Banelle struck the heart and brought a feeling of rejection. The act also reawakened the memory of her daughter, Jayenne, as the young child pushing Banelle away with all her strength, running and landing on the couch, her voice screaming, the buried-hiding-frightened face. This memory of feeling emotionally paralyzed rushed back and gripped Banelle.

She backed away a step, her arms still halfway reaching for Martee's face. Her instincts were ringing all the alarm bells inside her, warning despite Martee's strange condition and blatant rejection, that Banelle emphatically needed to separate Martee from Dollar. The feelings were so primal she had no words for them.

Banelle grappled with the ancient, paralyzing feelings, felt the shock of the primal alarms circulating with anger, and wrestled with them. Finally, Banelle was able to pull her eyes from Martee's cheek, the face hiding behind Dollar's arm.

Banelle looked at him, searching his eyes.

Dollar's face was quiet. "(I'll ride in back this time.)"

Banelle looked at his lips, backed away another step, feeling a twist in the palpable sense of rejection welling up from old memories. Was she the one who had to push someone away and run for the couch?

Dollar turned, put his left hand on Martee's left thigh and pushed her sliding to the middle of the passenger seat while he climbed in and settled himself.

Banelle felt jealousy hobnob with the anger and primal alarms — pity, compassion, the terror of reaching out and feeling pushed away like this — the urge to shove and run.

Dollar was watching Banelle quietly, impassive.

Banelle backed another step away.

She noticed her father was standing here, with Bernice half a step back and left of her father. Banelle looked within her father's eyes.

His eyebrows arched briefly, a sense of purpose on his face. "(Just drive.)" He nodded upward once, toward the driver's door.

Banelle backed away another step, and looked at Bernice.

Bernice averted her eyes, turned immediately and began walking around the back of the SUV.

Banelle looked at her father.

He nodded up gently, softness in his eyes. "(Come on, B.B. We've had a surprising, marvelous day and evening.)"

She realized her eyes were moist, and she blinked. She turned and opened the driver's door and began getting in.

Banelle heard the passenger door shut behind herself, presumed her dad had closed that. She heard her father's footsteps turn with a crunch of tiny rocks on pavement and begin walking around the back of the SUV.

Banelle got herself situated in the driver's seat, heard the right rear passenger door open and turned briefly to see Bernice climbing in.

Banelle turned and pulled the driver's door closed, began buckling herself in, and heard Bernice's door shut. *Dollar should be doing this.* She missed the thighs-warming feeling of security from his buckling her in every time he had done their ritual earlier in the day, the primal alarm bells still ringing inside her.

Her father opened the right front passenger door and climbed in. He closed the door, sat facing ahead, and averted his eyes from her when she leaned forward.

Banelle looked down, fiddling with her clutch, mist in her eyes. She opened the clutch, pulled out her keys, stuck the key in the ignition, and started the SUV. The automatic air system whirred up. She adjusted the rear-view mirror to see Dollar in the corner of the mirror and part of Martee's hair and face.

Banelle drove them back toward the block Bernice lived on. Nobody said anything the whole way there. Banelle drove quietly, thinking about their wonderful day together, felt how contrastingly weird the evening was at the moment. She looked in the rear-view mirror quite often.

———

Banelle stopped near Bernice's building, heard Bernice's door open, the feeling welling up how much she liked Bernice. Banelle turned and looked at Bernice and smiled. "We need to get together again."

Bernice looked at her, stopping halfway out the door. "Oh!" Bernice said, and looked toward Martee and Dollar, looked at the back of Banelle's father's head briefly, then looked at Banelle. "You mean it?" smiling, the excitement showing.

Banelle felt herself nodding several times, and felt the smile, even around her eyes. "Yes, definitely. Here." Banelle pulled her business card from her clutch and handed the card to Bernice.

"Jazzed!" Bernice said, hopped out, shut the passenger door, toothy smile, dance move, waved, and turned.

Banelle watched to make sure Bernice got inside the street-side entrance of the building.

Banelle checked the driver's side mirror, pulled the SUV away from the curb. She realized she was going to be the one taking Martee home also. "(Martee will just have to get her car tomorrow.)"

Banelle heard behind her the rustling and shifting of someone's body, and when she looked in the rear-view mirror, Dollar had a puzzled concentration on his face and was focused downward. Banelle risked a quick look around and saw Martee's legs sprawling across the passenger seat, turning to face backwards, left elbow in the air, head presumably in his lap, knees still in the motion of rolling into him, the sound of a belt clink and leather slap.

Banelle turned forward and watched the road while she drove, felt the primal alarms escalate and a spike of jealousy.

"(Please,)" Banelle heard Martee say in a mousy-sounding voice.

In the rear-view mirror, Dollar was focused, his eyebrows puzzled, busy with his hands. Banelle saw him pull Martee's left hand into view through the mirror, his right hand around her wrist, then he released Martee's left wrist and his hand disappeared.

"(Please,)" she heard Martee say.

Banelle glanced at her father briefly, then back onto the road ahead. Her intuition was pricking thickly at her, yet nothing was making sense within this accelerated moment, an anxiety empty of solutions. She wondered what her dad knew. "Dad. What the hell's wrong with Martee?"

Her father sighed, ran his left hand through his hair and across the back of his head, then he slowly grabbed the hair in a fist three times, pulled his hand down, and shrugged. "I guess she saw the Boogie Man," his eyes on the road. He turned and watched out the right side of the SUV.

What the hell's going on? Banelle thought. She looked in the mirror, Dollar continued busy, his attention focused downward, his shoulders shifting with effort, his lips pressed together purposefully.

"Martee." Banelle said, following her intuition. "MARTEE. Knock it off, Martee!"

"(Please,)" she heard Martee say in the mousy voice, a voice Banelle had never heard Martee use before. She felt her eyes go wide with understanding.

Banelle saw Dollar look at Banelle. He winked at her in the mirror. Before she could respond, he was focused down, and this time his face had a mischievous grin.

Banelle saw Dollar lift Martee's right hand with his left hand around her wrist, his right thumb in Martee's left palm, her left fingers splayed, and while he kept her hands in the air, he wrestled her left hand in front of his lips, took a deep breath and sighed, eyes on Martee's spread fingers.

Banelle felt her eyes go wide. She had to stop her foot from slamming the brakes. "Dollar!"

He placed the little finger of Martee's left hand deep inside his mouth, wrapped his lips around Martee's finger, slowly pulled Martee's hand away, drawing the little finger through his lips wetly.

"(Oh, Goddess,)" she heard Martee say quietly, the mousy voice, and the fingers of her right hand curled, Martee's left fingers spread in a spasm.

He repeated the maneuver on Martee's left thumb, slowly.

"(Oh, GODDESS.)" she heard Martee say.

Banelle felt shocked, her mouth open. There were no words.

He put the three middle fingers in his mouth and left them there, suckling. Banelle saw the sides of his mouth curl, his cheeks draw into valleys.

Banelle felt the agitation of her small left finger tapping arrhythmically against the steering wheel, the other fingers gripping, felt her own toes spread open in the sandals, tingles.

She watched his jaw move subtly back and forth, valleys of his cheeks shifting.

"(Ohhhhhhh… uhnnng…)" she heard Martee squeaking with the mousy voice, heard Martee's body tensely shush-sh-ing the fabric of the passenger's seat, felt the driver's seat jarred from the back, then jarred again.

Banelle's fingers gripped the wheel.

The fabric-shushing sound came fast, the seat jarred slightly forward and held, straining…

Banelle noticed the subtle aroma of pine.

…the seat relaxed, there was a sob, a mew of delight.

Banelle watched Dollar pull Martee's fingers slowly out of his lips, kissed the thumb, then pulled both of Martee's wrists together and tucked her forearms into the crook on the left side of his neck, held his right hand around both of Martee's forearms to keep them there.

His left hand disappeared. Were his fingers in her hair? His thumb brushing Martee's cheek and forehead?

Dollar glanced briefly at Banelle through the rear-view mirror, then immediately, levelly, calmly averted his eyes toward the left, turning his head to watch out the passenger window. He sighed, his eyes rolled, and continued watching out the left window, breathing deeply.

The shocked state Banelle had felt evaporated. She exploded inside, and with a quick, narrow-eyed glance at her father, who was still watching out the right passenger window, Banelle took all the anger and jealousy and rage and betrayal and… and… and DESIRE… "(Dammit.)" Banelle hissed, biting off the whispered word, packed the feelings into a knot inside her stomach all bunched up, the strain of shoulder muscles feeling angry, jiggle of her hair.

Banelle heard Martee's characteristic, road bump-interrupted soft sighing snore.

"(Martee, you shit.)" Banelle whispered.

Words were inadequate for the strong feelings roiling at Dollar.

And toward her father. She felt her lips press more tightly together, because she didn't have time for *him* right now, a strong sense of betrayal.

This impatience was all about Dollar, about Dollar's actions, Dollar's choices, ABOUT DOLLAR.

This can't wait! her resolute voice said, pleasuring in the intensifying perfume of an enraged Goddess.

Banelle couldn't help her making the Black Menace cruise a little faster, Martee's apartment was first on Banelle's offensive checklist.

"bye!" she heard her
father call

. . .

SATURDAY, dark of the morning. Banelle pulled the SUV into the driveway, stopped a little sharper than she counted graceful, and shut off the engine.

"B.B," her father said, "I'm going to head home."

"Dad." Banelle said shortly, riding her anger about Dollar. "Thanks, dad," Banelle clarified. *It was a great day.* She meant to say.

"Dollar," he said, while the two men got out on the passenger side. "It was interesting meeting you, and I hope to see more of you soon."

"Thanks," Dollar said. "I enjoyed chumming around. What a fabulous day!"

The men closed the passenger doors.

Banelle jerked the driver's door open and stepped out. She slammed the door shut, mashed her thumb on the remote lock button, the SUV beeped once and flashed the lights. She closed her clutch, turned her back and leaned her hips against the door and crossed her arms.

She heard her father's footsteps. The car beeped. "Bye!" she heard her father call. She heard the door of his car open, a pause, then the sound of the door closing. She heard the car start, back out, and a moment later heard the precision roar of the Cadillac driving away.

She heard Dollar's quiet-soled shoes pace around the front of the SUV and stop. "(Banelle.)"

"What?" Banelle said tersely. She waited. Banelle turned her head slightly, resisted looking directly at him. "WHAT?"

"Let's talk."

She felt the bile, the anger, the rage, the jealously. She didn't want to spit that out here, not in the driveway where the whole damn neighborhood could hear.

She didn't want him in her house, either, the safe place. She felt like shouting at him he should leave.

She felt like she wanted to strangle him in private, both hands on his neck, face close, his eyes only on her. She felt like she was being cheated, because she was also very, very turned on.

She had been all day, but that last thing with the fingers! If that didn't piss her off so completely! That had been the most erotic thing she had ever experienced in person.

The part of her aroused knew she was better than Martee's mousy voice shit, fingers tingling with chilly evaporation, toe alarms, sandals and panties in the way. "DAMMIT." Banelle spit out. "Get your dick into the foyer! If you want to talk so badly!"

She didn't hear him respond immediately.

"Love it!" Dollar said finally, and she could see with a glance he said so with the tensed jaws.

She pushed away from the SUV with great energy, walking loudly and briskly, fumbling with her keys. She unlocked the front door to her home and turned. He was right here with her. She glared at him, turned, and walked inside, throwing her clutch with the keys on the foyer floor and continued walking, entered the living room a step down, and snapped the switch for the lights. When she reached the center of the room she turned, ready to shout.

He wasn't in the room yet.

She exhaled, hands on her hips. She began tapping her right foot.

She heard the front door close finally. In another moment, he appeared at the edge of the foyer to the living room, darkness behind.

"WHAT THE FUCK WAS THAT?!" Banelle yelled at him, pointing

her left finger and jerking her arm in the general direction of where they'd just come from, from the SUV, from dropping off a drunk and sleeping Martee.

"THAT." Dollar yelled with the baritone resonance.

She felt the tingle of goose bumps.

Then he grew quieter. "That was your drunk girlfriend pawing me."

"Her *fingers*?! Dollar, what were you thinking?!"

He stepped down into the living room, walked toward a spot three feet from her, and stopped. "(I'm thinking,)" Dollar said, his voice even quieter, ever as firm as a few moments ago, "(That your girlfriend had her hands all over me, had my belt half off, and she was drunk.)"

"BUT YOU'RE MY..." Banelle yelled, and stopped. She wanted to say, *Man*, freaked. "FLAME." Banelle yelled, finishing.

He inhaled and became very quiet, barely nodding, continued nodding thoughtfully while looking within her eyes. Finally, he looked down toward the carpet, toward the empty space between them. "(Exactly.)" Dollar said quietly. "(Exactly.)" He looked within her eyes. "(There's your answer.)"

––––––

Banelle felt her eyes narrow, felt suspicious. She wasn't feeling particularly friendly. Unhappiness filled her mouth with a sour taste. Her lips pressed together, the taste of sleep needed, and there was stale beer to brush away from the teeth. She also needed processing time.

The desire for Dollar hadn't gone away either, and now here they were alone, and she wanted even more than she had the whole day to tear his clothes off, to feel his fingers undress her, to feel his bare hard arms hold her soft body, feel his lips wet around *her* fingers. The clash of jealousy with desire really, really pissed her off. "(What do you mean?)"

He huffed, dismissing her venom with a wave of his hand as being irrelevant for him.

"WHAT?"

He shrugged, breathed in deeply, looked down, and exhaled. He looked within her eyes. "Have you looked at the stones?"

She felt herself glower, her head slightly turned, trying to follow, feeling really, really angry inside also. "Speak more plainly." Banelle said through the clenching she felt in her jaws.

"She's your friend. Why is it she's in the campfire of intimacy with us?"

Banelle felt her eyes narrow, sliding deeper into touching this stunningly deep reservoir of anger. What really pissed her off inside was that she wasn't even sure the anger had come from him. Some of the anger was from years of dealing with Martee. Banelle had only known him, what, all day? Half the night so far? *All my life*, part of her offered.

Dollar pointed his left index finger at her. "YOU remind your friend to honor the stones."

"What stones?"

"The ones we put around our relationship to protect the flame."

She felt her eyes look down left, right.

His eyes widened. "What?! Did you two spin a deal?!"

She looked at him sharply, alarm couched in bold lies. "For Goddess' sake, Dollar!" Banelle yelled. "YOU were sucking her FINGERS!"

"YES!" Dollar yelled, his gray eyes dark with eyebrows. "THE WOMAN was trying to unzip MY PANTS!" His arm jerked right, free of the jeans pocket, thumb pointing over his shoulder.

She felt herself jump slightly, felt jolted by the sudden volume of his anger.

"WHAT ELSE was I going to DO?!" his hands open, both palms raised at elbow height.

Banelle opted to lower her voice. "Why did you do *that* then? Why not push her away?"

Dollar dropped his arms. "I spent the whole damn evening pushing her away. I SPENT THE WHOLE DAY CONNECTING to

YOU!" Dollar yelled, his left index finger pointing down, his whole body hammering energy into the floor, making his point, making that heard. "I pushed her hands away repeatedly in the back seat on the ride! She was drunk, I knew that! She's your friend, I knew THAT. Goddesses! She was horny! Hell, anyone could see that! It was the only thing keeping her awake!"

Banelle felt the lie of her next misdirection. She needed time to think. She needed him to calm down, when she would rather be harvesting his desire. "She fell asleep?"

"I saw you watching me and knew you were mad. But it shouldn't have been at me. NOT AT ME." Dollar yelled, his finger pointing at himself. "I figured I'd tease you. I figured I'd let you see something evocative while focusing Martee's attention on something besides my… besides my hard on. Hell, yeah, she fell asleep."

Banelle felt her eyes grow wide. "Did she get your zipper down?"

"Well, no," Dollar said, fidgeting and grinning.

"THEN WHY WAS IT SUCH A BIG DEAL?" Banelle felt her palms out, arms bent at the elbow.

"The deal?" Dollar looked unsettled. A grin slipped briefly, and he shrugged. "I was commando."

"What do you mean?"

"I don't wear underwear."

She felt her head move back slightly, surprised both at his turn from anger and his candid share. *He is just bringing us closer by sharing!* her resolute voice intoned. Banelle's eyes glanced at his crotch, a bulge only, and part of her felt she could increase his state of arousal.

Part of her mind was busy changing her own state of invitation. He was naked under the jeans and she was off track, if that was what she truly wanted here. "(You don't?)" Banelle said quietly, images stirring erect.

———

Dollar spoke quietly. "(Well, no, I don't wear underwear. Haven't in years. You?)"

Banelle felt her right shoulder shrug a little. "(Not all the time, no.)"

He shrugged both his shoulders. His eyes looked left and right briefly. "(How about now?)"

She was quiet a moment. "(I'm not saying.)"

He looked at her blouse and bee dangling, and stopped himself from saying something, closing his mouth. Instead, he rolled his left palm over, facing up, his eyes intent on her pelvis less than three feet away, his fingers drew together...

She felt an energy tingling, felt the moistness renew, fidgeted her feet, feeling her toes come up, the sandals rustling.

Subtle dimples appeared on Dollar's face. "(Feel that? If my best friend were trying to get your zipper down, and he was drunk, and you weren't wearing underwear?)" Dollar looked from Banelle's pelvis upward across her breasts, neck, then within her eyes. His eyebrows rose.

She felt this misdirection was irrelevant. She also felt unsettled. Whatever he had just done affected her so intimately she was curious what else he could do, as he had promised earlier in the day twenty feet away in the kitchen from where they stood in her living room now, a living room she inextinguishably wanted to share with him.

Banelle also felt her and Martee's habitual competition might be partly her own fault, and a part of her questioned her right to be having a fight with Dollar. It was also partly Martee's fault, and that was the part which Banelle didn't control, and hadn't since they were kids. It wasn't a game anymore, and she was feeling guilty.

She hid this anxiety automatically behind the anger, as she had for so many years. She felt the jealousy roar back. "Dollar, damn you! Stop that! She had an orgasm right there on the back seat! I felt it in my SEAT! DAMN YOU!" and the force of the yell and anxiety turned this protest into a screaming yell.

"She went to sleep, didn't she?!" Dollar yelled back. "And *I* did NOT have an orgasm, did I?! Banelle, if I weren't so damn mad at you right now! I'm frustrated! We should be cuddling! We should be kissing! I feel like cussing 'til I'm out of breath! YOU NEED TO TALK TO

YOUR FRIEND!" Dollar stomped his right foot, his whole body shaking.

"STOP YELLING AT ME!"

She watched the quickness of how livid his eyes became. "WHAT?! YOU'RE THE ONLY ONE WHO GETS TO DECIDE WHEN TO YELL?! DECIDE when I SHOULDN'T?!"

She was afraid of how angry he was, the way he moved, his sharply focused eyes with no lovingness at all now. She felt her head shake, the feeling of not being loved swamping her eyes, the horror of feeling empty…

He took a deep breath, then sighed that out.

…and the Wet.

He blinked twice, turned around in a circle where he stood, looked at her, then looked down. "I'm going to go."

"Go?" Banelle realized the mist was suddenly in her eyes. She blinked several times. She didn't want to yell at him, or to have received her own anger reflected from his reactions. She didn't like his anger added with hers and thrown back at her. She didn't want him here like this.

She didn't want him leaving, either, because this feeling unloved and left to herself scared her more than his being angry. Banelle's eyes widened. Pushing others away was just something she was good at. The thought of successfully pushing him away made her feel scared of herself most of all.

He glanced within her eyes. She saw how the anger was gone, put someplace else or exhausted, but his eyes weren't warm. He didn't smile. He didn't reach out with his hands palm-up invitingly like he had been doing all day. He hadn't leaned toward her recently either, and she missed that. Her eyes glanced down, hoping at least he was still aroused. He wasn't.

Banelle blinked wetly, with drops on her right cheek, and looked into his eyes. She blinked more because there was more moisture in her eyes than before. She didn't care anymore if he saw her cry. Maybe she wanted him to.

She felt the hot wet streak spill over her left eye's lashes down her cheek, sharing openly. She blinked the wetness, hugged herself with her arms, looked at his lips, looked at his eyes. She wanted to stop babbling.

She noticed he looked tired. "(What now?)" Banelle said quietly, and sniffed.

———

Dollar was slow to respond, quiet. "(Like I said, I'm going to go. We shouldn't be fucking in this crazy association of feelings or we'll have a fucked up start, for sure. But don't think you've succeeded. You can't push me away. I. Will. Call. You. Whether you like anyone being sweet on you or not.)" Dollar started turning.

Banelle wanted to reach out and stop him like she did the first time when they met earlier in the day, when her fingers and arm tingled with the energy of touching his biceps. She panicked, feeling unworthy having incited their anger falsely, visions of Jayenne running for the couch.

Banelle felt shitty, crappy, unlovable, heart aching, and rutty. She knew somewhere in a quiet place inside herself, knew with a certainty she was not going to stop him leaving tonight. She knew if he felt of his own damn accord she was lovable, worthy, a treasure, despite her own fucked-up proofs to herself, then *Yes!* he would call, and she would believe him to her toes.

A large part of her knew exactly what she wanted in her life. She felt the security of her choice now, this answering his call would happen. And Goddess help her, someday she'd feel that way, too, about herself. She could feel like he did, and finally believe for herself she was lovable, worthy, this reservoir full of treasures. And, if he didn't genuinely feel that way, well, here this tearfully was again.

"(Let the crying days begin,)" Banelle whispered, barely puffs. *What? A TEST?* Banelle's critical voice intoned.

Dollar turned around again and faced her

She felt her eyes rounding, was he aroused?

"(Banelle.)" Dollar said quietly. Almost softly, she imagined. Maybe he did care?

"(What?)" Holding her breath, balloon squeeze.

"(No offense.)" Dollar paused… Then changed his focus, turned around, stepped up into the foyer.

She exhaled, watching him leave.

Heard the front door… slam.

She put a hand over her eyes and freed the crying, getting her hand wet, felt herself sobbing with spasms from this agonized stomach. She felt the deep aching within the belly, down within the very fibers of muscles which normally made this sense of herself uniquely pleasant, and now this crestfallen woman.

She felt the awful emptiness, the clenched fist which would not relax yet couldn't hold firmly enough what had been thickly given to her, a falling wave crashing, unfulfilled. Tight. Empty.

She rolled her head back, looked at the ceiling, tears rolling past her ears, her left hand over the open mouth wordless with pain, open eyes of agony, felt the words which wanted to come out, yet they had no power now to speak. All the power was with the knot deep down in the empty, dark belly.

Banelle gasped for air, pulling through her mouth. With the gap from the quickening gasp, she quickly whispered, "(Dollar.)" The name mostly puffy air, throat clenched, no vocals. "(Fuck.)" Single word of silent prayer, a lonely buzzing leaving an empty flower brimming with nectar unused.

She wiped one eye with the back of her right hand, the other with the right palm, so wet, and blinked several times. She closed her mouth and swallowed. Her head rolled forward. She folded her arms and blinked at the floor, a splash falling on her arm. She looked around the empty living room, and blinked wetness. She walked into the foyer, just in case. The foyer felt empty, dark.

She turned, stepped down through the living room, strolled into the kitchen, and the flashing red light caught her eye. She remembered now there were phone calls. She counted the flashes standing there in the dark, nine messages. She breathed in slowly, shallowly, and sighed, arms hugging. There was no energy for messages. There was no one on earth she cared hearing from. "(Except Dollar.)" Banelle whispered.

Her eyes glanced out the kitchen window briefly, at the darkness of the tree and the glow of the familiar street light beyond, then at the floor where she was standing.

Eventually she felt thirsty, felt the rawness in her throat from the yelling and relived the shock of his being angry back. She felt restless, fidgety.

Banelle realized consciously there was the smell of chocolate in the air, and remembered the dark wonderful-smelling cake he and her father had made earlier in the day, back when things were so new and fresh, each surprise bringing her along into the next moment. "(It was a damn good day,)" Banelle murmured, smiling only a little, a mere dimpling of the corners of her mouth.

With the blink, her folded arms did the self-hugging. *Except that last part*, Banelle thought. Was that so bad, she wondered? Even that?

The fucker fought fairly.

———

Parts of the heated argument replayed in Banelle's mind, her eyes lost in the middle space of the dark kitchen floor. All the while she relived the argument, she felt the shallow breathing containing the stillness.

She wondered about this new stillness, how this just seemed to be here, down deep inside her in another corner. She wondered why this should be where the stillness was.

Banelle thought about her new friend, Bernice, about the fun she and Bernice had earlier in the evening, infectiously encouraging Banelle to loosen up and be self-expressive in dance. Bernice was innovative. She felt herself smile, then faded, remembering how Bernice was hungry for fatherly approval, and worse, Bernice's mom was dead, just like in the Disney movies. "(This sucks,)" whispered Banelle, sighing.

A waft of scent reminded her she had forgotten to wear antiperspirant. The bacteria had a field day unimpeded, ripe now on the nose.

Her eyes wandered around the dark kitchen, taking in the odd shadows from the strangeness of ordinary things like cupboards, chairs, the refrigerator humming, the curtains, the faucet with the slow drip.

The stillness of quiet hope was here inside. She wondered where she could have any hope at all in this moment.

Dollar had said he was going to call. She didn't know why she trusted this stillness, down in this one spot, yet she knew in a curiously profound way this was true as the earth the man worked with. Like rocks. Like nose-opening loam, freshly uprooted grass, sunshine through wavy green fluttering leaves.

She felt herself smile briefly, like a sunshine beam seen through a branch, for a moment blown by a soft breeze. She blinked with this breezy fresh feeling, cherry blossoms on the nose.

Then this feeling was gone, somewhere down inside herself. She felt too tired to chase the feeling out again and let the stillness simply be.

She breathed in more deeply, sighed, and wondered why she had come in the kitchen? "(Oh.)" Banelle said quietly, reminded of this very human thirst.

She walked slowly through the dark kitchen illuminated only in spots from reflections of street light. She felt for the cupboard where she kept the glasses, and selected one. She felt for the faucet and the lever, listened while the water poured into the glass, judged when to shut the water off, felt she needed less than the whole glass anyway.

She sipped, set the glass on the unlit gray counter in a clunk with a slide, then the hand released.

She turned around. The smell of chocolate was in the air.

She walked slowly back toward the living room. Her left arm moved from folded to diagonally across her soft breasts, her left hand cupping the right side of her neck, she pushed the kitchen door open with her right hand, remembered how he moved for her when he realized her hand was pushing on him.

She sat on the couch, and felt her way through the memories of the day. His eyes on her breasts, skin prickling alarms, laughter, touches, inside thigh thrills, sharing words, his *No Elephants!* voice.

But when in remembering she rediscovered the heated, angry argument, she found she wanted not to relive this part of the day.

"(Men suck. Maybe it's not important anyway,)" Banelle murmured in the surrendering, tired voice.

She felt like lying down for a bit, and let her body stretch along the cool cushions of the couch, the back of her hips against the couch back, her legs curled together with the knees by the edge of the cushions. She breathed in. She breathed out. She listened, laying with the quiet. She felt delighted after a busy, loud evening to simply hear the breathing.

In. "(How can I make every day be this full?)" Banelle murmured. Out.

Outside Banelle's home, seemingly in the distance, there was a rumbling. Part of the mind wondered what kind of storm that was, then the storm sound was leaving.

The sound seemed… Somehow that made the sad… She felt the long time filling the chest with fresh air, the long time sighing. "(Blue.)" Banelle murmured, and felt the nose scrunch briefly.

The air system, the soft sounds, breez'zzzes.

The dreams, thick choc'let cake in the hands, another hand tugging, intent on taking the cake away.

he nodded at her, smiled, "lovely."

. . .

SUNDAY, crisp spring chill. Dollar slammed the door of the green work truck. He stood in the parking lot looking at the Grape Hopper, the early morning Sun rising behind him, his and the truck's shadows stretching long on the tarmac along with the shadow of tall buildings behind him.

The Grape Hopper, two stories high, glowed with reflected morning sunshine, horizontal line of the metal roof wet with dew, glistening dew on the front wall, barn-red tongue-and-groove wood on the top half of the building, bottom left quarter of tall glass panels. The legs of the high tables and tall chairs stood against the inside of the windows, smoke-colored blinds pulled down to waist height hiding the tops of the tables. A walkway bridge enclosed from the elements and plush with glass walls joined the second floor to a nearby building adjoining the parking lot, a network of unique sky bridges from there across the metro.

The building's bottom right quarter portrayed a giant mural of the brown-saddled, light-tan Appaloosa towering over the center entrance below the horse's neck, the head above the double doors facing the parking lot, perked ears, shiny dark eyes, front quarters and part of the right side flank visible on the left of the doors. He smiled, feeling the welcoming of the second home called work.

Dollar started toward the front doors, breathed in deeply while he walked, appreciating the new morning and fresh air. He put the key in the door, turned his right arm looked at his watch. *Six-thirty.* Dollar nodded once. "Awesome." He had three-and-a-half hours before opening the doors for the public.

His Sunday morning regulars included a number of his friends who knew these were the only few hours in his week which were reliably predictable, and knew where he'd be. These friends included residents of an old folks' home two blocks away, along with any other local retirees who felt like walking over and enjoying a cup of fresh grind, ten a.m. coffee, free.

He stepped in, pulled the door closed with a firm steady pull rushing the hydraulic arm, then locked the door. On the right wall inside he used another key to open a panel, punched a 6-digit code to clear the alarm system, closed and locked the panel.

He turned around, visually surveying the main room. He felt himself nod taking in the small work-related details first, evidence of last night's crew, including Candy's and Katlyn's work setting the glassware clean and stacked, and Ric's attention cleaning the gloss-finish oak floors. "Excellent."

On the ceiling there were dollar bills from customers. There was a magick in the idea of having something there when they returned, something they had earned for themselves and could staple securely overhead, and staples were damn near free.

He turned and walked toward the jukebox and stopped, his right hand within his jeans pocket digging out quarters. He loaded four into the machine slot with his left hand, plucking them out of the loose change on his right palm, read again a yellowed sign over the juke box.

---

going into a fabulous song
   we find a courage

discarding every last word

He saw he had a piece of paper folded among the coins.

After the four quarters were loaded, he pulled the paper out of his right hand and shoved the rest of the coins into his pocket. He felt himself smile unfolding the paper, seeing with familiarity the torn piece Banelle had given him two mornings before, the only thing sweaty about the note being the lie he had told about how the ink had ran.

His eyes traced the hastily written, feminine handwriting, burning within his mind once more the entirety of her phone number, along with the emotions she evoked at the time she wrote the number for him: excitement, anxiousness, passion. He felt his head shaking in wonder, his eyes following the petite loop and impassioned sprawl of her handwriting, marveling how in such a brief handwriting moment he could see how a woman was feeling about their future together.

He refolded the paper carefully to display her handwriting and decided he would put her first note to him in his wallet, tucked within the soft plastic display panel on the left side. He closed the wallet with a satisfactory flip and slid the wallet into his left front pocket.

On the jukebox, he punched 1,1,3, then hit the random button for the other two song credits. He headed for the bar to get himself organized.

He was a third of the way across the main floor when the familiar trumpet riff, chased by an acoustic guitar, rolled out from the premium house sound system, leading him directly into experiencing the internal, on-tap brew of melancholy. The words, of course, known by heart:

> *In his room at the top of the stairs*
> *where disbelief lives an easy life,*
> *no perfume floats from*
> *the woman who loves him*

Selah, Kenya, my ruddy lover
my favorite socks have shrunk
in the Missing You River
please stretch them soon
you know you can

His shadowed walls pace sleeplessly
The old leather couch tries every corner
No clothes lie about of
the woman who loves him

Selah, Kenya, my ruddy lover
my favorite socks have shrunk
in the Missing You River
please clean them deeply
use your clever hands

His jeans alone on creaking footboard
the midnight blue candle ages dusty gray
no laughter rolls on the floor from
the woman who loves him

Selah, Kenya, my ruddy lover
my favorite socks have shrunk
in the Missing You River
please trust me once again
yes, yes, yes, I love you.

Seh-la-la, la-laaa, Ruddy, my only lover
mm, mmm, mm-mm-mmmm.
come swim agahh-ahh-ainn
my river-rrr-rr-rr-rr-rrrr
please trust me fresh and new
yes, yes, yes, I love only you.

. . .

With Banelle on his mind and Martee also on his mind, he realized he no longer identified with the chorus which once affected him profoundly. He could feel how the living alone parts of the song called to him, the bluesy wandering melody speaking hopeful and patient.

———

Listening evoked a memory of Dollar's childhood, and he felt himself smiling with a warm feeling inside while opening the door to dry storage. He began rummaging through the boxes of various brand name beers.

In the memory, he was coming home on the late afternoon school bus from elementary. Like so many times, the mare which his mom kept in the small pasture near the road would rear her head and perk her ears hearing the bus come. He would be hanging on the vertical stainless steel pole at the front of the bus, waiting for the driver to make the brief stop. He was glad to spend an hour or so with the mare before dinner, before the indoor, closed-in home experience which wasn't always so pleasant.

The mare expected the cup of oats and the brushing. The mare's favorite treat was their ride, and they would go through the woods which split the fields of the sprawling farm each afternoon and smell the drier pollen hilltops, the moister, cooler low spots deep in the woods, seeing every ride the changes the woods and hills secreted.

Dollar worked while the other two songs played, not paying any mind to lyrics or artists, just using the driving beat of each song to tap into his energy and move boxes.

He hauled boxes out toward the bar area, stocked coolers, broke down cardboard. He loaded the jukebox twice more, played 1,1,3 twice more with randomized followers, and kept working. Then he got involved reorganizing the stock room in the ensuing quiet.

He looked at his watch finally, the music long gone, saw how the time was a quarter of ten. Time for grinding fresh beans and brewing coffee, for a magick of intense smells. Five minutes before the hour, he walked across the main floor of the Grape Hopper and opened the door.

Three retired women were there waiting, along with one retired man. He'd seen them before many times, believed one of the women was the wife of the man in the group. He recognized the gray suit, white shirt, black shoes, recognized the white-dots red dress with the sharply watching blue eyes, nodded at both of them. Recognized the blue-on-blue jacket and skirt, flat black shoes, hazel eyes. An orange blazer and black skirt were new, white frills shirt, short black pumps, green eyes. He nodded at her, smiled, "Lovely."

They all smiled, and moved with careful gaited pace into the Grape Hopper while he held the door. "Go help yourselves," Dollar told the ladies, two of whom were smiling, staring at him and nodding like they always did.

Cheeky moms, Dollar thought, smiling, and nodded at them again. He didn't mind their gawking, feeling there mustn't be many tactile pleasures at that age, so what harm does a little cradle-gawking do, comparatively speaking?

He felt like they'd been there often enough he should get to know their names. Today wasn't the morning for that, though. There were many open issues on his mind and more than enough physical energy locked in anger mode by brooding resentment, more than he could ride down to engage pleasantly. He had no energy for exploring new friendships, he had been so involved with new relationships over the weekend already.

He worked his way around the main floor straightening chairs. Not much was in disarray, he just needed to do something with the energies. Before he got back by the bar area, he heard the main doors and saw the light change on the floor, Esk and Samone walking in for their shifts.

He smiled, seeing Esk's chop-cut blonde hair and blue eyes, half a dozen gold earrings staggered along her left ear's edge, a single earring on the right. She was wearing a black button-up shirt with blue jeans, and black running shoes. "You've got an hour to get the kitchen online," Dollar told Esk, nodding.

She rolled her eyes, already walking purposefully toward the kitchen door.

Samone wore her hair in a tasteful thick black taper-cut against her neck. Single pearl earrings glowed against her dark features, glimmer of intelligence on her dark brown eyes. Her lips and fingernails matched her red sleeveless shirt, over black slacks, black flats.

"The bar's stocked," Dollar said, looking at Samone. "It just needs that extra touch," Dollar winked.

"Good morning to you, too," Samone said.

He smiled. "Good morning, Samone! I'm glad you're here."

"A pleasure for you to see me again," Samone said, waving her hand regally. She smiled at the floor and slipped her arms out of the button-down cream sweater while she walked.

Dollar felt like sitting down. He shoved a final chair into place at a low table, walked to the bar, steamed a heavy stoneware mug, and poured himself fresh, dark roast coffee. He turned from the bar and went to sit on one of the tall chairs at his favorite table, the last of the high tables against the windows by the right wall looking out, sunshine angling in.

He noticed while getting comfortable the three women were visiting quietly, noted how the man sat across from the wife per usual. There was a chemistry in the group of the four of them, shoulder-shaking kidding going around, the old competition alive between the women.

Even so, there was a clarity about who the wife of the man was, grudgingly friendly deference. He wondered if they shared?

The four of them seemed thick with slow motion, not from frailty, the physical movements were deft, quick. There was more a sense of depth, like every move, every flirt had attached many memories, so many having-happened-before moments producing lightning displays of emotions flashing by, decades of history rippling.

Dollar turned in the tall chair toward the window, brought the mug under his nose to savor the rich smell and steam. He let his eyes wander idly watching out the window. He took the first sip and held the brew on his tongue.

Dollar saw a familiar red car zipping around the curve from the main street, entering the parking lot. He realized it was the same red Prelude he'd seen at Banelle's house the previous day. He didn't remember telling anyone that night about the bar.

Except Charlie, of course.

––––––

Dollar and Charlie had discussed damn near all of the high points of achievements in each other's lives during the times they were free of the women.

How had Martee retrieved her car, he wondered?

Dollar couldn't imagine how between dark of the morning Saturday and today Charlie could have been interrogated in any context whatsoever which would grant his divulging anything about the Grape Hopper to Martee, particularly not if what he sensed was *not* going on between Charlie and Martee was indeed not going on. That was still a puzzle for sorting out.

Dollar continued to breathe the rich steam in through his nostrils, deep within his lungs, and sighed with the pleasure.

He watched the Prelude park. The car door opened, and there with the bounce and swirl of dark wavy hair appeared Martee. He felt his eyebrows up, exhaled through his nose, the steam of the mug clearing off temporarily. His eyes automatically assessed her self-packaging while she swung the red door closed and started walking purposefully toward the Grape Hopper entrance.

Wow, Dollar thought, appreciating her stunning black form-capturing dress ending just above the knees, wide shiny black belt around her waist, shiny black sandals with short heels and a strap encircling each of the ankles. Except for the small black purse draped over her right shoulder, she wore no other accessories.

The neck of the dress was scalloped and ended the black material very close around her neck, which at first seemed quite conservative.

He scrunched his eyebrows and leaned forward slightly. He wondered if she was commando underneath: there wasn't any evidence of lines from the bottom of the dress all the way past her vivacious ass and exceptionally lively breasts – no lines at all, femininely smooth and full of motion, even on the shoulders. "(Delectable.)"

He leaned both elbows on the high table and cupped the mug with both hands, continuing to breathe the coffee's steam while he watched Martee.

That was a lot of intensity walking and pulling the door open, even for Martee, the little bit of time he had known her so far. She stepped inside the Grape Hopper, entering twenty-five feet away from where he was sitting and went straight toward the bar, and got Samone's attention. Samone directed Martee with an extended arm and a nod, pointing at Dollar.

Martee turned her head, saw him, and smiled brightly. She said something to Samone, then turned her attention back upon him, swirled her hair and walked across the floor. Dollar noted there might be more sassing in her skirt after she saw him than before. Like measuring earthquakes, he thought, and suppressed a chuckle.

He smiled and nodded his head upward while she drew near. "Hello."

Martee walked into his personal space, put her right arm around his neck, breasts against his arm, and kissed his lips, a wet chill and hot breath as she pulled away. "(Missed you.)"

The effect was immediate, his jeans suddenly feeling crowded.

Martee smoothed her hand across his back and shoulder until he just felt the fingertips, then her touch lifted as she stepped around the table end. He felt like he wanted to tell her to put the hand the hell back on his body.

She climbed onto the chair opposite him and bounced twice, situating herself. Martee propped her right elbow on the high table and set her chin on her fist, smiling.

Dollar extended his left palm toward the table in front of her. "Can I get you something?

"Maybe." Martee looked at his coffee. "Can I try that?"

He felt his eyebrows higher, blinked, relaxed his eyebrows, and reached the mug across the small tabletop.

She cupped both of her hands around his left wrist and hand, guiding the mug. She smelled with an inhale, her eyes looking within his, then she blew on the coffee. Her lips parted, she sipped briefly, pulled her head back slightly, her eyes upward, neck inviting, her eyes moving right, then left. She looked at him, nodded several times, smiled. "Yes, something like that would be great." Martee released his wrist.

He looked toward the bar and sat erect, waiting to catch Samone's eye.

Finally, Samone looked in his direction.

Dollar nodded upward once, raised his coffee mug, jerked his head toward Martee. Samone nodded and picked up a mug from the ready stack. Dollar turned back toward Martee.

Martee's lips parted, brief knit in the eyebrows. "Do you guys wait on each other here?"

He felt himself chuckle, felt the smile of his partially open mouth, and around his eyes also. He shook his head slowly. "Martee, you are here, do you know *where* you are? What kind of intel did you get?"

Martee looked at his lips, then back within his eyes. "About what?"

"Or are you just pretending?"

"Pretending?!" a bounce. "What are you talking about? The coffee?"

"Here I thought you did magick."

Her eyes narrowed.

"You must be good at some kind of magick, though. You knew where to find me, the same weekend twenty-three miles away, so maybe you're really good with the magick and just didn't think to look further?"

She smiled with dazzling vanity and shrugged her right shoulder. "I was here until late last night and you weren't. Coffee next, then magick. So what don't I know?"

"This is my bar."

———

Martee's eyes got round and she bounced, her head moved back. "Hell no! No, I didn't know!" Martee leaned toward her right, looking under the table, playfully kicked Dollar on the side of his left calf.

"What was that for?"

She swirled her hair and sat erect with a bounce. "You said you did lawns!"

"Lawn art." He pulled the mug near and inhaled deeply across the steamy top. There was lipstick on the far edge. "And I do." Dollar added with a single nod, took a sip.

"*Two* businesses?"

He felt himself nodding happily, smiling.

"When do you have time to date?"

"I don't. That's the arrangement."

He heard Samone approaching. "Here you go, Aaron."

Dollar looked into Samone's eyes with a nod and smile. "Thanks."

Martee accepted the mug with both hands, smiled at Samone, then turned her attention back upon Dollar.

He watched Martee holding the mug, much like he was, except she made sure to keep her face fully visible for him, except when she was actually sipping, her lips parting. "(By the way,)" Dollar said quietly, his eyes on her hands – noting everything behind the hot mug had movements of soft joy. He looked within her eyes. "(You're gorgeous.)"

Martee bounced, smiling, hair in a sweep. "(Thanks,)" continued smiling. Her eyelashes almost closed for a moment, then she looked at him. "(So, Friday night.)"

He chuckled, feeling his own nervousness, looked down toward the left, then down toward the right, at nothing particular, just remembering. "(Friday night? How about Saturday morning, just after midnight?)" Dollar looked at her. His eyes fell to her fingers, restless now on the mug she held. He remembered the dark of the night all right.

The fight.

Before that, Martee's orgasm, shaking Banelle's seat while Banelle was trying to drive; wrestling Martee's wrists to keep fingers off his belt buckle and zipper. Martee's clinging at the table; rubbing herself on him while dancing.

"(Did Banelle call you?)"

Martee's eyebrows knitted briefly. "(When?)"

"(Anytime after dancing that night.)" Dollar felt the resurgence of abs-tensing muscles remembering the flaming fight he and Banelle went through, remembered his insisting Banelle talk with her friend about where the rocks should be.

"(No. Why?)"

He looked down. His eyes scanned the tabletop, then focused on his hands cupped around the lonely mug. He was feeling disappointed. *Banelle didn't do a damn thing about the situation.*

Dollar looked at Martee. "(Nothing. Things just got a little weird later that night.)" Dollar wondered how much time Banelle needed for processing.

Martee was quiet.

He took a sip of coffee, then another, thinking as he felt the uptick of caffeine.

"(Dollar.)"

He looked at Martee, his poker game face. She put her arms on the table toward him, palms up, beckoned with her fingers for his hands.

He took another sip of coffee, watching her hands invite contact. He set the mug off on the right side, crossing left arm over right, collected his hands into a fold, swallowed the coffee he'd been savoring. He looked within her eyes.

She smiled, shrugged, beckoned with her fingers, palms up.

He put his palms on top of hers. Her hands slid under his, felt her fingertips brush the soft parts of his wrists, felt the soft insides of her forearms under his fingers.

Martee inhaled, spoke louder. "I apologize."

He remained quiet, looked at her lips, then looked within her eyes. "For what?"

"Dollar, I remember everything from our night together."

"Everything?"

"Yes. Even what you did to my fingers. And I needed that to help resolve a Goddess spell. I used you without asking when I needed a strong arm. I apologize." Martee slipped thumb and fingers around his wrists. He felt himself jump slightly at the feeling of being captured. She held him firmly. "And thank you for the energy assist. Ask me another time why it was so important to have your help during the night." Martee lifted his right hand, kissed his fingertips, rested their hands on the table again. "Thank you."

Dollar tried relaxing, his wrists held in her encircling hands, his curiosity playing with the words of her sharing in his mind.

His eyes fell slightly. He looked at her dress, at the way her breasts rose and fell with her breathing. He looked at her lips, how they would part briefly to say something, then close. He looked at her arms, her wrists, how small her hands were, felt how well they fit within his.

He brushed the bases of her wrists with his thumbs, stopped, felt himself melt a little. He looked within her eyes, smiled and blinked. "It was… upsetting, later, after getting you off." Dollar looked at her breasts in the dress, saw the rise of nipples pressing the fabric. He looked within her eyes. "So now. Tell me your name?"

She blinked, looked at his lips, then his eyes.

Dollar decided to confess. "I feel unexpectedly close to you. I continue to feel drawn to you despite trying to be respectful of a relationship I started earlier in the day Friday with Banelle, and I don't even know your full legal name."

———

"Yes!" Martee said, bouncing. She hunkered down, leaned forward, smiled at Dollar from under her eyebrows. "Marittia Emily Marlin," rolling the 'r' in the first name. She scrunched her nose briefly, then sat up with a bounce. "At work they call me 'Tim' or 'Top Cat'" bouncing twice. "Or 'Merle'" her hair swayed once in a flip of head. "My absolute favorite," squinted her eyes briefly, "is 'Martee.'"

"Marittia," repeated Dollar, fumbling the tongue rolling the rrr's, stopped. He searched for the rest of her name and couldn't remember that yet, so he looked at her.

"Emily Marlin."

"Marittia Emily Marlin. Marlin?"

She scrunched her nose, stuck the tongue out briefly, smiled, and bounced. "Marlin, as in I got that from my dad and I have no idea who started it before him. It could have been a joke at an emigration entry point a century ago, who knows?" Martee's right shoulder shrugged, her lips a mysterious smile.

He looked at her lips, then he looked at the soft curves shaping the black dress free of lines. His eyes traveled further down, looking at her trim midriff pressing against the tabletop where the honey-pine table framed, accented and drew out the curving of her breasts pressing against the black material. His eyes followed the soft lines of her arms flowing into his hands.

He realized consciously he had been feeling Martee's liveliness, his hands given to hers, noticed she was working a magick upon his body.

Dollar wondered if Martee knew nudging and tugging him with her ongoing wriggling was arousing him? Felt a brief scrunch of his eyebrows wondering if she was doing another magick on him also, something energetically deeper?

All the fun he'd had with Martee Friday talking, an evening with rocks and a gorgeous river, and while dancing at the club. The flirting had been fun. Fun times with the finger-sucking, also, getting Martee off, and the comforting delight of her sleeping against him on the ride to her flat.

The resulting fight with Banelle was so powerful. Banelle had been turned on, and still Banelle had her brakes on.

Dollar wasn't sure what to do next. He looked within Martee's eyes, felt like something had to be done though since his intention had been to pursue a relationship with Banelle, and Martee and Banelle were best friends.

Dollar realized with widening eyes he needed to take a few steps further along the bunny trail with Martee to be sure of his footing, consider his long-term choices carefully, because somewhere within the last twenty-four hours he had fallen rock-splashing wet at the fingertips in love with two women. What was he thinking? He had done fine for three years avoiding an intimate relationship with a female!

Here was something else to wrestle: how easy would it be to let Banelle go? To give himself relief from the energy-burning anger, relief from the socially compromising state of frustration he found himself in since the fight?

He had pulled out all the stops, though, and connected deeply as he could with Banelle. It wasn't fair to just dump her cold, especially with an unsettled fight. And hadn't that frustration been there all along? A little bit at a time Friday, into Saturday morning?

Banelle's words, "…butt out…" regarding Charlie were still echoing in his mind. Dollar liked Charlie. Then having to deal with Banelle's jealousy all day long?

Maybe it was for the best, learning that about Banelle up front. Maybe the luck was twofold, showing him the hazards of Banelle in contrast with potential pleasures. That was why he had a two-week rule for new relationships after all.

Dollar was beginning to suspect Martee didn't use rules when Martee wrestled for keeps.

With the twofold luck, he needed to see where the truest path lay. Something nagged at him, though, about Banelle's frustrating thwarting of his good faith advances toward Banelle. That wasn't just her attacking him out of all proportion over her perception of his offense. There was something deeper there. Banelle had not made the least effort at apologizing, either.

"(Martee had.)" Dollar realized he had just muttered out loud, and looked at Martee watching his lips.

Banelle had not touched or hugged him during the fight, even when he threw the 'I have to go' card on the table. He was surprised the door hadn't hit him on the ass after.

No. There was something which made even less sense. Perhaps he could make sense out of all that by interrogating the best friend?

Banelle seemed so full of lovingness and desire, smiles and hugs, and yet foot stomping on the brakes of her SUV, erecting brick walls, changing topics. It was like Banelle was fighting herself, blocking her own soft joys and happiness.

What did Martee know about all that?

Godessess! He could see the potential in Banelle, maddeningly out of reach. That made his mind determined to know what the secret was, yet feeling the hopelessness of not seeing anything he could fix or do there, so why bother?

What was he going to do with his so far unrequited love for Banelle?

Dollar's eyes focused, now sharp and clear. He watched the barely contained soft breasts and firmed nipples behind black night fabric calling to him across the table.

Inside himself, he felt a growing need to pull Martee's hands around the table, wrap that woman between his legs, and in the next moment kiss her.

Near-Goddess or crafty Independent Wiccan? Which was it going to be?

she felt the tingly excitement

. . .

MARTEE KNEW what strengths were in the shadows cast by her capacity to love.

Now, here at last her hands were clasped with those of a man of at least her caliber, and whether or not he was aware of his own shadows, she had poked her nose into them herself and had hit the Sky God's collection of subterranean treasures.

She was not afraid, knowing the strength of many of her own shadows, and also knowing only magnificent lights cast magnificent shadows.

Here she was holding hands with both.

Martee was also unafraid to tread with alert eyes through the outskirts of Virtue's hell, giving a watchful nod toward the three-headed dog guarding the Gate of Passion when she approached in her inner vision, her hands each full of rocks.

She waited, watching the dog's faces. Presently, she felt her own Shadow's hand cover her mouth with silence, as was their agreement, because there is not one word in any language that can be spoken near the gate of Passion which the three-headed dog will not find inflammatory.

She moved with shadowy hand over her mouth, her Shadow tight against herself, her two hands clenched with rocks, successfully passed by the three-headed dog, and entered the Halls of Passion.

Passion! Where she had felt most comfortably at play since the days of childhood when she would sneak out of the ground-floor bedroom window without her parents knowing, and run around in the dark and passionately throw rocks.

She knew, also, how the fires in this wing of Hell's grand halls only burned deeply if you played alone past the gates where words cannot be spoken.

She entered the grand Hall of Passion now in her inner vision while holding Dollar's physical hands across from her. Inside her vision, she felt renewed and youthful within the freshness and rustling of the air in the Hall.

Martee played for a moment silently, running around the chamber with her arms outstretched, clenching the rocks with passion. She felt the tingly excitement of waiting for the Lover's arrival for play, not knowing for sure when he will, no matter how clearly she could see him from the Hall.

She stopped her play and stood looking out at the universe, then stepped out through a shadow into the fresh night air, stepping into the open heart of the boy who cast such magnificent shadows. She waited for the feel of him, noticed with her physical eyes again his upper lip was wet from the steam of the coffee he had sipped moments before.

She felt him squeeze her hands gently.

Martee felt herself return the assurance, palms-with-palms, slipped her thumbs and fingers around his wrists to claim him, and held confidently as she felt him start in surprise.

Inside the vision of herself, she felt the Shadow's hand pull away, her mouth inside herself firmly shut. The quietness, feeling soft night breezes and hard rocks in the hands, with nothing for clothes.

Dollar took deep breath.

Martee waited, her eyes looking from one into the other of his eyes. She looked within the living black canvas centers, searching.

In the vision, the woman with the rocks in her hands felt teary in her eyes, blinked repeatedly, treasuring the waters of the eyes as the waters of the dark belly flowing with passion, such a free flowing feeling.

In her vision, Martee reached out with her naked right arm, dropped the palmful of rocks, pulled her right hand back and spanked the palm clean on the side of her naked thigh, the leg quivering as she passionately brushed off the rock dust. Her left hand clenched the rocks there reassuringly.

She extended her right arm, palm down, fingers spreading, and slowly turned her palm over. With the rolling, she felt through the bare soles of her youthful naked feet the unique, spiritually pure clear fire within the floor of this magick place, intimately knew of herself the important task of Union.

She extended her fingers, palm flat upward to receive the man, pulled the clear fire arcing through soles, ankles, calves, thighs, psoas, and then the magnificently subtle, redolent aroma of feminine pheromones entered her nostrils. She felt the clear fire through breasts, quickening heart, and neck. Her lips parted as she sucked air in shallowly, clear arcing through shoulders, arms, palms, and fingers. The luscious-feeling fire whorled invisibly, tingling around the fingers and nails of her hands, left hand clenching, right hand spread.

———

I love this part, Martee thought, a mere shadow blink of time from arc start to whirling. *Treasure consistency! Engage him with authority!* Her thoughts repeated the mantra, reminding herself over-and-over.

With the gentle night breezes of the internal vision, she reached for the shadowy night skies she saw within the black centers of Dollar's eyes. With the image of the hand reaching inside she felt her fingers pull slowly, drawing together, pulling on the black night with the whirling clear fire of shared passion, connecting their souls, more important even than sex, though that would come also.

Martee felt him respond. He pulled gently on her physical hands.

She slipped off the tall chair, clack of sandals, and stepped around the table. Dollar swiveled on the tall chair while she walked around and spread his knees apart. Martee stepped between his legs, moving into him so close she could feel the heat of his manhood on her ribs. She kept her eyes focused on his eyes, kept the vision inside herself whirling with energy and vivid, pulling at his soul with the image of her fingers.

She watched him lean forward into her and felt in answer the clear-hot fetish pulling at her psoas, felt the yearning to press her breasts against his chest. She pressed herself against his arousal, waited expectantly, her head turned upward, hair cascading, nipples taut.

His face came nearer, flare of his nostrils.

She watched him with eyes wide, watched until she could no longer focus on his eyes because he was so close. She smelled the aroma of coffee. She smelled also the scent she had smelled intimately of him before, that man's unique masculine smell rising on her nose, like rich, strong leather furniture rustling in her ears. She felt herself pulled into him, their lips meeting, felt a shiver down her spine, his chest pressed against her nipples grounding the tingling limerence. She closed her eyes, all the distant sounds she had been hearing dying away.

All she could hear now was his breathing through the nose with their continued kiss, heard the mousy whimper in her throat which came unsolicited, answering his energy reaching into her. She felt his tongue enter her mouth. She sucked on the tongue gently inside the wet lips, touched her tongue to his tentatively again in a swirl. She felt the breaths start to come with short sharp sissing inhales through her nose driven by clenching spasms, as if his fingers were stroking her psoas directly. She felt her left palm smooth behind his head, her fingers in his hair, forcefully holding him to continue kissing.

His tongue responded, energetically thrusting to fill her mouth, the tongue sliding against hers, sweeping her upper mouth, tracing her inner curves. She kissed while the spasms took her body further along the path of passion. She clung to their kiss with fear of falling down, pushed her breasts against the fabric, her calves tense, feeling that man hard through the thin black material of her dress, rubbing him.

She felt that man's right hand slide across her ass and grip, her skin caught in the thin dress, felt that man's left hand slide across her back bracing her, pressing her body against his.

From the pelvis she felt the clear energy rushing throughout her body. Her right hand joined her left hand holding his head, keeping that kiss through these hard surges, spasms, her whole body clenching tight.

Then came the downward crashing wave. She held on, these spasms deep within her gradually subsiding, the jerking shake resonating clenches throughout her body, her toes, her limbs, decreasing in frequency, until with one last shaking mousy whimper in her own ears she parted her lips from his.

She felt herself blink several times, the moistness flowing on her inner thighs. She swallowed, then opened her mouth. Martee wet her lips. "(Fuck!)" She kissed his lips briefly, then pulled her hands away from his neck, slipped them around his waist, hugged him with a whole-breasted wriggle. She relaxed her hug and just snuggled against him, head tucked into his neck. She felt his heat on her skin, his hardness had not gone away.

He was quiet.

Finally, she felt him release their hug.

She did also, sliding her left palm to protect the heat of his desire with the slight gap between them. She enjoyed feeling held in his arms and thighs, his eyes focused clearly into hers. The sounds of the Grape Hopper returned.

Martee heard Samone call across the floor, "Get a room!"

Dollar grinned. He glanced over Martee's head to the bar area, then returned his focus on Martee. He breathed in deeply. She felt that within her right arm, expansion pressing her breasts. She heard and felt him sigh out slowly.

Martee slipped her left hand around his back, relaxed her body against him and rested.

Dollar searched her eyes. "(You need to see my other business.)"

She felt her eyes opening wide, then she realized he meant the lawn business. She blinked and smiled, felt elated.

The shadows had become magnificent, a shared chill down the spine. "(Are you driving?)"

smoothed her palm along his arm, repeated

. . .

MARTEE WAS WALKING AROUND NOT FAR AWAY, orbiting, looking at Dollar occasionally while he processed what to do next about the dilemma he felt was on his hands, a choice to make.

He watched Martee investigating the collection of shrubs, trees, flowering bushes, and beds of plants, her sandaled feet walking on the lush grass mowed thick, the kind of grass requiring frequent mowing and daily watering. She paused at each of the nearby stonework accents, her eyes and head turning following the line and flow of symbols from and between each other.

The owner's mansion with the curved red tile roof was a hundred yards away from where he stood; the street where the work truck was parked fifty yards left.

This was his favorite landscaping artwork of all the ones he had created so far. The lawn was expansive, with eddies of stone symbols, and planted and hedged growth. All were comfortably spaced and rendered. There was a natural flow, the way the breezes were herded throughout the grounds.

There was also a carefully considered composition of smells which changed subtly from the earliest spring through the last leaves of fall, before the air became freezing, before hibernation overtook the garden.

Today, an exotic immingling scent of early summer blooms and moistly warm loam, rain recently fallen.

"You're doing magick here," he heard Martee say.

Dollar felt his eyes go wide, realized she would know. There had been the thunderstorm-door-busting soul moment, their souls touching in kiss.

She was looking sharply at him. "I'm not sure what kind it is. It's potent."

It's just honest earth.

Martee nodded her nose at him. "Admit it."

He paused, then he nodded. "Yes. Nobody's supposed to know."

She paused her restless orbit and looked at him thoughtfully. "Am I the only one who knows?"

He smiled. "Absolutely."

She breathed in and out sharply. "You aren't fooling me with that 'absolutely' crap anymore."

He couldn't help grinning. "Oh, really?"

"So tell me straight. Am I the only one who knows?"

Dollar nodded several times, smiled for himself. *Become honest as earth, vulnerable as wind.* "As far as I know, you are the only one aware enough to notice consciously."

She clapped her hands once and did a little bouncing skip, spinning around and stopping, her knees slightly bent, facing him, her hands palmed together near her breasts. "Perfect."

Dollar began strolling; they walked for a while. He was lost in his musings wandering among the various plants and trees and stonework accents. Some of the symbols he didn't yet have words for, they just *were.*

Being here among his creations was settling and reassuring. He was here to resolve an issue, full leverage to his advantage, intentional. "So, tell me about Charlie."

When Dollar said the name, Martee jumped, some of the color draining from her features. She was quiet.

He stopped walking. *Here,* Dollar thought, *this is a useful spot.* They could not be seen from the owner's house, driveway, or street. The daily mowing was already complete, the smell of fresh cut grass on the nose.

Martee walked toward him, eyes lost, stopped near him, half-turned away, and paused.

Inside his inner vision, wordless images stirred from the memory of his and Martee's soul-baring moment at the chalks Friday, restless shadowy images with fleeting scents attached. The images and scents had a foreign perspective he couldn't relate directly with. He knew they were not his memories. There was, along with the different perspective, Martee's love and self-love. That lovingness had a foreign texture he'd like to come to know more fully.

There was a sense of Charlie in the memory-evoked images also, and Dollar realized with widening eyes there was also a panicky sense of shame which wasn't his: there was the difference. "Something happened."

She nodded, her eyes down. Martee looked at him, then looked down, her eyelashes nearly closing. Then she closed her eyes completely. Martee slumped and sat on the lawn, her legs curled on her left, her right arm bracing her, hand on the grass, her bounce quiescent during the crumpling.

Dollar sat facing her, folding his legs and resting his forearms across his knees. His hands were close enough to touch her black hem, if he were to stretch the right fingers, or touch the skin of her legs with the left fingers. He determined to relax and wait, it wasn't his issue.

His eyes followed the lines of how Martee was sitting, tracing the curves of her feet and ankles, calves and knees, arrived at her hair, still except for a variable, directionless breeze around them. Her eyelashes were now opened slightly, downcast.

Martee noticed his watching her. She looked off toward the right. She pushed herself more erect and sat with her legs curled.

Her hands came together, clicked her fingernails, lefts against rights, fidgeted her fingers together, rested them on the bare skin of her legs below the hemline of the short black dress. "Nothing happened." She looked at him, then looked down, eyelashes almost closing. "But there was a day fourteen years ago when Charlie and I looked at each other..." Martee looked at Dollar. "Hadn't we, a thousand times? Ten thousand?" Martee said, leaning toward Dollar slightly. She sat erect, looked off toward the right.

She was quiet for a while. "That time." Her eyes became unfocused. After a while her eyes became sharp. Martee looked at him. "That time we knew."

Dollar was quiet, looking at her lips, looking at her breasts moving beneath the form-following black dress, muted energy of her wriggles and bouncing. He looked within her eyes. "Then what happened?"

———

"Nothing. A total bust!" Martee waved her hands in two circles, bringing them together on her lap. She watched her hands, her eyelashes almost closed. "We just knew. I freaked inwardly." Martee looked at Dollar. "That was my childhood girlfriend's father after all. Nothing happened. No kisses, no sex. Damn him. Damn me, also." Martee shrugged, "I had to let it go."

She looked away toward the right, quiet again. "Eventually..." Martee turned her head and looked at her hands. "It was just a habit not to think about him in that way. I created a spell, a daily mantra to forget what we both knew, consciously." Martee smiled briefly looking at Dollar. "Until Friday night." Martee's hands came apart, palms upward, fingers tensed in half-curls, "When I felt like I'd gotten hit by an elephant's trunk." Her fingers curled into fists, the color of strain, wrists upward.

Dollar cleared his throat. "Then all the memories came rushing back?"

"Rushing!" Martee bounced, suddenly alive. "Fuck! I wanted to damn well pull the man's zipper down right there in the bar!" bouncing herself with the words, extending her right arm, pointing at the work truck, at the way they had come from, pointing at that night.

Dollar grinned, wished he wasn't grinning. He didn't feel it was necessary discussing her later attempts at pulling his own zipper down. He chased the grin away, fought the smiling down with restless lips. He looked down, remembering when she had seized his arm and wouldn't let go, felt himself relax the smile until the mirth was completely calm.

Dollar looked at Martee. "I was a haven."

A beautiful, self-accepting frown came over Martee's face. She nodded briefly. She looked down, shrugged. "Maybe." She looked at him. "Maybe a little. But…" Martee said, bouncing, raising her left index finger in the air. "I…" her mouth open.

She shut her mouth, focused on his eyes, curled her finger down. She rolled backward, turning her legs, then rolled toward him, arriving on her knees. She walked her knees two short strides, put her hands on his shoulders and pushed against him.

At first he resisted; her pushing insisted. He uncrossed his legs and rolled backward onto the grass.

Martee landed on him, pulled her legs tucked under herself, sat erect on his abs. "Sometimes words suck."

"I see." He found his eyes were looking at her breasts, and he willed himself to look at her lips instead. He breathed in deeply and sighed.

He raised his hands, bending his arms at the elbows and bracing them on the lawn, opening his palms upward toward her.

She swirled her hair. The effect on his manhood was instant fulness from being so close to her. Her smells flowered on his nose, her breasts moved beneath the black fabric with the swirl, and her thighs rocked on him. The curves of her moving breasts lured his eyes, then his eyes were upon her neck and the kissable underside of her jaw, his eyes caught away in the flash of her smiling lips — all in a moment two heartbeats long, then her hair settled on her back.

Martee put her hands palm-down on his palms. He could feel her heat on his abs through his shirt.

He willed himself to talk. He had all but been won over by how delightfully Martee engaged with him, consistently alive with affection for him. He breathed in, touching the core of his resolve. "What about Banelle? And Charlie?"

Her eyes narrowed. "FUCK THEM." felt her thighs squeeze him saying so, felt her ass bounce slightly, keeping the contact between her soft parts and his abs, the strength inside her legs putting the sudden stop in her bounce. Her commitment sparked an instant yearning within him to disrobe, push her on her back, and feel her thighs slamming against his repeatedly.

Tears welled in her eyes. She looked down, the eyelashes almost closing. "Fourteen years of their hot mess!" He felt her left fist clench his right hand.

Dollar pulled Martee's left fingers to his lips, pulsed his energy and kissed her fingertips, felt Martee's thighs spasm against his waist.

She looked within his eyes, her lips parted, the normally happy smooth skin of her chin puckered. "By the Goddess, I ever am / as I ever do. It has been so long! My heart fell for yours in days, Dollar. Fourteen years and three days."

He saw how wet her eyelashes were, and there, his eyes moving, noticed there was a droplet paused halfway down her flushed cheek, a trail of wetness behind. He untangled his right hand from her hand, reached toward her face, snuggled his palm on her cheek. She cupped her left hand around his forearm.

He brushed his right thumb twice at the tear drop, feeling the wetness against his thumb, the moist area of her face which he had just helped release.

He fought with the urge to disrobe her completely and lay her down. His resistance slipped within the internal two-fisted grip he had on the Animal, then the urge transformed in his hands. He found he wanted her naked just as she was, on top, and he wanted to feel himself inside her, wanted her to slip onto him. His left hand wanted to pull on the back of her neck, pull the nippling breasts against his naked chest.

He fought with the desire, not letting the urge free of the Will, rooted in his resolve. He couldn't remember ever having been so mightily self-opposed. He looked within her eyes, one, the other.

Here it is in a nutshell, thought Dollar, internal eyes unrelentingly focused. *What I've been struggling with since Friday night,* feeling the dawning amazement. *Since falling in love!*

He felt the internal desire of the Animal trying to turn a trick on his resolve.

Why not *Martee?* He re-engaged his right hand with hers, both pairs of hands palm on palm, warm, delicious, relaxed. The disentangling was not going quite the way he had been hoping. Their time together was also going better than he had dreamed companionship could be with any woman.

He swayed his physical hands joined with hers gently back and forth, pivoting on his elbows, braced on the lawn, lying on his back with her seeping wetness straddling his stomach. Martee seemed content to keep her hands in his, be moved with his moving.

He let his mind wander creatively. He felt the earth beneath his back, smelled the loam and the grasses, smelled the various plants he had put in the area. The feeling of the earth with her straddling his belly, with the occasional breezes blowing her hair, the smell of her arousal, the sound of the relaxing breezes spinning and clattering the leaves of the trees, these things and the earth brought back to his awareness how eternal and long-lived a soul's life really was.

She looked at his lips and breathed in deeply, her breasts rising, pulling at his eyes.

"I'm in heaven here," Dollar said, allowing his eyes to enjoy the curves of her breasts.

"This is my art," circling his head as best he could, lying on his back, looking all around himself with his eyes. He resettled the back of his head on the grass and looked at Martee's eyes. "And this is Marittia Emily Marlin, in this lifetime. And she has chosen to be beautiful. And I have fallen in love with you."

He watched her vanity bloom with the magick words, looked at her breasts, the breathing. He looked in her eyes.

She was watching his eyes, looking at his lips.

"Now, tell me you don't love any other man while kneeling on this honest earth, your wet womanhood on my abs."

Martee squinted her eyes. "That's dirty."

———

Dollar felt himself shrug, eye's watching Martee's. "I just want to make sure we are both being completely open with each other and with ourselves. I actually don't know what to do next knowing I am in love with two women, and both women have expectations and a history with each other. Since you seem to have a similar dilemma with two men, I was hoping you had some idea what to do with the conundrum?"

He breathed in deeply, noticing a deliciousness in the air which he hadn't planted here or previously allowed to remain here. He treasured Martee's smell, burned that within his heart's memory, every rose distinct.

He looked at the sky, at the big white fluff wafting lazily by.

Martee pulled her hands free from his, leaned on him, her breasts near his chin where his tongue could have reached, and rolled over toward his left. She bounced herself more comfortably, rested the back of her head against his chest, also looked at the sky. Martee pulled his left arm across her breasts, wrapped her arms around his arm, and sighed. "My choice is clear."

He spoke the quiet internal words reminding the Animal their best interests were always served working together as a Team. Could the Animal understand, please? The Animal pointed out how well her smells blended with the work they had created *as a Team* on the grounds here.

He wasn't arguing with that, just held his resolve.

He liked the feel of being trusted by Martee. He liked the feel of her breasts against his arm. He particularly liked the feel of her head resting on his chest, the natural smell of her hair, burning beeswax candle wicks and simmering herb petals. He touched her hair with his right fingers, and stroked.

Both were quiet.

Martee's fingertips brushed his arm hair. "Do you know anyone else who actually does magick?"

"Not consistently."

"Ha-ha." He felt her palm pat his arm. She breathed sharply in and out, the feel under his arm so sublime. Martee took a very long and very deep lungful of air, raising his arm.

Dollar was going to have to admit to himself almost his entire Inner Team felt like he just needed to surrender the last mistaken sense of self-identity and release himself into the flow of her thighs, then share his words into the flow of her thoughts. Could they creatively collaborate a successful journey forward?

Martee's fingertips stroked Dollar's arm. "The man I met Friday has magick fingers."

Dollar felt himself laugh, felt her head jostled on the spasm of his laughter. "Are you accusing me of magick fingers?"

He felt her head roll against his chest, nodding in a circle. "Ohhhh, YESsssss!" Martee patted his arm twice with her right hand.

"Where did you deduce that from?"

"Besides all this?" Martee waved her right hand in a palms-up circle, looped her palm, put her hand back on his arm. "You remember at the sidewalk doing art? Wearing our artistic hats? You and I were sharing to each other?"

"Yes?"

"Did you feel that open house moment? Doors wide, soul to soul? Magick to magick? Feel stuck together yet?"

He didn't feel words were adequate. He pulled his left arm across her left breast, rubbed his left hand in a circle on her right breast, cupped, a new grip filled with soft joy. He relaxed. "I'm off my inner domain map here."

Martee licked her lips. "It is rare to see an egg yolk break *after* arranging the plate, to see hash browns practically woven together, except for a hairline tear along the ragged edge of someone's inner domain map, yours."

Dollar felt the energy of Martee's words. Was it love which hurt? Or was hurt from undermined self-esteem? Was his previous frustration with Banelle simply a projection of his own unconscious Brakes and Bricks?

Martee smoothed her palm along his arm, repeated. "I'm all yours, Dollar."

He felt something shift inside, an empathy, gentleness and kindness, self-acceptance to be intimately human.

He decided to adopt practical advice from someone he had rapidly learned to trust: *Sometimes words suck!*

I promise there is a way I can make you melt into a chocolate-drooling puddle and have hardly touched you. I am an expert in the natural energies some other people use for Reiki, and believe me there is a turn-on from these magick hands.

Dollar's left hand slid off the mound of Martee's right breast, fingers bumping across the fabric-covered nipple, tugged her dress higher. Martee's hips arched, and relaxed, releasing fabric. She unbuckled her glossy black belt and pulled it off into a looping pile near his feet. Her legs opened to his hand.

Dollar's fingers found Martee's wet self, swirled gently parting lips, brushed a sensitive bump, felt Martee's head roll toward him and the brief tension in her legs as she nestled her forehead into his neck. His two longer fingers sunk deeper into her secret self, soft curls falling on his chin, her forehead surging with the playful caress of his fingers, out, edge of the thumb across the bump, back over, fingers in, the emphatic grip of her palms, her fingers and thumbs tensing into his biceps at each surge, resting and resuming, repeating.

Below the feel of her, the chi of his hand harmonized her root chakra into a delicious chord building in intensity. The root spring of her own creative magick set to flowing, timpani vibrating beat by beat, accelerating, tensing drum head rising in pitch.

The glossy black straps of Martee's sandals flexed, happy around her ankles, toes spasmed, right heel off the ground, naked knees and thighs pulled together. She rolled toward him, closed around his hand, her right hand slid down his arm, and gripped his wrist. Martee's happy mousy whimper escaped near his left ear, and he felt the wet clench around his snuggled fingers, gush of wet release into his palm. Dollar murmured. "(What if I stopped trying to follow the rules?")

"(By the Goddess, Dollar. Let it be so.)" Martee whispered near the ear, shudder around his arm, hot breath puff onto the earlobe as another clench gripped his fingers, Martee's secret perfume on the nose seeping into taste buds.

Dollar bent his head, kissed her lips turned toward his, whispered. "(Can you come again?)"

Martee's right knee and thigh opened skyclad, enlarged irises considered his eyes, dimpled toothy smile, lips restless trying shapes of words. "(Are you driving?)"

Martee's hand guided the soft part of Dollar's left wrist to her tongue, the tongue licked shudders into his spine. Martee opened her smile, surrounded his thumb, pulled wetly through lips. Dollar's hips rose from the ground and collapsed again as the tip of his thumb emerged. Martee pulled his thumb into her wetness, kissed his lips with spasms as he played her mousy music. Her fingertips smoothed along his forearm in love.

"(we ever are / as we ever do.)"

Banelle and Dollar enjoy an intimate date in
Secrets 100, 105, 107 - Unbridled

Steam Rating: **Burning**
(vivid intimacy)

meet the author

. . .

MAURLLAN'S FASCINATION with the transformative power of language and storytelling has led him on a creative journey spanning multiple genres and forms. From exploring the shifting roles of gender in Historical Fiction to crafting immersive Paranormal Romances, his tales invite readers to question their assumptions, embrace the unexpected, and discover the magick woven between the words.

https://maurllan.com/

~ chasers ~

mundane lovingness
opened her craft book of spells
a sticky note was on the keys

mundane lovingness

. . .

DOLLAR CLOSED THE BOOK. He had needed to read the story again. Done. He felt weird *déjà vu* rereading what had happened to him, to see and know everyone's thoughts and feelings at the time, prior to the key parties becoming aware and acquainted with the Author.

"Martee, Martee, Martee." Dollar's fingers drumming a pattern of thruplets, a thump of the thumb stopping. They had taken time for fulfilling their respective ongoing appetites for mundane lovingness and magickal timings during their previous nineteen years of the Dragon turning on its heels and claws.

The World Canvas was stretched and had become a wee wiley wetter recently, though. He and Martee were going to start stacking spells at headquarters. Fun reminder.

opened her craft book of spells

. . .

MARTEE OPENED her craft book of spells compiled from her own research, and whispered, "(Dollar, Dollar, Dollar.)" Her left palm cupped his resting sex under content fingertips.

Her right hand flipped past the most recent three crafty spells in the book, came to the start of blank cream pages, pen in hand, wrote on the verso:

I suppose I must acknowledge the Rite of Spring.

To the man I loved and created a spell to forget, I offered my hand so he could give it my lover in Handfast.

To my best female friend ever, heft and lithe, children and blissfully childless, I offered my wit in jibes until she got over herself, and we solved for World Peace together, the three of us.

It is amusing for us to watch first one of her daughters then the other attempt to mimic what my friend used to be just yesterday, the punch line being my best friend changes every Moon now, learning more about herself in the joys of finally having freed herself from the curse of mistakenly self-entitled white men, the darkest gift my lover could grant her by the magicks currently suckling his fingertips. The daughters are maturing into power-houses of their own.

To the beeswax candle I sulfur-strike each nightly match. To the potpourri bowl I invest today's fructose-laden nectar petals simmering under the nose.

To tomorrow morning's reading of the free range eggs and caramelized hash browns I gift my salivating tongue after the appetites of another successful night.

To the Author and Goddesses, a heartfelt timpani-rushing request: bestir us new fun!

She squiggled a heart in large loops, with lips pressed. Whispered, "(Let it be so.)"

She felt his conjure rising under the left palm, felt her own smile, mist in the eyes with opening lips and shared love on the nose.

a sticky note was on
the keys

. . .

TWO HANDS, reaching from close by a black shirt, black buttons outward, moved forward with smooth habit to an anciently brown-painted machine with staggered rows of tan keys, many of them worn smooth of original symbols. A sticky note was on the keys. The left fingers snatched the note, the tug of adhesive releasing to a brief pop of the bright green paper square. He read aloud, "Remember, it is worth it!"

His right hand crumpled the note to himself, tossed the nub into the dry cavity of the Dinosaur's Left Rear Leg with a paper-rattling hollow sound. He knew she needed a bath, dried moringa tea residue from two days ago when he was up all night three nights in a row.

That April Mist needed a stroke or two of the magick from along the top row next, with shift key held down, not to typeset the point too heavily.

secret portals

Copyright 2022 Maurllan   iii

Volley   1
magnificent shadows   3
grabbing circling releasing   5
tangled in hurt and happiness   11

~ Goddess Perfume ~   21
Secret 099

whatever emotions were   23
surging up was an unusual commitment   29
only a different set of shortcomings   35
she heard male laughter   45
put her left hand on his biceps   63
the girl blushed and giggled   87
leaned back nonchalantly like she   93
had been struggling within herself   117
eyelashes almost closing, fingernails clicking   125
floating on an anxiety of gradual emptiness   133
eyes moved reluctantly from the jeans to look at
his eyes   143
his touching her there barely-familiar   161
she was indeed on the right track   167
pecked an air kiss   171
whipped her arm, twisting her body   199
selfishly dancing against his body   219
magick of a very real love potion   235
she slipped from the chair at his pull   243
"Bye!" she heard her Father call   253
he nodded at her, smiled, "Lovely."   265
she felt the tingly excitement   281
smoothed her palm along his arm, repeated   287
meet the author   299

~ Chasers ~   301

Retort 303
mundane lovingness 305
opened her craft book of spells 307
a sticky note was on the keys 309

www.ingramcontent.com/pod-product-compliance
Lightning Source LLC
Chambersburg PA
CBHW032002150726
47990CB00005B/1811